The Little French Guesthouse

Also by Helen Pollard

WARM HEARTS IN WINTER
HOLDING BACK

The Little French Guesthouse

helen pollard

bookouture

Published by Bookouture

An imprint of StoryFire Ltd.
23 Sussex Road, Ickenham, UB10 8PN
United Kingdom

www.bookouture.com

ISBN: 978-1-910751-88-6
eBook ISBN: 978-1-910751-87-9

For David

My love, my best friend, my rock

CHAPTER ONE

I wish I could tell you it happened like it does in the movies. You know the kind of thing. The heroine standing proud, oozing restrained fury. The audience's satisfaction as she delivers a reverberating slap across her lover's face. Her dramatic but dignified exit from the screen.

Believe me, there was nothing dignified about it. All I did was stand there shaking, rage and adrenalin coursing through my body like rabid greyhounds, my mouth flapping open and shut as I tried to find the words. Any words. Even a simple sound of outrage would have sufficed, but all I managed was a pathetic squeak.

'Emmy, it's not what it looks like,' Nathan spluttered, but of course it couldn't be anything other than what it looked like. My view as I stumbled through the door had been graphically explicit. Even he must have known how lame he sounded. Grappling for dignity and his belt, he tried again. 'We were... I mean, I didn't expect you to...'

I launched into a wronged-woman tirade as though someone had handed me a bad soap script.

'No, I *bet* you didn't expect me to...' An alarm bell clanged dimly at the back of my brain, but I ignored it. 'How *could* you? You cheating bastard! I can't *believe* you...' The clanging grew louder and more insistent, moving to the front of my consciousness. 'Shit!' With a guilty jolt, I remembered why I'd come all the way up here in the first place. 'Gloria, you need to call an ambulance. I think Rupert's having a heart attack.'

'What?' Adjusting her dress, Gloria greeted this sudden change of subject with bewilderment.

'Rupert. Your husband, remember? Heart attack. Ambulance.' I gave her bangled arm a nudge to see if her brain was still functioning or whether sex with my boyfriend was more spectacular than I gave him credit for.

'Ohmygod. Ohmygod.' The message finally got through to her lust-addled brain cells. 'Where is he?'

'Kitchen.' I headed for the stairs, my mind thankfully back on the emergency at hand and pushing visions of Nathan and Gloria romping on the roof terrace to the rear of my consciousness. For now, remarkably, there were more important things to worry about.

'What do you mean, a heart attack?' Gloria shouted after me. 'Why the hell didn't *you* call an ambulance?'

'I tried, but then I realised I didn't know the number, and besides, my French isn't good enough,' I called over my shoulder. 'I thought it would be quicker to get you to do it. I had no idea you'd be so *busy*.'

'Ohmygod, Emmy. He could be dead by now!'

She was right – he *could* be dead by now – but when we reached the kitchen, to my immense relief, Rupert was still conscious and sitting propped against the wall the way I'd left him. I'd done my best, but I hadn't expected to lose precious moments with the melodrama upstairs. I couldn't imagine how I would have felt if he had stopped breathing.

As Nathan and I watched the ambulance drive away, the panic subsided and the images I'd pushed away came crowding back in unwelcome and vivid detail.

Dinner at the guesthouse, the four of us laughing. Gloria absenting herself to "make a phone call." Nathan "just nipping to the loo – sorry, bit of a stomach upset." Arguing the merits of my favourite movies with Rupert over a glass of wine. His face turning pale and ashen as he fought for breath, the veins standing out on the back of his hand as he clutched at his chest. The way he twisted and fell from the tall bar stool onto the stone floor of the kitchen. My own heartbeat thumping like crazy as I racked my brain for some remnant of first aid, puffing and heaving as I manoeuvred him into what I hoped was the correct position for a heart attack victim.

And then that awful moment when I reached for the phone, only to realise I had no idea what number to dial for an ambulance and that my long-forgotten school French didn't stretch to asking for one. Calling out for Gloria. Silence in return. No answer from her room. Racing upstairs, along the landing, out onto the roof terrace on the strangely intuitive off-chance she might be making her phone call *al fresco*... And then that nightmare scene. Gloria's legs clutched around Nathan's waist. The ultimate betrayal.

Only four days into our holiday, our host was being rushed away in an ambulance and I had found my boyfriend indelicately joined with the lady of the house.

The tail lights disappeared, leaving the *gîtes* across the courtyard shrouded in darkness and the grounds deathly quiet. Three miles from the nearest town and with just a handful of cottages and farmhouses as neighbours, *La Cour des Roses* was idyllically peaceful during the day with bees humming and chickens clucking, but I still couldn't get used to the lack of noise at night. No continuous traffic, no groups of drunken lads ambling back from the pub, the background to urban life back home.

Shivering, I closed the door and turned back into the large farmhouse kitchen. Half-empty wine glasses stood beside the congealing remains of our evening meal on the pine table. The bar stool Rupert had fallen from still lay on its side. I lifted it upright.

Letting out the breath I'd been holding in some distant corner of my lungs, I considered my options. Should I scream and shout? Or should I be calm and understanding?

As it turned out, it didn't matter. Nathan walked through the kitchen and started up the stairs without a word. Thwarted, I followed him up to our room, where he began to undress with his back to me so I couldn't catch his eye. As he pulled off his jeans, so recently dropped for other purposes, my patience snapped.

'Nathan, this is ridiculous. We need to talk.'

'Em...'

I had always hated the way he called me that. *Em.* As if I were nothing more than an initial, a single letter.

'For God's sake, can't you at least look at me?'

He made a slow and reluctant turn, but his gaze didn't quite hit my eyes, landing instead on a spot somewhere near my left ear.

'What?' he asked sullenly.

'How can you ask "what"? Don't you think we need to talk about what happened?'

'Not tonight, I don't.' He met my gaze, but that was more disconcerting than when he'd avoided it. I couldn't read anything in his eyes. Remorse, love, misery. Nothing.

'Why not?' I persisted.

'Because it's late and I'm exhausted, that's why.'

'Yes, I bet you are – you and Gloria both!'

'Oh, for heaven's sake, Emmy, stop being so bloody childish.'

'Me, childish?' I gaped at him. 'How can you say that? I'm the one who wants to talk about this like grown-up people. *You're* the one who's being childish!'

He ran his hand through his hair in a gesture of impatience. 'There's nothing childish about recognising that twelve-thirty at night is not the optimum time for a serious discussion.'

'Don't you talk to me like you're planning a sodding business meeting! I want to know what you've got to say for yourself!'

A hunted look came into his eyes, and I balked. He shouldn't feel hunted, I thought. He should feel the need to explain, to apologise, preferably to grovel. That quiet, calm nature of his, so refreshingly un-macho when we first met, suddenly grated on my nerves.

'Did you hear me, Nathan?'

He scowled. 'You don't have to use that tone of voice, Em. You're not my mother.'

I blew out a ragged breath, enraged on several counts. His use of that damned single syllable again instead of my name. The implication that it would have been okay for his mother to interrogate him, but not okay for me to do so. The unbearable idea that I could be compared to that pompous, omnipresent, spiteful bag of a woman. The suggestion that I hadn't turned out to be as much like his mother as he'd hoped.

'No, I'm *not* your mother, thank heavens. But since we've shared the past five years of our life together, I think I'm entitled to ask why on earth you would have sex with that... that nymphomaniac? She must be at least ten years older than you!'

He bristled. 'I doubt that. Besides, I don't see what age has to do with anything. Rupert must be knocking on sixty, so that's quite an age gap between them, for a start.'

'Yes, and look how well *that's* going for them,' I retorted, at which Nathan at least had the decency to look sheepish. 'Anyway, we're not discussing the whys and wherefores of Rupert and Gloria's marriage. We're discussing the fact that you had sex with half of it.'

Nathan winced. 'Look, I... I had too much to drink.' He shrugged, as though that was a perfectly acceptable end to the matter.

I searched his face for traces of the funny, gentle, handsome-in-a-bland-kind-of-way man I lived with, but all I could see was a recalcitrant teenager in a thirty-three-year-old's body, who must know he was in the wrong but couldn't drum up the balls to admit it.

'Not good enough.' I shook my head so violently it hurt. 'People don't have sex with other people just because they've had one drink too many. You could have kept it zipped up if you'd wanted to.'

Nathan opened his mouth to reply, then closed it again. No doubt he realised he had no defence. Instead, he turned towards the bathroom. I was getting pretty tired of him turning his back on me.

'Don't walk away, Nathan,' I warned. 'We haven't finished this conversation.'

He looked back over his shoulder. 'You might not have finished, Emmy, but I have. For tonight, anyway. If you haven't noticed, a conversation needs two people.'

With that, he headed into the bathroom and closed the door. Not one more word about his escapade, just the sound of running water and spitting toothpaste.

Furious, I started to undress, but I was so angry that the seam of my favourite T-shirt ripped as I pulled it over my head. Great. Standing in the middle of the room in my underwear, I willed myself to calm down before I had some sort of seizure, and tried hard to concentrate on breathing evenly. When I was sure I wasn't about to follow Rupert's example, I finished undressing, pulled on a baggy nightshirt, then stared at the bed with distaste. Visions of Nathan and Gloria wrapped together flooded my tired brain.

What the hell was I doing? There was no *way* I could climb into bed beside Nathan as though nothing had happened. At this stage, I wasn't sure I ever wanted to share a bed with him again.

Maybe I could move to another room – there were no other guests in the house at the moment. Or maybe I should make Nathan move. Gloria could hardly complain under the circumstances.

Going out onto the landing, I cautiously opened the door of the room nearest ours. There was no linen on the bed. My explorations of the other two rooms revealed the same thing. I thought about trying to locate bedlinen and moving all my stuff. Nathan was right about one thing. It was late.

It should be him who moved.

When I went back to our room, he was still in the bathroom. Probably hiding. Or sulking. Or both. I started to strip the bed. One of us could have the sheets, the other the duvet.

When he finally reappeared, he stared at the disarray in bewilderment. 'What the hell are you doing?'

'*I'm* not doing anything. *You*, on the other hand, are moving to another room.'

'At this time of night? You must be joking!'

My blood bubbled unpleasantly. 'I'd hardly say it's a joking matter, would you?'

I was so frustrated with him, I could have stamped my foot like a two-year-old. Nathan and I rarely fought, but on the odd occasion when we did, he could be pretty stubborn about taking any part in it. Whereas I had a temper with a tendency to flare, thanks to my mother's redheaded genes, Nathan was adept at avoiding confrontation, letting my moods come and go without getting too involved. I'd always thought it one of his good qualities, being calm and placid in the face of my fluctuating emotions. Right now, I knew he was only burying his head in the sand, in the hope it would all go away by tomorrow.

'If you won't talk about this tonight, then you won't. But you are *not* sleeping in my bed.' I shoved his pillow and a sheet at him, dragged a spare blanket from the top shelf of the wardrobe and shoved that at him, too.

As he stood there wavering, his arms full of bedding, I half-expected him to ask why he should be the one to move out. Wisely, he didn't. Shaking his head, he opened the door, stumbled through it and slammed it behind him – a gesture which lost its dramatic impact when his blanket got in the way.

I perched on the stool at the dressing table. Cleanse, tone, moisturise. Just because my boyfriend had had sex with a woman he barely knew didn't mean I had to become sloppy. When I'd finished scrubbing, I viewed the results. Red and blotchy. Lovely.

I gazed at myself with a kind of fascinated detachment. Ignoring the self-induced redness, I didn't think I looked so bad for thirty-one. My youthful bloom may have needed a little cosmetic help now and again, and sporadic highlights might have been the only thing keeping my hair from being mousy, but I wasn't so different from the woman Nathan had asked out beside the photocopier five years ago. Gloria, on the other hand, came mainly from a bottle as far as I could see, with her mink-blonde hair, her foundation-filled fine lines, her spray tan. Why would he sleep with her when he had me?

When I'd brushed my teeth with a little more violence than my gums were used to, I climbed into bed already knowing there was no hope of sleep. I couldn't believe Nathan had been caught out like that and seemed to think it was okay not to talk about it. But then that was so typical of the way we'd been lately.

On the surface, our life was pretty normal. We got up, went to work, came home. Circled around each other pretending not to be hungry in the hope the other might offer to rustle something up, until one of us gave in and stuffed a ready meal in the microwave. Vegged out in front of the telly. On Saturdays, "we" did the shopping and cleaning. That was to say, I did the shopping and cleaning while Nathan found some urgent errand to run that involved dropping into the nearest computer superstore and playing with the latest gadgets. On Sundays, we read the papers in bed, which I enjoyed, and occasionally we visited his parents or mine, an ordeal neither of us enjoyed and had a habit of putting off until we were berated by one or both sets of them. I was all for a bit of routine, but even I'd begun to find it rather dull.

More insidiously, I'd noticed we weren't really talking any more. After only five years, were we already turning into one of those couples you saw down at the pub? The ones who sat for a whole evening barely saying a word to each other because they'd already talked about everything over the years and there was nothing left to say?

"Did I tell you about Derek's greenhouse and the...?"

"Yes."

"Oh."

"Marjorie said the vet told Doris her cat would have to have..."

"I know."

"Right."

Dinner in front of the soaps, a peck on the cheek at the beginning and end of the day, dutiful attempts to show an interest in something one of us was ecstatic about even though the other couldn't give a toss.

Didn't that happen to *older* people? *Much* older people?

Gloria came back at twelve minutes past three. Still wide awake, I heard tyres – presumably of a taxi – on gravel, a car door slam, a word or two of French to the driver. The crunch of her footsteps, the slam of the front door. The clatter of her heels across the hall. There was no indication that Rupert was with her, and I wondered if he was okay. He must be, I thought, otherwise she wouldn't have come home, surely?

A few minutes later, I heard another, more ominous noise. The creak of floorboards. A door opening along the landing. Nathan.

I shot out of bed and opened my own door so quickly, I nearly slipped a disc.

'Where do you think you're going?'

He spun around, one foot on the top stair. 'I...'

'*Don't* try telling me you needed a midnight snack or a glass of milk, Nathan, because it won't wash. I heard Gloria come back.'

'Yes, well, so did I,' he blustered. 'So I... I thought I should pop down and check how Rupert is.'

I rolled my eyes. 'A likely story. You can't tell me you're that worried about a man whose wife you were busy having sex with while he had a heart attack!'

Nathan curled his lip. 'It's not as if the two things were related, Em. He happened to collapse at the same time we happened to be having sex. The one did not cause the other. Besides, I've already told you I don't want to discuss this tonight. Even less so now that Gloria's back.'

Curiosity won out – briefly – over anger. 'Why on earth does that make the slightest difference?'

'We might be overheard,' he hissed. 'We're not in our own home. It wouldn't be proper.'

I couldn't believe his nerve. My blood boiled. You could probably have cooked eggs in my arteries.

'Proper! I think we already dispensed with *proper* behaviour earlier this evening. Don't you talk to me about proper!'

He shuffled uncomfortably. 'Emmy, you're raising your voice. That's exactly why I didn't want to do this.'

I raised my voice another notch for the pure pleasure of increasing his discomfort levels along with it. 'What difference does it make? There's nobody here but Gloria, and she's a whole floor down. Besides, in the event the woman has supersonic hearing, I think you'll find she's already in the know with regard to our current situation, seeing as she played one of the leads.'

'Oh, for crying out loud, Emmy, quit with the melodrama.'

He slammed into his room, leaving me with no apology, no promises, no satisfaction.

Back in my own bed, with both ears finely tuned to any further movement from the landing, I cursed Gloria and her sodding guesthouse. If we hadn't come here, this never would have happened. I cursed myself while I was at it, since it had been my bright idea. I'd thought a holiday would revive our flagging spirits. Help us relax. Pep things up a bit.

Nathan hadn't been enthusiastic about the prospect when I'd put it to him, but in my naivety, I'd taken that as an inability to prise himself away from the office.

'Oh, Emmy, no. You know how impossible it is. I've got deadlines. You've got deadlines. They never match. We've been through all this before.'

Nathan and I had met at work. With him an accountant and me assistant marketing manager at the same firm, it was almost impossible to plan holidays, but this time I had been determined. We *needed* this.

'Nathan, we haven't had a proper holiday for ages.'

He frowned. 'We went to Bath last year.'

'That was just a long weekend.'

'And Exeter,' he added, warming to his theme.

I sighed, exasperated. '*That* was a long weekend, too.' Our schedules had long since led us to give up on proper holidays and settle for exorbitantly-priced mini-breaks instead.

'Well, they were alright, weren't they?' Nathan said, with about as much enthusiasm as me being faced with the prospect of a weekend with his parents.

'Yes, they were alright, but we haven't had a *real* holiday since Greece.' I cast my mind back. 'Nearly two years ago.'

Nathan grunted. 'Too hot.'

I forced myself to be patient. 'We don't have to go anywhere hot, Nathan, but we do need a proper two weeks somewhere.'

'Two *weeks*!' he squeaked. 'By the time we've coordinated our diaries and booked it all, then killed ourselves finishing up before we go, and killed ourselves catching up when we get back, it's hardly worth the effort.'

Of course, hindsight was a wonderful thing. I could look back now and wonder whether Nathan's reluctance had all been down to job devotion. Maybe he simply hadn't relished the idea of spending two whole weeks away with me.

I'd persisted. 'I think it *is* worth the effort.' I was adamant, and he knew it.

'Fine, if that's what you want, but you'll have to do all the donkey-work.' The resignation in his voice depressed me beyond words. 'Go ahead and book something. Whatever you want.' He'd looked up from his laptop long enough to give a cursory smile that didn't reach his eyes, and then he was back in the land of spreadsheets.

Many women would have jumped at "whatever you want" and booked a fortnight in a five-star hotel in the Caribbean – and I can't say it didn't cross my mind – but I'd had a sneaking suspicion that secluded paradise could work both ways. Yes, it would mean being together, nothing to do but relax and talk to each other. But if we found out we had nothing to say, then two weeks of sun, sand and the new-found knowledge that our relationship was a boring pile of old crap could be two weeks too long.

No, what we needed, I had thought, was somewhere quiet and relaxing where we would have the opportunity to open up to each other, rediscover why we fell in love in the first place – and if that failed, some humanity in the vicinity and plenty of sightseeing to fall back on.

And so here we were at *La Cour des Roses*, "a delightful guest-house in the popular Loire region of France, where you will be welcomed and pampered by your convivial hosts, Rupert and Gloria Hunter. Relax in our beautiful garden or explore the tranquil countryside, colourful local towns, magnificent *châteaux*..."

Sounded great on the website.

CHAPTER TWO

The morning after Nathan's fall from grace, I was up with the larks – or more accurately, with the chickens. I hadn't thought to close the wooden shutters before I went to bed, and as dawn crept through the voile curtains, I reckoned if sleep hadn't come during the night, it was unlikely to come now.

Painfully aware of the empty pillow beside me in the bed, I sat up, glancing across at Nathan's shirt and jeans folded on the small upholstered tub chair in the corner of the room, his wallet and watch neatly laid out on the beautifully grained surface of the antique dressing table. A large matching wardrobe dominated the wall across from the foot of the bed, but the room was spacious enough to accommodate it. The soft blues of the bedlinen and cushions, and of the rugs on the polished wooden floorboards, added a cool, calming contrast to the warm honey tone of the wood.

Pulling on a sweatshirt, I crept downstairs and out to the patio where the chickens and I could commune in peace. The morning was still chilly, so I grabbed a throw from inside and lay on a dew-damp lounger with the warm wool pulled up to my chin like an old lady on a cruise. I stared at the expanse of lawn, its length broken by colourful flower beds and small ornamental trees, old flagstones sunk into the grass leading off to little hideaway corners and arbours amongst the denser shrubs and trees lining the edges of the garden... But I took little pleasure in what should have been a beautiful view.

No matter how lovely this place was, it was clear to me that moving to different accommodation had to be our number one priority. Nathan had strayed. I was entitled to be upset, but things like this happened to couples all the time. Gloria couldn't possibly mean anything to him. We'd been together too long to throw it all away over a lapse of judgment on his part. And we couldn't make any progress with the evidence of Nathan's infidelity under our noses.

I moved on to worrying about Rupert for a nice change of scene. I'd grown quite fond of him over the past few days, although I suspected he was an acquired taste. Nathan hadn't taken to him at all. Whereas Nathan was quiet (morose at times, now I came to think of it), Rupert was the exact opposite – loud and bumptious, sometimes outrageous. I would have put Nathan's instant dislike of him down to a simple personality clash if it hadn't been for the unnerving conversation we'd had the morning after we arrived.

We had been sitting in the garden recovering from our journey, and as I'd blissfully taken in the glory that surrounded us – neat lawns, late spring flowers, lush trees – I had been foolish enough to open my big mouth and voice my thoughts.

'Glorious here, isn't it?' I'd murmured.

Nathan scanned his surroundings, quietly assessing. 'Hmm. Wonder how much it cost him?'

I propped myself up on one elbow and looked across at him. Ever the accountant. If I put it down to professional curiosity, I could forgive him comments such as these.

'No idea,' I said dismissively.

'Last night at dinner, he said it was a wreck when they bought it, so he probably got it cheaply enough. But it must've cost him a fortune to do up.' Nathan craned his neck to look back at the house where deep green foliage crept up the grey stone walls. The stone looked older, almost crumbling, in some places, and patched in others – but red roof tiles added colour to the façade, and the blue-painted shutters which stood sentry at each window were smart and welcoming. Nathan swept his eyes across the newer whitewashed wing that was Rupert and Gloria's living quarters, built on the side of the house, with what was left of an old orchard separating it from the road. 'The renovation of the farmhouse itself. That extension,' he muttered. 'The *gîtes* across the way. Can't be cheap, converting an old barn like that. And the grounds were a wasteland when they moved in, apparently.'

I glanced over at the rows of lavender lining the courtyard between the house and the *gîtes*, a long building with a rough exterior of cream-and-grey stone and three wooden doorways, each surrounded by clambering grapevines. 'Well, they made a good job of it,' I said admiringly.

Nathan gave a cursory nod. 'Yes, but where did he get the money, Emmy, eh? He never said what he did for a living before they came out here.'

'Not our business, though, is it?'

Nathan curled his lip in an unpleasant sneer. 'Posh accent. Probably born with a silver spoon in his mouth. Doesn't look like the type who's ever had to work for a living.'

I raised an eyebrow in surprise. This was a side to Nathan I wasn't familiar with, and I wasn't at all sure I liked it.

'They must have worked pretty hard to create this,' I defended them, sweeping my arm to encompass our home for the next two weeks.

'I doubt he knows the meaning of hard work,' Nathan grumbled. 'I bet he paid other people to do it all while he just lounged around and watched. Jammy bastard.'

I frowned at him. 'Why does it matter? You'd be complaining if we were paying all this money and it *wasn't* nice here. Can't we just enjoy it?'

Nathan flopped down on his lounger in a sulk and I lay back too, my good mood dissipated.

I wondered if we would have been better off in one of the *gîtes*, thereby minimising Nathan's exposure to Rupert, but *that* thought didn't last long. I knew from bitter experience that Nathan's idea of self-catering was to grumble his way around the supermarket glaring at all the foreign brands, then stay out of the way while I did all the cooking and clearing up. *Self*-catering was the operative word. The first time it had happened, in Spain, I'd been so smug and self-satisfied with my newly-caught man that I hadn't noticed the one-sidedness of the arrangement. Not so in Greece, where we had a studio apartment so small, it would have been lucky to be classed as a bathroom in most hotels. After a fortnight of tripping over Nathan's feet as he lounged on the sofa bed while I cooked in a kitchen the size of a cupboard, I'd sworn I'd never put myself through it again. Here at the guesthouse, our booking included daily breakfast and three dinners a week, leaving us free to discover the local restaurants the rest of the time, and I thought that a happy medium.

Rupert did all the cooking at *La Cour des Roses*, and as I lay in my stupor the morning after his collapse, I wondered what would happen now. We were the only house guests at the moment, but more were imminent. Would Gloria take over? Casting my mind back over the past few days, I began to wonder what Gloria actually did – other than seduce other people's boyfriends. She was more your meeter-and-greeter than your do-er, looking decorative in a tight-jeaned, low-topped sort of way, fluttering and faffing. I suspected she was more skilful at the appearance of being busy than the real thing.

At least they had a cleaner. She was a tiny, elderly, weather-beaten woman who worked like a demon and chattered continuously at you, incapable of understanding that your French hadn't been used for years and had been inadequate in the first place.

Sounds began to drift across the courtyard from the *gîtes* – a toddler crying, a car door opening, a woman calling for her husband to bring in the map, the coffee was ready – and I felt a stab of envy. That should be Nathan and me, relaxed and ready to explore.

Heaving a sigh of self-pity, I levered myself up. That disembodied mention of coffee had woken my caffeine alarm. Like a sleep-deprived zombie, I ventured inside in search of a fix.

Gloria, all full make-up and backcombed bleached blonde hair, put in an appearance as I fumbled with the shiny technical wizardry that was the coffee machine.

'Here, let me,' she said, shoving me aside. She pushed buttons and twiddled knobs until jets of steam plumed up to the raftered ceiling, then handed me a cup. It was sludgy and tasted like something scraped from the bottom of the chicken house. Rupert was clearly the coffee whizz – another downside to his absence.

Squaring my shoulders, I prepared to tackle her over her coupling with Nathan. Such a time-honoured confrontation should have taken place the night before, of course, but Rupert's inconsiderate medical emergency had scuppered that.

It would have been nice if Gloria had made the first move and proffered an apology. After all, if she'd broken my necklace or insulted my favourite aunt or even trodden on my toes, I imagine she would have said sorry. Yet there she stood after having had rampant sex with my boyfriend, and not a sniff of one. Unbelievable.

Even so, I couldn't ignore the fact that the woman's husband was in a hospital bed. I reined myself in. First things first.

'How's Rupert?'

There was a flicker in her eyes, something icy and cold, but it was gone before I could decipher it. 'I phoned the hospital,' she said. 'They're discharging him this morning.'

'Did they say what was wrong?'

'It wasn't a heart attack.' Gloria shot me an accusing look, as if to criticise my incorrect diagnosis that had so rudely interrupted her extramarital activities last night. 'It's angina. They've given him some medication. He'll have to be more careful about what he eats and drinks.'

Rupert wasn't a light drinker, and I had a feeling this would be a bone of contention between them.

'Will he have to rest?'

'Apparently so. They think he damaged a ligament in his leg when he fell. He can barely walk.' Again, that hint of accusation, as though I'd somehow let everyone down by not throwing myself across the kitchen to catch a six-foot, fourteen-stone bloke all by myself.

'Well, I'm glad he's alright,' I said truthfully. And now on to the main attraction... 'Time for you and me to have a little chat, then, don't you think?'

The hint of shock in her eyes suggested she thought she'd got away without a confrontation. 'Oh?'

I found her brazen attitude astonishing. 'Don't you have *anything* to say for yourself?'

She shrugged as though she couldn't care less, but there was a wariness in her eyes. 'Shit happens, Emmy. You weren't supposed to see what you saw, but you did. I'm not sure what you want me to say.'

Flabbergasted, I slapped the undrinkable coffee down on the granite counter with so much force, I heard the cup crack.

'Maybe you could start by apologising for sleeping with my boyfriend?'

She folded her arms across her chest, a gesture which had the unfortunate effect of wrinkling the tanned skin above her cleavage so it looked like leather.

'There were two of us, Emmy – you saw that for yourself. Yes, I had sex with Nathan. And *he* had sex with *me*. Maybe you should look to him for an apology.'

'Nathan and I have already had words, thanks, which is more than I can say for you and Rupert. I presume you're going to tell him when he comes home?'

'Then you presume wrong.' Her eyes narrowed in threat. 'Nor do I expect *you* to tell him.'

I was impressed by her nerve. 'Don't you think you should discuss this vow of silence with all relevant parties first, rather than assume it?'

'I would have thought that even you would agree it won't do him much good to find out something like that. You wouldn't want to be responsible for a relapse, would you?'

She had me there. No matter how furious I was, I couldn't risk Rupert's fragile health just to get my revenge on Gloria. But being backed into a corner by her made me see red.

'You didn't seem so bothered about Rupert's health and well-being last night!'

'Are you suggesting I don't care about my husband?'

I barked out a strangled laugh. 'Let's just say that sleeping with the guests is a funny way of showing it.'

'Sleeping with *a* guest, Emmy. *One* guest. Get your facts straight.'

'You want me to get my facts straight?' I counted off on my fingers. 'You're married. You slept with my boyfriend. You're nearly old enough to be his teenage mother. There. Is that straight enough for you?'

Her mouth twisted in contempt. 'If your relationship is so solid and I'm so geriatric, then why did your boyfriend rip off all my clothes like a wild animal while you enjoyed your middle-aged reminiscences with my husband downstairs?'

I had no answer to that. Fortunately, I didn't have to find one. As I desperately searched my besieged brain for a biting riposte, the phone rang in the hall and Gloria shot past me to answer it.

I remained standing in the kitchen, dazed. Gloria's parting shot had hit its mark. Was our sex life really so deep in the doldrums that Nathan had felt the need to do this? Up until yesterday, I wouldn't have said so. I would have said we were probably the same as any other hardworking couple. We were often too tired, too busy, too stressed – but we still made love. Not as regularly as we used to. Not as passionately as we used to. But surely not many relationships could sustain the passion of a couple first getting together? I suddenly realised that I had assumed a gradual decline like that was normal. Even acceptable.

It seemed Nathan hadn't felt the same way.

Nathan made himself scarce the first half of the morning by pretending to sleep in, then moving all his stuff to his new room – something I only discovered when I went upstairs to see where he'd got to. The sheets and blanket I'd thrust at him last night were back on my bed, and when I peeped into his new accommodation, I saw that he had a full new set of bedlinen – which meant a) he had to have spoken to Gloria already and b) he didn't seem to be thinking along the same lines as me with regard to us moving somewhere else.

I couldn't say I was happy about either of those things, but with Herculean effort, I curbed my temper and impatience until we could be alone. Gloria had already had intimate knowledge of my boyfriend last night. What was left of my pride didn't want her walking in on a heart-to-heart and getting intimate knowledge of our relationship's failings as well.

The minute she drove off to the hospital, I collared Nathan at the bottom of the garden, where he appeared to be studying the habits of the chickens in minute detail.

'Nathan. We need to talk.'

He turned. 'We talked last night.'

I suppressed a sigh. 'No, we didn't. I talked. You said you didn't want to. It was a bit one-sided.'

'I'd say you shouted more than talked.'

I took a deep breath and counted to five. I really couldn't make it to ten.

'Of course I shouted!' I shouted. 'What did you expect? I found you having sex with another woman. What was I supposed to do, burst into song? I think under the circumstances I showed incredible restraint, what with Rupert and everything.'

Nathan nodded, conceding me that point at least.

'Do I get an explanation for last night's shenanigans or not?' I asked.

'I already gave you one.'

I choked out a laugh. '"Too much to drink"?'

He nodded.

'Pathetic.'

Nathan's jaw set in a stubborn line. It highlighted his resemblance to his mother. 'You really want to discuss this?'

'No, I don't *want* to, Nathan. Believe it or not, I'm just as reluctant to deal with what happened last night as you are. But I can't see how we're going to move forward until we do.'

'Okay. Fine.' He took a deep breath. 'The fact is, things haven't been right between us for a while, Em. We don't talk much any more. We don't do stuff together any more. I just don't think you've noticed.'

And with that one statement, the cold blood dripping through my veins turned into a red-hot, furious torrent.

I took a shaky breath. 'How *can* you have the gall to stand there and tell me I haven't noticed how crappy things have been lately? If you're so bloody observant, then why didn't *you* do something about it? Oh. No, wait. You did. You slept with Gloria. *Very* constructive, you faithless *prick*!'

Nathan paled at the onslaught. 'For God's sake, Emmy, keep your voice down. There might be people sitting outside the *gîtes*.'

'I will *not* keep my voice down. Don't you *dare* tell me to keep my voice down! I have spent the past year worrying myself sick about us, while *you* carried on in your smug little world. Not once have you said anything about being unhappy, while I've agonised and wondered whether it was normal to barely speak two words to each other. This holiday was *my* idea, remember? I'd hoped it would give us the chance to get to know each other again, to get away from work and stress and see if we could be like we used to be.' At that, my voice broke.

'Yes, well, we're not like we used to be, are we?' he said quietly.

'I should say not, after last night!'

He shook his head. 'You're not going to forget that, are you?'

My eyes widened. 'Do you honestly expect me to?'

'I'm not sure what I expect any more. I need to think. I'm going for a walk.' He stormed off in the direction of the lane.

Incensed, I stomped back inside. As I fought to bring my blood pressure into a safer zone, I looked around the kitchen with dismay. A huge room, it usually conveyed a sense of space and order, with its warm pine units and smart granite worktops fitted across the back half, and its large farmhouse table where guest meals were eaten set under the sloping roof of some kind of porch extension, well away from the cooking area. Now, the morning's dirty dishes were carelessly piled up next to last night's by the sink, Rupert's superlative sauce fit only for the flies gathering on the plates and pans, which stretched halfway around the kitchen. Naively, I'd assumed Gloria would do something about them before Rupert got back – something other than stack them in towering piles, that is. There was a rancid smell. Under the rubble, I discovered its source to be the leftover *crème brûlée*.

Mindful of how distressing the mess might be for Rupert on his return and desperate for something to take my mind off the fact that my relationship was now officially in intensive care, I filled the gigantic butler sink with steaming lemon-scented bubbles and took my frustration out on the dishes.

God knows, things hadn't been brilliant between Nathan and me, and I knew deep down that it takes two to allow a relationship to slide – but even so, you didn't go on holiday to mend bridges and expect your live-in lover to jump onto the first available life raft. We'd been together five years and lived together for three of them. Buying a flat had been a commitment. I didn't think it was unreasonable to expect fidelity and the occasional honest conversation.

Worst of all, I'd been so blindsided by his admission and accusations – and my own temper – that I hadn't even got onto the main topic for discussion: getting away from this place.

Two smashed plates, a cracked glass and a chipped cup later, I still had a fair amount of pent-up frustration to release on other household objects, so I looked around for more chores. I didn't have to look far. Either Gloria was so distraught about her husband that she couldn't bring herself to deal with mundane things, or it was as I suspected – that she left domestic matters to Rupert and Madame What's-Her-Name the cleaner, who must have been having a day off, judging by the state of things.

I'd located a broom and was about to brandish it when I heard a car outside. Assuming it must be Gloria returning with Rupert, I glanced out of the window, but didn't recognise the blue hatchback. As the driver unfolded his tall frame from the small car, I wondered how he could get in or out without doing himself some sort of injury. He must have been well over six foot.

He wasn't a *gîte* guest. Vacancy enquiry for the guesthouse? Maybe. He reached into the passenger side and brought out a laptop case, which he flung over one broad shoulder, then a file folder. Hmm. Insurance salesman? He wasn't wearing a suit, just chinos and a short-sleeved shirt.

He headed across the courtyard towards the house with long strides. I wasn't in the mood to deal with visitors or unsolicited callers, so when I opened the door, it was with a scowl – although that faltered a little as I took in the short brown hair and matching eyes in a rather handsome face.

'Yes? Can I help?' It came out sharper than I'd intended, but then my holiday – indeed, my life – wasn't turning out how I'd intended either, so he would have to lump it.

My appearance at the door seemed to have unnerved him. His brow furrowed. 'Hi. Er. Is Rupert in?'

I shook my head. 'No, sorry.'

He frowned. 'Gloria?' It could have been my imagination, but I thought he said her name with an element of distaste.

'No. Can I help?'

'And... You are?'

I didn't like the tone of inquisition in his voice. 'Emmy. I'm a guest here,' I snapped.

He stared at the broom in my hand in some consternation. 'Ah. I see.' Although clearly he didn't. 'Do you know when Rupert will be back?'

I could play the interrogation game myself. I didn't know this bloke from Adam, and I wasn't sure how much Rupert would want me to tell him. 'May I ask why you need to know?'

'I have an appointment with him. I'm Alain.' I was momentarily confused. Was he French, then? Because he spoke perfect English – although now I thought about it, there was the very slightest hint of an accent there. He held out his hand for me to shake, and I automatically took it as he added, 'I'm Rupert's accountant.'

I dropped his hand like it was poison. Accountants weren't currently my favourite kind of people.

'Well, I'm sorry, but Rupert's in hospital,' I told him. When obvious concern crossed his features, I softened my tone. 'He's fine and he's coming home later today, but he'll need to rest.'

'I'm sorry to hear that. Do you know what's wrong?'

I hesitated. 'Yes, but I don't think I should say.' When his expression turned to alarm, I hastened to reassure him. 'Please don't worry, it's nothing too serious. But I don't know you, and

I don't know if Rupert would want me blabbing all his medical details.'

Rather than take offence as I expected, he said, 'I understand. Thank you. I'll let you go back to' – he glanced in puzzlement at the broom – 'whatever you were doing.' He held out his hand again, which I took with the briefest of touches. 'Pleased to meet you,' he said as he turned to go – although as he went down the steps, I thought I heard him mutter, 'I think.'

When Nathan skulked back in, I was sweeping the kitchen floor. Staring at the brush and dustpan in my hands, he raised his eyebrows. 'I hardly think that's your job.'

'Someone has to do it, since Gloria's incapable of endangering her fingernails,' I snapped. 'I could hardly let Rupert come back to a pigsty in his state, could I?'

As if conjured by my words, Gloria's sports convertible swung up to the house. Rupert couldn't climb out of the low vehicle because of his injured leg. Glancing across the courtyard at his sensible estate car, I was exasperated by Gloria's lack of consideration. I shot Nathan a look of disgust at his lack of gallantry and went down to the car, waiting patiently until Rupert managed to swivel on his seat enough for me and Gloria to pull him out.

Huffing, we helped the invalid up the couple of steps to the kitchen and lowered him into an old easy chair by the window. I fetched a footstool from the lounge for him to raise his leg. Usually cheery and ruddy-complexioned from the sun, Rupert looked pale with all the effort, and I was shocked at how much older he suddenly seemed, his face unshaven, his wavy silver-grey hair straggly and uncombed.

Unsure what to do next, I turned to put the kettle on, but Rupert caught my hand.

'Emmy, dear girl,' he said, his voice shaky. 'I'm so sorry for what I put you through last night. You must have been terrified. Bet you thought I was a goner.' He winked.

'I'm just glad you're alright, Rupert.'

'Thanks to you.'

Aware that Nathan and Gloria were watching intently, I blustered, 'I didn't do much.'

'You did your best, and I'm grateful, love.'

He kissed my hand. I was so touched by the gratitude in this old-fashioned gesture that I felt an unexpected tear prickle, but Gloria's eyes were boring into me over Rupert's shoulder like drills. How she had the cheek to give me a look like that, I don't know. If she'd been where she should have been last night, he wouldn't have had to thank me at all.

Straightening up, I shot the look right back. 'Tea, anyone?' I asked.

Gloria shook her head. 'I have to get the Hendersons' room ready.' She turned to click her way upstairs.

I offered a cup to Nathan, but he looked so uncomfortable, I thought he might drop it, so I left it on the table for him. Had he found a conscience now Rupert was home?

Apparently not.

'I'd better help Gloria,' he declared and shot off after her, leaving me with an excess of tea, a wan invalid, and the instant resolve that I would be following him in precisely three minutes to make sure helping her was all he *did* do.

CHAPTER THREE

I couldn't recall the last time Nathan had offered to help *me* with any housework, and my overactive imagination didn't find it hard to stretch from envisaging him and Gloria making a bed together to them rolling around in one.

'Thanks, Emmy.' Rupert smiled appreciatively when I handed him his cup of tea. A few sips brought colour back into his cheeks. He was a tall man, and broad with it, but the way he sat hunched in the chair now, his usual vitality and the mischievous twinkle in his eye were noticeably absent. 'Your doing?' he asked.

'Hmm?'

He gestured around the now-sparkling kitchen. 'The cleaner's visiting her sick sister and Gloria hasn't got a domestic bone in her body, so I assume this is all down to you.'

'Oh, er, yes. I wanted something to do.' The minute the words were out of my mouth, I could have bitten my tongue, and sure enough...

'Something to do? Surely you're not bored already. Shouldn't you be out and about with Nathan, enjoying yourselves?' Rupert obviously didn't suspect a thing.

'Something to do to help,' I back-pedalled. 'I knew Gloria had to fetch you and you have guests arriving later.'

'Well, it's good of you, love, but I don't want your holiday spoiled any more than it already has been. You and Nathan both look like you need to relax a bit.'

Ha! He didn't know the half of it, the poor sod. Anxious to steer the subject away from our supposed holiday bliss, I pointed to his leg. 'How are you going to cope with more guests?'

Rupert shrugged philosophically. 'Madame Dupont will be in tomorrow to clean, and the gardener's due back at the weekend.' His brow furrowed. 'It's the cooking that's the problem. Gloria can't cook for toffee, I'm afraid.'

His laugh took me by surprise. 'What's so funny?'

'What's so funny, Emmy, is that Gloria was the manageress of a restaurant when I met her. Fancy place in London. You'd think working with all that food, something would've rubbed off, but alas no. She can't boil an egg. Guests who've booked for three gourmet meals a week won't expect to be given cold baked beans on chargrilled toast.'

'You mustn't worry about us,' I hurried to reassure him. 'Nathan and I can eat out.'

This would have been the perfect opportunity to tell him we wouldn't be a worry for much longer, since we would be moving on – but he looked so ill, I didn't have the heart. I didn't want him to think we were leaving because he was incapacitated. That would be like kicking him when he was already down.

'That's kind of you,' he cut across my thoughts. 'I know you'd muck in with any arrangement, but the Hendersons are another matter. Been here before. Fussy pair. Told me they come back every year just for the food. Heaven help 'em this year.'

'Surely if you explain...'

'It'd go down like a lead balloon.' Rupert patted my hand. 'I'll find a way around it when my brain gets back in gear. Right now, all I can cope with is a nap.'

'No lunch?'

He shook his head. 'Too tired. Would you do me a favour, Emmy?'

'Of course.'

'Pass me that pen and notebook, will you?'

I handed it to him and he started scribbling. 'Could you take this up to Gloria? She'll need to go shopping as soon as she's got the Hendersons' room ready.'

He tore off the list and I shoved it in my pocket. Helping him out of his chair, I passed him his crutches and we went down the hall to his quarters. It was a good job it was on the ground floor, because there was no way he could have managed the stairs.

Trying not to be nosy as we passed through his private lounge-kitchen, I helped him into the bedroom – a pink and floral monstrosity that Gloria presumably couldn't get away with elsewhere in the guesthouse. It looked as though she'd channelled all her feminine decorating frustrations into the one room. How Rupert could sleep amongst the lace curtains and chintzy duvet cover and nauseating dusky-pink walls was beyond me. The poor man's eyes closed the minute he lay down. If I had to spend any time in there, I thought, I'd want to close my eyes, too.

Back in the hall, I slipped off my shoes to minimise noise and crept upstairs. Nathan and Gloria had been alone far longer than I'd planned. Feeling ridiculous with my shoes dangling from my hand, I followed the sound of murmuring voices as I tiptoed along the landing and popped up in the doorway.

They were both fully clothed and genuinely involved in domestic chores – so far, so good – but they were also giggling as they battled to stuff a king-size duvet into its cover. Not so good.

They stopped what they were doing and looked up.

'Why are you carrying your shoes, Emmy?' Gloria's eyebrows rose into plucked arcs, her expression smug. She knew damned well why, and she was victorious because I hadn't got the evidence I'd come for.

'They're new. I have a blister. I came up to change them.' Time to set the proverbial cat amongst the pigeons. 'Rupert's worried about cooking tonight. It looks as though you'll have to do it.'

She stiffened in shock. 'But I don't... I can't... Rupert will have to manage!'

'He can't stand, and if he could, he'd fall over with exhaustion. He says the Hendersons will expect to be fed, so you'll have to do the shopping and then cook the evening meal.' I pulled the list from my pocket, wafted it at her and placed it on the bedside table.

Gloria wavered between terror and defiance. 'No, that's not possible. I mean – no, I don't think so.'

She looked to Nathan for support and I watched him squirm, caught between her plea for solidarity and his awareness that siding with Gloria in front of me wasn't a good idea.

'Perhaps Nathan could lend you a hand, Gloria, since he's suddenly so domesticated?'

I flounced out – but as I sought refuge in my room and flopped down on the bed, my petty victory soon faded. The cold reality was that in less than twenty-four hours, I'd plummeted from being in a boring but stable relationship to scoring minor points over my unfaithful boyfriend and his middle-aged one-night-stand.

The sooner we were away from this place, the better.

I knew when Nathan had successfully completed his domestic chores because I was standing in our bedroom with the door open a crack, watching until I saw Gloria go downstairs, presumably either to go shopping or to take care of her ailing husband – although knowing Gloria, neither was necessarily a given.

Nathan wasn't allowed the chance to follow. I intercepted him at the head of the stairs. 'I'd like a word.'

He gave an exaggerated sigh. '*Another* one?'

'Yes, another one. *If* it's not too much trouble.'

He followed me into our – my – room. 'What now?'

'We need to find new accommodation, Nathan. We can't stay here.' *Please don't say "why not?"*

'I agree.'

My eyes widened in surprise. 'You do?'

'Of course. It's clear that Rupert isn't able to run the place now. It'll be a complete shambles.'

I stared at him in disbelief. 'That's all that worries you? That you might not get a decent breakfast? Not the fact that you had sex with Gloria or that you're sleeping in a separate room from me or that I can't trust you or that you've ruined our holiday?'

'The difference is, Em, those aren't things I can fix.'

I felt my chin wobble and hated myself for it. 'Do you even *want* to fix them?'

He evaded the question. 'I guess we could look for somewhere else to stay, or we could alter the ferry and go home. But I do think we should leave it till tomorrow.'

There was a strange look in his eye that I couldn't quite pin down.

'We need to think properly about which we're doing,' he said. 'And about us. I'm not sure we should rush into anything.'

Hmmm. For a man who didn't want to talk things through, he certainly seemed to have been thinking things through. On the surface, his request fell just this side of reasonable. As to what was going on under the surface, I could only hazard a guess.

I couldn't see what staying one more night would achieve, but since this was the nearest he'd got to indicating he might be putting any effort whatsoever into our ailing relationship and was willing to at least think and talk about it, I was loath to complain.

I heaved a sigh. 'Fine. One more night, Nathan. But we are *definitely* leaving here tomorrow. And there had better be no more creeping about in the night from *you*.' I jabbed a finger in his direction. 'Lay hands on Gloria again and there won't be any discussing what's best for us, because there won't *be* any "us". Understand?'

Exhausted, I closed the bedroom door on his rapidly retreating back and was drawn by the inner sanctuary of the bathroom, where I could shoot the bolt and be alone with my thoughts. It was a spacious and soothing room with blue and white country tiles, honey-hued pine trimmings and a gigantic white claw-foot bath. Perfect.

Turning on the hot tap, I rummaged through the wicker basket of individual complimentary toiletries on the shelf until I found a little bottle of bath oil, which I poured lavishly into the running water. As I climbed in, melting into the bubbles, I imagined I could hear my poor tense back and shoulders sigh with relief.

As I lay with my eyes closed, the only sound that of the bubbles shifting and popping and the scent of the lavender oil soothing my senses, it occurred to me I was taking quite a risk, absconding like this, what with Rupert taking a nap and Gloria therefore unchaperoned. But since she had shopping to attend to, I really couldn't see how she would find time to philander with my boyfriend.

When I went downstairs after almost having drowned myself by dozing off in the bath, I was relieved to see that Gloria had indeed been shopping and therefore couldn't have been shagging my boyfriend. I was less relieved to see that Nathan was helping her unpack. This sudden domestic streak of his was beginning to annoy the hell out of me.

Just as I was formulating a suitably sarcastic comment, Rupert limped in on his crutches and sat heavily at the table, his eyes still sleepy from his nap. I put the kettle on.

When I placed a mug of tea in front of him, he gave a grateful smile, oblivious to the malicious undertow of ill feeling in the room. But as I grudgingly placed a mug in front of Gloria, she slumped dramatically in her chair, head in hands, and declared that she had a migraine coming on.

'I need to lie down until it goes away,' she whined.

'But what about the Hendersons? What about tonight's meal? I can't do it on my own!' Rupert looked decidedly ruffled. 'Can't you take one of your pills?'

She shot him a pained look. 'Yes, but they take forever to work. It won't subside unless I lie perfectly still in a darkened room.'

'Gloria, I appreciate you're not well, but can't you get by just this once?' Rupert wheedled. 'After all, the Hendersons – you know what they're like.'

'No, I cannot get by, unless you want me to vomit all over the food. I need to go to my room and I can't be disturbed under any circumstances!' She flounced off.

Rupert looked at the shopping strewn across the worktops and dropped his head in his hands. 'What am I going to do now?'

'We can go out for a meal tonight, can't we, Nathan?' I offered.

'If we must.' He gave me a disdainful look, and I wasn't sure what upset him more – the fact that he'd paid for three meals a week and his host had been inconsiderate enough to fall too ill to provide them, or the thought of having to spend an unexpected couple of hours sitting in a restaurant with me.

'That's good of you both,' Rupert said, 'but it doesn't solve the problem of the Hendersons.'

'The Hendersons could go out too, couldn't they?' I asked hopefully, already suspecting the answer.

'Yes – if I don't mind never having their business again and them denouncing me to all and sundry. They were promised a welcome meal and they'll expect to get one. They may be a pain in the arse, Emmy, but they come every year and recommend us to all their friends. I'm not sure I want to lose that amount of business over one meal.'

'Surely when they see what a state you're in...'

'It won't wash with them.' He sighed. 'Ah, well.' He hoisted himself from his chair, grabbed one of his crutches and headed for the mound of groceries on the counter. 'I'll have to manage.'

I watched in horror. He might be up to doing bits and pieces, but he certainly wasn't up to creating a gourmet three-course meal by himself.

'Rupert, don't be ridiculous. You've only just got out of hospital and you can barely stand up.' I gave Nathan the steely eye. 'Perhaps we could help?'

'Oh, Emmy, no, I couldn't possibly...' Rupert began.

But Nathan cut across him, his tone clipped and ice-cold. 'Sorry, Emmy, but no. Going to a restaurant is one thing. Cooking my own dinner when I've already paid for it is quite another. I'm off for a drive.'

He turned on his heel, snatched up the car keys from the windowsill and headed through the door.

I turned back to Rupert. 'I'm sorry.'

'No need to apologise, Emmy. It should be me apologising to you. You're on holiday. You shouldn't be put in a position where you feel obliged to help. If I'd known Gloria was going to fall by the wayside, I would've got someone in, but it's a bit late now.' He looked uncomfortable. 'On top of all that, I've caused you and Nathan to argue.'

I led him back to his chair. 'It wasn't you that caused the row. Nathan and I...' How could I make him feel better without giving him any insight into the real goings-on in this whole charade? 'We're still uptight from work, that's all. Nathan doesn't relax easily. He's not mean, just not very good at going with the flow.' I tried for a lighter mood. 'He's an accountant, used to everything being planned to within an inch of its life eighteen months in advance.' Which reminded me... 'Talking of accountants, yours dropped by this morning. Said he had an appointment.'

Rupert nodded. 'Never mind. Nothing that won't wait.'

'I told him you were in hospital, but I didn't tell him why – other than not to worry. Was that okay?'

'Alain's a good friend. You could have told him, but it's fine if you didn't.'

'Right, then.' As I glanced around the large kitchen with its shiny state-of-the-art gadgetry, expensive-looking pans dangling from one of the wooden beams and professional chef's knives ranged in size order on their magnetic strip near the double oven, I did my best to hide my panic. Cooking had never been my strong suit. 'You'd better tell me what needs to be done.'

When the Hendersons arrived, Gloria was still conveniently convalescing and Nathan was still out for his drive. That left Rupert and me skivvying in the kitchen – or more accurately, me skivvying while Rupert directed proceedings. The small voice in my head which agreed with Nathan that this was not what might be expected on the itinerary of an expensive holiday had been outvoted by my conscience. Nathan had slept with Rupert's wife, even if Rupert was ignorant of that fact. Didn't it occur to him that he owed Rupert a favour or two under the circumstances? Clearly not.

And so, by proxy, I was stuck with the sense of obligation. I'd always been a bit of a sap. Helpless kittens by the roadside that needed taking to the vet, lost children in the supermarket that needed reuniting with their mother – you name it, I'd never been one to walk away from a crisis. Still, there was a fine line between being a good Samaritan and a total doormat... Or maybe not.

Rupert got started on the main course while I was charged with chopping fruit for the fruit salad.

'Pineapple and mango on the counter. Apples and bananas in the fruit bowl. Grapes in the fridge,' he barked.

'Right.'

'Halve the grapes. Everything else in cubes.'

I turned the pineapple helplessly in my hands, wondering where to start. I only ever bought this stuff in tins.

Rupert sighed. 'Do you know how to core a pineapple?'

I shook my head.

'Okay. Leave that for me. Don't want spiky bits in it. God knows, the Hendersons are spiky enough as it is.'

I pushed the pineapple across at him and then stared glumly at the mango.

'Don't bruise it as you peel it, Emmy. Do the apples and bananas last or they'll go brown, then squeeze a few oranges and pour the juice over. Add a couple of tablespoons of honey.'

I gritted my teeth and got started. When the phone rang, I would have ignored it, but Rupert glanced at me expectantly so I dutifully answered, mango juice running down my arm.

'Er... *La Cour des Roses*?'

'Oh. Hello. Is that... Emmy?'

'Yes. Who is this?' At least it wasn't a babble of French I couldn't follow.

'Alain. We met this morning.'

Ah. The accountant. 'Can I help?'

'I was wondering if Rupert's back from the hospital. If he's alright?'

'Pssst.' This from Rupert. 'Who is it?'

I covered the phone with my mangoey hand. 'Your accountant. Do you want to speak to him?'

Rupert nodded and I took the phone across to him. He wiped the mango juice from it with a disapproving glare.

'Alain! Yes, fine, absolutely fine. Just a gammy leg. Nothing to get het up about. Sorry I wasn't here when you came this morning. I'll give you a call sometime to rearrange...'

I shook my head and got back to my allotted tasks. How he could be so blasé, I didn't know.

When the fruit salad was done, I went over to see what he was up to. He had meat browning in a large pot, and it smelled delicious. 'Next?'

'Veg for the casserole. Onions in the larder. Sliced, not chopped. Carrots, tomatoes, courgette in the fridge.'

'Hmmph.' I took out my frustration at being ordered around on the vegetables, chopping them with rather more vigour than they deserved.

Rupert looked across, presumably drawn by the vicious thwack of the knife on the wooden chopping board. 'For God's sake, Emmy, they all need to be even-sized cubes!'

'For God's sake, Rupert, if you don't shut up, I'll shove this even-sized carrot right up your...'

A flourish of flying gravel put an end to our bickering. As I watched the new arrivals climb out of their sleek, black, brand-new saloon, my heart sank. A smug-looking middle-aged couple, he in a navy blazer, she in a pure linen cream trouser suit, headed up the steps like they owned the place and looked me over as though I was the hired help – which, to be fair, was exactly what I looked like. I politely said hello and moved aside for them to come into the kitchen, where Rupert sat by the oven with his leg up, a packet of frozen peas balanced precariously across his swollen leg.

His prediction that the Hendersons would be unimpressed by his plight was more than accurate. He welcomed them with his usual gusto, explained that he was somewhat incapacitated but they weren't to worry, they would be looked after as well as always, Gloria would be here shortly, etc, etc... And that was when he came unstuck, because he had no choice but to introduce me as a fellow guest.

Mrs Henderson's eyes couldn't have got any wider without her eyeballs popping out of their sockets and rolling across the stone floor as she took in my dishevelled appearance – tomato-stained apron, tear-tracked cheeks from chopping onions, mango pulp in my hair. Her mouth turned down with displeasure and disbelief. Obviously she had not expected to find her host sitting around with his feet up, his wife conspicuously absent and a fellow guest roped in as slave labour.

'I see,' she murmured, glancing across at her husband.

Mr Henderson looked unfazed, and for a moment I thought we had at least one sympathetic guest between the two of them. Until he opened his mouth.

'Never mind, Hunter, I know you'll make sure we get everything we've paid for. Same room as always? See that someone brings the luggage up, would you? Come along, Anita, we'll go up and check the room's in order.' He led his wife upstairs, leaving me to gape after them in wonder.

'Really, some people!' I spluttered. 'What do they think this is, a five-star bloody hotel?'

But to my surprise, Rupert began to laugh. It started as a slow rumble deep in his chest, bubbling from his mouth in a delighted splutter. 'Ring for the bellboy, Emmy, there's a good girl.'

There was no option but to see the funny side. If I didn't laugh, I'd have to cry. In a glorious release of misery and tension, we laughed until the tears rolled down our faces. I hoped the Hendersons couldn't hear us, but they were probably too busy inspecting every square inch of their room for dust and defects.

When Nathan returned from his drive, Rupert's face was purple, and when he laughed, pain shot through his leg so his laughter was interspersed with shouts of agony. The stitch in my side had me doubled up so badly that I'd subsided into an untidy heap against the pale yellow wall. The distaste on Nathan's face only made us laugh harder.

'Bellboy!' Rupert stage-whispered to me, pointing at Nathan. I howled with merriment.

Nathan glared at us. 'What's so funny?' he snapped. 'For crying out loud, Em, get a grip.'

'Can't,' I spluttered. 'Ouch!' Clutching my side, I tried to get myself under control as Nathan waited impatiently for an explanation. I couldn't be bothered with one. He was hardly likely to see the funny side. 'You need to bring the Hendersons' luggage in and take it up to their room.'

'What?'

'The Hendersons' luggage. You...'

'I heard. You must be joking! I'm not ferrying luggage about. I'm a guest here myself.'

His high-handed response sobered me up quicker than a hard slap.

'Rupert can't do it and Gloria's still lying down,' I told him. 'You could wake her up – I'm sure that would make you popular. As for me, I'm messy and tired and I've just spent the last two hours mincing and chopping while *you* went for a drive. It won't kill you, surely?'

Nathan's face was mutinous as he stared me down. Contempt was written across his face in capital letters. 'Emmy, I haven't paid good money to come on some sort of working holiday. I'm sorry Rupert isn't well, but he's running a business and he needs to sort it out. He'll have to get hired help in. It's not your job to slave away cooking and cleaning, and it's not his job to sit and watch while you do it.'

I opened my mouth to point out that he'd been more than happy to offer his bed-making services to Gloria, but thankfully Rupert cut across me.

'You're quite right, Nathan,' he said, his voice steady. 'Emmy has gone above and beyond the call of duty, and yes, I do need to sort something out, but I hadn't expected Gloria to be so indisposed. This is a one-off, I assure you. I appreciate Emmy mucking in, and I'll make sure it's reflected in your bill.'

'Oh, Rupert, that's not necessary,' I chipped in, upset that Nathan had made him grovel.

'If Rupert wants to make the gesture, Emmy, then of course it's necessary,' Nathan said. 'It's a matter of principle, after all.'

Uh-oh. Bad choice of words, Nathan.

'A matter of principle? Well, of course, you'd know all about *principles!* I stopped. 'Oh, just bring the bloody bags in.'

'Why can't the bloody Hendersons bring their own bloody bags in? Are they crippled?'

'No, but you will be if you don't...'

'I can hear that racket down the hall.' Gloria appeared in the doorway, freshly coiffed and made up. It was good to know her conveniently-timed lie down had resulted in a full recovery.

CHAPTER FOUR

Somehow, we ended up with delicious antipasto – juicy olives, vine-ripened tomatoes, slivers of smoked chicken, vegetable crudités (chopped into perfect matchsticks by me as per Rupert's instructions) with balsamic vinegar to dip them in – followed by a tasty country casserole. I enjoyed this very much, until Mrs Henderson enquired what the meat was. She might have been used to eating rabbit, but I certainly wasn't. I paled at the revelation, but since it was too late for the rabbit, and I'd already eaten some, I recovered my poise and finished what was on my plate, declining seconds.

As I contemplated the tropical fruit salad, I tried to swallow my resentment towards Rupert for such a labour-intensive menu. I knew the poor man couldn't have guessed his wife wouldn't be at his side helping him, but there'd been an inordinate amount to do.

The large kitchen table was welcoming as usual, with its matching pale blue linen tablecloth and napkins, the cut-glass wine glasses glinting in subdued lighting... But the atmosphere was less than jovial. Hardly surprising, since most of us weren't talking to each other. Gloria unkindly left it to Rupert to make the evening swing, but his face was etched with tired lines and he ate very little.

It was the Hendersons, oblivious to any undercurrent of strain or malice, who unwittingly saved the evening by regaling us with horror stories of the "dreadful" B&B they'd stayed in on the journey down and their lavish plans for living it up in Paris on the way back.

'Honestly, I have never stayed anywhere with such cheap, nasty bed sheets,' Mrs Henderson exclaimed with disgust. 'Heaven only *knows* what the cotton count was. The towels were bald, and there was a chip in my water glass – disgraceful. Almost cut my lip. I'm positive the bedroom shutters had woodworm.' She shuddered. 'And the breakfast!'

'Cold bread rolls and jam,' her husband chipped in. 'And coffee. That was it. No fresh pastries like you have here, Hunter. No offer of eggs. Not even a decent cup of tea. Bloody disgrace. Never again!'

I suspected the owners of the B&B were probably saying the same thing about the Hendersons.

Soon after the meal, for which they managed a cursory compliment, they retired to their room. Exhausted from cooking and keeping up a pretence in front of Rupert, I was desperate to do the same – but I had to wait until Nathan retired to his. I wanted to know exactly where he was for the night.

I followed him up the stairs. 'So have you thought yet? About what's happening tomorrow?' I asked him, closing his door behind us.

He frowned. 'I thought that was the point of staying another night. To give us time to think.'

My eyebrows shot up. 'You're hardly going to be thinking when you're asleep. You've had time today, surely?'

He stared at his feet. 'Of course I have, but... All I know is that it's obvious things aren't going too well between us.'

'I think we've already established that.' I sighed. 'Maybe we need to try to remember the good times. When we were first going out together, we wanted to see each other all the time.' I tried a smile. 'You used to ring me from accounts to tell me how much you fancied me in my suit. We had a sandwich together instead of working through. And deciding to buy the flat... We felt good about that. We had fun choosing the furniture, getting things how we wanted them. Having people round. It's only this last year or so that it's... deteriorated. I think we need to be asking ourselves why. And where do we take it from here?'

He looked up. 'Where do *you* want to take it from here?'

'I don't know. But I do know we need to get away from here so we can talk about what we both want, how we might make things work. Is that a problem?'

A sad look crossed his eyes. 'I think the problem, Emmy, is that you're obviously not going to forgive or forget what happened with Gloria.'

I balked. 'Of course I'm not going to forget! I might forgive, but that takes time and work. From *both* of us.'

He nodded. 'I'm tired. Let's sleep on it. We'll talk in the morning.'

By the time I staggered down for breakfast, the Hendersons had already set off on a *château*-and-culture hunt.

'Nathan not up yet?' Rupert asked as he handed me a cup of wonderfully strong coffee.

I'd heard Nathan go downstairs before I had my shower this morning, but since I'd assumed Rupert would be up to deal with the Hendersons' breakfast, I hadn't worried about it.

'Yes. Well before me,' I answered carefully.

'Hasn't had any breakfast. Nor has Gloria. Hope they're not sickening for something.'

They were pretty sickening, alright. What were those two up to? A quickie in the henhouse, maybe?

When they both came into the kitchen a few minutes later, I found myself looking for evidence of straw in their hair or chicken poop on their backs – but Gloria wasn't at all dishevelled, and

Nathan was smartly casual as usual in tailored shorts and polo shirt. Hmm.

Rupert, bless him, was as oblivious as ever. 'Changeover day for the *gîtes* tomorrow,' he announced. 'Two to clean out, and we're full next week so all three to get ready.' He looked across at Gloria.

'Madame Dupont will be here, won't she?' she asked defiantly.

'Hope so, but it usually takes her *and* the two of us. Do you want me to ring her? See if she can get anybody to come with her tomorrow? That niece of hers might want a few euros. What do you reckon?'

For a moment, Gloria seemed distracted. Then – completely out of context, it seemed to me – she smiled.

'Don't worry, Rupert. I'm sure Madame Dupont and I will manage.'

'Sure, Gloria? It'll be hard work.'

'We'll be fine.'

You could have knocked me over with a chicken feather.

After breakfast, Rupert and Gloria disappeared to their quarters, leaving Nathan and me to stare at the table or floor – anywhere but each other.

'So what's it to be?' My question hung between us, suspended on air thick with animosity.

'Not here.' He grabbed me by the elbow to steer me upstairs. It was the first time he'd touched me in days, but there was nothing loving or intimate about it.

As he pushed me indelicately into his room and closed the door, trepidation uncurled in my gut. The sun shone brightly through the window, highlighting the dust motes that danced above the dark wood furniture. I thought how quaint and pretty they made the room look.

Nathan stood with his hands shoved in his pockets. He looked slightly sick, his Adam's apple bobbing up and down when he swallowed. Despite the warmth in the room, my arms felt cold and goose-bumped. I rubbed them absent-mindedly.

'Nathan?'

'I'm leaving.'

'Sorry?' I looked at him blankly.

Nathan let out an exasperated sigh, as though I were a child who couldn't understand the simplest concept. 'For heaven's sake, Em.' He gestured past the bed to his open suitcase on the floor by the window, and to drive his point home, he started emptying drawers and shelves and packing his case in that neatly-folded, anal way of his.

I experienced a wave of relief that he was finally thinking along the same lines as me.

'Thank goodness for that! Do you want to try and get a room somewhere else, or should we cut our losses and go home? I'm veering that way myself, but I think we should phone the ferry company first to make sure we can get the booking changed.'

Nathan stood across the room from me, his arms full of socks. 'You're not listening. I said *I'm* leaving. Not we. Me. And I'm not going back home. Not yet, anyway. I'm just leaving this place.'

There was a sickening pause. My heart thudded in my chest. I knew what he was going to say a split second before it came out of his mouth.

'I'm leaving *you*, Emmy.'

The silence in the room was so stifling, I thought I could hear my own heartbeat, yet proof that everyday life was still going on all around us drifted in through the open window. Chickens clucking in the garden, a tractor rumbling over a nearby field, that indefinable scent of early summer: a promise of flowers and sunshine and all things sweet.

It took a moment for his words to sink in. When they finally filtered through my misfiring synapses, I said, 'You're kidding, right?'

'For God's sake, Emmy. You're standing here watching me pack. Does it look like I'm kidding?'

I stared at him, wide-eyed with disbelief. I'd lain awake for two nights trying to find the heart to forgive him his indiscretion, worrying about how we could patch things up, wondering whether we were worth it. And he was planning to just jack it all in?

'That's it? No discussion?'

His mechanical folding and arranging faltered. I couldn't understand how he could pack with the same precision with which he approached his working life, whilst telling his partner of five years that he was leaving her. 'What's the point?'

Unwanted tears rolled down my cheeks. I brushed them away with the hem of my T-shirt. 'But that was why I wanted us to have a holiday – to discuss things, to try to make things better!'

Nathan shrugged – a gesture of indifferent finality. 'Well, the holiday served its purpose. We tried, but let's face it, it's no good.'

'Tried? Tried what? You must be joking!' Anger rose in my throat to choke me, and droplets of saliva shot in his direction as I fought to fire the words out. '*I* tried. *I* suggested this holiday and made all the arrangements. You only went along with it for an easy life. We argued all the way here, spent half the week barely speaking to each other – as usual – and then you slept with someone else's wife. You call *that* trying? You lazy, emotionally-stunted bastard!'

As I fought to catch my breath, I searched his face for any clue as to why he was doing this. I just couldn't get my head around how swiftly everything had deteriorated.

Then I heard the distant clatter of heels, and a wave of nausea and realisation swept over me.

'You're not going alone.' It was a statement, not a question. I'd never been so sickeningly sure of anything in my life.

Nathan stared at the toe of his shoe. 'No. Gloria and I are going together. She's leaving Rupert and... We're going together. Somewhere. For a while.'

He looked like a confused teenager, determined to stick to the path of rebellion he'd embarked on while perhaps already beginning to regret it. The brief flicker of sympathy that flashed through me faded as fast as it came. I hoped he damned well *would* regret it. It was one thing to be asked for a trial separation because you both needed a bit of space. It was quite another to be left for a woman substantially older than you, with bleached roots and impractical footwear and spider-mascara.

'You're leaving me for *Gloria*?'

'Yes. Well, no. What I mean is, I'm leaving because things between you and me aren't working. Neither is Gloria's marriage. Obviously. So it seems logical to go together. But not because of each other. If you see what I mean.'

'Bloody hell, Nathan, how many times did you rehearse that?' I suspected he had no idea what he wanted – that Gloria was merely a catalyst, and he was being carried along by the excitement of taking action for a change. 'You know you have no future with her, don't you?'

His rebellion sparked back. 'That's not fair, Em. You don't know that. Besides, we haven't thought that far ahead. But with due respect, I can't see a future with you at the moment, either.'

He had me there. I couldn't imagine how we would ever claw back from this. To think I'd been almost pleased yesterday, when he'd said he wanted time to think things over. I'd hoped he felt some remorse – that he was willing to find a way to put things back together between us. But no. He'd been planning his departure with Gloria.

I was tired of shouting. Tired of listening. Tired of caring. Who was this man? The man I'd once thought sweet and handsome and romantic, the man I'd thought would be my best friend and lover for a lifetime? He wasn't my best friend any more. I didn't think he had been for quite some time. As for my lover – I realised now that our love-making had long since drifted into the realms of the functional. I wasn't losing a lover or a best friend. It seemed I'd already lost them some time ago.

Well, I'd wanted something to happen to shake up our relationship, and sure enough, something had.

Downstairs in the kitchen, Rupert sat in the easy chair by the patio doors, his complexion as faded as the upholstery. He stared bleakly out into the garden, his hands clenched tightly together in his lap, his shoulders slumped. The poor sod. If this had come out of the blue for me, it must have been one hell of a shock for him. At least I already knew things were rotten and had only been plunged from misery into worse misery. Rupert had been dropped directly from the heights of assumed marital bliss into total betrayal.

I made him a cup of tea.

'How very English of you,' he said. 'Tea for a crisis. Thank you.' He patted my arm. 'Don't worry, love, we'll get by.'

'I know. Although I'm not sure how.'

He winked. 'Darling Emmy, I'm an entrepreneur. I always think of something.'

I couldn't help but smile. 'Ever the optimist.' Hesitating, I asked, 'Are you very upset, Rupert?' then shook my head. 'Ignore that question. It's none of my business.'

I watched him warily, thinking he might be cross with me for being so nosy, but instead he let out a large snort of laughter.

'What's so damned funny?' I demanded.

'You're so damned funny, saying it's none of your business, you silly girl. Your wet dishcloth of a boyfriend has had sex with my wife, under our noses, under my roof, and they're currently in the process of leaving us both high and dry. If that doesn't qualify as your business, God knows what does!'

'I'm so sorry.'

'What the hell for?'

'For Nathan's behaviour. For booking the bloody holiday. If we hadn't come here, this never would have happened.'

'It might not have happened to you, but it probably would've happened to me, sooner or later. If not with your delightful partner, then with somebody else's. It should be me apologising to you for *her* behaviour.'

'Don't be ridiculous, Rupert. You can't be held responsible for your wife's behaviour.'

'No. And neither can you for his.' He jerked his thumb towards Nathan, who was coming downstairs with his suitcase and studiously avoiding eye contact with the man whose wife he was stealing. 'Perhaps we're both better off, love.'

I stood in the doorway for the grand departure, looking out across the courtyard at the rows of lavender and the pretty *gîtes,* where normal people must be having normal holidays. Gloria had yet to make her appearance. No doubt she was busy deciding between her designer shoes and handbags, and squirreling away all her jewellery so there was no chance of Rupert claiming it back.

Thank goodness the Hendersons were out soaking up the grandeur of whichever *château* they'd chosen to bless with their presence. Since they were already unimpressed by Rupert's injury, I couldn't imagine what they would make of this sorry spectacle.

Nathan loaded his suitcase into Gloria's sports car, then came back in for her luggage. Despite my misery, I almost laughed at his furious attempts to cram it all into the woefully inadequate boot space. Gloria was high maintenance and probably took four suitcases for a simple weekend away, but even so, it looked as though she'd packed for the long-term. My heart sank. I turned to look at Rupert, but he wouldn't catch my eye, instead staring out at the scene with a stony indifference on his face. It was impossible to tell whether his heart was breaking or if he was glad to see the back of her.

Gloria came clattering down the hall and stopped as if to say something to him, then seemed to think better of it. Instead, she teetered off to the car, whispering something to Nathan before climbing into the passenger seat. My God, they really were an item – she was letting him drive her precious convertible.

Nathan came back over, scuffing at the gravel with the toe of his shoe. 'Right, we'll be off, then.'

What did he want? A medal? A pat on the head to tell him I didn't mind him deserting me, less than a week into our holiday, to run off with an ageing, over-sexed adulteress?

I clutched my arms across my chest in a vain attempt to hug myself warm. I felt so numb and cold I couldn't speak.

'Gloria said to tell Rupert she'll be in touch about the rest of her stuff,' Nathan muttered, unable to look me in the eye.

'I'll tell him.'

And still he stood there. 'Emmy...'

I wanted him to go. I couldn't stand the sight of him. Or her.

'What do you want me to say, Nathan? *Bon voyage*? You need to leave now.'

For a brief second, I thought I could see regret in his eyes – maybe even a change of heart. But then Gloria beeped the horn, the impatient bitch, and that flicker of connection was gone. He went back to the car, squeezed in beside her, started the engine and set off across the courtyard and down the lane.

Closing the door, I glanced at Rupert, but I didn't think he was in the mood to be comforted by the woman whose boyfriend had run off with his wife. Leaving him in peace, I went up to my room to lick my own wounds.

Rupert and I got exceedingly drunk that night. It was the only decent thing to do. Whether we were celebrating or grieving, we weren't sure – but after several large glasses of Beaujolais, it didn't seem to matter. I did express my reservations about him combining too much alcohol with his newly-prescribed medication for his newly-diagnosed angina, but he told me to bugger off, so I left it at that.

'So what needs to be done tomorrow?' I asked him cautiously.

His shoulders slumped. 'One *gîte* to freshen, two to clean out. Shopping. Meal to cook.' It was as though the effort of just thinking about it left him no energy for anything more than monosyllables.

'Well, then, I think you should phone Madame Dupont right now. See if she knows anyone who can help us out tomorrow.'

'Help *us* out?'

'Yes. Us. You can hardly mange by yourself, can you? Even with Madame Dupont here.'

'No, but I can hardly ask you to...'

'You're not asking. I'm offering,' I told him sternly. 'And I have no intention of arguing about it. I'm too tired and very probably too drunk.'

There was a pause. 'Then I'm grateful,' he said quietly. 'But we need to come to some sort of arrangement about payment...'

'What did I say about arguing? Make the phone call. If you leave it any longer, there'll be no chance.'

He nodded and did as he was told. The call lasted far longer than I felt was necessary for a simple enquiry, but I could only hear Rupert's side and it was all in lightning-speed French, so I could make neither head nor tail of it.

As he yammered on, with long pauses where I could hear Madame Dupont's less-than-dulcet tones yammering back, I cursed every bone in Gloria's bony body. At breakfast, when she'd been all sweetness-and-light and had stated that she and Madame Dupont would manage perfectly well, she had *known* she wouldn't be here tomorrow. She could have let Rupert make the call when he suggested it, while there was still a chance. Even if he'd got someone to cover his share of the work, we still would have been one down when Gloria left. But no, that wasn't good enough for her. She'd deliberately put him off so he'd be doubly in the shit. I could have killed her.

When Rupert put the phone down, I demanded to know how a straightforward request for casual labour could take fifteen minutes.

'Things work differently around here, Emmy,' he explained patiently. 'First, I had to enquire after Madame Dupont's health and she had to enquire after mine, then I had to check that she was still coming tomorrow, then I had to ask if she knew anyone who could help. Then she had to run through every last person within a ten-mile radius who might have been willing to do it but can't and give a reason for each of them. Her daughter's away visiting a friend, her niece's husband's a lazy pig and wouldn't look after the kids even though they could do with the money, and the girl who lives two farms away might have but she's got a Saturday job at the *tabac* in the village. She can't think of anyone else at such short notice. Then she said she understood that I was incapacitated and she would be happy to work longer hours than usual to help Gloria, so I had to admit that Gloria wouldn't be available but you were willing to chip in, so she demanded to know why, and when I told her why, she had to ask for every last detail and I had to fob her off with as little as I could get away with. And finally, she had to give her lengthy and vitriolic opinion on the whole sorry subject. See?'

My mouth gaped open. I took advantage of my parted lips to pour more wine through the opening. 'You told her that Gloria's left?'

'What else would I tell her once she asked?'

'Couldn't you have come up with some other excuse?'

'Couldn't be bothered. Too hard to keep up a pretence. Besides, we only need one person to have spotted Gloria and Nathan riding off together, and the cat would've been out of the bag anyway.'

I blanched. 'You told her that Nathan left?'

'No choice. It'd be obvious tomorrow, what with you helping and no sign of a chivalrous man at your side. She may be getting on a bit, but she's still as sharp as a knife.'

For a moment, the shame was unbearable, but I pulled myself together. If I was embarrassed, how must he feel, knowing all his friends and neighbours would soon get word that his wife had left him for one of his guests?

I gave him a small smile and lifted my glass. 'Well. Here's to...' But I really couldn't think of anything to toast.

Rupert chipped in drunkenly. 'How about to laughing in the face of adversity... And unexpected friendship?'

I clinked my glass against his.

CHAPTER FIVE

When my balance became impaired, I made the executive decision that the wine sloshing around our empty stomachs must be mopped up by French bread – an excellent sponge for alcohol – and put together a makeshift supper.

'How did you and Gloria get together, then?' I asked, as I stuffed some rather smelly cheese into my mouth. It wasn't something I would have touched with a bargepole if I'd been sober – but I wasn't sober.

Rupert's eyes glassed over, as though he were transported back to his and Gloria's heady days of romance. Or maybe it was the alcohol.

'I was out at a restaurant with friends in London. Gloria was the manageress there. Asked her out. She was younger than me, but in those days the heart used to overrule the head more.'

'How long ago was that?'

'Ten years.' He swirled the ruby-red healing waters around in his glass, watching the whirlpool. 'Proposed to her after three months. Couldn't believe my luck when she said yes. That place where she worked was full of City types. She could have had her pick.'

Privately, I thought Rupert wore rose-tinted glasses. Gloria's airs and graces were a thin veneer, one those City types probably saw right through. They would have viewed her as a possible good time, not a marriageable commodity. Besides, she must have been at least mid-thirties by then. If she was that good a catch, why hadn't somebody snapped her up before?

'Gloria had already been married,' Rupert answered my unspoken question. 'Too young, and it didn't last long. I'd never been married. Plenty of opportunities, of course.' He winked. 'But I always got cold feet when things got serious. Didn't feel that way with Gloria, though. Maybe it was my age – nearly fifty and never married, and here was someone daft enough to have a go at it with me.'

'You did okay, being married ten years,' I comforted. 'That's not bad going nowadays.'

'No, I suppose not. How long were you and Nathan together?'

Fleetingly, I noticed we were both talking about our relationships in the past tense.

'Five years. We met at work and went out for a year or so, then Nathan saw a flat for sale that he liked, so we bought it and moved in together. We've been there just over three years.'

Rupert glanced at my left hand. 'No engagement? No wedding plans?'

I glared at my ring finger as though it lacked something. 'No, not really. We were busy with the flat and work's always so hectic and we both work long hours and...' I realised I was making a string of excuses. Perhaps if we were meant for each other, Nathan *would* have proposed by now. After everything that had happened, I could only be grateful he hadn't.

'No talk of babies? Starting a family?'

I shook my head. 'We never really discussed that either. If it cropped up, Nathan would shrug it off and say we were a bit young – not ready yet. That we were happy enough as we were.' God, I must be drunk. I was telling Rupert things I hadn't even discussed with my mother. 'I did wonder about it sometimes. I mean, I'm thirty-one. Nathan's thirty-three. We've been together five years. How long were we going to wait?'

'You didn't try to persuade him?'

'No – and I think that might be your answer right there.'

'How do you mean?'

'I mean that whenever he evaded the subject, I took it personally. I thought: doesn't he love me enough to want to raise a family with me? *But* I never pushed back very hard. I thought that was because I loved my job and wasn't ready to settle down to that extent yet. But maybe it just meant that I didn't love *him* enough, either.' I shrugged. 'Or that I didn't want children enough.'

Rupert inclined his head to one side as he drunkenly pondered the implications. 'Or maybe it means that you would like children one day, but subconsciously you knew Nathan wasn't the right man to be their father?'

'Perhaps,' I mumbled.

Valiantly, Rupert tried to change the subject. 'You said you met at work. Do you still work at the same place?'

'Yes, but in different departments, obviously...' Nausea hit me like a brick, the cheese and wine roiling in my stomach, as the implication hit home. 'Oh God. What am I going to do when I go back?' I jumped up from my chair and started pacing – well, weaving – around the kitchen table. 'How is *that* going to work, with both of us at the same place? It's going to be *awful.*' A couple of big fat tears escaped and rolled down my cheeks.

Rupert shifted awkwardly in his chair. 'Don't cry, Emmy. It'll be uncomfortable for a while, but you'll find a way. Nathan has a great deal more to feel uncomfortable about than you. You have the moral high ground, and don't you forget it!'

He fell silent for a moment while I swiped at my tears with a napkin, streaking my face with breadcrumbs. My legs weren't too happy about keeping me upright, so I sat back down.

And then Rupert asked the question I'd been dreading. 'Did you know about Nathan and Gloria? Before today?'

I toyed with the idea of lying to him, but we were both past that. What would be the point?

'Yes.' I tried to look him in the eye, as best I could after three large glasses of wine. 'But not all of it.' His questioning expression encouraged me to go on. 'I knew they'd done it once, but I thought that was it. I never dreamed they'd leave us. I'm sorry.'

'What for?'

'For knowing when you didn't. The night I found out was the night you fell ill. I could hardly tell you then. Besides, Gloria didn't want us to say anything.'

'No, I bet.' He patted my hand. 'At least Nathan had the decency to fess up.' He picked up on my discomfort. 'That isn't what happened, is it?'

'Trust me, Rupert, you don't want to know.'

'Yes, I do. It'll do you good to get it off your chest. Come on. Out with it.'

I spilled the beans. My race up to the roof terrace, the scene I found there (although I spared him the details), Nathan's pathetic excuses, kicking him out into another room – the whole caboodle. My brain was too fuzzy to come up with an alternative version. When I'd finished, for a moment I thought I'd done the wrong thing. Then Rupert laughed, a sharp bark that made me jump.

'Ha! It's better than one of those dreadful soaps.' He shot me a look of sympathy. 'You poor girl. When I thanked you for doing your best when I collapsed, I had no idea how much more I had to thank you for. You did well, keeping your head like you did. A lesser woman would have gone to pieces over a discovery like that and forgotten all about me and my old ticker struggling away down in the kitchen.'

I grinned. 'It was touch and go for a couple of minutes, believe me.'

The Hendersons made an appearance around ten, by which time Rupert and I were well and truly plastered. I thought we made a passable show of not slurring our words too much, but I couldn't stay upright in my chair, and Rupert's glazed eyes were as red as his cheeks. Their disapproving looks indicated that our attempts at sobriety were less than successful. After the required pleasantries, they headed for their room, but as we heaved a sigh of relief, Mr Henderson poked his head back around the door.

'Dinner at seven tomorrow, Hunter?'

Rupert valiantly fought the stricken expression creeping across his face. 'Seven. Absolutely.' When the door closed again, he flopped his head back. 'Oh, Emmy, what am I going to do?'

'You're going to bed. We'll worry about it tomorrow.'

'Tomorrow's too late. There won't be enough time for planning *and* doing. And we'll be hung-over.'

'Then we'll make sure we get up early enough for a conference. If we feel crap, we feel crap. Can't do anything about it tonight. We could solve world hunger right now and neither of us would remember it in the morning. C'mon.'

I helped him out of his chair. He was exhausted and his limp was severe as he headed to his room.

'Night, Rupert. Don't worry. It'll work out somehow.'

'Night, Emmy. Thanks, love. For your support. You're a real trooper.'

I stumbled up the stairs, but as I swayed into our room – my room, now – I was grateful for the alcohol blurring the edges of stark reality that assaulted my senses everywhere I turned.

One suitcase on top of the wardrobe, one toiletry bag in the bathroom, one toothbrush by the sink.

Nathan had gone – and it felt like he'd taken all the good memories with him. The day he'd asked me out across the photocopier, when I'd punched my hand in the air in delight the minute he'd turned his back. Our first date in a candlelit restaurant, when he'd told me he'd fancied me from the minute he saw me. The summer he'd fallen in the river trying to climb into a rowing boat. Reading the Sunday papers in bed with a vatful of coffee. The evening he'd asked me to buy the flat with him. The day we'd moved in, when there were *two* toothbrushes by the sink, along with an implication of forever.

All those memories had been overwritten by images of Gloria's legs wrapped around him; his sulky face as he told me he was leaving; him driving away in her sports car.

At that moment, in my drunken haze, I hated him for that.

When the alarm clock penetrated my fuzzy brain, I felt like death and pretty much looked like it. A whole bottle of wine? I should have known better. Still, it was the only thing to have done under the circumstances, and despite the nausea and pounding head, I didn't regret it.

Crawling out of bed and into the shower, I hoped Rupert was in a fit mental – if not physical – state today. I needed his interpreting skills to help me communicate with Madame Dupont, and he would have to get his head around a menu for tonight – assuming I could find my way to the supermarket and back without ending up in Paris.

As I walked back into the bedroom and dropped my damp towel on the floor, I caught sight of my reflection in the ornate full-length gilt mirror and glared at it. I may have been on the untoned side (that gym membership was definitely a waste of money) and had a tendency to go pink and freckled before getting a tan, but I didn't think I looked much worse than any other woman in her early thirties.

It's easy to sympathise with fifty-something women whose husbands leave them for someone younger, traded in for a newer model. What sickened me was that my thirty-three-year-old man, somewhat on the young side for a midlife crisis, had left me for a woman at least a decade *older* than him – a woman who, although glamorous and well-preserved in an artificial sort of way, surely couldn't compare to still-reasonably-fresh me.

I stared at the offending image in the mirror. Nathan hadn't just slept with Gloria – he'd run off with her. What if it wasn't only about looks or make-up or calorie-counting? What if it was just... me? I didn't think I'd changed since we first met, but perhaps in his eyes I had. Was I more impatient? A tad grumpier? Less fun? Less caring? Less interesting?

Pulling on a long, baggy T-shirt, I let out a heavy sigh. There was a three-person, twelve-hour day ahead to share between an ancient cleaner, a novice and an invalid. I already had a headache and felt sick. Getting depressed wasn't going to help.

Deciding coffee and breakfast might be of more practical use, I staggered downstairs, my hair still dripping from the shower. I'd guessed – correctly – that Rupert wouldn't be up and about yet, but in my hung-over state, I'd completely forgotten about the Hendersons until I was in the kitchen. Belatedly remembering my state of dress, I glanced through the window in a panic, letting out a sigh of relief that their car wasn't there. Presumably, they'd already left to forage for their own breakfast because their irresponsible host had failed to get up early enough to prepare one for them. Another black mark against Rupert.

I groped for the espresso machine, made a strong one and, clutching it in my hands as if my life depended on it, trundled to the patio doors to look out over the garden.

And there he was.

At least six feet tall, strong but not too beefy, over-long sun-streaked blonde hair, work jeans – and no shirt. As he chopped at the hedge with shears, his muscles rippled and a slight sheen of sweat covered his tanned torso. What a sight for sore eyes. After the last few dreary months, it was like stumbling onto an oasis in the desert of my suppressed senses.

Somehow aware of my arrival, the vision turned and smiled – and what a smile. White teeth, blue eyes, chiselled jaw... Okay, forget the "chiselled" because yes, I knew it, I was beginning to sound like a romance novel.

I smiled back, then remembered how little my T-shirt covered and how bedraggled my hair was.

He put down the shears and started towards the house. Uh-oh. Too late to run away and slip into something more suitable. Since he'd already seen what there was to see, I opened the patio door a fraction.

He held out a tanned, rather soily hand. 'Morning. You must be Emmy. I'm Ryan.'

I shook his hand. My fingers went numb, and I wasn't sure whether it was because he had a grip like a vice or because all the blood had rushed from my hands to other departments.

'Er, yes. Hi. I – er – I'm sorry, I didn't expect anyone to be here.' I gestured apologetically at my sparsely-clad person and, to top off my embarrassment, blushed like a schoolgirl.

'No, so I see.' There was no way of knowing whether the amused tone in his voice stemmed from my looking cutely messy, as I hoped, or crappy messy, which I suspected was more likely.

'Didn't Rupert tell you about me?' he asked.

My mind was a blank. 'I don't think so.'

Ryan gestured behind him. 'I do the garden in the summer, except I missed last week because I was back in England. Rupert keeps it at bay himself in the winter.'

'Oh, yes, he said something about the gardener being due back soon. Well, that's good. One less thing for Rupert to worry about, what with his leg and everything.' I floundered. 'You do know about his leg and everything?'

'Word gets around.'

I saw a trace of pity in his eyes and flinched. He knew all right, and not only about Rupert's leg. Madame Dupont must have been clogging up the local telephone wires half the night after Rupert called her.

'Ah, so that's how you know my name. Local gossip.'

He pointed at my cup. 'Smells good. Any chance of one?' Deliberately or not, he was giving me a way out of the uncomfortable turn the conversation had taken.

I was grateful. 'No problem. I'll get dressed and bring you one out.'

'Thanks.' As he headed back to the hedge, he looked back, a cute smile on his handsome face. 'By the way, no need to get dressed on my account.'

I couldn't get to my room fast enough. Ten minutes later, I'd tousle-dried my hair, pulled on slimming denim crops and a low-cut T-shirt, ladled on nude lip gloss and made him his coffee, which I carried out onto the patio.

He came back up the garden when he saw me. 'Thanks.' Taking a sip, he let out an exaggerated sigh, as though he'd gone to coffee-shop heaven. 'You make good coffee.'

'Just one of my many talents,' I trilled girlishly, then winced at how flirtatious it sounded. The boy could be ten years my junior, for goodness' sake. Flirting was definitely out – life was far too complicated as it was. Making a fool of myself by fawning over a handsome youth could only add to my pain. Besides, I imagined he had girls throwing themselves at his feet wherever he went. I wouldn't be surprised if good old Gloria had tried it on. Poor lad.

Thankfully, Ryan didn't appear to notice my gaucheness. He was too busy savouring the sensory marvel that was my coffee. 'Far superior to Gloria's,' he said. 'Not that she offered too often. I was glad she didn't, after tasting it. Awful stuff – sludgy and bitter.' He made a face.

'I know. I think she bought the cheapest she could find. I'm using Rupert's secret stash of the good stuff now that she...' I hesitated, then ploughed on. 'Now that she's gone. The grapevine announced to you that she left, I presume?'

'Yep. Good riddance. Rupert's better off without her.' He grimaced. 'Sorry, that was an insensitive thing to say. I heard your boyfriend went, too. This must be a pretty crap time for you.'

'Well, it's not been much fun so far. But I'm okay. I've got so much to do helping Rupert today that I won't have time to wallow.'

'You're not leaving?' he asked in surprise.

I stared at him for a moment. The truth was, I was still processing the fact that Nathan had left me. The idea of cutting my losses and actually leaving hadn't yet filtered into my beleaguered brain.

'I don't think so. Not yet, anyway. I couldn't do that to Rupert so soon after... Well.' No need to go into detail. 'The least I can do is stay until he's a bit better and we can sort out some help around here.' *Because I feel so cripplingly guilty about what my boyfriend has done. Because I have nowhere else to go. Because I don't want to drive across France all by myself and go home to an empty flat and face up to family and friends and colleagues and reality in general.*

Ryan drained his cup. 'That's good of you, under the circumstances. If it makes it any easier for you, I'll spread the word that you're capable and coping and couldn't give a hoot that your man ran off with the wicked witch.' He smiled – a real full-on, handsome-guy smile that crinkled the corners of his blue eyes. 'I'll see you around. I promised Rupert I'd do a couple of extra stints to make up for missing last week.' He handed me his empty cup, started to walk down the garden, then turned back. 'If you find yourself losing that stiff upper lip, come and see me. I don't mind being a shoulder to cry on. Rupert's not very good at that sort of thing.'

'Thanks, Ryan. I'll bear it in mind.'

Come and see me. What the hell was that supposed to mean?

Still musing over gorgeous Ryan and his flirty manner, I went to rouse Rupert. When there was no response to my discreet knocks on the outer door of his quarters, I let myself in and rapped on his bedroom door. That didn't wake him either, so I barged in to shake him out of his sleep. Strangely, I didn't hesitate. A week ago I hadn't even met the man, and already I had no qualms about invading his personal space. The way I saw it, there was no alternative. We were like two survivors shipwrecked on an island, thrown together to conquer impossible circumstances.

Even so, I was eternally grateful he wasn't in the habit of sleeping naked on top of his sheets. There is a limit.

Ten minutes later, he was hung-over but showered and caffeined-up, and we sat at the table to draw up our battle plan.

'Right. The guests in the *gîtes* aren't obliged to vacate until ten, Emmy, but in reality they often take longer, so you need to use the time before that to shop for the new guests' welcome baskets and the house guests' evening meal.'

Rupert sounded decisive, but as he started scribbling a shopping list, I noticed his hand was shaking. Hangover? Nerves? Shock? I had no way of knowing – and no time to ask.

'Madame Dupont can freshen up the empty third *gîte* if you get delayed.' He spoke as he wrote. 'There's plenty of spare linen, so the laundry can wait until tomorrow.'

I took the shopping list with trepidation. The truth was, I didn't like driving abroad. I could do it – I wasn't a danger to the continental public or anything – but I certainly wasn't as confident as at home.

But Rupert misunderstood my anxious expression. 'Emmy.' He reached across and patted my hand. 'You don't have to do this, you know.'

I straightened my spine. 'I know. But you can't manage by yourself.'

Rupert gave a small smile. 'Then thank you.' He hesitated. 'Are you... Are you planning to stay the week?'

There was a hopeful note in his voice that I couldn't ignore. I glanced at his fingers, still shaking lightly as he held the pen. His shoulders were slumped, his unshaven face ashen. Only a few short days ago, the man had been in the hospital with heart problems.

I thought back to what I'd said to Ryan, about waiting until Rupert was a little better and we could get help in. My ferry was booked for next weekend. If I left sooner, I'd have to mess about altering the booking, and since I had no idea what awaited me at home – if anything – I was more than happy to put off the inevitable. Besides, despite the events of the past few days, I liked it here. It was sunny and colourful and comfortable. Why head home to rain and explanations any sooner than necessary?

'Yes, I'm staying,' I said decisively. 'I can't be bothered to change all my plans, and I need to keep an eye on you or you'll do too much.'

'Well, I'm glad – but I do *not* want you slaving away on my behalf.' A pained expression crept across his face. 'I don't want you to feel obliged, Emmy.'

'I was thinking more along the lines of helping than slaving. At least it'll give you time to sort something out. *And* it'll keep my mind off Nathan.' When he looked like he might argue, I added, 'It's my holiday and I shall do what I like with it.'

'All right, if you insist.' He looked too tired to argue. 'But we'll review it on a day-to-day basis, and if you don't build in some me-time, as those ghastly life coach chaps call it, I shall have something to say about it. I'll transfer what you paid for the holiday back into your bank account, and I expect to pay you for whatever you do for me this coming week.' When I opened my mouth, he held up a hand to stop me. 'I would have had to pay for local help anyway.'

I shook my head, adamant. 'No way, Rupert. The holiday charge – okay. Wages – absolutely not.' Seeing the mutinous look on his face, I pointed at the clock on the wall. 'We can argue or I can shop. Which is it to be?'

I took myself utterly by surprise by driving the lanes past rolling fields and farmhouses to the outskirts of town, remembering Rupert's directions to the supermarket, parking without crashing, finding everything we needed and arriving back safely by ten-thirty. The rest of the day was a blur of sweat and hard labour, but since it meant I had no time to brood over Nathan's perfidy or Gloria's barefaced cheek or Rupert's dismay, I didn't mind. There was simply a job to be done with numerous deadlines – my speciality – along the way, and concentrating on the tasks at hand kept me from self-pity.

By the time I got back from the supermarket, Madame Dupont had already sorted out the unoccupied *gîte*, so we got to work on the other two, waiting politely until the occupants drove away and then piling in.

I might have been mortified last night that Rupert had told Madame Dupont everything on the phone, but today I was grateful. It meant no explanations were necessary.

Her face was brown and wrinkled from the sun and her old-fashioned floral dress, support stockings and black lace-up shoes gave me the impression of a strict grandmother. Her stern demeanour made me a little nervous about the day ahead – but as we muscled our way into the first *gîte*, she gave me a semi-toothless smile, patted my arm, pointed at the basket of cleaning accoutrements in my arms and said a simple *'Merci,'* rather loudly, as if I were deaf.

I smiled. We may not have understood each other linguistically, but it seemed she knew I was doing my best for Rupert. Heaven knew I had to be preferable to Gloria, who had probably let the poor old woman do the lion's share of the work while she rearranged the potpourri or trimmed stray cotton strands off the curtains.

Getting access to the *gîtes* brought out the nosiness in me. I'd seen photos on the website when I'd considered booking one for myself and Nathan, but they hadn't fully conveyed the delightfully rustic interiors. Rough whitewashed walls, stone fireplaces, wooden bed frames, beautiful patchwork quilts and soft woollen throws – they all exuded carefully-thought-out charm. Paperbacks and a smattering of board games on the shelves added a nice touch.

Curious, I went through the back door to where each *gîte* had its own outdoor space with a table, chairs and parasol, separated from its neighbours by trellises wound with climbing plants not quite yet in flower. A gate led to a communal lawned area which, screened from the courtyard and therefore from the danger of cars by a tall hedge, curved back around towards Rupert's garden – a lovely area to sunbathe or for kids to safely kick a ball around. I hadn't even known that part of the garden existed. No wonder this place kept Ryan busy in the summer.

The grass here was newly mown, but I could hear a motor still running. Unable to help myself, I peeped through the hedge that divided the *gîte* garden from Rupert's, to see Ryan pushing a large lawn mower, his muscles flexing as he swivelled around the flower beds. It took some effort to turn away. I strode quickly back to the *gîtes* before gawking could turn into stalking.

Limited to communicating with gestures and simple phrases, Madame Dupont and I got by, and I was surprised at how quickly my long-forgotten French seeped back into my consciousness as she chattered at me without expecting me to fully understand. While she dusted and swept, I mopped. She cleaned the oven while I cleaned the fridge. Since she knew where everything was kept, she checked the toiletry supplies while I scrubbed the bathroom.

As we changed the bedding together, my elbow knocked the shallow dish of potpourri on the bedside table, and I only just caught it before it scattered across the floor. Madame Dupont reached over and took it from me, then crooked her finger, beckoning me to follow. In the kitchen, she stood on the pedal of the bin and with a wink and a flourish, she poured the potpourri from a great height with a rapid-fire diatribe of which I only understood maybe every tenth word – but Gloria's name featured prominently, and I gathered that this was a symbolic cleaning out of her toxic presence.

I grinned along with my new ally as we dragged the bin bags outside and headed for the next *gîte*.

CHAPTER SIX

By late afternoon, all three *gîtes* were done, with two occupied and one awaiting an arrival, and I was pooped. Poor Madame Dupont was pooped too, so much so that I offered her a lift home. She only lived half a mile down the lane, but I was worried her varicose veins wouldn't get her there.

As I pulled up outside her dilapidated cottage, she let out a string of Gallic invective, then she patted my cheek and said *'Merci,'* several times. Despite the language barrier, I understood the gist. It was good to know that she, and ergo the rest of the neighbourhood, was on our side.

As I waited for her to get safely indoors, a cacophony of noise drifted through the open car window and I craned my neck to see over her fence, looking for the source of the racket. Dozens of scrawny, evil-looking black hen-like creatures scurried about her yard and the land beyond. I pulled a face. I couldn't imagine having to look at and listen to them all day. Good job her neighbours weren't too close.

When I got back, Rupert made me a well-deserved cup of tea.

'Get Madame Dupont home alright?'

'Yep. That cottage should be under some sort of historic preservation act.'

Rupert laughed. 'You should see inside.'

'What are those ghastly creatures she's got in her yard? Hens or something. What on earth does she keep those for?'

'They're a sort of chicken. Madame Dupont has several grown-up children and therefore numerous grandchildren and great-grandchildren. That's a lot of mouths to feed.'

'Mouths to feed?' I looked at him questioningly, although I had a nasty feeling where the conversation was going.

'They're good eating birds. When she has family to visit or she visits them, they get a chicken. I wouldn't get too friendly with her if I were you, or you might find yourself on the receiving end of her generosity.' He twisted his hands in a wringing motion.

I shuddered at the thought of the ugly birds' bald necks. 'Wish I'd never asked.'

Taking a gulp of reviving tea, I kicked off my sandals and put my aching feet up on the chair opposite. Now that the flurry of the day was over, my mind latched straight back onto Nathan's desertion.

I looked across at Rupert. 'Do you mind if I ask you something?'

He shrugged. 'Depends what it is.'

'I wondered... Were you and Gloria having problems already? Before Nathan?' But then I stopped and held up a warning hand. No matter how desperate I was to find reasons for being abandoned, I didn't have the right to pry into Rupert's marriage. 'Actually, no, don't answer. Sorry. Nothing to do with me.'

'If it'll stop you feeling so guilty about his behaviour, I don't mind telling you.' He shot me an exasperated look. 'Yes, we were having problems. Things were good at first. Gloria gave up work and we rented out her little house and split our time between my flat in London and the house in Mallorca. It was a perfect life for her – sunning herself on the coast half the year, shopping and fancy restaurants the other half. Then, about six years ago, I decided to buy this place. You should have seen it, Emmy. It was a wreck, but I fell in love with it the minute I saw it. I knew it could be beautiful and I needed a new project. I was bored with Spain, and London was only a bolt-hole to me. Several of the pies I had fingers in had come to a natural conclusion and this place seemed like the perfect investment. It could earn us an income for as long as we wanted and would be worth loads more than we'd shelled out on it if we wanted to sell. So I went ahead and bought it.'

I took a sip of tea, sighing in appreciation, and nodded at him to continue.

'Gloria liked the idea, but she didn't know what she was letting herself in for. We had to live here to oversee the work, and it wasn't the relative luxury she was used to. When it was finished, we advertised to upmarket types and she quite liked the idea of being the lady of the manor. She wasn't so keen on the hard work it entailed, though – and of course, it tied us down. I rented out the place in Mallorca because we didn't have time to go there any more. Gloria sulked about that. She made sure we still went to London, but I wasn't bothered about gallivanting over there too often, so sometimes she went on her own.' He poured more tea. 'I was blind, Emmy, or stubborn, or both. We're not exactly next door to Paris here. The novelty wore off for Gloria, but I loved it so much, I stuck my head in the sand.'

'That's understandable.'

'Maybe, but also terribly complacent. I knew when I married her that it was probably my lifestyle she found attractive.' He smiled ruefully. 'But then it all seemed to go a darned sight better than I expected. Lulled me into a false sense of security.' He sighed. 'I should have seen things from her point of view. She married a reasonably dashing middle-aged man of independent means who could offer her the nearest she was likely to get to a jet-set lifestyle, and ended up in the middle of nowhere with a bunch of noisy chickens and an ageing stick-in-the-mud.'

So much for the rose-tinted glasses I'd thought Rupert had on last night.

'You're not being fair on yourself,' I told him.

'No sympathy, please. I only told you so you'd get it into your head once and for all that Nathan's poor decision – and that's what it was, Emmy, because he must have been mad to cheat on you – had nothing to do with breaking us up. My marriage was already foundering on the rocks. Nathan was merely the catalyst to an inevitable conclusion.'

'Funny. That's exactly the same way I see Gloria. As a catalyst. Nathan and I were fine at first – we had a lot in common, working at the same company, and we enjoyed the same things. But then it started to slip, and like you, I didn't pay enough attention – at first, anyway. This past year, I'd noticed it more. Fewer conversations that weren't about things like the energy tariff or replacing the boiler. And working at the same place meant we tended to spend our evenings telling each other about our day at the office in vast detail. It got kind of depressing. But lately, even that tailed off. Less talking. Fewer evenings out. Less...' I blushed furiously.

'Less sex?' Rupert asked gently.

I nodded, miserable and embarrassed. 'I put it down to tiredness, working too hard... But it's obvious now that the spark had died a bit. I just didn't think it had died enough for him to sleep with someone else. And it would have been so much better if Gloria was a nubile twenty-three-year-old. It's not good for the ego when your boyfriend runs off with someone older than you.' I gave him a curious look. 'How old *is* Gloria?'

'Forty-six,' Rupert admitted apologetically.

I made a face. 'I can't imagine what's got into their heads. A bit of illicit lust is one thing, but running off together? It can't last.'

'No, I don't imagine it will,' Rupert agreed. 'I think they're probably using each other as an excuse – a way out for them both. For now.'

He finished his tea, and we heaved ourselves back to our feet for kitchen duty. I was grateful to see that he'd planned his menu more sensibly this time: homemade spring vegetable soup from the freezer to start, followed by a cold seafood platter – plump prawns, lobster tails and crab, surrounded by salad leaves – and fresh fruit salad for dessert. Three delicious courses that looked and tasted fantastic but were mercifully light on hard work, and all of which we could prepare in advance. We worked amicably side by side, defrosting, chopping and peeling. At least there would be no standing over a hot stove co-ordinating numerous dishes to come together at once – something Rupert wasn't up to and I was frankly incapable of. One-pot Emmy, that was me.

'I met your gardener this morning,' I said casually.

Rupert nodded. 'I like Ryan. He's a hard worker, that's for sure. Done wonders with the garden. Usually comes in two or three times a week, so you'll likely see him again before you go.' He glanced sideways at me, a mischievous twinkle in his eye. 'Good-looking young man, wouldn't you say?'

'I suppose.' I gave a nonchalant shrug, although certain nerve-ends were tingling at the vision I still had in my head from this morning. 'If you like that sort of thing.'

Rupert grinned. 'Not your type? Prefer a nice, studious accountant?'

I grimaced. 'Ha! Not any more. I think Nathan's put me off accountants for life!'

Rupert nodded. 'Understandable. I doubt I'll be chasing after any blonde restaurant managers in the near future, either.'

As we finished off in the kitchen, we decided the new *gîte* guests need know nothing of Rupert's current situation. They had the accommodation they'd booked, a welcome basket as promised, and the owner was available to provide information and deal with any problems as advertised. The fact that only one of the owners was around would probably go unnoticed.

The Hendersons were a different matter, however. It would be too much to hope *they* wouldn't notice the place being run by one incapacitated member of the team, while the able-bodied one was permanently unavailable. I didn't think a couple who could spot a speck of dust at twenty paces would be blind to the fact that my partner was suddenly missing too, while I was permanently up to my elbows in household chores.

'We'll get 'em drunk tonight,' was Rupert's solution. It seemed to be his solution to most things. 'I'll dig out the Chablis.'

Piece of cake.

The Hendersons were indeed impressed by the wine, but not by the news. I admired the way Rupert handled it. He may have come across as a jovial buffoon, but I was beginning to see that this was a front he put on for the guests' benefit, to put them at ease during their stay and presumably to soften the brittle edges of Gloria's manner.

Rupert kept his announcement factual. 'Well, I imagine you're wondering why Emmy and I were somewhat... inebriated when you came back last night.'

Mrs Henderson's eyebrows shot up, and her husband shifted in his chair.

'I would apologise for our behaviour,' Rupert went on, 'but I'm sure when you hear the reason behind it, you'll understand.' He refilled their glasses. 'I'm afraid my wife has taken it upon herself to leave me at what is rather an inconvenient time. Emmy has kindly agreed to help me over the next few days, so I hope you'll bear with us.'

Clearly amazed that a paying guest would offer to do any such thing, Mrs Henderson's eyebrows shot up even higher. 'I see,' she managed. 'Well, we're both...very sorry, of course.'

'Absolutely, Hunter,' her husband chipped in. 'Rotten luck. Bad timing, as you say.'

Mrs Henderson's pursed lips as she glanced sideways at her husband confirmed that Rupert knew his stuff. Lies would have been seen through and put him in a bad light.

To break the awkward silence, Rupert launched into one of his tales. 'Did I ever tell you the story behind the name for this place?'

I smiled encouragement. Anything to get us back onto neutral ground.

'*La Cour des Roses* – courtyard of roses. Straightforward, you'd think. And when we first saw the place, it seemed an obvious enough name. There was a courtyard, and there were roses. Millions of the things. Trouble was, they'd taken over the whole garden, strangling themselves and everything else in sight, especially the climbers. So what was the first thing we had to do? Have 'em all taken out. Every last one of 'em. Someone came in with a digger, and all we were left with was a mud bath. It was pretty depressing, I can tell you. There we were with a property named after roses, and not a blasted rose in sight!' He laughed. 'But the name sounded so pretty, we didn't have the heart to change it. Besides, what would we have changed it to? *La Cour de la Désolation* doesn't have quite the same appeal, does it? So I had to get the landscaping chap to train those rambling roses over the doorways of the main house, and Ryan's been introducing a few new bushes in the garden each year...'

I listened to him ramble on with a smile on my face. Last night, he'd called me a real trooper. Well, he was quite a trooper, too.

The next day, I revelled in a much-deserved Sunday lie-in. I eventually surfaced around noon, groggy and grumpy, my body complaining that its caffeine fix was a good three hours overdue. As I dragged on some clothes, I glanced at my phone on the bedside table. The message screen was devoid of contact from Nathan. I hadn't expected any different. I wasn't sure if or why I wanted to hear from the cheating bastard anyway.

I wondered if I should be making some calls myself. My parents, for a start – but I wasn't sure I was strong enough for that yet. My mother was... strident, and she would have an awful lot to say and no qualms about saying it. My dad would only worry, and as an accountant himself, he'd always got on so well with Nathan. I'd never understood half of what they talked about, but they seemed to enjoy themselves. Why tell them any sooner than I needed to? Maybe that was best left for when I went home.

I could phone my little brother, but although Nick would express sympathy, as a committed commitment-phobe, he could never fully understand. Besides, he'd probably think Nathan leaving was a cause for celebration – he and Nathan had never got on.

My best friend Kate, on the other hand... With a pang that hurt, I wished I could meet up with her for a latte to sob out my woes, but since that couldn't happen, a phone call would have to do. I flicked up her number and clicked on it.

She answered immediately. 'Emmy! How's France? I wasn't expecting you to phone! Is everything okay?'

At the sound of her voice, the emotion I'd been holding in check for Rupert's sake – and mine – flooded over me in a sudden wave. 'No!' I wailed. 'Nathan left me!'

'He *what*?'

Ten minutes later, she was up to speed with a fairly incoherent account of Nathan, Gloria and Rupert.

'Bloody Nathan. Bloody disgrace,' she pronounced. 'You're better off without him.' There was a pause. 'Sorry. I shouldn't have said that.' Another pause. 'Do you think he'll come back?'

'I don't know,' I admitted, exhausted after my rant. 'I'm still so angry with him, I can't think straight. It's all been so unexpected.'

'I know,' Kate soothed. 'You've told me a few times that things were getting a bit dull, but I never imagined Nathan would do something like that! He's always been so... straight-laced.'

'You were going to say boring,' I muttered.

Kate and Nathan got along passably for my sake, but they didn't have much in common. Kate was bright and bubbly and passionate about things like the environment and equality. Nathan was the epitome of conservative capitalism. Chalk and cheese.

'I wasn't. I only meant it seems out of character. Maybe he just needs some space. A trial separation.'

'He didn't say that,' I pointed out.

'Will you try to phone him? In a few days?'

I shook my head, then realised she couldn't see me. 'No. Absolutely not. It would look like I was begging. And since I don't know how I feel about him, other than sodding livid, I don't see the point.'

She sighed. 'I wish I was there, Emmy. But...'

'Don't remind me! Ten days in the Maldives with Jamie. What time do you fly?'

'Later this afternoon. Jamie's collecting me around two.'

'Okay, well, have a lovely time.' I was going to cry again. 'Thanks, Kate. I feel better.'

'You don't sound better.'

I straightened my spine. There was nothing more she could do for me for now. 'I'll see you when you get back?'

'I'll phone you as soon as I can. Promise.'

I powered off the phone and put it in the drawer, where I wouldn't be tempted to check it for messages from Nathan.

Downstairs, there was no sign of Rupert – although he must have been up and about because the washing machine was taking off on a supersonic spin cycle.

The Hendersons were just leaving.

'Where to today, then?' I asked politely.

'Le Château d'Ussé,' Mrs Henderson announced. 'It was the inspiration for Sleeping Beauty, you know.'

'No, I didn't know. Well, enjoy.'

She managed a small wave and off they went. Two people I would be less likely to associate with fairy tales, I couldn't imagine.

I stuffed down a croissant while I waited for the washing machine to come in to land, dragged out the king-size sheets we'd stripped from the *gîtes* yesterday, and trudged outside to peg them out on the line at the bottom of the garden.

No sign of Ryan or his muscles. Shame. Still, it was a Sunday.

Mentally telling myself off for even thinking about him, I trooped back inside to shove another load of washing in, then scanned the bookcase in the hall. The worthy tomes I'd packed along with my good intentions held no appeal, so I plucked out a thriller and went outside. I wandered down the garden, skirting islands of bright pink azaleas and pale yellow roses until I found a wooden Adirondack chair under an arbour of sweetly-scented lilac. The warm sun slanted through the leaves and flowers, just the right temperature for soaking up some vitamin D without roasting, and it was the perfect hideaway for losing myself in the happy world of murder and mayhem in Rupert's book. The plot tore along at quite a pace and I got so wrapped up in it that I jumped when my stomach gurgled loudly.

Taking heed, I headed back to the house. As I crossed the patio, someone called out.

'Excuse me.' A woman stood at the gate between the courtyard and the garden. 'Hi, sorry to disturb you. I'm Jenny Brown. I'm in the *gîte* at the end over there. I didn't get to meet you yesterday.'

Realising she must have arrived while I'd driven Madame Dupont home, I crossed to the gate and shook her hand. 'It's nice to meet you. I hope everything's all right for you.'

'Gorgeous. Just what we were hoping for. Harry's been working too hard. We both have. I found this place on the Internet and it looked so scrumptious and I thought, gosh, that's just what we need. A little R & R, a *château* or two. You know.'

'Yes. I know.' I plastered a smile on my face to hide the fact that my heart had plummeted to my feet. Her words were an echo of mine to Nathan – and look how that had turned out. I hoped Jenny and Harry would have a better time of it.

'Feel free to come over if you need anything,' I told her.

'We will.' She turned to go, then swung back round. 'By the way, I'm sorry about your husband's leg.' She paused. 'And I hope you don't mind me saying so, but you could do with updating the website a bit. You don't look anything like your photograph.' Her eyes widening, she quickly added, 'Oh, I meant that in a good way. You look much younger in real life.'

I frowned. My husband? My photograph? The fog cleared.

'Oh, no, Jenny. The chap you met yesterday – Rupert – he's not my husband. What I mean is, that isn't me on the website. That's his wife. She's not here at the moment. I'm... helping out while she's away. Rupert's a friend.'

'Oh. Right.' Jenny's sunny smile faltered. 'I hope I didn't offend you. I *thought* Rupert seemed an awful lot older than you. See you later.' She waved and skipped back to her *gîte* across the way.

As I threw a sandwich together, I made a mental note to tackle Rupert about the website sometime. If Gloria wasn't coming back, he could do with removing her hateful image from it. And I could do without being mistaken for Gloria again.

Peeved, I bit into a plum tomato. It promptly exploded juice and seeds all over my T-shirt – clean on today *and* white. Great.

I'd just put all the lunch items away when Rupert came into the kitchen to forage.

'What do you want me to do with all that bedlinen when it's dry?' I asked him tetchily.

'Just shove it in one of the unused rooms out of sight for now. I'll get Madame Dupont to deal with it next time she comes in.'

This seemed rather *laissez-faire,* even for a Sunday, but if he couldn't be bothered, I didn't see why I should.

'Besides, other things to worry about first,' he said. 'The Stewarts are due on Tuesday.'

'Why is that a worry?'

'Madame Dupont isn't in today – church. Or tomorrow – sister's. Could you do their room for me, love?'

I frowned. 'Today? Why not tomorrow?'

'Because tomorrow is market day,' he stated, as though this was a perfectly obvious answer. When all he got from me was a bewildered expression, he explained, 'I always go into Pierre-la-Fontaine on market day. I get my fresh and specialist food there.'

I blew out a frustrated breath. 'Can't we stick to the supermarket this week?' I'd only just mastered that little hurdle. Driving to the outskirts of town and parking in a large supermarket car park was one thing. Negotiating my way into a proper French town on a busy market day was quite another. Besides... 'Haven't you heard of doing your grocery shop online?'

He had that stubborn look in his eye that I was coming to recognise all too well. 'Of course. But I wouldn't like it.'

'Why not? Wouldn't it be easier?'

He shook his head. 'I like to see what's fresh. What's on offer. I don't even write a list – I've only been doing that for your benefit. I wouldn't dream of confining myself to the supermarket, anyway. I like to use the shops in town. Go to the market when it's on. Bump into people I know and have a chat. I'm getting cabin fever, Emmy. I need to get out, get back to normal a bit. And it would do you good, too. Give you a break from this place.'

He gave me a pleading look, and I couldn't help but laugh. He looked like one of those dogs with the wrinkled faces and huge eyes that you can't say no to.

I sighed. 'All right.' The idea of getting out and about was beginning to appeal to me, too. Other than the first couple of days pottering about nearby villages and taking strolls along country lanes with Nathan, there had been a distinct lack of traditional holiday activity so far. 'But only on the condition that you treat me to coffee afterwards.'

Rupert shook his head. 'You're getting so you're anybody's for a coffee, Emmy.'

'I know. You've corrupted me with your big shiny machine.'

He raised an eyebrow. 'I wish!' But to his gratification, I'd already blushed bright scarlet before the words were out of his mouth.

CHAPTER SEVEN

Resigned to my afternoon fate, I went up to what would be the Stewarts' room, opened the windows to air it out, then glanced into the bathroom. It had been cleaned since the room was last occupied, but I wiped it over. Spotting that the complimentary toiletries were running low, I went to ask Rupert where he kept his supplies.

'No bloody idea,' he admitted. 'Gloria always dealt with that girly stuff.'

I was going to say it was good to know there had been at least *some* useful task in Gloria's remit, but he had such a defeated look on his face – whether at Gloria's absence or his gap in knowledge with regard to toiletry stocks, I wasn't sure – that I kept my remarks to myself.

Methodically, I went through every cupboard and drawer in every communal area. First, the kitchen units I hadn't yet explored, then the inbuilt broom cupboard in the hall. No joy there. I glanced at the tall wooden desk unit by the front door where the phone and diary resided – not enough storage space, but I did a double take anyway. I'd admired its polished elegance every time I passed, but it was only now that I realised what it was – a restaurant antique, one of those counters where the *maître d'* would stand sentry with his reservations book and a haughty look. Fabulous.

Trooping upstairs, I had a quick root through the large *armoire* on the landing, but it only held bedlinen and towels. With all the obvious places covered, I went back downstairs for an unlikely foray into the guest lounge, a slightly formal affair with upright upholstered chairs and sofa, and an imposing sideboard in dark wood. I'd only poked my head in here a couple of times, but I'd rejected it as a place to linger – it was quite a contrast to the warm and welcoming atmosphere of the kitchen, and since the bedrooms were spacious enough to include a small armchair, I hadn't felt the need to use it. Looking through the sideboard, I found napkins, tablecloths, candles, and finally came up trumps with two deep drawers stuffed full of individually-wrapped soaps, sachets of shampoo, and tiny bottles of bath oil. Why toiletries should be stored in a sideboard in the guest lounge, I couldn't begin to guess.

I emptied them into two empty plastic storage boxes I found in the hall cupboard, left one there to be nearer the *gîtes* and took the other upstairs so it would be handier for the guest rooms.

That done, I set to doing what I should have already finished by now – vacuuming, dusting, polishing and making the bed in the Stewarts' room. I took a leaf from Madame Dupont's book and defiantly binned Gloria's clichéd and dusty potpourri, then went down to the garden, cut fresh flowers, found a glass vase for them in the kitchen and placed it on the now shining antique dressing table. And on the basis that less was more, I relegated several hideous ornaments to the top shelf of the wardrobe while I was at it.

Finally, I admired my handiwork with a sense of pride. The room was as it should be: a clean, tastefully-decorated haven within the restful cocoon that was *La Cour des Roses*.

I was looking forward to resuming reading in the sunshine when I heard a knock at the door. Talk about never getting any peace!

Rupert's accountant was on the doorstep. Again.

'Hi. I – er.' His gaze fixed on my chest, which ordinarily would have either flattered or annoyed me, depending on what mood I was in and who was doing the staring. This time, it did neither, since I realised it was only because of my sloppy eating habits. I'd forgotten to change, and the tomato pulp was now dried on like cement.

'Sorry.' I wafted at the carnage down my front. 'Rogue tomato.'

He nodded. 'Is Rupert in?'

I crossed my arms over my chest, partly in confrontation and partly to hide the salad spillage.

'Yes, but I'm afraid he's convalescing and can't be disturbed. If it's *that* urgent, perhaps I can make you another appointment?'

His brow furrowed. 'No, I don't think you understand...'

Bloody accountants. Didn't he have any patience? 'No, Mr...?'

'Alain.'

'Alain. I don't think *you* understand. Rupert really isn't well. Not only that, but...' I stopped. It wasn't my place to tell him about Rupert's marital misfortunes. 'Look, unless Rupert's about to be clapped in irons for not paying his taxes, I *really* can't see what's so important that you need to come here on a *Sunday*...'

'Friendship.'

'I'm sorry?'

'Friendship is what's so important. Not taxes. I may be Rupert's accountant, but I'm also his friend. I didn't come to do his books – I came to see how he was. I heard there had been some... trouble.'

There was a tinge of annoyance in his voice, but his caramel gaze remained calm on mine, despite my rudeness. Those soft brown eyes were the kind you could lose yourself in if you weren't careful, with their warmth and unexpected seductive quality.

Hmmph. I wasn't inclined to associate any accountant with warmth *or* seduction, thank you very much.

'I'm sorry. I didn't realise,' I managed.

'Don't worry about it. It's good to know someone's looking out for Rupert's interests – which is more than Gloria did. If he's resting, I'll come back another time. Could you tell him I was asking after him?'

I gave him the first genuine smile he'd had from me. 'Of course. I'd ask you to come in and wait, but I've no idea how long that would be.'

He shook his head. 'I'll go. Thank you.' He pointed to my T-shirt. 'Good luck with that stain.' He winked and was down the steps before I could reply.

Back upstairs to change the wretched T-shirt, I put it in the bathroom sink to soak, in the vain hope that Madame Dupont might know some ancient French trick for rescuing it. That done, I dragged more laundry out of the machine and hung it out, brought the dry linen inside to dump it in a spare guest room as instructed, and finally – *finally* – went back outside to the patio to read.

I was musing as to why the heroine was so quick to sleep with the hero when he was such a misogynistic pig when I heard footsteps coming across the gravel and looked up. Adonis, aka Ryan, leaned against the garden gate, his jeans anchored on his slim hips, a tight-fitting T-shirt clinging to firm abs, his bare arms tanned and muscled and lightly covered in blonde hair.

I think I may have inadvertently licked my lips.

'Ryan, hi!' I called, too brightly, desperately trying to cover my wicked thoughts with a casual greeting. Indeed, since I'd barely come to terms with being abandoned, it occurred to me that I shouldn't be having wicked thoughts at all. 'What are you doing here?'

'I promised Rupert I'd do extra to make up for last week, remember?'

Either I'd forgotten, or I'd blocked our encounter yesterday from my mind in the spirit of self-preservation. But there he was – and here I was, once more unsuitably attired, this time in a pair of baggy linen trousers that hid my widening hips but probably made me look the size of a bus, and a T-shirt that must have shrunk in the wash and now clung unflatteringly to my stomach. Self-conscious, I crossed my arms in front to spare him the sight.

'Oh, right. Didn't think you'd come on a Sunday.'

'Makes no difference to me. I'm not a churchgoer.' There was a hint of devilment in his voice. I swallowed hard as he waved a pair of secateurs at me. 'I can come back another time if it'll disturb you.'

'No, go ahead. It won't bother me. I'm going to fetch a cold drink. Can I get you one?'

'Sure. Thanks.' He strolled off, snipping at bushes and trees as he went.

I fixed iced juice and took it outside. When Ryan saw me, he stopped what he was doing and came over, taking a seat on the edge of the lounger next to mine. Since he'd only started five minutes ago, I didn't think this was very productive of him, but it wasn't my place to say.

'So, Emmy, how's it going?' he asked. 'I gather yesterday was a whirlwind of activity.'

'You... How... What?' I asked intelligently.

Ryan laughed, his teeth white and even in his tanned face. 'Madame Dupont cleans for my parents over at their summer place. She bumped into my mother this morning at the *boulangerie*. Mum speaks excellent French.'

'Oh, I see.' A blush rose. 'Isn't anything private around here?' I bleated.

'Don't worry, Emmy. Rupert's not stupid. He knows what an old gossip Madame Dupont is – he won't have told her any more than she needs to know.' As I sighed with relief, he added, 'Doesn't stop her adding her own embellishments, though.'

I watched as he took a long gulp of his juice and swiped the drips from his extremely kissable mouth.

'Do you live with your parents?' I asked in an attempt to change the subject, then immediately regretted the question. I hadn't meant to insinuate he was a stay-at-home mummy's boy, but thankfully he didn't seem to take offence.

'Yes and no. They spend about three months a year out here, on and off. I come out for the gardening season, March through to October, so I often have the place to myself. When they're out here, I move into the barn.'

'The barn?' An image of Ryan sprawled out naked in the hay, barely covered by an old blanket, popped unbidden into my mind.

'Well, it's not a barn any more. They've been converting it. Eventually, it'll be a couple of *gîtes*. Right now, it's only an open space with a kitchenette and shower room, but it's coming along.'

'You're helping with it?'

'They get workmen in for the technical stuff, otherwise I do what I can when the gardening allows or when it rains.'

'You really are a jack of all trades, aren't you?'

Ryan looked me so straight in the eye that I squirmed in my seat. 'I'm good with my hands.'

Oh, Ryan, I bet you are. As I stared at his broad hands and long fingers with their soil-ingrained tips and work calluses, I realised I could have said the words aloud. *Get a grip, Emmy. He's just a baby!*

'How old are you?' I blurted before I could stop myself, immediately giving myself a mental kicking for not stopping my thoughts from becoming audible speech.

'Twenty-four. Why do you ask?'

He knew damned well why, but we were playing some sort of cat-and-mouse game, and I had no intention of being the mouse.

'Just wondered. You seem to have a lot of skills for your age.' Great. Now I sounded like my mother.

'I'm a quick learner.' He hoisted himself up from the chair. 'I'd better get on. Thanks for the drink.'

He handed me his glass and as I reached out to take it, his fingers brushed mine. Raising an eyebrow, he headed down the garden before I could stop gawping.

I closed my eyes in despair. For heaven's sake, why couldn't a woman whose boyfriend had deserted her for a middle-aged nymphomaniac be left in peace to wallow in self-pity? Why did there have to be gardeners like Greek gods popping up out of the shrubbery?

I spent the next couple of hours alternating between the excitement of my book and the excitement of glancing surreptitiously across at Ryan, allowing myself the luxury of observing the way the muscles in his arms bunched and tightened while he worked; how his jeans stretched across his thighs as he crouched; the slide of his waistband as he bent.

Oh, I knew I was in a vulnerable emotional state and should be wary of such lascivious thoughts. Plus, he was seven years younger than me. I had no intention of making any moves on him or anything. But since I'd been starved of sexual fantasy for a while now, I figured I was at least allowed to look. After all, when you're on a diet, there's nothing to stop you drooling through the bakery window – as long as you don't go inside to sample the éclairs.

Ryan gathered up his tools and headed back my way.

'Finished?' I asked, trying not to stare at the sweat trickling down through the hairs on his chest.

'For today.'

'Would you like another drink?'

'Please.'

I fixed iced grenadine for us both and brought it out. He downed his in five seconds.

'Thanks. Thirsty work. What are you doing tonight?'

'Hmm?' His question took me by surprise.

'No meals to cook for the guests?'

'No, but...'

'How about eating with me?'

'Well...' I couldn't think straight. Was he being neighbourly, or was he asking me out on a date?

'You and Rupert must be spending way too much time together,' he went on. 'Surely you could do with an hour or two away?'

I wondered what Rupert would say about me dining out with his gardener. 'I don't know if he'll cope on his own. I mean, he's still...'

'He'll be fine. He can scramble himself some eggs or whatever it is that invalids eat. I'll pick you up at seven.'

My mind desperately sought a way out, but by the time it had got a grip and begun to process any coherent thoughts whatsoever, Ryan had already waved, closed the gate and started his engine.

What had I let myself in for now? No good could come of this, whatever Ryan's motives. If his intentions were honourable and he was simply being kind, then I appreciated the sentiment but didn't relish being an object of pity. On the other hand, if his intentions were *dis*honourable, then I was in real trouble, because either he was sadder than I thought and there must be something wrong with him – why couldn't he find a nice girl nearer his own age? – or he was a heartless gigolo, happy to take advantage of a vulnerable woman without caring about the consequences.

Two hours later, my book abandoned, I was still stewing it over. I wanted to duck out and cancel, but that would involve phoning Ryan, which would involve asking Rupert for his number. Besides, I had no excuse to give. If Ryan was only being nice, I might hurt his feelings, and there had already been enough hurt feelings around here to last a lifetime.

I reconciled myself to my fate. The best that could happen? I might enjoy a pleasant evening with a nice young man, possibly struggling to restrain myself from drooling if he looked as good fully clothed as he did half-naked and sweaty. And the worst? Well, I was a big girl now and quite capable of rejecting the advances of a misguided youth.

In the meantime, there were more immediate problems to contend with, namely Rupert. What was I going to tell him? *"By the way, I'm off out with your under-age gardener tonight. Not sure if he's offering me a shoulder to cry on or a shag, but either way, I'll be leaving at seven."*

I tracked him down in a small den at the back of the house: a cosy retreat with a large leather-topped antique desk and captain's chair, a small leather sofa scattered with bright ethnic cushions and a fading Turkish rug across the wooden floor. One wall was lined with ceiling-height bookshelves, stuffed to overflowing. Rupert sat at the desk, a look of open self-pity on his face, which he was quick to hide when I poked my head around the door.

'Emmy. All right?'

I wanted to ask him the same question, but since he was pretending nothing was wrong, I didn't feel I should push.

'Yes, thanks. Your accountant called round again while you were resting.'

'Oh?'

'He wanted to know how you are. The local grapevine works remarkably efficiently around here, doesn't it?'

Rupert nodded. 'I'll get back to him soon. It was good of him to call. He's a nice chap.'

I grimaced.

'You don't think he's a nice chap?'

'I didn't say that, but being an accountant is already a black mark against him in my book.'

'Only in your twisted, bitter, post-rejection world, Emmy. You can hardly hold that against the poor bloke!'

I harrumphed and changed the subject. 'I threw out the potpourri in the Stewarts' room and used fresh flowers from the garden. Is that okay?'

Rupert's brow furrowed. 'Did you leave a bald patch in the flower beds?'

'No. I was careful.'

'Then that sounds lovely. Thank you. Did you manage to find the toiletry stores?'

'I did. *Eventually.* You know, Rupert, they're fiddly and small. They can't be economical, and they're certainly not environmentally friendly with all that packaging. To be honest...' I stopped. 'Sorry. None of my business.'

Rupert gave me a look. 'It's your business for the next week. What did you want to say?'

'Well, I think they're a bit tacky. Like people are staying in a motel chain or something. Everything else here is so classy, it seems a shame.'

'What would you suggest?'

I shrugged. 'Not sure yet. I'll think about it.'

'I appreciate it. Any walls you want knocked through? Any furniture that needs replacing?'

'I'm only trying to help,' I muttered.

'And I'm only teasing. Anything else?'

There was no point in putting it off any longer. I tried for a bright, breezy and matter-of-fact tone.

'Yes, actually. I – er – wanted to let you know that I won't be around to eat with you tonight. I'm going out.'

Rupert raised a surprised eyebrow. 'Oh? Anywhere nice?'

'I have no idea. Ryan asked me out to dinner. I think he feels sorry for me. Not that I told him about Nathan, of course; it's that wretched Madame Dupont. Anyway, he asked me to dinner and I wanted to refuse, I mean I was going to refuse, and I tried to, but he left before I could...'

'Emmy. There's no need to explain. Of course you should go out and enjoy yourself. Ryan's a pleasant young chap.' He frowned. 'Bit young for you, though, if you don't mind me saying so.'

'I wouldn't mind you saying so if it was likely he was looking for a long-term relationship, Rupert, but as far as I know, his intentions only stretch as far as dinner.' Now it was my turn to frown. 'I hope.'

Rupert laughed, a loud guffaw that dispelled my nerves. 'Don't worry, love. Ryan's a well-brought-up young man. I'm sure he only wants to give you a bit of company and get you out of the house for the night, not out of your pants. Here, put this in your handbag in case you need to fend him off.'

He reached behind him for an antique sword mounted on the wall over his head. I threw a cushion at him and left.

Up in my room, I showered, slathered on body cream, then screeched to a halt as I hit the perennial problem of what to wear. My holiday clothes stared forlornly out at me from the antique wardrobe, looking lost now that Nathan's were no longer hanging alongside them. Overriding the sudden wave of misery and loneliness that threatened to engulf me, I rummaged through them. By rejecting anything unflattering or over-revealing or too casual, I was left with two summer dresses I'd packed for the express purpose of dining out with Nathan. Little had I known I'd be choosing between them for a date with a cute gardener.

After much soul-searching, I went with the blue, made my make-up as natural as I could get away with and hurried downstairs. The last thing I wanted was for Rupert to answer the door to Ryan and have them both shuffling uncomfortably around the lounge waiting for me, like an overprotective father with his daughter's prospective suitor.

In the kitchen, Rupert was munching his way through a salad, and his glass contained sparkling water. Good for him. I raised an eyebrow.

'Don't start,' he muttered, reading my mind. 'Thought I ought to have an evening off, that's all.'

'It's good to see you've decided to be a good boy for a change.'

A horn beeped out in the courtyard and Rupert grunted. 'Hmmph. Yes, well, you be a good girl, for that matter.'

Blushing all the way from my sandals to my split ends, I shot him my best glare and left before he could embarrass me any further.

Despite the many and varied scenarios my anxious mind had dreamed up for the evening, its worst fears remained unrealised.

Ryan had cleaned out the front of his estate car so I didn't get soil all over my dress (although the back was still a mucky gardener's paradise). He was charming without being smarmy, and his easy-going manner soon calmed my nerves.

We drove into Pierre-la-Fontaine and dined in a hotel restaurant where I enjoyed the formal waiter service, crisp tablecloths, fanned napkins and, well, the *Frenchness* of it all. The *porc en croûte* oozing mustard butter, served with crisp green beans and potatoes piped into pretty swirls, was heavenly – and the dainty *tarte au citron* was a stratosphere beyond the pale imitations I'd tried back home.

The irony wasn't lost on me that dining out in France with my own boyfriend had involved struggling to find common ground or any enthusiasm for conversation, and yet here I was with a sun-streaked blonde gardener of tender years who I'd known for less than two days and with whom there seemed to be no problem finding topics to talk and laugh about. Life could be funny sometimes. Funny peculiar, that was, not funny ha-ha.

'So how did you end up gardening here in France?' I asked him, over coffee. 'Was it because your parents have a holiday home here?'

'Kind of. I started studying landscape design at college but dropped out after a year. Didn't like the idea of sitting behind a desk when I could be out doing the real thing all day. So I'm self-taught – I picked up a few jobs and learned as I went along. My parents had a smaller holiday home in the area when we were kids – we came out every summer – but three years ago, they sold it and bought somewhere bigger that they could develop and have a couple of *gîtes* to give them some income when they eventually retire. The house needed modernising, but the gardens were totally neglected, so they asked me to come out and do my stuff. People saw what I was up to and liked it, and of course we knew quite a few people from spending our summers over here. I built up quite a client base.'

'With the Brits?'

'Yep. They're not always fluent in French and prefer to deal with someone they can understand – but some of the locals use me, too. I'm reliable and I know what I'm doing.'

'So what do you do in the winter?'

'I usually go back to the UK and pick up some labouring work. I have a couple of mates who are in the building trade.'

I nodded, trying hard not to imagine him shirtless in a hard hat.

'What do you do?' he asked.

'I work for a marketing agency in Birmingham.'

'Creative stuff, I imagine?'

I laughed. 'Sometimes. But it can be as much about tact and persuasion with clients, and organisational skills with your projects and your team.'

'You have a team?'

'Kind of. I'm only the assistant manager, but my boss is happy to take a back seat. He's not too hot on people skills.'

'But I bet you are.' There was a hint of devilment in Ryan's voice. 'I also bet you're sexy when you're bossy.'

I blushed and rapidly changed the subject.

After the meal, we strolled around the quiet streets to work off dinner. Enjoying glancing in the shop windows, I was relaxed enough not to think anything of it when Ryan took my hand to cross the road and kept hold of it as we walked. It was... friendly, that was all.

When we pulled up at *La Cour des Roses*, Ryan turned the engine off. 'Any chance of a coffee?'

'You already had one. You'll be up all night.' Suddenly I was cautious again.

'You're not going to invite me in?'

'Is there any reason why I should?' I looked him in the eye. 'Or why I shouldn't?'

He smiled sweetly. 'No to either question.'

I heaved a sigh. We couldn't sit in the car all night like teenagers. 'Fine. You'll have to be quiet, though. Rupert will be asleep and the Hendersons are upstairs.'

He followed me in. I made tea to limit our caffeine intake, and we went through to the lounge. The rest of the house was unnervingly quiet.

'See? It wasn't so bad, was it?' Ryan's eyes sparkled at me as he settled on the sofa next to me.

'What do you mean?'

'I mean, you can stop panicking. I didn't bite, you didn't get drunk and pour out your life story, and nobody asked if you were my mother.'

There was I, thinking I'd been so sophisticated all evening, hiding my insecurities, and he'd read me like a book. 'What made you think I was panicking?'

'The way you gripped your glass so tight your knuckles went white? All those glances to see if anyone was giving us funny looks? Oh, and how you shifted so far away from me in the car that you nearly fell out?'

I didn't like the merriment dancing in his eyes at my expense, no matter how hypnotisingly blue they were, and I bristled with indignation. 'I don't think...'

'Emmy, I'm teasing you. Haven't you heard it said that people only tease people they like?'

'Perhaps I'm not in the mood to be teased.'

Ryan shifted closer on the sofa. 'What *are* you in the mood for?'

Staring him down, I tried hard not to laugh. 'That has got to be the cheesiest line I've ever heard!'

He gave me a boyish grin, and I was close enough to notice the tiny dimples in his cheeks. They made my stomach flip.

'You're right,' he agreed. 'Perhaps I should stop talking.'

'Isn't it time you were going?'

'No. Ever since I first saw you standing at the window in that ridiculous T-shirt, I've wanted to do this.'

CHAPTER EIGHT

He moved in until our bodies were touching. I didn't protest, but I did have misgivings. He was so much younger than me; I was still raw from Nathan's rejection; Rupert was in the house; what if the Hendersons came down? But the wine I'd had at dinner took the edge off the swirl of thoughts, allowing me to acknowledge them without caring enough to do anything about them.

Ryan tilted my face up to his. 'Do you mind?'

He didn't wait for a reply – but since I didn't mind in the least, I allowed him to carry on. I'd forgotten how wonderful a first kiss could be. After five years with Nathan, our kisses had become... familiar, maybe even a little perfunctory. Don't get me wrong, we could still be excitable after a drink or two if we were in the right mood – but this was different.

I could feel Ryan's desire emanating through his shirt – and his jeans – and it was genuine. His lips transmitted that delightful sense of urgency I hadn't experienced for quite a while with Nathan (not without several units of alcohol inside me, anyway). Ryan began to explore with those dextrous hands of his, and that was okay, too, because it was good to know someone wanted to explore me at all.

But then there was a distant thunk from somewhere in the house, and I jumped back. Ryan put a finger to his lips in a shushing gesture as we waited for further developments – and that was when it all began to unravel for me. Everything about him was so damned *perfect*. His eyes, his mouth, his kiss...

The realisation suddenly made me acutely self-conscious. I knew I was passable for a stressed-out woman in her early thirties – but I also knew I didn't have the airbrushed glamour of the young, flat-stomached French girls of Ryan's own age who I imagined he must be used to. Making the comparison with such imagined perfection – and the reality of it sitting right here next to me – caused me to freeze in my tracks.

Ryan sensed it. 'Emmy, is anything wrong?'

'No, not really, it's...'

How could I explain? Ryan was young and full of himself. How could I tell him that only a few short years down the line, he too might be in a clinch with a model-like vision, unable to give in to the moment because he couldn't compete with his lover's usual quarry, lacking in confidence because he'd been dumped for what should have seemed a much worse prospect? Why burst the boy's bubble?

He waited patiently for an answer. I had to come up with something plausible, fast.

'I'm sorry.' My mind raced and lit on half-truths that would do. 'But what with the guests upstairs and Rupert down the hall and...'

Ryan planted a light kiss on the tip of my nose. 'It's okay, Emmy. I understand.'

'You do?'

'Of course. And I'm sorry for making you uncomfortable. I didn't mean to. I asked you out because I thought you might need a friend to help you through the rest of your stay. Someone nearer your own age than old Grumpy Boots down the hall.'

I kissed his cheek. 'I do. Need a friend, that is.'

He stood, and as he straightened his shirt, I experienced a pervading sense of loss – the feeling that an opportunity had been missed. I began to wonder if I should have let it go by.

'Ryan, I'm sorry. It's just that...'

'No. *I'm* sorry.' He pulled on his jacket. 'This is more than too soon for you, after Nathan. I only meant to take you out to dinner, not to kiss us both senseless.'

Who said the youth of today were insensitive?

'That's okay. I shouldn't have let it get started.' I walked him to the door. 'Goodnight, Ryan.'

'Goodnight, Emmy.'

With a heavy sense of regret, I watched him walk to his car.

'So, how did it go last night? Did you have a good time?' Rupert wiggled his eyebrows, making me laugh.

'Fine, Rupert. I had a good time, thank you.'

'Any exciting nookie I should know about? I require all the gory details.'

I did my best to remain nonchalant. 'No gory details.'

'Emmy, my life is distinctly lacking in excitement at the moment, above all in the bedroom department. If I can't have my own thrills, I need to hear about yours. Come on. Spill.'

I gave him a stern look. 'There's nothing *to* spill.'

'Where did he take you?'

'The hotel with the cream front off the *Place du* something-or-other.'

'Very specific, Emmy. What did you eat?'

I told him. Anything to shut him up.

He nodded his approval. 'What did you do after dinner?'

'We strolled around town.'

'Then what?'

'For heaven's sake, Rupert. What is this, an inquisition?' I wanted to tell him to stop being such a nosy bastard, but that would make him think I had something to hide. Besides, there was a chance he'd heard us come into the house – or worse, heard Ryan leaving a good hour after he'd brought me home. That gravel left an awful lot to be desired in the stealth department. 'He drove me home and came in for a cup of tea.'

'A cup of *tea*?' Rupert snorted with derision, which had the unfortunate effect of causing his orange juice to shoot up his nose. The ensuing sneezing and coughing fit was not a pretty sight. When he'd recovered his composure, he gave me the eagle eye. 'You're telling me that a handsome young man, who fancies the pants off you, took you out for an elegant dinner, strolled you gallantly around town, drove you to your door, escorted you in – and you made him a cup of tea? Oh, Emmy, you *are* out of practice.'

I bristled. 'It's not a question of being out of practice, Rupert. Ryan is a great deal younger than me, Nathan and I have only just split up and...'

'You're not denying he fancied the pants off you, then?'

'Do you have to be so crude?'

'Indeed I do. You're so delightful when you blush.'

Unwillingly, I obliged. 'I think we'll leave this discussion alone, thank you. Now, do you want to get off to this market or not?'

Happy to be out and about, Rupert directed my driving in typical dominant-male manner.

'How are you going to cope when I go home on Saturday?' I asked.

'Fine, Emmy. Don't you worry.' His bluster didn't fool me. I could read him pretty well by now, and I knew when he was only saying what he thought I needed to hear.

I called his bluff. 'Stop talking bollocks. I'm serious. You're going to need help and we have to find a solution. I know the Hendersons leave on Thursday, but you've got the Stewarts for a week and the Kennedys on a long weekend from Thursday. Who's going to help Madame Dupont do the *gîtes* on Saturday? What about next week's guests?'

'Madame Dupont might do some extra hours.'

'Madame Dupont is a good, loyal cleaner, Rupert, not a miracle worker. The woman must be seventy if she's a day. And even if she did do it all – which would probably kill the poor soul – who's going to do all your errands? You can't even drive yet.'

'I'll ask Madame Dupont if she knows anyone.'

'When is she in next?'

'Tomorrow, probably.'

I nodded. Tomorrow was good enough.

Rupert navigated me into Pierre-la-Fontaine and a very tight parking spot that I would never have dreamed of attempting if I'd been on my own. He had dispensed with his crutches for the trip and was trying to manage with a walking stick. The quiet streets I'd enjoyed on my evening stroll with Ryan were bustling now, and when I saw the market stretching up the main square and branching off onto cobbled side streets, my heart sank and soared at the same time. The holidaymaker part of my soul that had been damped down out of necessity took it all in hungrily – but my common sense reminded me that we were limited by Rupert's energy and his leg.

I glanced at stalls selling African statues, bohemian floaty linen tops, leather handbags – and one, bizarrely, selling every manner of girdle and corset known to womankind.

I snorted. 'Does anybody still wear that sort of thing?'

Rupert grinned. 'They must do. That stall's here every week. Makes you wonder what Madame Dupont has on under her skirts, doesn't it?'

I shuddered. 'If she straps herself into vicious gear like that, I'm amazed she can move or bend at all!'

'Emmy, if you want to have a look around, I don't mind,' he said kindly. 'Heaven knows, you deserve it. Although if you're tempted by something from that particular stall, I'd rather not know about it. I'll just...'

'Rupert!' A shout halted us in our tracks as a middle-aged couple headed towards us.

The woman kissed him on both cheeks. 'It's good to see you. How are you? We were *so* sorry to hear about everything.'

'Hello, Brenda. Richard.' Rupert shook the man's hand. 'I'm fine, thanks. I'd like you both to meet Emmy – my guest and, it turns out, my saviour.'

Brenda turned to me and held out her hand. 'It's good to meet you, Emmy. Both Madame Dupont and Ryan have been singing your praises.'

I gulped. 'Ryan?'

'Brenda and Richard are Ryan's parents, Emmy. They have a holiday home a few miles down the road.' Rupert grinned, enjoying my discomfort.

'How nice to meet you both,' I said, fighting the urge to bolt down the street.

'We'll be going for coffee soon. Will you join us?' Rupert continued to torture me.

'Sorry.' Richard unwittingly came to the rescue. 'Just had one, and we need to get to a few places before they shut. Some other time, though? It would be lovely to see you properly. Call us if you need anything. Nice to meet you, Emmy.'

I let out my breath, grateful for the glorious continental tradition of businesses closing for lunch that prevented them from joining us.

Rupert nudged my arm as they walked away. 'That was fun. Do you think they know who Ryan took to dinner last night?'

'You have a warped sense of entertainment, Rupert Hunter, do you know that?'

'Yes. It was one of the things Gloria disliked about me. I might develop it further to spite her.'

'Well, don't bother today. You have shopping to do.'

Rupert pointed up the street with his walking stick. 'Most of the food stalls are at the top end. Why don't you have twenty minutes looking around here, Emmy, then come and find me. You can't miss it – just follow your nose.'

He shuffled off without waiting for a reply, and once I'd watched him to make sure he was coping with the cobbles, I decided to take him at his word and enjoy myself.

Choosing between the brown handbag or the teal cost me five minutes more than Rupert had allowed me. I caught up with him at a cheese stall, where he was sampling something crumbly and chatting away to the stall owner.

'Emmy! Try this,' he greeted me, shoving a morsel in my mouth before I could stop him.

Bravely, I hid a grimace. 'What is it?'

'Goat's cheese. Like it?'

Glancing at the cheese man, I forced a smile. 'Mmm. Ah. Delicious.' I swallowed it down with difficulty. Rupert laughed uproariously, as did the stall owner.

'You haven't bought any, have you?' I muttered as we walked away, peering dubiously into his carrier bag full of wrapped cheese mysteries, then glancing up at the next stall. 'God, how many types of sausage can the world need?'

A great many, it seemed. They dangled on strings like candles – cooked sausages of every variety possible. I gawped as Rupert made his choice and stuffed the package in the bag with the cheese. He looked exhausted.

I took the bag from him. 'Where do you want to go for coffee? If you don't sit down soon, you'll fall down.'

'Just across the street.'

He led the way at a snail's pace, limping badly. We grabbed a table outside and I sank down with a contented sigh. Not for long.

'I recognise that voice,' Rupert said. 'Come on, Emmy. I want you to meet my good friend, Jonathan.'

Rolling my eyes, I heaved myself back to my feet and followed him into the dim interior, all dark wood wall panels and tables. An elderly man with a shock of white hair propped up the bar, regaling the owner with some story in what even I recognised was not the best French in the world – but he did it with a flourish, punctuating his tale with dramatic arm gestures and comical facial expressions, and the Frenchman laughed along, clearly able to follow the gist. As we approached, the story-spinner turned towards us.

'Rupert, my old friend!' he exclaimed, stretching out his arm to shake hands and then pulling Rupert to him in a tight embrace which Rupert stoically accepted. I pulled a bar stool over and pushed Rupert onto it.

'Emmy – Jonathan. Jonathan – Emmy,' Rupert introduced us.

Jonathan beamed and subjected me to the same treatment as Rupert. 'So *you're* the angelic Emmy.'

I gave a tentative smile. 'I'm not sure I'd go that far.'

He waved off my modesty. 'Nonsense. I've heard all about you. And no offence, Rupert, but you're well shot of Gobby Gloria.'

Rupert seemed to take this in his stride, while I suppressed a smirk.

Jonathan leaned in to me. 'Between you and me, lovey, she and I never got on.'

Rupert turned from ordering our coffees and something alcoholic-looking for Jonathan. 'Between you, me and this entire *département* of France, Emmy, I think you'll find that Jonathan struggles with women in general,' he said jovially.

'Ah. I see...'

Jonathan laughed. 'He's trying to tell you I'm gay.' He laid a hand on my arm. 'But I can still recognise an angel when I see one, and you are definitely one.'

'Well, thank you.'

'So, Rupert, how's it going?' Jonathan asked, jabbing at Rupert's leg with his walking stick for emphasis.

Rupert hid a wince. 'It's going well, considering, but that's all down to Emmy here.'

'So I hear.' Jonathan raised his glass in my direction. 'We could do with someone like you on a permanent basis, young lady. A Girl Friday. Someone who'll muck in and get on.'

'Oh? Do you have *gîtes*, too?' I asked him.

Jonathan shook his head. 'Alas, no. Wish I did. The old pension doesn't stretch that far. No, what I meant was, it'd be nice to have someone to call on from time to time. You know: when the cleaner's away, or when the car breaks down and I need a lift, or someone to go shopping on the days I'm not up to it. Maybe keep an eye on the house when I'm away.'

'You get all your friends to do that!' Rupert laughed and turned to me. 'He has an informal rota system so no one friend feels too put upon at any one time.'

'But that's the problem,' Jonathan said. 'I'm getting on now. And I *am* putting on people. You should set yourself up over here, Emmy. A Girl Friday agency to help out old codgers like me.'

Rupert snorted. 'What, so you could pay her a pittance to run round after you?'

'Pretty much, yes.'

'Sorry to disappoint you, old boy, but Emmy's already got a job to go back to. *And* it pays a decent living wage.'

Jonathan let out a melodramatic sigh. 'I had a feeling she would. Ah, well.'

When Jonathan had satisfied himself that Rupert wasn't suicidal, and he'd enjoyed some of the juicier aspects of gossip surrounding our mutual dilemma, Rupert and I headed back outside.

'I had to leave my shopping at some of the stalls 'cause I couldn't carry it,' Rupert announced. 'Fetch it for me, will you? I'll sit here and wait.' He grabbed an empty table on the terrace.

I shot him a glare. 'Which stalls?'

'The meat stall over there.' He pointed. 'And that veg one there.'

'And how am I supposed to ask in French?'

'They're expecting you. I gave them my name.'

Resigned, I started across the street. When I got to the butcher's stall, I felt a bit absurd just saying Rupert's name, so I dredged my memory banks and bravely tagged on *'Un sac, s'il vous plaît?'* to great success. Dragging the heavy bag of meat over to the veg stall, I tried the same again – and was given two large bags that weighed a ton. I looked inside. Melons, oranges... Rupert and I were going to have words. Lugging them back to the café, I dumped them at his feet without much care for his toes.

'Rupert, this is ridiculous!' I snapped. 'What do you think I am – a weightlifter? You can't tell me this stuff's so much better than at the supermarket where you can use a *trolley* to get it to the car...'

'I quite agree.' I jumped at the voice behind me and spun around to find Alain towering over me. He smiled at me and shook Rupert's hand. 'You're taking advantage, Rupert.'

Rupert shifted uncomfortably. 'Yes, well, I didn't expect to buy so much. Haven't been out and about for a bit.'

I shook my head. As if *that* was a legitimate excuse for giving me a hernia.

'So I hear.' Alain settled himself at our table and ordered a coffee.

Rupert ordered us another small one each, and I winced. I was going to be awake for the next forty-eight hours at this rate.

'I wouldn't mind hearing the correct version from the horse's mouth, though,' Alain went on. 'So far I've only had it fifth-hand, and it's starting to get a little outrageous and difficult to believe.'

Rupert laughed. 'Oh, I think you'll find that outrageous and difficult to believe isn't so far from the truth.'

As Rupert began on his tale, I studied Alain from the corner of my eye. He didn't fit the general stereotype of an accountant at all. His casual trousers and shirt were at odds with the suited businessman you might expect. No paunch from sitting at a desk all day. No sign of grey in his brown hair. If I were to guess, I'd say mid-thirties at most.

When Rupert had finished, Alain cocked his head to one side and said, 'As your friend, I'm sorry for what you're going through. I wish there was something I could say or do to make it easier. As your accountant...' He hesitated. 'Rupert, we need to talk sometime, now Gloria's left. We ought to look at what might happen if she doesn't come back, or if she files for divorce.'

I almost shook my head in disbelief. Typical accountant. Two words of sympathy and then straight into bank balances and the bottom line. I bet he was already juggling Rupert's finances in his head, playing with figures, moving things around to maximise advantage and minimise damage.

Alain looked at his watch. 'I have a client to see in fifteen minutes. Just enough time to get you and your shopping back to the car, I should think.'

And without waiting for a response, he stood and hefted the two heaviest bags from the floor.

My opinion of accountants as a species went back up a tiny notch.

'What was all that about?' I asked Rupert as I manoeuvred the car out of the busy centre.

'What was all what about?'

'Bumping into all those people. It was like a meeting of the nations! When I'm out shopping back home, I don't bump into everyone I know like that.'

'Market day in a small town, Emmy. Nearly everyone I know goes in on a Monday. And we all know who favours which café. I was bound to bump into someone. In fact, I'm surprised we didn't meet anyone else.'

'Yes, well, I'm glad we didn't. Partly because my bladder couldn't have coped with any more coffee and partly because you said we were just nipping to the market. We've been gone for hours, and you're knackered. It's done you no good at all.'

'On the contrary, Emmy, I may be physically tired, but I have been socially and mentally stimulated and I enjoyed it very much. Leave me alone.'

Back at *La Cour des Roses*, Rupert – despite his protestations – was too tired even for lunch. He headed straight for bed, while I snaffled some fruit and yogurt and took them out to the garden, seeking out my favourite spot under the lilac. Hidden away out of sight and sound of the house, here I was enclosed on three sides by shrubs and hedge. The small patch of lawn I could see from my hideaway led to the end of the garden and the chicken run. I breathed in the scent of the lilac flowers draping over me like a canopy and sighed with pleasure.

The Hendersons were out – as usual. How *did* they keep up the pace? I was surprised we hadn't bumped into them at the market along with everyone else. A sudden vision of straight-laced Mrs Henderson trying to seduce her husband by wearing a skin-coloured girdle and suspenders popped into my mind, and I nearly choked on my yogurt.

The chickens were quiet, there was no noise from the *gîtes*, no Ryan doing his manly chopping and digging. Had I hoped he would? That would be ridiculous. He was easy on the eye, and there was no doubt it was enjoyable to lounge around watching him work and sweat, but I couldn't expect him to be here again today. Besides, I'd had my chance last night. It had been there for the taking – *he* had been there for the taking – but I hadn't been ready for it.

Now, as I lay on the lounger with the afternoon sun warming my skin and melting my tired, stressed-out bones, all I could think about was the feel of Ryan's hands running over me, his lips demanding... Demanding what?

Too restless to sit still, I went back up to my room with no sense of purpose. A warm bath to soothe? A cold shower to punish? Sexual frustration coursed through me like a torrent now, and I didn't know whether to kick myself for not scratching the itch last night, or give myself a pat on the back for showing such heroic restraint.

Opting for the happy medium of a warm shower, as I stood under the spray, I wondered what Ryan was thinking. Had he already forgotten about it – would've been nice, but never mind? Did he still pine for my body? (This, I appreciated, was the least likely scenario.) Or was he offended by my sudden withdrawal? He'd seemed understanding, but I didn't like to think he might be feeling insulted or rejected. We'd had a good evening, something I wouldn't mind repeating before I went home, and I didn't want an atmosphere between us for the rest of the week, both for my sake and Rupert's.

Coming out of the bathroom, as I crossed to the dressing table for fresh underwear, I realised I ought to do some washing. There wasn't much left except... Scrabbling to the back of the drawer, I pulled out a matching bra and briefs set and stared at them in surprise.

It had completely slipped my mind that I'd brought these. Hidden away from Nathan's prying eyes, they were my seduction gambit, their purchase prompted by dismay as I'd packed my motley collection of white (and off-white) underwear for the holiday. Realising such garments were hardly conducive to unbridled passion, I'd felt guilty and to some extent responsible for our physical cooling-off of late. I may not have been at the granny-pants stage yet – I liked to think I was a good decade or two away from that inevitable decline – but there *had* been a slow and unnoticed creep into an era of sensible cotton pants and plain T-shirt bras.

Staring into my half-packed suitcase, horrified by how much I'd let things slide, I'd felt compelled to dash out to the extortionate lingerie shop on the nearest high street and splash out on this little set. Handing over my credit card, I'd imagined waiting for the right moment – after a meal in a restaurant; coming back to our room mildly intoxicated; peeling off my dress to reveal the sexy underwear and a tan. Nathan's surprise and appreciation. His enthusiasm. A much-needed spark.

That moment had never come. Instead, Nathan had had *his* moment with Gloria, who no doubt made a habit of spending Rupert's money on expensive Parisian underwear and thought nothing of showing it off to paying guests. Was hers lacy and black, like this? Satiny red? Or did she have the gall to go for pure and innocent white? Perhaps Nathan had seen her in all three by now.

Flooded with sudden emotion, I sat down on the edge of the bed to finger the delicate black lace and tiny red rosebuds. Self-pity turned to anger and then defiance. Discarding my towel, I pulled on the pants, wriggled into the balcony bra and braved the results in the mirror.

With these on, I had curves mostly in the right places, the balcony bra creating more where I wanted them and the pants giving enough coverage to hide those I could do without. They did what I'd wanted them to do when I'd bought them – they made me look and, more importantly, *feel* sexy. Trouble was, the person intended to admire me in them wasn't here any more.

His loss. He might no longer find me attractive, but there were others who did. Ryan, for starters.

What a stupid expense.

Or was it? The underwear was bought and paid for. The body wearing it was desired, judging by last night's kiss. It would be a shame to let it all go to waste... Wouldn't it? I thought about how Ryan had looked at me last night – the way I'd felt when he'd kissed me, run his hands over me – and it was enough to make me squirm. Just because Nathan and I didn't have that spark any more didn't mean I was ready for the scrapyard. If he could feel free to rekindle his love life with someone unsuitable, then so could I.

CHAPTER NINE

With an exhilarating mix of bravado and defiance, I pulled on tight jeans, a low-cut top – great cleavage with the bra doing the work – and heels. No point in going at it half-cocked, so to speak. I headed downstairs before I could change my mind. When I poked my nose around the door of Rupert's quarters, the light snoring coming from his bedroom confirmed he was still having a nap. As I'd hoped. No explanations required.

Leaving a scribbled note in the kitchen saying I'd gone out for a drive, I went into the hall to rummage in the desk for Rupert's address book. I had an idea where Ryan's parents' house was from our conversation last night, but the last thing I needed now I'd made my mind up was to drive around the French countryside for hours, only to come back empty-handed. Riffling through the dog-eared pages, I realised I didn't know Ryan's surname, but then a streak of inspiration led me to R and, hey presto: Ryan. A mobile number *and* an address. Bingo.

My hands shook slightly on the steering wheel as I drove along the country lanes past regimented rows of vines, deserted in the middle of the afternoon. I'd never done anything like this before, and I wasn't sure whether I was excited or petrified.

With one eye on the satnav, I wondered if I should have phoned first, but what would I have said? *"Hello, Ryan, will you be in this afternoon, because I fancy having sex?"* Too direct, too much laying of cards on tables. He might have changed his mind, and

I wouldn't be able to tell over the phone. If he was out, I would have to turn round and go back for a cold shower. If he was in, I could say I happened to be passing and was curious to see the progress on the barn. Nothing obvious. Keep it casual.

The house stood alone along a narrow lane with a convenient sign at the gate. Turning in, I veered towards the barn, one end still ramshackle, the other in the process of improvement. Ryan's car was parked outside. Good. No other cars in sight, so his parents must be out. Even better. Adjusting my cleavage, I knocked tentatively on the heavy wooden door, my prepared speech going round in my head on a repeat loop.

Ryan opened the door, bare-chested and in his work jeans, his hair ruffled. He looked dopey, as though he'd been asleep – but as he looked me over from head to toe until I tingled, the dopey expression was replaced by wide eyes and a predatory smile.

'Emmy. Come on in.'

'Hi. I was just passing and thought I'd pop in and have a look at the place.'

'Right. Sure. Do you want a drink? Beer? Wine? Tea?' The last was said with a tease in his voice.

'Wine would be nice, if it's chilled.' I was beginning to feel hot and bothered – and to second-guess this oh-so-brilliant plan of mine. Cold alcohol wouldn't go amiss.

He poured two glasses and handed one to me. I took a large gulp.

'This is coming along.' I gestured at the room.

'I'll give you the tour.'

He did. It took all of two minutes. He was right when he said it was a work-in-progress. The tour consisted of poking my head around the door of the finished bathroom – nicely done in earth-hued country tiles with a walk-in shower – and then back to the main room, which for now had a neat new kitchen area near the door, an old sofa, a TV, and Ryan's bed at the far end.

'It's lovely,' I said. 'So far.'

'So are you. So far.' Ryan turned me to face him, all trace of teasing gone. 'Why are you here, Emmy?'

I couldn't speak. Instead, I took another gulp of wine before Ryan relieved me of my glass, placed it on the coffee table, took my face in those capable, hard-working hands and pressed his lips to mine. I all but melted into the kiss as he backed me up to the bed and lowered me onto it, then pulled away, his expression questioning.

'No pressure, Emmy. Really. I'm happy to do whatever you want, but I don't want to take advantage. I'm not that kind of guy. Just a bit of fun, okay?'

He was so sweet. And gorgeous. Shirtless and muscled and mine for the taking if I wanted. And oh boy, I wanted. I'd had enough of pedestrian lovemaking. I wanted my share of passion for a change.

'I'm sure. Come here.'

Jeans were removed between kisses and Ryan was as gorgeous naked as I'd imagined he would be, his body lean and tanned, his muscles strongly defined – and then those twinkling blue eyes and oh-so-kissable lips.

When I wriggled out of my top, Ryan took in the lingerie with hungry eyes and let out a whistle.

My eyes narrowed with momentary cynicism, unsure if it was meant for me or the underwear, but then the thought struck me that it didn't matter. He didn't need to flatter me – I was his already. I smirked. Every penny spent on these damned things was going to be worth it.

Ryan didn't relieve me of my fancy lingerie straight away. Oh no. We got our money's worth first as he ran his hands over the lace, then under the lace, until they were finally discarded with a flourish. Even in the desperate heat that followed, Ryan was kind and attentive, roaming my body as though he wanted to explore every inch, and I revelled in it.

Lying together afterwards, I stared up at the high-beamed ceiling, my heart pounding, trying to catch my breath. Spectacular. That was the only word I could think of.

'Spectacular,' I said. This was becoming a bad habit, speaking my thoughts out loud.

Ryan hovered over me and smiled, revealing those cute dimples of his. 'Yes, it was. You are. God, Emmy, there was a store of pent-up energy in there. I can't say I'm sorry you chose me to release it on.'

I gave an embarrassed smile.

He planted a light kiss on my lips. 'Don't worry, I can handle it.' His hands slid down between us. 'Want to go another round?'

I did, so we did – another round in the bed, and when I went for a shower in the walk-in, he followed me and we had another round in there amidst the steam and pounding water and fragrant masculine-scented soap. Ryan was insatiable and so, I was surprised to find out, was I.

When I'd dried myself off and was too exhausted for more, I started to dress.

'Do you want to stay?' Ryan lounged against the wall, a towel anchored on his slim hips. 'I make a decent spaghetti bolognese.'

'No, thanks. I ought to get back. Rupert will be wondering where I am. He thinks I went for a drive.'

Ryan rolled his eyes. 'You two are developing rather a strange relationship, Emmy. You do know that, don't you?'

'Nathan ran off with his wife, Ryan. I don't want him to worry about me on top of everything else.'

'You could phone. Tell him you're safely tucked up in bed elsewhere.' His smile was slow, lazy... Wicked.

'If I stay any longer, one or both of us is likely to have a stroke.' I pulled on my jeans.

Ryan's dimples flashed. 'Okay, have it your way. I may be around at Rupert's tomorrow. Feel free to wear that sexy underwear again. You could pretend it's a bikini. Sunbathe on the patio in it.'

I shot him a withering look. 'Rupert already has heart problems. I don't want to be responsible for adding to them.'

'Great way to go, though.'

'Bye, Ryan.'

As I drove home, an image of Ryan standing in his doorway wearing nothing but a towel around his waist still imprinted on my brain, I couldn't stop smiling. I'd had a great time. I'd rediscovered sex, and the icing on the cake – surprisingly, for a girl who had a complex the size of France – was that I had no trace of guilt to plague my enjoyment.

It was almost seven when I pulled up at *La Cour des Roses* and glanced in the driver's mirror. Oh dear. I could probably wipe that smug smile off my face, but there was no mistaking the flush across my cheeks, and the clothing I'd chosen this afternoon for seduction was hardly suitable for my alleged solitary afternoon drive. Rupert was no fool. As I climbed out of the car, I fervently hoped he wasn't around, so I could scoot upstairs and change.

When I peered around the kitchen door, Rupert had his head in the fridge and was busy rummaging. Cursing my luck, I took advantage of his blind position to shoot past him.

'Back in a mo. Need a pee,' I shouted, before he could turn around and catch me in vamp mode, flying through the kitchen and up the stairs at a speed not suited to the height of heels I had on.

Crikey, I hadn't experienced so much excitement and subterfuge in years.

The next morning, with the sun shining through the curtains, I stretched like a cat. A contented cat that had got the cream.

Nathan may have deserted me, and there may have been many ramifications still to be faced, but for now there was nothing I could do about any of it. I'd had incredible sex – *three times* – with a hunky gardener; I had the tacit approval of the doyenne of the community, Madame Dupont, something I suspected she didn't dole out lightly; and I was earning major brownie points in my role as good Samaritan to my host, with whom I was developing a genuine, solid friendship. I'd even managed to deflect his suspicions about my afternoon drive over supper last night. All in all, I felt decidedly chipper.

I thought about texting Kate to reassure her that I was doing better – far better – than she might expect, but I worried it might cost her a fortune to receive or reply from the Maldives. Then I decided her peace of mind was worth the price.

Her reply came back soon after. *So glad to hear it, my friend. Wish you were here. Bet you do, too! xx*

Smiling, I dressed and followed my nose to the kitchen.

'Ah, just in time.' Rupert handed me an espresso.

'Hendersons out?' I asked. My communication skills were limited nowadays until the first cup was absorbed into my circulatory system. I had rapidly become addicted to Rupert's healing brew.

'Of course.'

Apart from guest meals, the Hendersons had been noticeably absent, invariably leaving soon after breakfast for a full day's sightseeing, and I worried that this stemmed from the inconvenience of Rupert's personal difficulties.

'Are they always like this?' I asked him.

He gave me a knowing look. 'You're worried that all this business with Nathan and Gloria hasn't gone down too well.'

I nodded miserably.

'They're culture vultures, Emmy. You heard what they're planning to do when they get to Paris – fifty-three museums in a day or whatever. They've always been like this. And they always look as though they've got pokers stuck up their arses. Don't worry about it.'

'But I don't want you to lose business. And you said they recommend you to all their friends.'

'They were cheesed off when they arrived, but even they can't complain that things haven't run like clockwork around here, thanks to you. I'm not sure they were over-fond of Gloria anyway. They leave on Thursday, thank the Lord, and I'm not going to go bankrupt or die of disappointment if they never cross my doorstep again. Okay?'

'Okay.'

Since we'd shopped for tonight's guest meal at the market yesterday, my morning was free – and I had a good idea of how to spend it.

'Is it alright with you if I go out?' I asked him.

'Of course. Anything exciting planned?'

'I spotted a hairdresser's in town yesterday. Mine's a mess.' I scraped a hand through the split ends for emphasis. 'I thought I might see if they can fit me in.'

'Do you want me to phone for you first?'

'No, thanks. If they can't manage it, I'll have a mooch and a coffee.'

'Good for you. It's about time you did something for yourself.'

I drove the now-familiar roads past gently rolling farmland into Pierre-la-Fontaine. The streets were more sedate without the market, and as I walked towards the main square, I took time to look at the buildings – so characterful with their cream or whitewashed fronts and red or grey roof tiles, their doorways and balconies sporting colourful containers of bright flowers – pinks, red, yellows. The square, with its stone fountain, was neat and similarly festooned with blooms, lending it civic pride. I peered into a *pâtisserie* with its glorious tarts and pastries, watching in awe as locals thought nothing of handing over an arm and a leg for a beautifully-boxed *gâteau*.

When I reached the hairdresser's, I took a deep breath, then opened the door. A pretty woman somewhere around my age left her customer to greet me. Knowing my French wasn't up to the task at hand, I pointed dramatically at my unkempt yet somehow still boring hair like a manic mime artist.

Thankfully, her English was much better than both my French and my miming.

'I'm Sophie,' she introduced herself with a smile.

I smiled tentatively back. 'Emmy.'

'So, Emmy...'

She studied my hair. Between us, we came to the conclusion that I was a disgrace to my nation for not having had it trimmed before I came on holiday, and that my fading highlights left substantial room for improvement. Taking pity on me – I think she saw it as her sworn duty as a Frenchwoman – she told me I could take up a last-minute cancellation if I came back in half an hour.

I filled in the time with a coffee in the square. As I soaked up the morning sunshine, I fancifully imagined I could breathe in the life and noise and history surrounding me. This was what I'd come to France to do, after all. I watched the old men outside the *tabac*; listened to animated chatter as women exchanged news, a small fussy dog under their arm or in their shopping bag (a strange phenomenon – the French did love their little dogs); and found myself wondering how it was that French women were always so immaculately dressed, even at their most casual. No pottering around the supermarket in paint-covered jogging bottoms and ketchup-stained hoodies like we British. I envied them their casual elegance and their perfect haircuts. At least I would be joining them on one of those counts soon. I hoped.

'So, what do you want me to do?' Sophie asked when I was back and settled in the chair.

'A trim? Highlights?'

She tutted in a Gallic manner and shook her head with disapproval. 'I think we need to do a lot more than that, don't you? Layers. Lots of them. Three different highlights. Light blonde, gold, darker blonde. Very... What's the word?'

'Colourful?' I suggested in alarm.

'Subtle. What do you think?'

I stared at the mess in the mirror and compared it with Sophie's wavy, highlighted blonde bob. 'Fine. Do your worst.'

'My *worst*?'

'Just an expression. I'm happy to go with whatever you think.'

Delight lit her face. She rushed off to mix her magic potions and got to work with brush and foils. 'So, Emmy. I will do my *worst* and you will soon be very chic. Very sexy. Very French.'

I gave a disparaging laugh. 'Hardly.'

Sophie patted my shoulder. 'You wait. You will see.' Her eyes twinkled. 'You said you are on holiday. With a friend or a boyfriend?' she asked as she worked.

'I *was*,' I muttered. 'Not any more.'

She frowned. 'No? What happened?'

'My boyfriend slept with another woman and left me.'

I gasped before she did. It had just popped right out of my mouth. What was it about hairdressers? They were like psychiatrists – five minutes in their chair and you were telling them all your darkest secrets. Maybe this was why I tried not to visit one too often.

Sophie met my look of horror in the mirror with a reassuring smile. 'Tell me about it. Tell me everything.' When I shook my head, she asked, 'Have you talked to a friend from home?'

'I phoned my best friend,' I admitted.

'What about your *maman*?'

I shuddered. 'If you'd met her, you wouldn't ask me that.'

Sophie laughed. 'Then tell *me*. You can pretend I am your best friend from home and that you are sitting next to her here at the salon, having your hair done together. It will make you feel better,' she insisted. 'You know it will.'

I doubted that, but even so, I found myself pouring out the entire tale – well, everything except rolling around with Ryan. I felt I was entitled to keep *that* to myself.

Sophie was right – it did make me feel better. She provided all the proper girly understanding and sympathy and moral outrage I needed. She gasped in all the right places, let out a French swear word or two when required, and above all, she was wholly sympathetic to the point where, when I'd finished the tale, I burst into tears. Tutting, Sophie passed the tissues, clicked her fingers at her junior to fetch me a cup of tea and waited until the waterfall dried up.

'I'm *so* sorry,' I stuttered, mortified.

'Don't be. You needed to do that. But you did not have someone to do it with. A phone call is not the same. I am pleased that I could be that person for you.' When I looked up, she too had a tear in her eye.

The doorbell tinkled as a customer entered. Sophie looked around and greeted her, then turned back to me.

'Sit for forty minutes for the colours. Here are some magazines.' She dumped a pile in my lap and winked. 'If you can't understand all the words, you can look at the pictures.'

She whisked off to deal with her next customer – a middle-aged woman whose hair already looked perfect – while I pulled myself together and braved the mirror. The sight was not pretty – red eyes, blotchy face, hair wrapped in squares of tin foil sticking out at all angles. I was mortified by my outburst, but it seemed I *had* needed a proper cry, and since Sophie didn't mind being the one to set me off, perhaps I shouldn't mind either. And since I was never going to see her again, it didn't matter that I'd spilled my life story or made a fool of myself.

I flicked through the magazines. Fabulous fashions, fabulous interiors, celebrities I'd never heard of ... I tried reading a paragraph

or two and was pleased to get the gist here and there. By the time
the junior took me to the sink, I'd regained my equilibrium, and
when Sophie waved off her immaculate customer – now even more
immaculate – and came back over, I was ready to face the world.

'Why is your English so good?' I asked her as she chopped
and snipped.

'I learned it in school, of course, but when I was eighteen,
I went travelling around Europe with friends. I met a boy in
England – a student – and stayed with him for a few months.
Naturally, his French was not very good, so we spoke English all
the time.'

'What happened with him?'

Sophie caught my eye in the mirror. 'I found him in bed with
another student.'

I stared at her in horror. 'Oh God, Sophie, I'm so sorry!'

She patted my shoulder. 'It was a long time ago. And my story
is just as dramatic as yours, you know. The student he was in bed
with was a boy.'

I spun my head around, but she firmly twisted it back into
place and carried on cutting.

'Apparently, he needed to "experiment".' She made quote
marks in the air with her scissors and comb. 'I came back to
France with much better English and a much worse opinion of
men.' She bent to whisper in my ear. 'But I got over it. And so
will you, my friend.'

'It may take a while. I could have understood it if he'd left on
his own – but with Gloria! He barely knew her! And it's upset-
ting – her being older than him. She's so artificial, so... made up.'
My voice hitched. 'Do you think that was the problem? That I
didn't do all that? I wear make-up for work and going out, but on
evenings and weekends, I tend to slob around in baggy jogging
bottoms and sweatshirts. I didn't think it mattered – I didn't think
we needed to impress each other any more.'

Sophie gave a cynical snort. 'And what did Nathan look like at weekends?'

I managed a laugh. 'Unshaven, with holes in his socks.'

'Well, then. Why should it be different for you than for him?'

'He *used* to tell me my bed hair was sexy. That my old pyjamas with the sheep on were cute. But this woman... I never saw her with a hair or an eyelash out of place.'

Sophie tutted. 'If that was all that bothered him, then he didn't care enough about you, Emmy. And anyway, I am going to make you look fabulous now – more fabulous than you *already* look – and that will serve him right.'

With that, she turned on a supersonic hairdryer and, through necessity, the conversation ground to a halt.

When she'd finished, I gawped in the mirror at the result. She'd worked wonders with a shorter, choppier cut, and the three different tones of highlights made my newly-tanned face glow.

'There. You see?' Sophie surveyed her handiwork with an expert eye. 'Chic, sexy and *almost* French.'

At the till, my credit card wept a little, but I owed her for so much more than a hairdo.

Sophie scribbled a number on one of her business cards and handed it to me with my receipt. 'This is my mobile number. Now give me yours.'

When I looked quizzically at her, she reached out and touched my arm. 'You might feel like some company while you're here, and I enjoyed yours today. Maybe we could have coffee or a drink sometime.'

'Oh. I...' I was about to decline when I realised that I would like to meet this kind, bubbly woman again. 'That would be lovely. Thank you.'

I gave her my number, realised that meant I would have to actually charge my phone, turn it on and carry it with me, and added the number for *La Cour des Roses*.

She smiled. '*À bientôt*, Emmy. I will phone, I promise.'

I left the salon a new woman. Glancing in the shop windows on my way back to the car, I couldn't stop smiling, and I drove to the house in a daze of self-admiration, using each junction and traffic light as an excuse to preen in the driver's mirror – so much so that I nearly missed the turning. With a manoeuvre worthy of a local, I swerved in and parked up with a spray of gravel.

'Great hair, Emmy,' Rupert commented the second I walked in.

I grinned. 'Thanks. Sophie had a cancellation.'

Rupert raised his eyebrows. 'You're on first names with the hairdresser?'

'Why not? She's lovely. We had quite a chat.'

There was a pause before Rupert nodded. 'Well, as long as it's done you good, love.'

I winced. Rupert and Sophie had never met, but I suspected he would rather she didn't know the blockbuster version of his recent woes. I opened my mouth to say something reassuring, but Madame Dupont bustled through from the hall, pulling on her old cardigan.

When she saw me, her eyes opened wide and she made an expansive gesture. I expected a gabble of unintelligible French, but what I got was a compliment I understood, followed by 'Where did you have it done?'

With Rupert looking on, an amused expression on his face, I haltingly provided a version of the morning's events in mangled French.

Nodding, she painstakingly corrected what I'd said and encouraged me to repeat it, smiling broadly when I did so. Then she told me she had no need of a hairdresser because her daughter-in-law did it – which was why she had to wear it in a bun. I think.

'Your French is getting better, Emmy,' Rupert commented as Madame Dupont left.

I was going to make a self-deprecating comment, but stopped. He was right. It *was* improving.

A car drew up in the courtyard. As I went out to help the Stewarts with their luggage and we introduced ourselves, I breathed a huge sigh of relief. A quiet, self-effacing couple in their late forties, they couldn't have been more different from the Hendersons if they'd tried, thank goodness.

When I'd helped them up to their room with their bags, I took them back downstairs to show them the guest lounge and the dining area of the kitchen.

'There'll be a welcome meal for you here this evening at seven,' I told them.

'How many other guests are there?' Mr Stewart asked.

'Just one other couple at the moment. Mr and Mrs Henderson.' In case they were put off by their fellow guests at dinner, I added, 'They're due to leave in a couple of days,' to give them light at the end of the tunnel.

They were delighted with every aspect of the guesthouse, and I felt inordinately proud on Rupert's behalf – but when I took them out to the garden, Mrs Stewart sighed. 'Oh. Oh dear.'

'Is anything wrong?' I asked her, alarmed.

Quickly, she shook her head. 'No. Not at all. It's just that...' Her gaze took in the loungers on the patio, the pots of lilies, the neat lawn, the blossom on the small fruit trees. 'I thought I was keen to visit all the *châteaux*, but now all I want to do is sit here and never budge!'

'Take a seat if you like. I can bring you a cup of tea?'

Mr Stewart shook his head and smiled. 'Thanks, but we haven't had lunch yet. We'd better get off, explore a bit. We can unpack later.'

Rupert and I agreed to convene in the kitchen at four, and he went for a nap while I went to lie in the shade on the patio. The early June sun was pleasantly warm, insects hummed, roses

wafted their gorgeous scents my way. Paradise. Closing my eyes
in contentment, I started to doze, but as the minutes ticked by,
a small storm cloud started brewing in the recesses of my mind,
half-thoughts and unformed worries swirling and eddying until
I sat up in alarm. My breathing was fast and shallow.

Reality hit me like a thunderbolt. I was due to go home in
a few days' time. I'd been so busy with Rupert and the guests
and the work – and Ryan – that I hadn't thought much about it.
Now, it struck me that I would have to navigate to Calais all by
myself *and* drive the car onto the ferry without veering off the
ramp and plunging spectacularly into the Channel. That could
cause me sleepless nights all on its own.

If I managed that, there was the drive back to Birmingham.
Facing the empty flat, or worse, Nathan. Filling people in. As for
work... How could I walk past Nathan in the corridors, bump
into him in the break room? People would find out we weren't
together any more. What would I tell them? More to the point,
what would *he* tell them? There would be questions and gossip
and people talking behind my back. Resentment towards him
bubbled up like acid in my throat. It was bad enough that he'd
slept with someone and left me for her, but I *loved* my job, and
now he was ruining that, too.

And then there was Rupert. He was still getting used to his
medication and although his leg had eased, he wasn't fully mobile
yet. Apart from his little foray to the market yesterday, which
had worn him out, I was doing all the shopping and errands and
half the chores. Even with Ryan doing the garden and Madame
Dupont's ministrations with bleach and polish, I couldn't see
how he would get by.

As if to prove my point, if not batter me around the head
with it, the phone rang and I shot indoors to answer it before it
woke him. My prayer that whoever was on the other end of the
line spoke English was answered. As I riffled through the diary

to answer their enquiry about dates later in the summer, cursing under my breath as an avalanche of loose pieces of paper and receipts fluttered to the floor, I was both gratified and shocked to see how booked-up *La Cour des Roses* was over the coming weeks. I added the caller's provisional booking for August with mixed feelings. It was great to know this season would be a success for Rupert after everything that had happened, but it could all come clattering down around his ears at this rate.

As I headed back outside, Ryan was lugging his kit through the gate.

CHAPTER TEN

A slow thrill curled in my stomach, mixing unhappily with nerves and worry to make me feel slightly sick.

'Hi.' His eyes went straight to my hair, widening with gratifying approval. 'Wow! You look amazing.'

'Thanks.' I mentally gave him several brownie points for his observational skills. Nathan wouldn't have noticed for days, maybe weeks.

His brows knitted together as he came closer. 'Are you okay?'

'Fine.' I tried to smile, but it wasn't one of my better efforts.

'No, you're not. Here.'

He led me to the loungers, pushed me down by the shoulders and sat opposite, his face full of concern – not that of a lover, but a friend.

'I go home on Saturday,' I blurted. 'I'm due back at work on Monday.'

'Could you delay it for a few days? Exceptional circumstances?'

'No way. Nathan's due back on Monday, too. We work for the same company.'

'Ah. So if Nathan turns up on Monday but you don't, it won't look good.'

'No.'

'And if you turn up but Nathan doesn't, people will want to know why.'

'Yes.'

'And if you both turn up, it's going to be pretty uncomfortable.'

'Yes.'

His expression was sympathetic. 'You've no way of knowing what he plans to do?'

'No. I haven't tried to contact him. I don't see why I should. He's the one who left.'

He nodded. 'And?'

'I'm worried about Rupert, Ryan. I don't think he can cope. He's not facing up to things.'

'Rupert will be alright, Emmy. You've done a hell of a lot for him.' He brushed a stray hair from my face. 'You need to learn to relax more.'

'I know. I'm not very good at it.'

'I could help.' There was a wicked light in his eyes, and when he smiled, my stomach flipped over at the sight of those tiny dimples of his.

'You could? How?'

'You know how.'

His lips met mine with a hunger that took my breath away. I allowed myself a few moments, then pulled back.

'That isn't going to solve anything,' I scolded.

'You can't think straight because you're worrying so much, right?'

I nodded.

'Well, then. Let me clear your mind, Emmy. Let me relax you.'

'Ryan, we can't. Rupert's inside having a nap, and there are guests who could be back any minute.'

'Who said anything about going inside?' Ryan tugged me to my feet. 'Come on. I know a place.'

Breathless with anticipation, I allowed him to lead me around the side of the house to the old orchard, where we weaved between the trees to a dense stand of bushes between the house and the roadside hedge. He ducked under and around until we were in a magical little clearing in the midst of all the greenery.

I gasped. 'How did you find this?'

'I know every inch of this garden. And every inch of you.' He sat on the small patch of grass and pulled me down next to him.

'I bet this is where you bring all the girls.'

He laughed and shook his head. 'Nope. Never. This is private property.'

'But you've brought me.'

'Ah, but you're not trespassing. You belong here.'

I shivered with something like pleasure at his choice of words. 'You're sure nobody can see us?'

'Positive. For goodness' sake, stop worrying and start relaxing, or else.'

'Or else what?'

'You'll see.'

And then his mouth was on mine, teasing away any misgivings I might have about *al fresco* lovemaking, and his hands were roaming my body, unzipping and unbuttoning, until I forgot where we were and revelled only in what we were doing.

Afterwards, we lay on the grass in the dappled sunlight, out of breath and sheened with sweat.

'Relaxed now?'

'Mmmm.' Words were a distant thing, too hard to grasp in the afternoon warmth. My bones had melted and I couldn't move.

'You still seem a little tense, if you ask me.'

'Hmmm?'

He stroked my thigh. 'Perhaps I need to work on you a little more.'

'Mmmmm.' If he worked on me any more, I might turn into a molten puddle, but it would take too much effort to resist.

My God, the boy had stamina.

I arrived for kitchen duty twenty minutes late and looking like I'd been dragged through a hedge backwards – which wasn't too far from the truth.

Ryan and I had drifted to sleep, and although it almost gave me a heart attack at the time, I owed a debt of gratitude to the anonymous dog that had squeezed through the hedge to bark outside our secret hideaway. Thankfully, it was an obedient mutt and lolloped back to its owner before we could be discovered, but my heart shot from rhythmically slow to alarmed thudding in a split second as I peered at Ryan's watch.

'Shit! I should've been in the kitchen ten minutes ago.'

'Rupert's not your boss. He won't mind.' Ryan rubbed the sleepiness from his eyes and stretched that gorgeous torso.

'What if he went up to my room to look for me? I hope he hasn't searched the garden.' My eyes were wide with panic.

'Calm down, Emmy. I doubt he's sent out a search party yet, and he can't get up the stairs. Tell him you fell asleep in your room.'

'But if he's in the kitchen, he'll see me come in from the garden.'

'Tell him you fell asleep in the chicken run.' He grinned.

'It's not funny, Ryan.'

'Okay.' He forced a serious expression. 'Tell him you went for a walk and went further than you meant to.'

'That's good. Will he buy that?'

'Well, since you're covered in grass and leaves, it'll have to be a country pursuit of some sort.'

I rolled my eyes. 'Brush me down. And hurry up.'

'Yes, Miss.'

He brushed me down so intimately that I started getting all hot and bothered again.

'Stop that!'

'But you told me to.'

'Not like that! Oh, for goodness' sake. How's my hair?'

He combed it through with his fingers, pulling a leaf from the back. 'If you can't get to a hairbrush before he sees you, you'll have to tell him a stiff breeze sprang up while you were out.'

I slipped my sandals back on. 'Right. See you.'

'Emmy.'

'Yes?'

'I had a great time.'

'Me too.'

Rupert took my bumbling explanations with his usual pinch of salt. 'Well, the walk must have done you good, Emmy. Brought a flush to your cheeks.'

I flushed even deeper. 'The sun's hotter than it looks.'

He glanced through the window. 'Ryan's out in the garden.'

I managed an expression approximating surprise. 'Oh, is he?'

'Hmm. Odd. I went to look for you on the patio earlier and Ryan's gear was there, as if he'd just dumped it. Couldn't see him anywhere.'

I gulped. 'Maybe he was at the bottom of the garden. Or around the side. Or up a tree.' I pulled on an apron and changed the subject. 'I took another booking for you earlier. Five days mid-August. They wanted a full week, but it wouldn't fit in.'

'Thanks.'

I thought about the cascading crap in the diary and my organisational hackles rose. 'Why do you insist on keeping that dreadful diary?'

Rupert looked up from his pastry in surprise. 'I can't run the place without a diary, can I?'

I shot him a look. 'Obviously. But a manual diary's such a pain in the arse. Entries rubbed out and crossed out until nobody can make head or tail of it. Bits of paper blowing all over the hall every time you open the damned thing. I don't understand how you haven't double-booked or accidentally turned someone away before now.'

'The diary was Gloria's baby. She dealt with the bookings.'

'Hmmph,' I murmured noncommittally. No doubt she chose this above more manual tasks which might involve chipping her nail varnish.

'Why, what would you suggest?' he asked.

'How about a spreadsheet?'

Rupert laughed. 'Gloria was a complete technophobe. Hated computers.' His brow furrowed. 'Although she mastered the art of Internet shopping successfully.'

'Yes, well, Gloria isn't here any more, is she?' I said sourly, then clapped my hand over my mouth. 'Sorry.'

Rupert patted my shoulder, leaving floury fingerprints on my T-shirt. 'You're only stating a fact.' He deftly separated an egg and swirled the yolk into his pastry, working it in with nimble fingers.

I mused as I chopped. 'I'm surprised you haven't thought of using a spreadsheet yourself. I bet you do all your accounts on spreadsheets, Mister Financial Whizz.'

'True. But Gloria liked it the way it was and we muddled by. I admit a spreadsheet would be easier to follow. Trouble is, I'd end up scribbling notes to myself and not updating it.'

I conceded this was highly likely, knowing him. 'Why not leave your laptop next to the phone in the hall as a plus-point for your guests – instant Internet access for looking up *château* opening times or local restaurant menus? If you need to work on stuff in private, you could take it into your den as long as you remember to bring it back out again.'

Rupert blanched. 'And what's to stop people looking at all my private documents and financial dealings?'

'Password your files.'

'You don't like that diary, do you?'

'No. It's archaic and dangerous for business.'

'Okay. You can borrow the laptop and set it up for me.'

'Good. Are you going to do anything about the website?'

'How do you mean?'

'I wondered whether you were thinking about updating it.'

'Why, do you think it needs updating?'

I shrugged, as though it was neither here nor there to me. 'Maybe. A little.'

Rupert laughed. 'You're not good at hiding your hand, are you, Emmy? What's the matter with it?'

'When did you last give it an overhaul?'

'I haven't. Wouldn't know where to start. Got a fellow to design it for me when we first got going, but nothing's altered much – he showed me how to change the prices, and that's all I needed.'

'But the place *has* changed, Rupert. You're probably not aware of it, being here all the time, but I noticed straight away when Nathan and I arrived. The photos were different to the reality.' When his face fell, I hastened to reassure him. 'Not in a bad way. The gardens and buildings have matured. Why not take advantage of that? If nothing else, I think you should change the photos, take some shots at different times of year.'

Rupert considered. 'Fair point. What else?'

'You haven't got an availabilities page.'

'People phone or e-mail.'

'Yes, but an availabilities page would be an instant answer for them.' I wagged a finger at him. 'But you'd have to be religious about keeping it up-to-date.'

'I'll think about it. And?'

Unable to bring myself to say what I really wanted to, I started to bluster. 'Well, the font and layout are a bit old-fashioned.'

'There's something else eating at you. Out with it.'

I took a deep breath. 'I think you ought to consider removing all reference to Gloria.'

'Ah.'

'That is, if you think she's not coming back.' I softened my tone. 'It's misleading for people when they come, and if they ask about her, it'll be awkward for you.'

In an attempt to cheer him up, I told him about Jenny mistaking me for Gloria, at which he laughed uproariously.

I glared at him in reproach. 'It's not funny, Rupert.'

'Yes it is, and you know it. Would you know how to do all this, Miss Marketing?'

I looked at him in surprise. 'If you gave me access, I could probably figure it out. It might depend how it was originally set up, but...'

'Good. The chap I used before has moved back to England. Can't be bothered to find anyone else. I'll pay you, of course.'

'It isn't that.'

'What, then?'

'Well, assuming I can get to grips with it, a tweak is one thing, but a complete overhaul takes time. With everything that's going on around here, I don't think I could manage it.'

'I understand. Tell you what,' he said in that decisive tone I'd learned to dread. 'Why don't you just rid us of Gloria and then do the rest when you get back home? I could e-mail you photos. It'd give you something to do at the weekends instead of moping.'

I sighed, beaten. 'Okay. That sounds good.' Actually, it sounded like hard work on top of catching up with my proper *paid* work, but it served me right for opening my big mouth. Still, there would be something decidedly therapeutic about erasing Gloria from *La Cour des Roses*.

With the preparation for dinner done, we sat down for a well-earned cuppa.

'Did you ask Madame Dupont about getting help in?' I asked him.

He looked sheepish. 'No. Forgot.'

'For goodness' sake, Rupert, get it done. I go home on Saturday!'

His shoulders slumped and I felt guilty for haranguing him, but it wasn't just for his own good. I needed peace of mind, too.

Since Nathan and Gloria had left, I'd put my heart and soul into making sure Rupert didn't suffer because of their actions. I couldn't leave without knowing he'd be okay.

'You're right.' He sighed. 'It won't be like having you around, though. You always know what's needed and how to do it, and you put up with all my moods. Can't see how some local girl would match up to that.'

His forlorn expression made me laugh. 'You mean you won't have a live-in slave at your beck and call twenty-four hours a day for you to bark orders at.'

'Well, if you must put it like that.' His smile faded. 'Couldn't you stay another week, Emmy? I might be better by then, and if not, it would give me more time to put something in place. Might do you good, too. I know you've had a crap time of it and you've been working like a dog, but it's settled down now. You could relax, recharge your batteries. It's not going to be easy for you, heading back to face up to it all.'

I studied him. Did he know how much I dreaded going back? Not that he'd have to be a qualified psychiatrist to work it out. Well, it didn't matter. The return ferry was booked for Saturday, and I was expected back at work on Monday.

'I can't, Rupert.'

He looked me in the eye. 'Didn't any of your teachers ever tell you there's no such word as can't, Emmy?'

And off he limped, leaving me to sit stewing with my dilemma. Any more, and my brain might explode.

When dinner was almost ready, Rupert went off to change while I set the table. I was startled to find myself humming. My boyfriend had run off with a cradle-snatcher, my new best friend was a demanding, limping near-sixty-year-old with a dicky heart, I was involved in sexual relations with his youthful gardener, and

I had a gazillion problems to face. Why on earth would I hum? Humming would mean I was happy, wouldn't it?

That was when the sudden, crippling certainty that I wasn't ready to go home hit me, and I sat down in the nearest chair to bite my nails and nibble at my cuticles. Perhaps my decision not to stay longer wasn't as set in stone as I thought.

My private agonising continued throughout the evening. The Stewarts were nice people – although it wasn't possible to ascertain much more than that, since for most of the meal they were obliged to listen to the Hendersons' restaurant and sightseeing recommendations.

'You need to be careful when it comes to *châteaux*,' Mr Henderson informed them. 'Some look fabulous from the outside but there's not a stick of furniture inside. Not like our stately homes back in England. And yet some of them are quite the opposite – they look unprepossessing but are well worth the visit once you're in.'

'*Chenonceau* would be your best bet if you want the best of both worlds,' his wife chipped in. 'Rather a long drive from here, but very impressive – built across a river and with incredible gardens...'

With my head in turmoil, I felt incapable of rescuing the Stewarts from this cultural onslaught. I thought about phoning work to tell them I needed to stay another week, and flinched.

"Oh, hi, Carl, I wondered if you'd let me ignore all my deadlines and stay in France for another week? I'm looking after a middle-aged stranger with angina, I have to clean the bedrooms and feed the chickens, and Nathan's run off with a skeletal over-tanned tart."

No, I didn't think so.

I lay awake most of the night, finally falling into a deep sleep as it started to get light, then woke at nine feeling like I'd done several rounds in a boxing ring. With bags under my eyes and aches in every part of my body – although that might have had something to do with the unorthodox location of my romp with Ryan the day before – I threw on a sundress and headed for the kitchen, where Rupert was clearing up after breakfast. I greeted him with a grunt and pointed at the coffee machine. As he obediently worked his magic, the phone rang. Since Rupert was busy with the coffee, I picked it up with a less-than-confident, *'Bonjour.'*

'Emmy? It's Sophie.'

'Hi! How are you?'

'I have a few minutes before my next customer, and I want to ask how *you* are. I was worried about you after you left, because I insisted you tell me your story and then you were so upset.'

I was touched by her concern. 'I'm fine, thank you. Honestly. It was good to talk. And it's kind of you to phone.'

'Not kind. I wanted to. And I want to ask if you would like to go for a coffee or lunch one day this week. Maybe you could drive into Pierre-la-Fontaine and meet me for my lunch hour?'

'I'd love to.' I couldn't think of a reason why not. I liked Sophie. It was impossible not to.

'Great! Which day do you prefer?'

I thought about my sleepless night. 'Any reason I can't go out to lunch today?' I called across the kitchen.

Rupert frowned. 'Don't think so.'

'Would today be too soon?' I asked Sophie.

'Of course not! Twelve-thirty?'

'Thank you. See you then.' I clicked the phone off.

'Got a date?' Rupert enquired.

'Ha! Wouldn't you like to know?'

'Yes, I would, which is why I asked. Who is it, then?'

I arranged an enigmatic expression on my face. 'Someone I met in town. Someone kind, friendly and extremely attractive.'

'Oh?' Rupert looked disconcerted. 'Does he have a name?'

'Sophie.'

'What?'

'Sophie. The hairdresser. So you can get your mind out of the gutter.'

Rupert guffawed. 'I reckon it could stay in the gutter. For a minute there, I thought you might be so sick of men after Nathan that you were thinking of swapping sides!'

Sophie was locking up when I arrived. Her face lit up when she saw me, and I tried hard not to envy her that winning smile, or that petite figure and bouncy blonde hair.

'You made it!' She kissed me on both cheeks. 'There's a nice place along the street.' She linked arms with me as though we'd known each other for years.

The little restaurant was informal and crowded, but we got a table for two.

'Your hair looks fabulous,' Sophie stated. 'But of course I would say that!'

I grinned. 'It does. Thank you. I love it!'

'I'm glad. Now you must promise you will not allow it to become so dreadful ever again.' A dimple flashed in one cheek.

'I promise.' And I meant it.

'If you come back to France sometime, maybe you could let me do it for you?'

'Of course.'

'Will you come back, Emmy? For a holiday? Or are there too many bad memories?'

'Actually, I have more good memories than bad, now. The first few days were awful, but I've made such a good friend in Rupert, I can't imagine not visiting him. And I absolutely love *La Cour des Roses*.'

As the waiter hovered, we turned our attention to the menu.

'The *croque monsieur* is very good here,' Sophie told me.

'Isn't that just a toasted cheese sandwich?'

Sophie rolled her eyes. '*Mon Dieu*! You must be educated, Emmy!' She ordered for both of us, then sat back. 'You look tired. Is everything okay?'

I sighed. 'Not really. Rupert's being a real pain.'

'Oh? Why?'

'He's been dragging his feet over getting help in for when I leave, so I tackled him about it.'

'And?'

'He said he would, but then he asked me to stay another week.'

'What did you say?'

'I told him I couldn't. The ferry's booked for Saturday and I'm due back at work on Monday. I have an important meeting on Wednesday.'

Sophie studied me as she sipped her mineral water. 'But you want to stay?'

I flung my hands out in despair. 'I don't know! I've felt a real sense of accomplishment here, since Nathan left. I could have gone to pieces. I could have packed up and gone home.'

'But you didn't.'

'No, I didn't. At first, because Rupert needed me. After that... Well, I *wanted* to be here and I *wanted* to help. I've enjoyed the change.' I stopped myself from adding that my romps with Ryan had increased the appeal somewhat.

'And now?'

I sighed. 'I should get back to where I belong. There'll be a mountain of work piled up on my desk.'

'What do you do?'

'Marketing.'

'Do you like it?'

'Very much. It's interesting and varied.' I grinned. 'And pressured and riddled with deadlines.'

Sophie laughed. 'You enjoy that?

I cocked my head to one side. 'I love facing a challenge and finding a way around it. Maybe that's why I've enjoyed helping Rupert. God knows, he can be a challenge sometimes!'

'You're worried about leaving him.'

'Of course. But he's not my responsibility, is he? He's a grown man, not a child. If I weren't here, he'd have to manage. But I *am* here, and now he's my friend. I'm not the type to desert a friend in a crisis.'

She reached across to touch my hand. 'What will your boss say if you try to stay another week? Will he let you?'

I chewed my lip. 'Well, he can't stop me, I suppose. I'm still owed holiday. But he won't be very impressed, especially with the presentation midweek.'

My heart sank. I'd spent months trying to drag the Kelly family's shoe business into the twenty-first century. If I stayed in France, that meeting would have to be postponed or someone else would have to do it. I couldn't say I was happy about either option – but after all, the team had been carefully primed for my two-week absence. Surely I should be able to trust them for one more week?

As the waiter arrived with our lunch, Sophie said, 'Well, of course, I can't tell you what to do. But maybe an extra week's sunshine at *La Cour des Roses* will make you stronger to cope with everything when you go back. And we could have lunch again.' She winked and took a bite of her *croque monsieur*.

I did the same.

'So. Is it "just a toasted cheese sandwich"?' Her dimple flashed as she smiled.

I shook my head, unable to speak. I was too busy stuffing another heavenly bite into my mouth.

'Is it okay if I use the phone?' I asked Rupert when I got back. 'Mine's out of charge and I can't find the charger.' *And I have no intention of switching it back on, only to find messages from Nathan – or worse, no messages from Nathan.*

'Are you calling Australia or Guatemala?'

'England.'

'Then you have my blessing.'

Clutching my cup, I stumbled off to the den for privacy. Part of me hoped Carl would be stuck in one of his interminable meetings. No such luck. He answered his extension on the second ring.

CHAPTER ELEVEN

I cleared my throat. 'Carl? It's Emmy.'

'Emmy?' The surprise in his voice came across the Channel loud and clear. 'Aren't you in France? Is everything alright?'

'Yes, I'm in France and I'm fine, but no, everything's not alright. I've got some problems here and I need to stay another week.'

'You need to *what?* Another *week?*' His voice headed into the realms of a girlish squeak.

'I'm sorry, but there's no way around it. I wouldn't ask otherwise, you know that,' I simpered, hoping to butter him up with a tone of voice that suggested I couldn't imagine he would ever be anything other than understanding.

'But a week, Emmy, on top of the fortnight already. What could be so important? Are you unwell?'

This was the tricky part. If I made up an illness so severe that it prevented me from coming home, Carl might ask for proof that I'd visited a French doctor or something. And of course I had no idea what tale Nathan would spin when he got back. I decided to stick with embellishment rather than outright fabrication.

'To tell the truth, it's all been a bit of a disaster. I'm – we're – staying with a friend over here and he's had a terrible time of it. A heart attack...' *Well, that was what we'd thought at the time, wasn't it?* '...and a damaged ligament in his leg. He was in hospital, but now he's out and he's incapacitated and he lives on his own and there's nobody else to look after him.' I slowed down, trying not to babble. 'If I could stay another week till he's back on his feet, it would make all the difference.'

There was an ominous pause. 'Well, I can see your predicament, Emmy, but you know it's not company policy to allow such a long stretch at once.'

'Carl, I've taken less than half my holiday allowance each year for the past three years.' I knew this to be true because I'd worked it out in my head at two in the morning.

'Be that as it may, Emmy, holiday leave can't be carried forward from one year to the next, you know that.'

You tight bastard.

'I'm well aware of that, but I still have another two weeks owing for this year, and nowhere in my contract does it say extended leave is forbidden, only that it must be negotiated with my boss. I work all the hours God sends when we have a deadline, you know I do.'

I could hear the cogs turning. Carl was one of those blokes who delegates and then pretends to senior management that he's done most of the work. Another week of my absence wouldn't be easy for him.

He sighed. 'Okay, Emmy. If you must, you must. But if you're not back a week on Monday, there'll be hell to pay for both of us.'

'I understand. You'll need to go through my desk and find the file for the Kelly account. The meeting's midweek.'

'*Midweek?* But who's going to do the presentation if you're not here?' There was an edge of panic in his voice. The Kellys were not easy people to deal with, stuck at least a decade behind the times, stubborn as mules, and I seemed to be the only person they would listen to.

'Dave knows all about it. He's been working closely with me and he did a lot of the legwork. He needs to get more experience with presentation, so perhaps he could take that on. If you give him a hand, I'm sure he'll sail through it.'

'Well, I don't know about that, Emmy. You've always dealt with the Kellys.'

'I know, but...' I hesitated.

The kernel of an idea had been brewing in the back of my mind for a while, but with everything else that was going on, my brain hadn't properly latched onto it. Now, as I gazed around Rupert's study and took in the vintage, masculine feel of the leather-topped desk and captain's chair, the brass pen pot on the desk, the antique blotter, it began to burn that little bit brighter.

'You know, Carl, I'm beginning to think we should take a different direction with that company. They're paying us to help them move on, but they're so hesitant about everything we suggest, we never seem to move forward. I'm thinking about maybe helping them move backwards instead.'

'You're... *What?*'

I grinned. 'The Kellys produce good quality – if old-fashioned – footwear. Maybe it's time we played on that instead of glossing over it. Vintage is in right now. Talk to Dave – that kind of thing's right up his street. He can give them both options and I'll work on the detail when they choose the vintage route.'

'Well, I don't know, Emmy...'

'We won't lose them, Carl. They're old-fashioned and stick with what they're used to. That's usually a pain in the arse, but this time it suits us – it means they're not going to move the account just because I'm not at one meeting. Honest.'

'Well, if you're sure...'

'I'm sure. And can you chivvy Heather with that price research I left her with?'

Carl huffed. 'Okay, but really, if you were here where you're supposed to be...'

'Thanks, I really appreciate it. Bye.'

'Emmy, wait! What about Nathan? He's not staying out there for another week as well, is he?'

Ah. Should have anticipated that one. 'To be honest, Carl, I don't know.'

'You don't *know?*'

'He's not here. He – um – went to stay with a different friend this week.' *True enough.* 'But I had to stay to help with this sick friend, so I – er – assume he'll be back on Monday.'

'Can you get hold of him?' Carl persisted, oblivious to my discomfort. 'Derek's going mad up in accounts. He's been trying to contact Nathan for two days over some problem, but his mobile's always switched off. I gave Derek your mobile number.'

'Oh. I – er – haven't checked my phone today.' Crikey – the last thing I needed was a phone call from Nathan's boss. 'And I'm sorry, Carl, but I don't know the friend's number.' *Lame.* 'It's Nathan's friend more than mine.' *Indisputable.* 'Maybe he lost his charger or something?' *Get out now, Emmy, before you make it worse.* 'If I hear from him, I'll tell him Derek was after him.'

'Fine. See you when you get back.'

'Thanks, Carl.'

But he'd already gone, presumably to let Derek know that Nathan was irresponsibly uncontactable and I was a babbling idiot.

As I sat recovering from my ordeal, I wondered what Nathan would think on Monday when he turned up to work – assuming he *did* turn up to work – and I didn't show. My main problem was that he would get first run at telling his side of the story, although I couldn't imagine he would announce to everyone that he'd slept with someone else's wife while on holiday with his own partner and then run off with said floozy. That sort of thing didn't go down too well in the accounts department.

Up in my room, I braved turning my mobile on long enough to text Sophie with my decision, then broke the happy news to Rupert, who was ecstatic that his live-in help was daft enough to stay on.

'I appreciate it, Emmy. I know it must've made things difficult for you at work. Take as much time for yourself as you can. Maybe we should get out more. Or we could have people over for dinner. I could introduce you to some of my friends. Get you a bit of a social circle going.'

I looked at him in surprise. 'I'm only here for another ten days, Rupert. I'm not going to pine for lack of company in that time.'

He frowned. 'No, I know, but there are lots of lovely people around here, Emmy. Might be fun for you.'

He gave me a strange, considered look, and although I wasn't sure what was behind it, I was pretty sure I would live to regret it.

Feeling I'd earned a rest, I went outside, all the way to the bottom of the garden to my favourite hideaway where I could sit in the shade of the mauve and white lilacs and doze.

Telling Carl I was going to stay another week was the right decision. I had a fabulous haircut, I'd made a new friend in Sophie, and I was having a... stimulating affair with a gardening god. I felt genuinely happy.

I should have known it couldn't last.

'Mother, please. I don't need you to... Of course it would be good to see you but I don't think there's room for you here, it's fully booked. Oh. You already asked the owner? Well, why didn't you say so? No, I'm not trying to put you off. Yes, I'm managing perfectly well. How did you find out about all this, anyway? I might have known. Yes, I am eating properly. No, I'm not going to do anything stupid. How will Dad get the time off work? Fine. See you tomorrow. Yes, love to Dad. Bye, Mum.'

That was my side of the telephone conversation I had with my mother later that afternoon. My mother's side was somewhat longer. How did she know what was going on?

To cut a long and garbled story short, it seemed Carl had not got as far as telling Nathan's boss about Nathan's new whereabouts, because Derek, still unable to contact Nathan on his mobile, had phoned the number at *La Cour des Roses* which Nathan had furnished him with in case of accounting emergencies. So much for our agreement not to worry about work on our precious holiday together.

Rupert, woken from his nap and unable to spot me at the bottom of the garden from the house, assumed I'd gone for a walk and took it upon himself to inform Derek that Nathan was no longer on the premises, so Derek had looked up Nathan's emergency contact on the personnel database and – foolishly, in my opinion – phoned Nathan's mother in the hope that she might know how to reach her son.

We can all imagine her reaction – one minute under the impression her son was on a nice holiday with his girlfriend, the next in a state of confusion bordering on panic. Derek, belatedly realising he'd put his size nines where they shouldn't be, had bowed out as gracefully and tactfully as he could and scuttled off to deal with his accounting dilemma on his lonesome.

There was nothing graceful or tactful about Nathan's mother, on the other hand. Assuming that whatever had happened was all my fault – as usual – she'd got straight on the phone to *my* mother, first to find out if she was in the picture, then to put her in the picture, then to say what a disgrace I was to ignore her poor darling son so much that he'd absconded in the middle of his holiday.

My mother was not one to take such an onslaught lying down. She could hold her own, even against Nathan's mother – an ability that had me in awe. Leaving the woman in no doubt as to what she thought of both her and her son, she immediately tried my mobile, which of course lay neglected in my bedside drawer.

Mum always prised contact numbers out of me before I went away – 'In case your father has a stroke or something, Emmy' – so she phoned *La Cour des Roses* to verify that Nathan had left and to find out where he'd gone and why.

Rupert, having just dozed off again, was caught unawares – not a good state to be in when speaking to my mother. Even so, his underused tact radar must have won out over his thick skin for a change, because he realised she was not to be toyed with and refused to confirm anything other than the fact that Nathan had indeed left and his current whereabouts remained unknown – although, under her remorseless questioning, he did confess that I wasn't returning home on Saturday as planned and would be staying another week. This, of course, was enough to make my mother demand a room for the weekend and insist I phone her back the minute I was located.

Heaven forbid that the airline gods should look kindly upon me and ensure no last-minute flights were available. My parents were due to arrive mid-afternoon the next day.

With my ears still ringing from the verbal onslaught that was my mother in full panic mode, I laid into Rupert about interfering in other people's affairs.

'I need to know what you told Nathan's boss. Exact words, Rupert.'

'He asked to speak to Nathan. I told him Nathan wasn't here. He asked if I had a forwarding number and I said I didn't. Then he asked if you were still here, and I said you were and you'd spoken to your boss this afternoon.' He hesitated. 'Was that okay?'

'Yes. Good. Okay.' I was grateful for Rupert's unusual restraint. At least he hadn't said anything that could clash with what I'd told Carl. 'That's it?'

'That's it. Scouts' honour. I wanted to tell him his feckless employee ran off to shack up with a woman old enough to be his...'

'Tell me you didn't.'

'But I didn't.'

'Thank the Lord for that. Right. Next.'

'There's more?' Rupert shifted from foot to foot like a guilty schoolboy.

'Yes, there's more. Did you *have* to tell my mother I'm staying on? Did you *have* to invite them here? Couldn't you have told her you didn't have any vacancies?'

'You would've had to tell them you were staying another week sooner or later, and you know it. As for inviting them, I didn't. Your mother invited herself. All I did was confess under vicious interrogation that there would be a room free tomorrow. If you hadn't been hiding at the bottom of the garden, you would have ended up doing the same.' His voice softened. 'She sounded worried about you, Emmy. I got the distinct impression she wouldn't take no for an answer. I don't see what else I could have done.'

I heaved a sigh. He was right. We'd been well and truly steamrollered – but that didn't mean I had to like it.

With an innocent look on his face, he added, 'You never told me your full name was Emmeline.'

This was what came of allowing people to talk to my mother. When she was distraught, she had a habit of reverting to the name on my birth certificate.

'I don't use it. I only answer to Emmy. Bear that in mind if you want to live long enough to meet my mother.' You could have balanced a coffee cup on my bottom lip, I was pouting so much.

'I think it's delightful.' Rupert dodged clumsily before I could hit him. 'But I can see that you don't. Where did she get that from?'

'A film. Mum was pregnant with me and raging with hormones when she saw it. She decided the name was romantic.'

Rupert laughed.

'At least I wasn't named after a bear in checked trousers,' I shot at him.

He smiled in that aggravatingly mild-mannered way of his. '*Touché*, Emmy.'

Still feeling that Rupert was somehow to blame for the disastrous way things had panned out and knowing I was being unfair, I stayed out of his way for the rest of the afternoon, occupying myself with making up the room for the Kennedys who were due to arrive tomorrow. My parents would have to take the Hendersons' room, and since there was nothing I could do about that until the hateful, stuck-up pair left in the morning, the following day would be far more hectic than I'd anticipated.

Dinner was a somewhat strained affair, with Rupert still shell-shocked from his dealings with my mother and me still sulking. In a sudden stroke of genius that would get me out of the house *and* reduce tomorrow's workload, I demanded his shopping list for the following night's guest meal and went out to do a late-evening shop.

By the time I started back from the supermarket, I was exhausted, stressed out, furious with Rupert and furious with my parents. As I rubbed at the tension in my neck, I remembered Ryan's healing touch in the garden yesterday. Ryan. Mmm. His place was only a little out of my way. It would be rude not to drop in and say hi, wouldn't it? A slight detour here, another little detour there...

'Sorry to drop in without phoning first,' I said as he opened the door. Belatedly, it occurred to me that he might have company. 'Are you busy?'

'I am now.' He took my hand and pulled me in. 'Any particular reason for your visit? Anything I can do for you?' His eyebrows wiggled suggestively, and my tension began to melt away like a switch had been flicked.

I flopped down on the sofa. 'I'm staying another week. I phoned work this afternoon. My boss wasn't happy.'

Ryan perched on the arm of the sofa. 'That's good. That you're staying another week, I mean – not that your boss is pissed off. I'm glad you'll be around a bit longer.'

I looked up at him. He seemed to mean it, and inwardly I sighed with relief. Ryan and I hadn't yet defined the boundaries of our...

liaisons, and as I'd driven to his place, I'd worried my news might panic him. I didn't want him to think I was staying because of him, and I made a mental note that we ought to discuss it sometime. But for now, he seemed at ease with the situation – and I had enough on my plate without rocking my already-capsizing boat.

'There's more,' I said sulkily. 'Nathan's boss phoned *La Cour des Roses* and Rupert told him Nathan had left, so Nathan's boss phoned Nathan's mother who phoned my mother who phoned Rupert, and now she and my father are descending on us tomorrow.' My shoulders slumped in defeat.

'Ah. All that tension we got rid of yesterday has come right back, hasn't it?'

'Mmm-hmm.' I rolled my shoulders. 'I wondered if we could have another therapy session. You know, so I could relax.'

'No problem. I'm feeling kind of tense myself.'

I slapped playfully at him. 'You're never tense.'

'I hide it well. I get tense here.' He lifted my hand and placed it on his chest, where I could feel his heart thudding against my palm. My mouth went dry. 'And here.' He placed my other hand... Well, it's safe to say there was nothing relaxed about where he put it.

'In that case, I'd better get to work on you,' I said in my best sultry manner. 'You obviously need a thorough going-over.'

'You think so?'

'I know so.'

'I like a woman who knows her own mind.'

'That's good, because I know exactly what I want right now.' And I took it. And Ryan had no complaints.

It was late when I got back, and as I ferried the shopping from the car to the kitchen, I hoped against hope that Rupert might have gone to bed early so I wouldn't have to explain myself.

No such luck.

'You've been a long time, Emmy,' he said, limping into the kitchen to give me a hand shoving the now thoroughly-unchilled chilled items into the fridge. 'I was beginning to think you'd got arrested for shoplifting.'

'Ha ha. It took ages, that's all. There was *such* a queue at the deli counter. And the cheese counter.' I grasped at straws. 'Then the girl at the checkout put something through twice and it took me forever to get her to understand, and she had to call someone over.'

'Still, the supermarket closed an hour ago. Get lost on the way home?'

I gulped and tried to ignore my suspicion that there was a glimmer of mischief behind his innocuous enquiry. 'No, but it was such a nice night that I decided to go the long way round. I was enjoying the drive and the breeze through the window.' *Change the subject, Emmy, before you dig yourself any deeper.* 'Anyway, let's get this lot unpacked. I need to get to bed. I'm exhausted.'

'Yes, you must be.' He allowed a melodramatic pause. 'You go on up. I'll do this.'

'Thanks.'

'No worries. You'll need all your strength for tomorrow. Parents coming and all that.'

I groaned and headed off to bed. I was shattered. I thought holidays were supposed to be less stressful.

By the time I flopped down for lunch the next day, I ached all over. My body wasn't used to all this continuous physical activity. The frenetic combination of housework and rampant sex was either going to leave me incredibly fit or finish me off altogether.

Madame Dupont had come for a cleaning stint in the morning and soon picked up on my agitation.

'What is wrong, Emie?' she asked as we made *thé au citron* and took a break. 'You are working too hard!'

'My parents arrive today,' I explained in my halting French. 'They found out about Nathan and they're coming for the weekend.'

'Won't that be nice for you?'

I shrugged. 'Maybe. My mother... She asks a lot of questions.'

Madame Dupont gave an unladylike cackle. 'And you don't want to tell her all the answers, no?'

'No.'

She reached across to pat my hand. 'Mothers always know the truth.'

'You're right.' I sighed. 'I need to get back to work.'

'Why do you need to clean so much? Because your mother is coming?'

'I want to please her, I suppose.'

Madame Dupont shook her head. 'You will please her by being *you*, Emie. Not by polishing.' When I frowned uncomprehendingly at the last word, she mimed it and showed me the tin of polish, making me repeat after her.

I finished my tea. 'You don't know my mother. It could go either way.'

Rupert wasn't at all remorseful about being partially responsible for my mother and father descending on us. He delighted in making me miserable throughout lunch by regaling me with all the outrageous things he would say to them, including hinting that he and I were involved in a passionate affair to make up for our partners' infidelity.

'That's hardly likely with your leg,' I told him as I devoured my sandwich.

'Tell me about your parents. After that conversation with your mother yesterday, I feel the need for advance information so I can prepare my defence strategy.'

I grinned. 'Mum's in charge of that partnership, if you hadn't already guessed. She's the one who organises us and gets things done.'

'And how does your father survive this onslaught?'

'Quietly and uncomplainingly.' I hastened to jump to his defence. 'He's not downtrodden, though. He's placid, I suppose, and contented – happy to let Mum take charge because he can see that's what makes her tick. He works hard, and I think he has enough of being in charge at work. When he gets home, he's happy to hand over the reins to Mum.'

'What does he do?'

'He's the accounts manager at a big manufacturing company.'

Rupert spluttered out a laugh. 'What is it with you and accountants? I thought you'd had enough of them with Nathan!'

'Yes, well, Dad came first, didn't he?' I scowled. 'It was Nathan that was one accountant too many in my life.'

Tactfully, Rupert changed the subject. 'Does your mum work?' He shuddered, as though imagining what devastating effect she might have on her work colleagues.

'No. She was a secretary when they first met, but Dad earned enough for her to stay at home when we were small, which she dutifully did, although I don't think she enjoyed not being in the thick of things. By the time we were old enough for her to go back to work, she ran so many committees and charity whatnots, she didn't have time.' I smiled. 'When I was a teenager, I was *so* embarrassed by them. I thought my mother was too loud, too bossy, and I wished Dad would stop being a wimp and stand up to her. But then I had relationships of my own, and I developed a kind of admiration for what they have. They both *like* the way things are. That's all that matters, isn't it?'

'Yes, I suppose it is.'

We both fell silent, as I contemplated my *so* not-made-in-heaven match with Nathan, and Rupert no doubt did the same about his relationship with Gloria.

'You look tired, Rupert. You need to go for a rest.'

'Yes, Nurse.'

He winked as his mobile rang. Digging it out of his pocket, he answered as he limped off to his room.

'Alain! Good to hear from you. I've been thinking about what you said, and you're quite right. We do have a lot to discuss. Yes, maybe we should meet...'

God, that accountant was a pest. Like a dog with a bone.

I hurried upstairs to clear out the Hendersons' room. Since they were supposed to vacate by ten, I'd hoped to get it done earlier – but of course the wretched couple didn't leave until midday. They made no apology, just took their own sweet time packing their fancy matching luggage and distracting Rupert from his chores with a detailed itinerary of their imminent assault on Paris. Heaven help the Parisians.

At least they paid up without a quibble. I'd half-expected them to demand a discount for mental trauma caused by their fellow occupants' domestic crises, so I was startled when they complimented Rupert on how well he'd provided for them under the circumstances. They shook his hand, asserted they would be back next year, shot me a curt nod and left.

'I didn't even get a thank you!' I spluttered.

Rupert surprised me with a kiss on the forehead. 'You can have one from me instead. For helping me keep the hardest customers of the year happy.'

I'd just finished their room when the phone rang. Knowing it was too much to hope that my parents' flight might have been cancelled, I picked it up with a gruff, *'Bonjour.'*

There was a pause. 'Emmy?'

'Yes?'

'Hi there, big sis. Wasn't sure it was you, for a minute. Had visions of a sexy French maid.'

I rolled my eyes. My little brother, the playboy. 'Hi, Nick. What's up?'

'I believe it's me who should be asking you that question. At least, that was one of the many instructions I received at seven minutes past eleven last night.'

'Ah. Mum got to you already. Eleven-o-seven precisely?'

'Yup. I know, because I was in the middle of something important and didn't appreciate the interruption. You have a lot to answer for.'

'Sorry. Who was it this time?'

'Ginny. You don't know her. Neither do I, now – not in the way I wanted to. Has Nathan really sailed off into the blue yonder?'

'I'm afraid so.'

'How're you holding up?' His joshing tone was gone. My brother might be a perennial teenager despite his twenty-nine years, but he wasn't uncaring with it.

'I'm okay, considering. I'm over the shock, getting past the anger and heading into oh-my-god-what-am-I-going-to-do-now.'

'You'll be fine. We Jamiesons are resilient folk. Besides, Mum has no intention of letting you fall apart. Are they there yet?'

'No. They're due any minute, though.'

'Don't let her bully you. Phone me if you need moral support.'

'Okay. I will.' I felt the tears threaten and swallowed hard. A big hug from my little brother wouldn't have gone amiss right now.

'Oh, and Emmy? Just so you know. I always thought Nathan was a bit of a dickhead.'

I laughed. 'I know you did.'

'Oh. Do you think he knew?'

'Yes.'

'Ah. That might explain why we never hit it off. Bye, sis.'

'Bye, Nick.'

As I put the phone down, I glanced in the hall mirror and winced. I looked awful. My hair was scraped back in a stubby ponytail for cleaning purposes, the dark bags under my eyes could rival Rupert's, and now my eyes were red from the effort of fighting back tears. Conscious that my ever-perceptive mother would be here soon, I ran upstairs to shower, apply concealer and blow-dry my hair into some vague semblance of the style Sophie had so effortlessly achieved for me. I needed to look confident and capable and serene. My mother was already fired up by the melodrama of my predicament. I didn't want to add fuel to it by looking like death warmed up.

CHAPTER TWELVE

My parents landed at three, although it was clear they'd hoped to arrive sooner – I could hear my mother berating my long-suffering father for his snail-pace driving before she even got out of the rental car.

'Hello, Mum.' I ran down to give her a kiss.

'Hello, darling.' Holding me at arm's length, she scrutinised my appearance. 'You've had your hair cut.' She tilted her head to one side as though to judge better, then made her pronouncement. 'I like it. Makes you look younger.'

I heaved a sigh of relief. Not wanting to risk her spotting something she *could* make an issue of – such as the luggage-sized bags under my eyes – I broke away and went round to my father's side.

'Hello, Dad.'

'Hello, love.' Dad gave me a peck on the cheek. While he unloaded their bags, my mother's eagle eye took in the house, the garden and the *gîtes* across the courtyard.

'Lovely, isn't it?' I said brightly.

She pursed her lips. 'I suppose so.'

Dad winked at me. 'It looks delightful. I can see why you wouldn't want to rush away, even after... Well.' He coughed and hoisted the bags up to the house.

I led them upstairs. Their room was the best in the house, as befitted the Hendersons. It overlooked the full sweep of Rupert's garden, from the patio with its ceramic pots of lilies to the lawn dotted with random flower beds like islands of colour in a green ocean, the odd weeping pear or willow adding graceful height and shade, and on to the chicken run amidst the shrubs down at the far end.

'It's beautiful, Emmy,' Dad said. 'Are you sure Mr Hunter didn't mind us coming at such short notice? Your mother was rather forceful with him on the phone.' He shot her a look of disapproval, but it was like water off a duck's back.

'No, Dad, it's fine. The people who were in this room left at lunchtime. Another couple – the Kennedys – are due today for a long weekend like you two, and the Stewarts leave on Tuesday. Rupert's pretty busy – he gets a lot of repeat business.'

'Yes, I imagine he does.' Dad stared dreamily through the window.

'Did Nick phone you?' Mum asked, keen to know whether her instructions had been obeyed.

'Yes, he did,' I assured her.

'Good. He seemed rather distracted last night. I wasn't sure if he was listening properly. He must have been asleep when I rang.'

'Maybe.'

Suppressing a smirk, I caught Dad's eye and saw that he, too, was trying not to smile.

'Come down when you've unpacked,' I said. 'I'll go and make a pot of tea.'

As I turned away, I saw Mum surreptitiously run a finger across the dressing table. I almost laughed at the disappointment on her face when her finger came away clean.

As I headed downstairs, I heard Dad say, 'Well, she seems happy enough, Flo,' followed by my mother's impatient 'Oh, for heaven's sake, Dennis, you can't judge by appearances. I hope the shower works.'

Those two never changed. My dad, so quiet and thoughtful and calm, permanently bossed around by my larger-than-life, opinionated mother. And I'd never come across a happier couple.

When they came downstairs, I had tea waiting for them on the patio. There wasn't a better way to show off the place than this. The late afternoon sun cast a deep yellow glow across the garden; the hens clucked peacefully; insects buzzed and zinged around the roses.

Dad sighed contentedly. 'The garden's glorious. Does Mr Hunter do it himself?'

'Some of it, but there's a bloke who comes in the summer.'

'French chap?'

'No, English. His mum and dad own a holiday house a couple of miles away, and he spends the summer out here doing gardens. In the winter, he goes back to England, labouring or something.'

I blushed, trying hard not to think about Ryan's taut muscles and tanned torso, and prayed he wouldn't turn up for a stint in the garden.

'Sounds like a grand life,' Dad said wistfully.

'How are things at work?'

'Oh, okay. We have a new client taking up all my time. He's an awkward old sod, actually...'

'Never mind all that, Dennis.' My mother bristled impatiently. 'We didn't come all this way to listen to you witter on about work. Now, Emmy, what's all this about Nathan?'

'You didn't have to come all this way, Mum. I could have explained over the phone.'

'Rubbish. I know you, Emmeline Jamieson. You'd have told me bugger-all over the phone. This way, we can sort it out face-to-face.'

I poured tea and settled myself in for the long haul. 'There's not a vast amount to tell. Nathan thought we should separate. He's gone off and I stayed here. Then I decided to stay an extra week to help Rupert, because he's damaged his leg and can't get about.'

Mum huffed. 'Now, Emmy, that's not all there is to it. People don't just go off in the middle of their holidays. Nathan's mother tried to blame you, of course, what with her thinking the sun shines out of her son's backside, but I gave her what-for.'

I bet you did. Perhaps it might be easier if you tell me what you've heard already, Mum. You were a bit' – I searched for the least offensive word – 'overwrought when you rang.'

She sipped her tea, then put her cup back in the saucer with relish. 'Well, the first *I* heard was when Dorothy phoned. Heaven forbid I should hear major family news from my own daughter' – her accusatory glare bore right through me – 'but no, I have to hear it from that dreadful mother of his. Anyway, she told me...'

Mum was an expert at monologues. I'd got the gist when she phoned, but this was the unabridged version and took a good ten minutes.

I was happy to listen. It delayed me having to give my side of the story, and besides, I needed to know everything she knew and where she'd heard it from so I could decide how much I could tell her without giving away any more than necessary. There was always a great deal of strategic planning involved when dealing with my mother.

She finished her tale and poured more tea to rehydrate her voice box, waiting with ill-disguised impatience for my version.

My mind raced. She was right – boyfriends don't disappear in the middle of a holiday just because things aren't going too well. And Madame Dupont was right, too – there was no point in lying to her. She had that innate ability, as all mothers did, of knowing when I was not being entirely truthful. I couldn't avoid telling her that Nathan had run off with another woman, but I certainly wasn't going to tell her in lurid detail about the night I found Nathan and Gloria having wild jungle sex.

Tweaking the timeline of events, I explained that there had been some strain at the beginning of the holiday due to the owner being rushed into hospital, and Nathan had injudiciously decided that comforting the owner's wife was the way to go.

Mum butted in at this point. I was amazed she'd stayed silent for so long. 'Do you mean to tell me that Nathan has run off with Mr Hunter's *wife?*'

'Yes, Mum. Her name is Gloria.'

She raised her eyes heavenwards. 'Well, that explains it.'

I wasn't quite sure what Gloria's name had to do with anything, but logic had never been my mother's strong suit.

'And how old *is* this dreadful creature?'

'Mid-forties.'

'Well, for goodness' sake, I can't imagine what's got into the boy, going off with a woman like that when he's got a perfectly good *young* girlfriend.' She squeezed my arm in sympathy. 'Don't you worry. It's just some silly midlife crisis. He'll soon be back.'

The idea that she might pity me made me feel queasy. I didn't want her to see me in the role of helpless victim.

I took a deep breath. 'I'm not sure he will be back, Mum. And to be honest, I doubt I'd want him.'

My mother looked flabbergasted. 'Well, really. What are you talking about? Men dally around all the time, don't they, Dennis?'

She looked across at my father, but he remained his usual implacable self. 'It's no good asking me, dear. I wouldn't dream of it.'

I smiled, but Mum was not to be waylaid.

'Well, they do. It's a disgrace, of course, but that's the way they are. You'd be in a different position if he'd run off with some young secretary he'd got pregnant and intended to set up shop with, but as it is, it sounds like this *Gloria*' – she spat the name out – 'is far too old for him. He'll get it out of his system. Nathan knows which side his bread's buttered. Once he realises she's mutton dressed as lamb, he'll come running back with his tail between his legs, you mark my words.'

She paused for breath, sipping more tea to lubricate her throat before the next onslaught, while I wondered how many more clichés she could squeeze into the conversation. But all we got was, 'Well, Emmy, I don't know what to say.'

She sighed, patted my knee, then drew me into a voluminous hug. As I looked across at my father, I saw the glint of a tear in his eye.

'I don't want you to worry about me. I'm fine.'

Her soppy moment over, she said, 'I don't see how you can be fine.'

'Well, I am. I wouldn't say I'm turning cartwheels in the garden, but I'm okay under the circumstances. I know you're both cross with Nathan, but I've had longer to think about it than you. I can't say I'm not upset – I was livid at first, and surprised because it seemed out of character for him. But things were pretty rubbish between us already.'

Mum looked me in the eye. 'You don't love him any more.'

Returning her honesty, I shook my head. 'No. Not any more.'

She reached across to take my face in her hands. 'If that's the case, Emmy, then there's nothing you or he can do to change it. Life's too short to go through it pretending to love someone. You deserve better.'

I was spared further interrogation by Rupert's timely appearance. Looking much better for his rest, he limped out with his best greet-the-guests smile fixed in place.

'Mr and Mrs Jamieson. What a delight.' He shook their hands. 'Welcome to *La Cour des Roses*. I'm so glad you came.'

Dad jumped up, smiling warmly back. 'Mr Hunter. Good to meet you. You have a beautiful place here. It's good to know Emmy is somewhere like this at such a difficult time.' Ever the gentleman, he pulled out a chair for Rupert to sit.

My mother's polite smile was on the glacial side. No doubt she thought Rupert was more than a little to blame for what had happened; that he should have kept his wife on a shorter leash.

Rupert sensed it and turned the charm up a notch. 'I can only say what an absolute godsend Emmy has been the past few days, Mrs Jamieson. She's a real gem. You must be incredibly proud of her.'

Amused, I watched my mother thaw, despite her attempts not to. Pouring Rupert some tea, I sat back to enjoy his expertise as he melted the last of her defences with compliments, concern for their wellbeing after their journey and hopes that they would enjoy their stay.

I caught Dad's eye and he winked. He liked Rupert, I could tell, and I couldn't be more pleased. It was important that he understood why I wanted to stay and help. And once more, it highlighted the chasm between Nathan and me – that my dad and I could both appreciate the man's charm and fun, taking him with a large pinch of salt along the way, while Nathan hadn't taken to him at all.

Lost in my thoughts, I dangerously took my eye off the ball for a moment. When I came back to the game, I was horrified to hear where my mother was headed.

'...can't think what's got into Nathan, running off like that. And with a woman nearly old enough to be his mother.'

'Mum!' I shot her a stricken look.

'What?' she retorted. 'I'm only stating facts.'

'Quite so.' The advantage of Rupert's thick skin was that he was rarely offended.

'Haven't you heard from either of them?' Dad asked.

'Not a peep,' Rupert admitted.

'Well, we know Nathan's phone has been off for days. That's how I found out about this mess.' Mum shot me a reproachful look. 'Although I suppose we would have found out eventually, when you didn't come home on Saturday.'

'I only decided I was going to stay two hours before you rang! Of course I would have phoned. You beat me to it.'

Mum turned her frustration back on Rupert. 'Have you tried to contact your wife at all, Mr Hunter?'

'Mum! That's none of our business.'

'Of course it's our business, Emmy.'

'Your mother's quite right,' Rupert put in smoothly. 'And please, it's Rupert. Yes, Mrs Jamieson, I have tried to contact Gloria.'

My eyes widened in surprise. This was news to me. Since I'd taken the stance that I would make no effort to reach Nathan, I'd assumed Rupert felt the same about Gloria. I'd no idea he'd been trying to get hold of her. Rupert played his cards pretty close to his chest, but so far he'd given me the impression he knew deep down that she'd gone for good. Had he tried to contact her to beg her to come back? Or to tell her to go to hell? I resolved to find out the next time I could get him alone.

'Her mobile's always switched off,' he said now. 'I also phoned some friends who live further south, but she isn't there. I don't know where she and Nathan are. They'll resurface when they want to, I suppose.' Rupert reached across and patted my hand. 'The important thing is that Emmy and I are coping perfectly well without them.' He hoisted himself to his feet. 'Talking of which, we need to make a start on dinner. Couple of minutes, Emmy?' He limped back into the house.

'Seems like a nice chap,' Dad said. 'Shame about his health. I hope he gets better before you leave.'

'So do I, Dad.'

'What did he mean, make a start on dinner?' Mum queried.

'Just that. I need to help Rupert cook. You and Dad relax out here. You must be tired.'

My mother, won over during Rupert's presence, frowned again. 'Exactly how much are you having to do here, Emmy?'

Taking a deep breath, I weighed up the pros and cons. She knew I'd agreed to stay another week to help Rupert, but she had no idea how much hard graft I was putting in. I knew she wouldn't like it – that she would think Rupert was taking advantage of her darling daughter's better nature. I could play it down, but since they were going to be here until Sunday, they would see for themselves.

I opted for vagueness. 'I do what needs to be done at the time, Mum. I'm enjoying it. Don't worry.'

Before she could respond, I popped a kiss on her cheek and shot into the kitchen, leaving her to mutter to my father out of earshot.

'So what was all that you told my mother?' I asked Rupert as soon as I caught up with him indoors. 'About trying to contact Gloria? You never told me that.'

'Ah, well, your mother has a much more vicious interrogative streak than you, young Emmy. You need to practice more. Hone your skills.'

'You're evading the question.'

He sighed. 'I didn't tell you, Emmy, because you had your own problems to contend with. And I know for a fact that the reason your mobile is never on your person and never charged is nothing to do with early-onset middle-aged forgetfulness. You're assuming Nathan hasn't tried to contact you, but the truth is, you don't want to know.'

'If he wants to get hold of me, Rupert, all he has to do is ring the landline here.'

'And he hasn't. But the point is, I knew how you felt and I respected that, so I didn't see the point of burdening you with my attempts.'

'But that makes me feel awful. You should have told me. God knows we've told each other all sorts!'

He looked me in the eye. 'Ever heard of male pride, Emmy? If I'd got anywhere, I would have let you know.' He turned to the fridge and started to get everything out, a subtle indication that he'd shared as much he was going to.

But I wasn't finished yet. 'Can I ask *why* you want to get hold of her? Do you want her back? Is that it?'

When he turned back to me, his whole face collapsed a tiny fraction, and I finally understood what people meant when they said that someone looked crestfallen.

'The truth, Emmy? I don't know. But I don't think what I want makes any difference. Gloria's the one who's taken action, so it's what Gloria wants that's the issue. Was she just making a point? Attention-seeking? Is she trying to pay me back for something I've done – or haven't done? Has she left for good? Does she want a divorce? Will she come back?' He held out his hands in a gesture of surrender. 'See? Too many questions. They're making my head hurt and they're stopping me sleeping. So the answer to *your* question, Emmy love, is that I'm trying to get hold of Gloria simply to remove some of the questions from the equation. I'd like to know where I stand, so I can come to terms with whatever that is. But in her usual contrary fashion, Gloria isn't playing ball, and there's nothing I can do about that.'

The meal that evening was a huge success. We had a full house, and the atmosphere was relaxed and jolly. The Stewarts, noticeably more animated this evening without the overbearing input of the Hendersons, told us about their newfound love affair with the Loire, an area of France they'd never tried before. The Kennedys arrived just in time for the meal and happily gave in to the food and chatter.

Mum defrosted again with the aid of several glasses of wine and complimented the food at every opportunity. No one knew better than my own mother that I had never been a natural cook, so she was somewhat taken aback that I'd contributed in any way whatsoever to the gastronomic delights on the table.

My father's tired lines were smoothing out, and I was glad. What with his demanding job and my demanding mother and worry over his abandoned daughter, the stress had been clear to see when he arrived, but now he leaned back in his chair, smiling.

It was dark outside. Rupert had turned off the harsher spot-lights around the kitchen units, cleverly hiding any detritus from the meal and leaving us in the mellow glow of the overhead light and wall lamps in the dining area.

He was on top form, with plenty of tales to tell and an easy way of telling them. A natural raconteur, his stock supply of anecdotes was brought out, but there were others I hadn't heard before and I laughed helplessly along with everyone else.

'If you lovely people are wondering why I don't supply candle-light to add to the ambience, then I shall tell you,' he announced over coffee. 'I used to do all that, when we first started up the business. Thought it added a touch of class. And so it did – until one of the guests had their fiftieth birthday here. The woman's husband had paid serious money to a *pâtisserie* in town for an absolutely fabulous cake, which he placed on the table in front of his wife. He'd also spent serious money on the gift, by the looks of it, all decked out in fancy tissue paper and ribbons. He handed it over with the flourish it deserved, she opened it with the flourish it deserved, the wrapping paper dangled in the flame of one of the candles...'

There was a collective gasp around the table.

'In her panic, she started wafting it about, which of course only made the flames spread up towards her hand. The smoke alarm got itself in a tizzy, deafening us all, and I was hopping about, desperately trying to grab it from her before she dropped it – I had visions of the whole table going up in flames!'

'Did you get it off her?' Mum asked, eyes wide.

'Couldn't get near the bloody woman – she was hopping about too, and of course the more she moved, the more the flames grew.'

'So what on earth did you do?'

Rupert gave an exaggerated sigh. 'Chucked the water jug over it. There was nothing else I *could* do. It put out the flames alright, but it also drenched the birthday girl and ruined the cake – one minute a superbly crafted tower of white swirls and delicate iced flowers, the next a waterfall of cream and soggy sponge. The sleeves of her dress were singed, as was the box – although thankfully not the gift within. It rather spoiled the evening, and caused a god-almighty row when they left the next day. The chap was a solicitor and fancied the notion of suing me for the cost of the cake, the cost of his wife's dress – a designer label, naturally – and possibly mental distress.'

'And *did* he?' Meg Kennedy asked, agog.

'Thankfully, no. We came to an arrangement over the bill. Well, less an arrangement and more a full refund for their stay.'

'That's disgraceful!' Frank Stewart chimed in.

Rupert winked. 'On my part or his?'

Frank grinned. 'His, of course.'

Rupert shook his head. 'I was only grateful the kitchen hadn't burned down. Didn't fancy a legal wrangle. But hence no more candles. If you lot want ambience, you'll have to create it yourselves with your delightful company and scintillating conversation.'

'Dare I ask what the gift was, after all that?' Karen Stewart asked.

Rupert shook his head in despair. 'A dress from a Parisian boutique, clearly at least two sizes too small and two decades too young for its recipient. I could hear them arguing all the way up the stairs! Funnily enough, they haven't been back since. Can't think why…'

Mum and Karen were helpless with laughter. I caught Dad watching me and quirked a quizzical eyebrow at him, but he just shook his head and joined in.

It was midnight when we broke it up. As I started to clear the table, my mother began to frown again, but my father tactfully guided her away by the elbow. On their way upstairs, I heard him stop her before she could complain.

'Leave it, Flo. The girl's never been happier.'

I piled the debris by the sink with a light heart. My father, in his usual quiet way, had hit the nail on the head. Though my circumstances should most definitely suggest otherwise, and though this may be but a brief interlude, I *had* never been happier.

CHAPTER THIRTEEN

The next morning, I decided to take my parents sightseeing. Since Saturday would be the usual flurry and they were leaving on Sunday afternoon, I needed to show my mother that I could enjoy a day out like any other holidaymaker.

'I'll drive, Dad. You have a rest and enjoy the scenery.' This offer took my father by surprise as we headed across the courtyard towards the cars.

'Oh no, Emmy, don't worry. We have the rental car.'

'Mine and Nathan's is bigger. You can't swing a cat in that sardine tin you turned up in.'

Dad looked aghast. 'But yours is right-hand drive, Emmy. Wouldn't we be better in this one?'

I gave him a look. 'Don't you trust me to drive?'

'Of course I do, sweetheart.' His expression belied his words. 'But you don't like driving abroad. You always make Nathan do it.'

I patted his arm, took their stuff (my mother always packed for all eventualities, even on a day trip) and piled it into the boot of the car.

'Yes, well, Nathan hasn't been available for chauffeur duties, so I've had to get on and do it myself. You can navigate. You know I can't read a map for toffee.'

Mum and Dad exchanged a glance and climbed delicately into the car as though it might fall apart. With a spray of gravel, which was unnecessary but fun, we headed off.

Rupert had scribbled a manageable itinerary, which would take us to several little towns with *châteaux*. When it became apparent to my parents that their daughter was no longer reluctant behind the wheel and was unlikely to crash into a ditch or drive into a barn, they began to relax, my mother oohing and aahing at the fields and villages from the back seat, my father staring rapt out of his window without a murmur.

At our first stop in Montreuil-Bellay, we found a café where we could sit outside and overlook the *château*.

After coffee, we circled the *château* to stroll alongside the river for a while. I suspected Dad had given Mum the hard word, because both of them were careful to pick neutral topics. Nathan wasn't mentioned once.

With our limbs stretched, I drove on – still competent and thereby still startling my parents – to Chinon, where we found the restaurant Rupert had recommended on a cobbled street leading up from the river. I couldn't remember the last time we'd sat in the sunshine having lunch together. Life back home was always so busy with work that at weekends I just wanted to flop. And whenever I dragged Nathan with me to spend time with my parents, there was the unspoken payback that I would have to spend time with *his* parents – a fate worse than death. Nathan's father always looked like he would rather be somewhere else (heaven knows, he wasn't the only one) and his mother... Well, how do you describe the indescribable?

I might not have wanted Mum and Dad to come, but now they were here, I was glad.

'So, Emmy, what'll happen when you go back to work?' Dad asked gently.

'There'll be a pile of stuff dumped on my desk and Carl will sulk because I took the extra week, I suppose.'

'Yes, but what about Nathan, Emmy? Will he be there? Will people know what's happened?' Mum asked bluntly. If Dad had given her the hard word, the effects had worn off predictably quickly.

'I don't know. If he's back, he's back, and I'll have to take it from there. If not, well, it all depends on what he's told them. I'll have to play it by ear. I haven't got much choice, have I?'

My mother huffed. 'It's a disgrace. Not just leaving you like that, but leaving you in the dark. He's making it hard for you on purpose.'

'I don't think he is doing it on purpose, Mum. To be honest, I don't think he knows what he wants.' I picked at my bread, shredding it into crumbs and sweeping them from the table. 'But it's a going to be a pretty crappy few months sorting the whole mess out.'

Dad spoke quietly. 'This mess was of Nathan's making too, Emmy. Stand up for yourself.' He took out his wallet and beckoned the waiter. 'And while you're fighting your way through those crappy months ahead, keep your eyes on the prize. Freedom. Peace of mind. Being true to your heart. Those things might be clichés nowadays, but they're worth the fight, love.'

We spent the afternoon pottering, all awkwardness behind us. My parents could relax. They had completed their mission. From the moment they'd arrived, they had somehow managed to sympathise, comfort, see for themselves that I wasn't suicidal – indeed, that I was content for now – and help me clarify my thoughts and direction. Not an unremarkable feat in twenty-four hours.

We arrived back culturally replete and still in one piece, despite the fact that I'd driven the whole way. Looking forward to a lie-down before we ventured out to eat, I didn't take kindly to Rupert's accusatory tone the minute we got in.

'Emmy. You forgot to take your mobile again.'

'Sorry.' I tried to sound sincere. 'Why, did you need me? Anything wrong?'

He let out an exasperated sigh. 'Nothing urgent, but I've had to make a decision on your behalf, so I hope it wasn't the wrong one.'

'Oh?'

'Richard and Brenda rang to ask if we'd like to join them for a meal. I told them your parents are here and they suggested we all go. The more, the merrier and all that.'

'Richard and Brenda?' Tired from the long day, my brain wasn't in full gear.

'We met them at the market, remember? Ryan's parents.'

His eyes were full of mischievous glee as my face blanched and then followed up with a blush for good measure. I said a silent prayer that he'd had the good sense to refuse. Then again, why should he? It wasn't unreasonable to assume my parents might like to meet a pleasant middle-aged couple for a convivial meal. And in theory, of course, Rupert couldn't know I'd have any reason to feel uncomfortable in the presence of said couple. In practice, the glimmer in his eyes suggested he had his suspicions and would enjoy any discomfort that might be served up alongside the food at dinner.

Rupert turned to Mum and Dad. 'Nice couple. They run a business back in the UK but they have a holiday home and spend a good few weeks a year out here. Their son does my garden for me in the summer. But if you'd rather have Emmy to yourself, I'm sure they'd understand.'

'No, that would be lovely,' Mum said, sealing my fate. 'We were going to ask you to eat out with us anyway, Rupert. Two more won't make any difference.'

'That's settled, then. Good job, because I'd already accepted.'

By the time we piled into the restaurant – which was elegant, but with a touch of the countryside in its sage green tablecloths and napkins, and wicker and dried flower arrangements on the walls – I was calm and collected again. A long shower had helped me regain my equilibrium, and I'd given myself a stiff talking-to while I got ready.

How hard could it be? Ryan's parents seemed nice and presumably had no idea I'd been shagging their son. Rupert was, admittedly, a loose cannon, but he was hardly likely to voice his sordid little suspicions. I was making a mountain out of a molehill.

Brenda and Richard rose from a large round table by the window to greet us. As I frowned at the extra place set and a jacket flung over the back of the upholstered chair, out of the corner of my eye I saw the door to the gents' open, and Ryan strolled over to the table.

Oh, no.

As further introductions ensued, I did my best not to spontaneously combust with panic whilst at the same time shooting Rupert a vicious look.

'Didn't know you were coming, Ryan,' he said jovially, shooting me an innocent look back.

Ryan didn't even have the decency to look uncomfortable. 'Neither did I. Mum and Dad decided it was time I was seen out in public in something other than muddy jeans.'

Everyone shuffled around choosing seats until, inevitably, I found myself next to Ryan. This didn't appear to have anything to do with Rupert's mischievous leanings, for once, but with my parents. The old folks must have thought I needed someone nearer my own age to talk to.

Wine was ordered, tasted and poured. In desperate need of an anaesthetic, I snatched up my glass and gulped a large mouthful.

Ryan smirked, and I kicked him forcefully under the table. He mouthed a dramatic "ouch" and continued to smirk.

Once we'd studied the menu and ordered, the table settled into polite chatter. Brenda and Richard were friendly and unpretentious – like their son, who seemed to have inherited all their good qualities.

Neither Gloria nor her departure were mentioned, but I couldn't help wondering how the evening would have gone if she and Nathan had still been here. Brenda and Richard were clearly fond of Rupert, but I didn't think Gloria would have been their type. Too dolled-up, too waspish. Nathan would have complained that he didn't want to spend the evening with a bunch of strangers, and by this time he would have had his fill of Rupert's bumptiousness. Then again, I would have been forty times more relaxed because I wouldn't have slept with the young man sitting next to me who was currently running his hand up my thigh under the table.

I slapped it back. 'Stop that!' I hissed, smiling madly in case anyone noticed.

Ryan turned to me, propping his head up with his arm to block anyone from reading his lips.

'What's the matter with you tonight?' he asked. 'At the risk of sounding like my mother, you're acting like you've got ants in your pants.'

I glowered as subtly as I could. 'Has it occurred to you that I might be uncomfortable with your mum and dad because of...'

He made a mock production of getting the point. 'Ah! Not ants in your pants. Me in your pants.'

'*What?*' I couldn't believe he'd said that in the present company, even if it was under his breath. The others were in full swing discussing the merits and complications of buying property abroad and paying no attention to us, but even so.

'That's the problem?' Ryan asked, his voice still low and conspiratorial.

'Well, don't you think this is all a little awkward?'

'Not really. Nobody knows. I'm not sure it would matter if they did. Chill out a bit.'

My eyes flashed fire in place of raising my voice. 'I appreciate this may not be a big deal for you, Ryan. For all I know, you sleep with older abandoned women all the time.'

'Not at all. You're my first. Cross my heart.' He made a slashing motion across his chest, and I let out an exasperated sigh. It was hard to stay mad at him for more than two minutes.

'Yes, and about that. Why me? Why aren't you out with some flat-stomached girl your own age?'

Ryan laughed. 'I'm not ageist, Emmy. I go out with women I find attractive, women I can talk to and feel comfortable with. You fit into that category. Stop selling yourself short.'

'I'm not.'

Ryan squeezed his hand on mine under the table. 'You've had a knock to your self-confidence, that's all.'

'I know. But this is all a bit weird, and it's giving me the jitters. Rupert, I can cope with. My parents and your parents are another matter.'

As if they could tune in, both couples directed their attention to us. Dragged back into the group chatter, I tried hard to settle.

Rupert was the star turn as usual. Brenda and Richard were like new-found soul mates to my mum and dad, and Ryan was relaxed and charming with all of them. I envied him his easy-going personality and wondered whether he'd always been that way or whether it was down to the lifestyle he'd chosen – the lack of authority and structure, the outdoors, the summers in France?

In juxtaposition, my own lifestyle seemed positively dreary. I thought about drizzly days and lacklustre evenings in front of the telly with Nathan, with no energy or inclination to liven things up... But by the time coffee landed, my common sense had kicked back in. Ryan's lifestyle wouldn't suit me. For a start, I couldn't keep a plant alive for love nor money. I viewed the outdoors as suitable for relaxing in, not for sweaty hard labour. And having been brought up by an accountant and then living with one, I couldn't imagine not having the comforting predictability of a regular pay slip. Each to his own.

As the wine and coffee filtered through to my bladder, I excused myself and went to the ladies'. Catching my reflection in the mirror on the way back out, I pulled up short. The pink sunburn I'd been lamenting had given way to a golden glow, my hair was now pristinely French, and all the fresh fruit and salad (and possibly worry) must have offset the croissants and sauces, because unless my eye deceived me, I looked almost svelte. Bemused by the idea that Nathan deserting me in foreign lands should have had such a beneficial effect, I was still preening as I pulled open the door and ran headlong into Ryan in the small space that separated the toilets from the dining room.

'Have you been lurking?' I accused him when I got my breath back.

'Maybe.' His hands came up to my face and he planted his lips on mine. 'You look more delicious than the food. I wanted a taste.'

I blushed at the compliment and tried to push him away. 'We have to get back to the table. They might get suspicious.'

'Of what?'

'That we both came in here at the same time.'

Ryan laughed. 'Emmy, we've been sitting at the table for three hours. Nobody's going to think anything of the fact that we needed the loo at the same time.'

I tried not to respond to his kisses, but it wasn't easy. With his body pressing me against the wall, my limbs began to turn to warm jelly.

'What if someone comes in?' I hissed when I came up for air.

Ryan spun me round so he was against the wall. 'I'll watch the door.'

There was a small pane of glass for him to see any approaching intruders, but my stomach fluttered from the combination of nerves, rich food, caffeine, alcohol and, surprisingly, excitement at the possibility of being discovered. I doubted it was good for the digestion.

As Ryan worked his magic, I opened my eyes and was gratified to see that he dutifully had one eye on the door. I closed mine again to savour the moment, but as his hands strayed downwards, I reluctantly pulled away.

Ryan may have been relaxed about all this, but I certainly wasn't. And if I was uncomfortable about the idea of people knowing, then perhaps I should be uncomfortable with the thing itself. I hadn't even told Sophie, despite telling her everything else under the sun.

I didn't think Ryan saw this as anything other than a quick fling – at least, I hoped he didn't – but I didn't know for sure, and I would hate for one or both of us to be hurt through mis-understanding the situation. The problem was, we hadn't really discussed it. Maybe it was time we did.

'We need to talk,' I blurted.

He cocked his head to one side in enquiry. 'Okay. What is it?'

'Ryan, this... thing between us has been great – wonderful, actually – but I'm in a pretty crap place at the moment. I'm not looking for a long-term relationship, and I assume you aren't either. That first time we... got together, you said, "Let's have some fun," and I took you at your word.' God, I hated having conversations like this. I sighed. 'Maybe we should have talked about this sooner, but I didn't want to spoil things.'

Ryan laid a hand on my arm. His face was open and honest. 'Emmy, that's okay. I'm not expecting anything of you and I never did. But I *am* worried you might think I took advantage of you. If I did, I didn't mean to.' He hesitated. 'I know you go home next week, but you'll be back at some point to see Rupert and I *would* like to stay friends. I'd hate for things to get awkward between us.'

I managed a wobbly smile. 'Me too.'

His gaze was direct. 'So where do you want to go from here? We can carry on the way we have been until you go, if you want. I'd be happy with that.' A shadow crossed my face, and he nodded. 'But I can see you're not.'

I shook my head, feeling slightly sick. 'I can't explain why. I don't think this evening has helped. I... I'm just not comfortable with it any more.'

'The last thing I want is to make you feel uncomfortable.' He put on a mock pout. 'Shame, though. Now I might have to do some actual gardening when I go round to Rupert's!'

I grinned. 'So we're good?'

'We're good.' He reached for the door, then turned back and winked. 'I can't tempt you to a farewell quickie in a cubicle? Fine. We'll go back to the table.'

I started to follow him out, but he wagged an admonishing finger at me. 'Not together or they might get suspicious,' he said in a girlish imitation of me. And then, in his own voice, 'Besides, it wouldn't make sense. Everyone knows women spend twice as long in here as men.'

I scurried back into the ladies' to brush my hair and reapply lipstick. My head and my heart both declared their approval at my decision to call it quits with Ryan... but certain other elements of my anatomy couldn't believe I was turning down a few more days' hot sex with Adonis.

'What a lovely couple,' Dad commented as he drove us home, the lanes quiet and the fields invisible in the dark beyond the roadside. 'And Ryan seemed like a nice young man. Polite. Interesting. It's good to see someone his age so enthused about the outdoors. Handsome, too. Pity he's not nearer your own age, Emmy.'

I could sense Rupert tensing in the back seat next to me and guessed he was fighting a merry outburst. I tensed along with him, but there was no humour on my part, merely panic.

'Hmm,' I said noncommittally.

'Oh, don't be silly, Dennis,' Mum came unwittingly to my rescue. 'He's a nice enough lad, but even if there wasn't such an age gap, he's hardly Emmy's type.'

Rupert's shoulders were shaking now, and I punched him just in time to convince him to turn a threatening guffaw into a cough. God, he could be so bloody childish sometimes. It was difficult to believe he was nearly an OAP.

Dad went on, oblivious. 'If what you mean by that, Flo, is that he's not like Nathan, then all credit to him is all I can say. She's tried the steady, boring type and look how that turned out.'

The following day involved quite a juggling act. There were no rooms to sort out – we were full to the brim already – but I still had the supermarket run, three *gîtes* to help clean and two to make ready for new arrivals, plus the evening meal to help cook, and all this while plastering a smile on my face and taking several noticeable breaks to pacify my mother.

My schedule was put back ten minutes when I bumped into Jonathan at the supermarket.

'Emmy! I heard you were staying another week. So glad!'

I accepted his over-familiar hug with stoicism. 'Thanks.'

'Bob! Come and meet the lovely Emmy!' he yelled across the dairy aisle. 'Had to ask yet another friend to help me today,' he muttered crossly. 'Leg playing up. Didn't dare drive, but the cupboard was bare.'

Bob ambled over, an ageing hippie with long, straggling grey hair, a beard to match and jeans that had seen at least a couple of decades' wear. We shook hands.

'So you're on Jonathan duty today?' I asked.

He grinned. 'I usually get away with it when it's a driving task, seeing as I ride a motorbike.'

They both laughed when my eyes widened at the prospect of Jonathan riding pillion, clinging on for dear life.

Bob put me out of my misery. 'Don't worry, I drove Jonathan's car today.'

'So how do you two know each other?'

'We frequent the same bar. Everyone gets dragged into Jonathan's circle sooner or later. He's like an inexorable force that sucks you in.'

'Talking of which, will I see you again before you go home?' Jonathan wanted to know.

'I wouldn't be at all surprised.' I was getting used to this everyone-bumping-into-everyone thing.

'Then we'd better let you get on. I know Saturday's a busy day for you.'

Back at *La Cour des Roses*, Madame Dupont and I set to work, following the same routine as last week.

'Where do you live back home?' she asked me as we worked. 'In a village or a city?'

'In an apartment, near a city,' I told her.

She wrinkled her nose in disapproval. 'Is it busy and noisy?'

I laughed. 'Yes, but I like that.' I dredged through my mental French dictionary for the right words. 'I like being in the... centre of things.' I glanced through the window. 'But I like it here, too. Birds singing in the garden – I don't hear them in the city. And Pierre-la-Fontaine is perfect. Not too big. Not too small.'

She nodded. 'Bigger is not always better.'

I couldn't argue with her there.

When Dad realised Mum was driving me mad with her eagle eye and her interrogations between each task I performed as to why I needed to do this or help with that, he winked conspiratorially and whisked her off for an afternoon drive, gallantly offering to drive Madame Dupont home on the way – giving me extra kudos with the old lady for possessing such a considerate parent.

The phone rang as Rupert and I started on the guest meal, and since he was up to his elbows in flour, I went to answer it.

'Emmy? It's Sophie. I was so glad when I got your text. Would you like to go out for a drink or a meal this weekend?'

'I'd love to, but my parents found out what happened and they arrived on Thursday for a long weekend, so...'

Sophie chuckled. 'So you must spend time with them and show them you are perfectly fine?'

'Exactly. I'm sorry. It would be lovely to see you again.'

'No problem. I understand what parents are like. Especially when you present them with such a drama! Why don't you phone me after the weekend?'

'I will. Thanks for phoning, Sophie.'

'You're welcome! Good luck with your parents!'

'Sophie again?' Rupert asked. 'Best friends already?'

I grinned. 'Not quite. But I think we could have been, if we lived nearer. She's kind and vivacious and...' I made a face. 'And disgustingly pretty, by the way.'

Rupert waggled his eyebrows. 'In that case, maybe I could join you and this extremely attractive hairdresser for lunch sometime next week?'

I threw a chunk of courgette at him. 'Forget it. She's way too young for you. In fact, I think she's probably a bit younger than me.'

Rupert winced. 'Been there, done that. Won't be doing it again.'

I glanced at him. 'You'll meet someone eventually.'

He leaned against the counter, his fingers covered in shortbread mixture. 'You know, Emmy, I'm not convinced I want to bother with all that again.'

'You're just saying that because Gloria treated you so badly. But you'll get over her. It may take time, but then you might feel like dating again and...'

Rupert shook his head. 'I'm beginning to think I was a bachelor till I was fifty for a reason. Maybe I was meant to be on my own.' He wafted his hand at me, dropping spots of flour mix at my feet. 'And I'm not saying that to be melodramatic. I can be selfish and I want my own way a lot. That's not an ideal quality in a relationship.'

'Oh, and Gloria was the queen of selflessness, was she?' I pointed my knife accusingly at him.

'Certainly not. But maybe that's the point. Maybe neither of us were really suited to wedded bliss. Anyway, I think I'll be more than happy on my own for a while. As long as I have my friends to bitch and complain to – and about.' He winked.

I forced a smile and attacked a large red pepper, imagining it was Gloria. Maybe Rupert was right – maybe he would be okay on his own. But I hated to think he might rule out the chance of future happiness with someone else just because of the way Gloria had behaved, stomping on his heart like that.

CHAPTER FOURTEEN

By the time we were tucking into dinner, I was tired and didn't have much of an appetite. That didn't mean I could pick at my food, however. With my mother watching me like a hawk, I had no choice but to steadfastly work my way through the hake in sauce and oven-roasted vegetables, occasionally resorting to mushing it around my plate so it looked like I'd eaten more than I had – an old childhood trick which I was sure wouldn't fool her at all. Luckily for me, she was distracted by the delicious food, lively conversation and the wine top-ups my dad surreptitiously foisted on her, bless him.

It seemed the Stewarts were more in love with the Loire than ever.

'We're thinking of looking for a holiday home in the area,' Karen Stewart announced over heavenly home-made ice-cream and melt-in-your-mouth shortbread.

'Really? That's fantastic news! I can recommend an excellent estate agent,' Rupert told them. 'Her name's Ellie Fielding. She's the English half of the agency, Philippe's the French half. Ellie can be a bit scary at first, but she knows her stuff. If you like, I'll give you her phone number. Maybe you could find time to meet her before you leave on Tuesday.'

'That's kind of you,' Karen said, beaming, as Rupert wrote down the number. 'Now we've had the idea, I can't wait to get started. It might be sensible to have a quick chat with someone before we go home. It'd be so good to have a bolt-hole here in France.'

She squeezed her husband's hand on the table, and I fought my resentment. It wasn't the Stewarts' fault they were happily married – or that they were well-off enough to buy a second home. Even if Nathan and I were still together, the idea of him agreeing to a holiday home abroad was laughable. For a start, we didn't have that kind of money. Then there was the small matter of a holiday home not being much use if your job meant you never took any holidays.

Physically and mentally exhausted, I escaped to my room as soon as I could clear away without actually snatching plates from under everyone's noses.

Sunday was thankfully a more laid-back affair. After breakfast, while Mum got settled outside, Dad helped me hang out some of the laundry from yesterday's mountain of washing at the bottom of the garden, where we took advantage of the cover of billowing sheets and the distance from my mother to converse in conspiratorial whispers.

'Is Mum okay with all this?' I asked him anxiously. Her many disapproving looks yesterday had begun to get me down.

Dad patted my arm. 'She's shocked and cross with Nathan, as we all are, but she'll get over it. And so will you.'

'I appreciate the confidence, Dad, but that wasn't what I meant.'

'I know,' he mumbled through a mouthful of pegs. 'Rupert could charm the birds out of the trees, but your mother isn't that easily taken in. To tell the truth, she thinks he's taken advantage of you.'

'How about you?' I asked.

'Me?' Dad considered a moment. 'I think helping is doing you good, taking your mind off things while it has a chance to catch up with itself. I suspect Rupert is taking advantage, but I can't blame him after all he's been through. He'd be in a terrible mess if you weren't doing all this.' He gestured at the snowy white sheets for emphasis. 'In any event, as long as you're both benefitting, it doesn't matter, does it?'

I shot him a grateful smile. He could always size up a situation in a trice and make the best of it. A rush of emotion came over me for the one man who had always been there for me, no matter what. Giving in to it, I threw my arms around his neck and hugged him tight as I breathed in his familiar aftershave.

'I love you, Dad,' I murmured.

Taking this in his capable stride, he hugged me tightly back, then pulled away. He took my chin in his hands. 'I love you, too.' He smoothed a tear from my cheek with his thumb as he blinked away his own. 'Come on. Your mother will be wondering where we've got to.'

Rupert brought us a tray of coffee and disappeared back indoors, presumably because his trouble radar had picked up on my mother's disapproval of his enslaving her daughter and he didn't fancy being in the line of fire.

She looked upset.

'What's up, Mum?'

'I don't know, Emmy. What with your brother a permanent gigolo, and you and Nathan splitting up, it seems this family's not having much success in the relationship department.'

Her eyes glistened, and in that moment my strident, ever-practical mother looked decidedly vulnerable. It tore at my heartstrings that Nick and I could still cause her so much worry.

'Well, that's where you're wrong.' I squeezed her hand. 'Nick hasn't tried anything long-term yet, so how he can be a failure at it? Besides, you and Dad have been married for decades without killing each other. I'd call that a success, wouldn't you?'

Mum cocked her head to one side as she thought about it. 'You're right,' she said. 'Yes, you're right.'

● ● ●

As my parents' little car disappeared down the lane late that afternoon, I thought about what I'd said to my mother. Their visit had served to remind me how much they loved each other. They weren't just fond of each other, or used to each other, or putting up with each other, or taking each other for granted. After thirty-five years, they were still *in love*.

What if I never found what Mum and Dad had? Could I settle for anything less, having been a witness to their relationship, knowing it might be out there for me somewhere if I waited long enough for the one-in-goodness-knows-how-many who might be the person I could share it with?

I sat and watched the sun sink slowly behind the field across the road until the midges and mozzies and beasties came out to feast on my bare arms and then, with a self-pitying sigh, I hoisted myself upright and returned to the house.

Feeling out of sorts and unable to settle, I wheedled Rupert's laptop from him, took it to the kitchen and set to work on that atrocious booking system of his.

Creating a spreadsheet was simple enough, but transferring the manual diary onto it was another matter. I'd never seen such a mess. When Rupert came in to see how I was getting on, the table was covered with little piles of date-sorted booking enquiries and letters of confirmation and goodness knew what else.

'How's it going?' he asked, halting cautiously at the doorway as he took in the paper mayhem.

I glared up at him. 'Fine.'

'Would it help if I helped?'

Glancing at the diary with its spider scribbles and eraser smudges, I shoved it at him. 'Absolutely.'

It was after ten when we sat back with a celebratory hot chocolate to admire our pretty-coloured spreadsheet and neat file of correspondence.

'Okay, you were right,' Rupert said grudgingly. He picked up the diary and tossed it in the general direction of the waste bin. 'I admit it. I couldn't have followed that lot.'

'You've always managed so far. Never a hitch, you said.'

'Yes, but what I didn't tell you is that I always asked Gloria because I couldn't understand anything she'd written. Since she left, I've only looked ahead a few days at a time. If I'd tried to plan any further, I wouldn't have stood a cat in hell's chance. You've stopped me from coming quite a cropper.'

'I'm glad.'

'Now for the other bit.'

I stifled a yawn. 'What other bit?'

'Website. Gloria.'

'Ah.' I still felt guilty about suggesting that, which was why I hadn't pushed it. 'Are you sure?'

'Yes.'

It was late and we were tired, so I kept it simple. The photo of the two of them was removed. Rupert found one of him on his own – taken at least five years ago, but it would do – and we removed any mention of Gloria from the text. That was all that was needed for now.

'Thanks, Emmy,' Rupert said quietly as we shut the laptop down for the night.

'No problem.' I studied him. 'Are you okay?'

He gave a wan smile. 'I'm fine. Thought I was, anyway. It's just... Doing that...' He wafted a hand at the screen. 'It seems so final, somehow.'

'I can change it back, if you like.'

'No. I'm a realist, Emmy. No point in showing something other than the way it is.'

Figuring that was enough for one night, I stood and popped a kiss on his cheek. 'Night, Rupert.'

'Night, love.'

And now there was another expression I understood better. I couldn't honestly say I was heartbroken when Nathan left, but as I climbed the stairs to my room now, my heart was breaking for Rupert. His defeated expression, the tired lines, the shadows under his eyes would haunt me for quite some time. That moment when I'd deleted the photo of him and Gloria – happy, smiling at the camera, arms around each other's shoulders – had been nothing other than awful.

Still, as I climbed exhausted into bed, I'd have been lying if I hadn't admitted I rather liked the idea of Gloria logging on to her own website, only to find out that she was missing in action.

My lie-in the next morning was rudely interrupted by Rupert bawling my name up the stairs, presumably in lieu of the fact that he hadn't yet ascertained how much pain and effort might be involved in climbing them.

I staggered out onto the landing looking like a sleep-deprived witch. 'What? *What?*'

'Were you still asleep?'

'No, of course not. I have every intention of spending the rest of the day looking like this,' I declared, pointing at my tangled hair and slouchy T-shirt for emphasis.

'Sorry. I thought you'd be up by now.'

I glanced at my wrist. Goodness knows what for, since I wasn't wearing a watch. 'Why? What do you want?'

'I need you to drive me into Pierre-la-Fontaine. Market day. Errands to run. Accountant.'

'Accountant? *Again?*'

'Last week was just a social bumping-into-each-other, Emmy. This is business. Alain's right – there are things I need to discuss with him now that Gloria's gone. I've sweetened your chauffeur duties by arranging to meet him at the café, so you can be placated by continental atmosphere and caffeine.'

I shook my head. 'Rupert, you don't need me listening in on your personal financial discussions. Couldn't he have popped round here sometime?'

'He didn't have time between appointments.'

'Well, can't I just see you to his office and then disappear?'

He tapped his leg. 'First floor. Too many stairs.'

'I'll look round the market while you two talk at the café, then.'

Rupert looked stricken. 'I'd really like you to be there, Emmy. My memory... I think this medication's affecting my brain a bit. It'd be helpful to have an extra ear.' Before I could respond, he added, 'Get a shift on. We need to leave at nine if we're going to get the other stuff done first. You need to do something with your hair, though.'

'That wasn't so bad, was it?' Rupert demanded on the drive. Fields gave way to small groups of houses, gradually increasing until we were on the outskirts of town.

'What wasn't?'

'Your parents this weekend. Not so bad, after all.'

'I suppose not.'

Rupert gave me a sympathetic glance. 'At least you've got them out of the way. Now you can relax a bit.'

'Ha! Of course I can relax. There's only my job and my flat and my finances to worry about.'

'That's the spirit!' Undaunted by my expression – which should have conveyed that I was struggling to cope with his chipper mood this morning – he carried on. 'Anyway, you can put all that behind you for now, and we'll have a nice morning out.'

I shook my head. The man had the strangest outlook some-times. Why he thought lugging ton-weights of vegetables around and listening to an incomprehensible accounting conversation would be a bundle of laughs, I had no idea.

Even so, I enjoyed the market – although this time, I stayed with Rupert to help carry the bags. To make it more fun – for him, anyway – he made me ask for everything in French while he tutored me. I wasn't at all happy at first, but I got into it and by the time we'd finished, I was feeling rather proud of myself.

We were almost done when I spotted a stall from the corner of my eye. 'That's it!'

Rupert jumped. 'What's what?'

'Down there.' Without waiting, I shuffled along the cobbles with my bags, leaving Rupert to follow more slowly with his stick.

The gift stall had glass bottles of every size and shape filled with pretty bath crystals, a cork in the top and a ribbon around the neck.

'*That's* your solution,' I whispered to him as he caught up with me.

'My solution to what? Do I smell or something?' Rupert looked disconcerted.

I gave him a look. 'Not that I've noticed. I'm talking about that stupid toiletry system of yours. This would be *so* much better. Really classy and pretty.'

Rupert glanced at a price tag and blanched. 'Pretty expensive, you mean. They're nice for a gift, Emmy, but not in every room.'

'Obviously.' I kept my voice low. 'But we can copy the idea. Get some glass bottles like these, buy some good quality bubble bath and body lotion – decent stuff but in economy sizes – and refill the bottles when needed. *Et voilà!*'

'Hmm.' Rupert studied the stall. 'It would look much nicer. And less nickable than sachets.' He nodded. 'Can you sort it?'

'Of course!' I almost turned to go, then stopped. The girl behind the stall had looked so hopeful as we stood there muttering to each other. Choosing a tall, elegant bottle of pale green bath crystals, I paid and waited while she wrapped the gift in pretty paper.

'Who are they for?' Rupert asked.

'Sophie.'

'The hairdresser? What for?'

'For being a friend when I needed one.'

Alain arrived at the café just as we were ordering. I'd forgotten how tall he was – he towered over us in greeting, then folded himself into a chair.

'Rupert tells me you're staying another week, Emmy,' he said by way of an opening. 'That's good of you.'

I shrugged. 'I'm only pleased I could help.'

'Emmy is being ridiculously modest as usual,' Rupert chipped in. 'She's been a complete star. You name it, she's mucked in and done it – cleaning, cooking, organising, making suggestions, changing things...'

'Oh?' Alain smiled. 'What sort of things?'

Rupert rolled his eyes. 'Well, she's got rid of Gloria's diary for a start. Complete bloody shambles, that was. It's all on a spreadsheet now. Emmy's the spreadsheet queen. *And* she got rid of Gloria from the website.'

I glanced at Alain in a panic. Did he think I was being bitchy? Apparently not – he suppressed a smile.

'Fresh flowers in the guest rooms,' Rupert went on. 'Individually wrapped guest toiletries soon to be banished for aesthetic and environmental reasons; solution decided upon this very morning. *And* she's going to work on my website when she gets back home.'

Alain raised an eyebrow and rested that soft brown gaze of his on mine. 'Impressive. Are you in hotel management back in the UK?'

I laughed. 'Not at all. Marketing.'

'Well, it's good to know your skills are benefitting Rupert to such an extent while you're here.' His smile was warm and approving.

Our coffees arrived. Alain curled long fingers around his cup and brought it to his lips. He had a full mouth, I realised – none of that tight-lipped seriousness you might imagine in an accountant – and his face was tanned. Shouldn't an accountant be pale from being stuck behind a desk all day, I wondered? Not that I was staring at him or anything.

As he got down to business, I resigned myself to my fate. Since I was here to help Rupert with his listening and retaining skills, I supposed I'd better pay attention.

Alain was concerned about Rupert's financial situation now that Gloria had upped sticks, and it sounded as though he'd spent considerable time covering all bases. Rupert, ever the entrepreneur, had no trouble following all the possible scenarios and permutations. As for me, although I was a) pretending not to pay too close attention to Rupert's personal business and b) mathematically lost, I followed the gist enough to understand that although *La Cour des Roses* was doing well, things might get tight if Gloria decided to take him to the cleaner's – something not one of us around the table doubted would happen.

'I know you're doing well, Rupert,' Alain concluded, 'but you need to ensure you're fully booked mid-season as well as at peak season. Maybe find a way to attract people in low season.'

Rupert looked taken aback. 'I like being quiet in low season,' he muttered. 'Gives me chance to catch up – spring clean, decorate, sort stuff out.'

I shot Alain a sharp glance. After all Rupert had been through, he was being too pushy.

But he carried on regardless. 'I'm not saying you should be busting at the seams all year round. I'm saying you should extend the season, that's all.'

'*La Cour des Roses* pays its way,' Rupert said sulkily.

'It *did*,' Alain pointed out, 'when you only needed to cover costs and boost your income. But if you have to pay Gloria off, you'll need to maximise your profits.'

Alain looked across at me for support, his gaze holding mine as though I was the only other person in the café. Because he was interested in what I had to say? Or because of something else? I ignored my accelerating pulse and retuned his look with a glare. What did he think he was playing at? Rupert wasn't well. His wife had just left him. He didn't need to hear this right now.

'Any thoughts, Emmy?' Alain asked.

Oh, I had plenty of thoughts all right, but they weren't remotely polite. I closed my eyes for a moment, corralling them into something constructive, then turned to Rupert.

'Well, obviously I haven't seen your books – and I don't want to,' I hastened to add. 'But...' I thought about the bath salts by my chair. 'Gloria didn't necessarily do things badly, but I suspect she didn't put much thought into them either. Maybe you could start by looking at whatever she dealt with. Those motel toiletries are a prime example. I know she ordered them in bulk, but they can't be economical. People use them once and chuck what's left, then put the rest in their suitcases. Even if they only stay a couple of nights, you've lost everything you put in that bathroom. I suspect the difference in cost will be small, but taken over time, it could add up. Besides, we're not just talking cost here. We're talking about something far more valuable, which has a knock-on effect – image.'

I was getting in the swing now, despite myself.

'You're tied down to the service you offer – for example, you have to cook three guest meals a week whether you have one room full or four. In which case, you might as well have all four booked as often as possible. Think about what image you want to convey and go for it, especially if you want to increase bookings through repeat business and word-of-mouth recommendations.'

I lifted my purchase from the floor and waggled it at him. 'Those crappy toiletries do not convey class. The glass bottles do. Potpourri does not convey class. Fresh flowers in antique vases do. You have good quality linen on the beds, but a duvet cover is a duvet cover. Add character. Those throws you have in the *gîtes*? The patchwork quilts? Gorgeous. Put them in the guesthouse as well. Get rid of any ornaments and pictures that don't scream "class". It will cost money, but you can do it a bit at a time and it's an effective, long-lasting change. What about local artists? They may be willing to donate a piece if you leave their business cards out...'

I paused for breath, only to realise that Alain and Rupert were both staring at me open-mouthed – Alain in surprised admiration, Rupert in sheer panic. Oh dear. Once the ideas got running, it was hard to stop the flow. I immediately felt guilty. Five minutes ago, I'd been livid with Alain for haranguing Rupert. Now I'd done the same... Which made me even more livid with Alain for leading me into it.

I thought fast. I'd got carried away with minutiae, when we needed to look at the bigger picture first. I had to give Rupert something simple and solid to think about.

And then I needed to collar Alain in a quiet corner and thump him.

I wafted a hand to indicate that my verbal diarrhoea was of no consequence. 'Small things can be done over time. If you want to fill vacancies, the main question is how you're advertising. I booked via an online site – although I looked at your own website before I went ahead. Do you only use the one?'

Rupert nodded, back in his comfort zone. 'I pay a yearly charge to list the *gîtes* and a link to my website. And I'm listed with the local tourist board here. It's done the trick so far.'

'Okay. But now...'

'More ideas?' Alain asked with a smile.

I narrowed my eyes at him in warning.

'The problem with the site I booked through is that it lists thousands of properties,' I explained. 'Maybe you need to advertise on more than one site. Or look at the *type* of site – see if there's something more select, specialised to the region, so you're less a drop in the ocean and more a splash in a pond. And we need to increase your chances of being found on search engines. What about social media?'

He grimaced. 'No, thanks.'

'You don't have to tell everyone your darkest secrets or what you had for dinner, Rupert. Although maybe that isn't such a bad idea. A photo of the food you cook for guests posted up three times a week might be quite tempting...'

Rupert suddenly stood. 'I'm off to order more coffees.' And without waiting for our response, he limped away to the counter.

Shit. I'd gone too far. Again.

Happy to share the blame, I rounded on Alain like a mother tiger who'd caught him too near her cub. 'What was all that about?' I hissed.

The look of surprise on his face would have been almost comical if I wasn't on my high horse.

'What do you mean? I've hardly got a word in edgewise for the last ten minutes!'

'I know that,' I said crossly. 'But I wouldn't have got started if you hadn't been haranguing the poor man about profits and loss and how much he's going to lose in the divorce, would I?'

He frowned. 'You didn't have to join in.'

'Actually, I did, because by the time *you'd* finished with him, I wanted to give the poor man something practical to think about. What you were telling him was unsubstantiated at best. We have no idea what Gloria might do. Don't you think this is all too soon for him? He needs time to gather himself together. All you've done is make him worry about things he needn't worry about.'

We stared at each other as he absorbed my tirade, and I bit my lip before I said something I might regret. I turned to check that Rupert was still out of earshot, but he was nowhere to be seen, presumably at the gents'.

Alain held my gaze the minute I turned back. For the first time, I noticed golden flecks in the brown – and I desperately wished my pulse would behave. I was so mad with him I could spit, so the way my stomach flipped when he looked at me like that was just downright annoying.

I compensated by venting my spleen. 'Nor do I think a café is the ideal place for a discussion like this.'

Alain gave me a disparaging look. 'Neither do I. But I think you and I both have our suspicions about why he chose it.'

'He *said* he couldn't manage the stairs to your office, but that you didn't have time to come out to *La Cour des Roses*.'

'The first bit's true enough. The last is pure fabrication. I offered to come to the house, but he insisted on meeting in town because he was visiting the market. With you.'

I took my time absorbing that one. It stretched into an awkward silence.

Alain sighed. 'Emmy. I know you and Rupert have had a crap time, and I'm beginning to see how much you care about him. But, at this point, I would like to remind you that I have known him for six years. He was one of my first clients when I moved down here. That means I have also known Gloria for six years. And believe me, what you think of her is nothing compared to what I think of her. I have had to spend those six years biting my tongue every time I did Rupert's books and saw what she'd spent on a new car, or some cocktail dress she was hoping I'd write off as a business expense, and her insistence on not renting out the London flat so she could use it for the occasional shopping weekend. Can you imagine the lost income on that?'

'But that's all you're bringing it down to, isn't it?' I spat, incensed. 'Income and profit and loss. Rupert's comfortably off, from what I can gather. He has no aspirations to be mega-rich.'

'No, but what I'm telling you – and what I'm trying to get across to him – is that he needs to start thinking about where Gloria will leave him at the end of all this. He needs to prepare himself for the worst.'

'And what I'm telling *you*' – I jabbed a finger in his direction – 'is that he doesn't need to hear this right now. Couldn't you have had the decency to wait a few weeks?'

Alain's lips thinned. '*I* could. *Gloria* might not. Look, Emmy, you go home soon, but I'm one of the people who will have to see him through this. I'm only trying to help a friend.'

'Well, that friend has been seriously ill, Alain, and I would have thought you'd take that into consideration.'

He shook his head. 'It's a pulled ligament, Emmy. It's hardly life-threatening!'

'Oh, so you don't see being dragged off in an ambulance with a suspected heart attack as serious?'

Alain paled. 'What are you talking about?'

CHAPTER FIFTEEN

I took in the shock in his eyes. 'You didn't know?'

He shook his head. 'No. So perhaps you'd better tell me before he gets back.'

The barman came over with our coffees, and I waited till he'd left.

'The night Gloria and Nathan... Well, Rupert had what I thought was a heart attack. We called an ambulance and he spent the night in hospital. They said it's only angina, but he's on medication and he's supposed to adjust his lifestyle. I presume that includes less stress.'

Alain ran a hand over his face. 'Shit. I had no idea. He only told me about his leg! And the grapevine hasn't told me any different. He must be playing it down to everyone.'

'Then I'm sorry for what I said – but only to some extent. Even if he wasn't ill, Gloria leaving has been more of a blow than you think. Just because *we* can't stand the woman doesn't mean...'

He kicked me under the table. Rupert was back.

'Sorry about that. Someone I know through Jonathan. You two getting on alright?'

I narrowed my eyes at him as he settled back down with his coffee. Was he really trying to set me up with his *accountant*?

I glanced back at Alain. He was shaking his head at Rupert in friendly despair.

'We're having a few people over for dinner tomorrow night,' Rupert said smoothly as Alain prepared to leave. 'Can you join us? Around seven?'

Alain looked taken aback. He hesitated a moment, no doubt toying between showing support for his friend trying to resume his social life after his set-backs, and the prospect of having to spend an evening in the company of a woman who had just accused him of being an insensitive prat.

'I...' His shoulders slumped a fraction. 'Sounds good. I'll look forward to it.'

As he negotiated his way through the crowded tables to the door, Rupert elbowed me in the ribs.

'What the hell have you done to him?' he hissed. 'Can't I leave you for two minutes? He was all over you like an adoring puppy dog, lapping up your creative genius and that lovely smile... And by the time I got back from the loo, there were thunderclouds hovering over your heads!'

'We... disagreed over something.'

'What?'

'Nothing you need worry about.' I hurriedly changed the subject. 'If the thunderclouds were so bloody obvious, why did you invite him to dinner?'

'Because I fancied some company.' He gave me a look. 'And because Alain fancies you.'

'Oh, for goodness' sake, Rupert.' Although, I had to admit Alain had given me that impression at the beginning – but I suspected the attraction had worn off after the way I'd lashed out at him.

But Rupert carried on, oblivious. 'He's half-French, half-English, you know. Best of both worlds, if you ask me.'

I rolled my eyes heavenwards. 'Rupert Hunter, may I remind you that it's not even a fortnight since my boyfriend ran off with your wife. I need time to lick my wounds, not to be on the lookout for a new bloke.'

'That hasn't stopped you romping in the bushes with my gardener,' Rupert shot at me, his eyes twinkling as my skin went from delicate pink to an unbecoming puce.

'What are you talking about? I haven't... I didn't...'

'No point denying it. Heard the mating noises through my open bedroom window last week. Woke me from my nap.' Delighted by my discomfort, Rupert patted my hand. 'Don't fret, Emmy. I don't blame you. Ryan's a good-looking young chap and you could do with a bit of fun after being with that stick-in-the-mud.'

'It was only a rebound thing, a bit of comfort,' I said sullenly. 'Anyway, we've both agreed to call a halt to it. I just... I wanted to feel attractive again.' Thinking I might have shared a step too far, I bit my lip.

But Rupert smiled. 'I can understand that. Don't take this the wrong way, Emmy – I should stress that I see you more as a sort of goddaughter than anything else – but someone needs to tell you because that blind boyfriend of yours obviously didn't: you *are* attractive. You're natural and curvy in a lovely, uncomplicated sort of way. A lot of men like that. Alain certainly seems to. We'll find out when he comes to dinner.'

'Yes, and about that. Who *are* these people who are supposedly coming to dinner tomorrow? Other than Alain?'

'No one yet. I made it up. Don't worry, I'll think of someone. You could invite Sophie, if you like. I don't want to end up playing gooseberry all by myself. Wear that floaty sundress with the low-cut neckline. Plump up your cleavage a bit.'

I rolled my eyes. Rupert the matchmaker. Heaven help me.

Rupert behaved strangely all the way to the car, throwing little compliments my way – how well I'd squeezed into a small parking space, how I knew the streets like the back of my hand, how I'd ordered everything in French at the market stalls. It was the same on the drive back – how confident I was behind the wheel, how well I knew the road home. This was a side of him I wasn't used to, and I found it rather unnerving.

True to his word, he spent half the afternoon on the phone, ringing round his cronies to see who might be free for his dinner party tomorrow, and he insisted I phone Sophie to do the same.

She was available and delighted to accept. 'Now I will be able to picture where your exciting holiday has taken place and meet your Rupert!'

'He's not *my* Rupert, thank heavens. I'm only his temporary guardian.'

'Cheer up, Emmy. It's about time you had a change of company,' was Rupert's response to my long face as we ate dinner. I refrained from pointing out we'd only just got rid of my parents, and our night out with Ryan and *his* parents had held more than enough excitement for me. I knew I would be wasting my breath. When Rupert set his mind to something, it had a habit of staying set.

'How much are your mortgage repayments?' His question came out of the blue after supper.

'Why do you ask?'

'Just wondered.' He tried for nonchalant disinterest, but I knew him too well.

'Well, you can keep wondering, my friend.'

He ignored me. 'Fixed rate? Variable? Tracker? Maybe I can help. You know I'm a financial whizz.' He flashed that infectious smile of his.

I frowned. 'Rupert, at no point since your over-tanned bony wife ran off with my no-good dull boyfriend have I mentioned any of my financial worries. What hidden agenda have you got whirring around in that under-occupied brain of yours?'

Rupert arranged his face into an indifferent mask. 'No agenda. But it occurred to me that while I'm sitting here – under-occupied, as you say – with you scurrying around after me, I might be able to pay you back with financial know-how. Fetch me another beer, will you?'

I got him his drink. It was easier than arguing.

'Thanks,' he grunted. 'So, how much is your mortgage?'

'You're not going to leave this alone, are you?'

'Nope. What do you think I'm going to do with the information – sell it to the highest bidder? Imagine I'm your independent financial adviser, except I'm doing it for free. A lot of people would pay highly for my services, you know.' He wiggled his eyebrows.

I laughed. 'To be honest, I've been trying not to think about it. Besides, I haven't heard from Nathan yet. How can I plan ahead without knowing what he intends to do?'

Rupert's expression softened. 'How you deal with Nathan isn't any of my business. But if I give you some good advice, you'll have things straight in your head when you discuss where you stand with him. You need to face up to the future. After all, you go home soon.'

'I know.' My heart plummeted southwards. Any impartial outsider would think I should be glad to be heading for home and some kind of normality, but the thought filled me more with trepidation than anticipation. I liked it here. I'd had a chance to just *be*. I'd grown used to Rupert's low boredom threshold and demanding nature, and although he often irritated the hell out of me, we'd built up a good way of doing things, considering. And there was no denying the beauty of the house, the gardens, the weather.

But Rupert was right. Life at *La Cour des Roses* had been a surreal experience in many ways, but it was time I got to grips with reality.

I took a deep breath, a large gulp of wine, and looked Rupert in the eye. 'Alright, maestro. What do you need to know?'

Rupert actually made notes. Our mortgage rate, the bank we were with, what we paid for the flat, its postcode and number of rooms. Our bills, our salaries.

Numbed by alcohol, I let him get on with it. Bless the old soul, he was probably bored and needed a project to get his teeth into. Besides, Rupert was pretty savvy about this stuff. His advice wouldn't go amiss.

'What's the diagnosis, doc?' I poured myself another glass in case there was bad news to come.

Rupert sat back and rubbed his eyes. 'Well, it all looks pretty sound to me. The question is what to do if you and Nathan go your separate ways.' He gave me a searching look. 'I presume that's what's going to happen?'

I thought about the first time Nathan took me to view the flat: my pleasure and anticipation at the prospect of owning a home of our own, sharing our lives together. Nathan presenting me with a moving-in present – a picture I'd seen in a catalogue but thought we couldn't afford.

And then I remembered his betrayal on the roof terrace. His non-existent effort to make amends. Driving off with Gloria.

I looked Rupert in the eye. 'Without a doubt.'

We sat brooding for a moment, then Rupert startled me by slapping the table with his large hands, making our drinks slosh.

'In that case, we need to carve you out a new future.'

I mopped up the spills with a napkin. 'I wouldn't go that far, Rupert. I just need to know what you think I should do about the flat and stuff.'

'My dear Emmy, you need to broaden your vision. What savings have you got, and which are in your name?'

I was surprised to realise Nathan and I had saved quite a bit – although the pleasant feeling this evoked was dampened by the realisation that it was only because we'd worked so hard and had been too tired to spend our disposable income on going out or holidays or anything fun. Our main indulgences seemed to be expensive ready meals, Nathan's attraction to the latest electronic gadgets and my habit of thinking that PMS justified extensive retail therapy. With a jolt, I remembered a small inheritance from my grandmother. I wasn't sure Nathan even knew about that, since the old dear had died before we met. I told Rupert.

He jotted it down and sat back with a flourish. 'Right then, here's what I think you should do.'

Sitting forward in my seat, I eagerly awaited his sage advice.

'In an ideal world, you could do with being rid of Nathan, cutting off all ties, but with your salary, I don't think you could afford to buy him out. Not without substantial hardship.'

I'd already come to that conclusion during one of my many sleepless nights. 'So?'

'Either he could buy you out, or you could force a sale – but both of those options would throw you off the property ladder. Better still, you could persuade him to rent the flat out for now. It's in a good area on a commuter route into the city centre. The rent would cover your mortgage and then some.'

'And where would I live?'

'Here at *La Cour des Roses*.' He said it as though it was the most obvious answer in the world.

'*What?*' I stared at him, wide-eyed.

'I've been thinking.'

'Oh, God, no.' I put my head in my hands. So much for sage advice. Rupert had cooked up one of his schemes, and I was the guinea pig he was roping into it.

'There's no need to be like that, Emmy. I haven't got the hard facts and figures yet, but here it is in a nutshell. You rent out the flat which pays the mortgage, keeping you on the property ladder – albeit jointly with an unfaithful prick, but beggars can't be choosers. Any leftover can be used towards maintenance, repairs, bills. Then you come and live here, and I pay you to help me run the place.'

My mouth gaped open and I had to make a conscious effort to close it. 'You want me to give up a career in marketing to work part-time cleaning the *gîtes* for you?' I couldn't see where he was going with this, other than insane.

'Not just cleaning. There's more to it than that, and you know it. You'd be a sort of manager – of a much smaller enterprise than you're used to back home, admittedly. But there's advertising, bookings, hosting, tourist advice for the guests, bookkeeping. All those ideas you had today – you'd be able to implement those. And yes – shopping, cooking, errands and cleaning, I suppose.'

He cleared his throat. 'I don't want to give all this up, not yet, but I can't do it on my own – nor do I want to. You've already proven yourself more than capable. I can't imagine what it's going to be like without you, and I can't think of anything I'd like more than to have you here.' He held up a hand to stave off the protests I was about to make. 'You'd be living rent-free with no bills, so the money would be better than you think.'

I frowned. 'Rupert, I know you do well here, but I don't see how you could afford to pay me much. And if you give me a room, you'll be lowering your income.'

He shook his head. 'Actually, no, because you could have Gloria's mother's room.'

'What?'

'When we had that wing built, Gloria insisted we allow for her mother coming to stay. She said it wouldn't be fair to bung her in with the other guests, so we had a room built specially.'

'Crikey, that's devotion to the in-laws. Did she like it?'

'No idea. The old bat refused to come unless Gloria flew back to accompany her out here. When we'd made all the arrangements, she got pneumonia to spite us, turned up her toes and that was that.'

I knew I shouldn't laugh, but the thought of an awkward, elderly version of Gloria giving them the run-around and then popping off out of spite made it hard not to.

Despite my better judgement telling me not to give Rupert's ridiculous plot the time of day, my brain whirred dangerously. I hadn't realised his private extension was so big, but I wasn't sure I could countenance living in such close proximity to my wannabe mentor. Not that I was considering this with any seriousness whatsoever, of course.

He took advantage of my lack of protest to hurry on with his sales pitch. 'It's a bit chintzy and old-ladyish, but I'd have it redecorated. It's quite big. And en suite. And right at the far end. Looks out over the orchard at the side of the house. I could put a private entrance in. I know you wouldn't want anyone to think we were... Well, you know.'

'All right. I understand I wouldn't be taking a guest room. But I still don't see how you could afford to pay me much.'

Rupert gave me a patronising look as he topped up my glass. 'Emmy, darling, how much do you imagine Gloria cost me to run?'

I thought about what Alain had said this morning. Thought about the clothes, the jewellery, the suspected Parisian lingerie, the designer luggage that Nathan had loaded into the expensive sports car.

'Hmmm,' I murmured circumspectly.

'And if you were to tot up how much actual work she did around here?'

I got the picture. 'But if you get divorced, she'll cost you even more!'

Rupert shot me a wry smile. 'I don't doubt it. But only in the short-term. I'm well-placed financially, Emmy, and I can stand a few losses. But you heard what Alain said this morning – I need this place as a going concern. If you weren't here, I'd have to cough up for local help anyway. Surely even you can see that if you take that into consideration, and if you compare all Gloria's little expenses against paying a decent wage to someone I trust, I couldn't be worse off?'

I was still trying to compute this when he added, 'Besides, I could get a dog.'

This threw me for six. 'I'm sorry?'

'I've always wanted a dog.' He had a wistful look in his eye.

'And that's relevant to this conversation because...?' Perhaps his beer had combined in some horrible way with his medication to make him go prematurely senile.

'Gloria wouldn't let me,' he explained. 'High heels don't go with dog-walking, and she didn't like the idea of picking up poo.'

This, I could well believe. In fact, it was the most plausible thing he'd come up with in the last ten minutes.

'But if *you* were here, Emmy...'

'Oh, so now you want me to live here so you can pay me to pick up dog poo?'

'Hardly. I'll pay you to help run the place, which will free up my time, allowing me to commune with nature and share the trustful companionship of man's best friend as befits someone of my advancing years. Would you deny me that pleasure?'

I rolled my eyes. 'Okay, Rupert, enough with the dog. To get back to business. You'd have to allow for the off-season, so it's not like I'd be earning what I earn now, would I?'

'You wouldn't need to, with no rent to pay and only a few living expenses. Besides, you'd also be starting to build up your own business.'

'Business? What kind of business?'

'Well, I haven't pinned that down yet...'

I snorted with derision.

'What I *can* tell you, Emmy, is that there are plenty of ex-pats out here. They might need help with advertising their holiday homes, websites, brochures, liaising with agencies. Keeping an eye on their properties. Organising cleaning and maintenance. The possibilities are endless for a practical girl like you. All you have to do is identify a need that can be met with the skills you have, get your head around how to offer it and charge a sensible rate.'

I shook my head, then stopped when it spun a little. 'Rupert, I couldn't make a living doing piecemeal work like that.'

'At the end of the day, Emmy, I wouldn't know for sure. But you'd have plenty to be getting on with here at the house and I'd be paying you a living wage, so you could explore the possibilities in your own time.'

'I don't speak enough French,' I declared, not wanting to get carried away, and also acutely aware we'd both drunk too much – as usual. As far as I could see, the main drawback to moving out here would be the inevitable ravages of alcohol abuse.

'I could help you. You've already come on in leaps and bounds.'

'I have no idea how to set up a business in a foreign country. I wouldn't know where to start.' Sulky now, I was keen to find obstacles before my brain started computing it as feasible.

'I could help you with a lot of it. Alain would help you with the rest – it's his speciality.'

I clutched at straws. 'How could I afford his services before I'd even earned anything?'

'He'd be more than eager to help you, young lady. I think our Alain is rather smitten with you.'

'Oh, for heaven's sake!'

Rupert looked me in the eye. 'Don't you like it out here?'

I sighed wistfully. 'You know I do, but I'm on holiday. It's not the same as giving up a good job to come out on some pie-in-the-sky whim.'

'Wouldn't it be good to have a change, a new challenge, one where you can use your skills in a way that's satisfying to you? Be your own boss? And, best-case scenario? You move out here, love it, never look back and make a decent enough living doing something you're good at.'

'And worst-case scenario?'

'Think positive, Emmy, that's the ticket!'

CHAPTER SIXTEEN

Tuesday dawned bright and sunny. The days were rarely anything but. Rain tended to come at night, leaving the garden dewy and green and the days clear. Sitting up in bed for a few minutes to allow any unprocessed alcohol to drain away from my head, I could almost feel the weight of the bags under my eyes.

I remembered my conversation with Rupert the night before and groaned. In the odd patches of the night when I'd managed to sleep, one minute I'd dreamed of a glorious life of sunshine, fantastic food and coffee at pavement cafés and the next minute, I was buried under a mountain of king-size sheets that needed washing, being suffocated by a gigantic hound that sat on top of me and wouldn't budge.

In the many waking moments in between, I had cursed Rupert and his tipsy, enthusiastic ramblings. What he'd suggested was nothing but a pipe dream. Of course it was tempting. That was why people went on holiday – for a taste of something different. But holidays were a brief respite, an escape that couldn't be sustained in the real world. You couldn't compare one with the other.

My life and what defined it – my home, my job, my family and friends – were in England. All Rupert had done was muddy the waters in an already difficult situation. God, he could be a pain.

Refusing to give his outrageous suggestions any more space in my brain, I staggered into the bathroom, and when I couldn't stand the pounding of the shower on my aching head any more, I dried, dressed and made a beeline for my favourite kitchen appliance.

Taking my coffee outside, I padded around the garden in my bare feet, content to feel the wet grass between my toes and admire the explosion of colour everywhere I looked. The bleeding hearts dotted amongst the shrubs at the edge of the garden were out, their flowers dangling prettily, and the early June day was already beginning to warm up. The chickens, locked in the henhouse overnight for their own safety, were fussing to get out, so I entered the run to allow them their freedom and give them breakfast.

I backed out bottom first – into Ryan.

'Oomph. Sorry. Didn't see you there.'

Ryan laughed. 'You're becoming more domesticated by the minute. Bet you didn't imagine you'd be feeding chickens when you came on holiday.'

'I didn't imagine ninety per cent of the rest of it, either. You're early.'

'I know. Rather busy at the moment. I have a lot of gardens to catch up with after my week back in England and... Well, my other clients were somewhat neglected last week.' He gave me a cheeky grin.

'Oh.' I blushed. 'Ryan...'

'Don't worry, Emmy. I'm still okay with what we agreed on Friday, if you are.'

I sighed with relief. 'Yes.'

He removed any awkwardness by taking my cup from my hands and draining what was left of my coffee in one gulp.

'Hey! Now I'll have to make another!' I yelped.

'Make me one while you're at it.'

I glanced sideways at him as we headed towards the house. There was something I'd wondered since the first day I'd met him. As his lover, it hadn't seemed appropriate to ask – but now we were officially just friends, my curiosity won out.

'Do you mind if I ask you a personal question?'

'I'd say we've already been pretty personal. It'd be a bit odd for me to mind at this stage. Go ahead.'

'Did Gloria ever... You know... Try it on with you?'

A delighted guffaw burst from his throat. 'Now, what on earth would make you think that?'

I suspected it was a rhetorical question, but I answered anyway. 'The woman was a flirt, Ryan. If she could go after Nathan, I can't imagine for one minute she could ignore a sex god like you working in her garden!'

He grinned. 'Sex god, eh? Is that how you see me?'

I slapped playfully at him as I blushed bright red. 'I was seeing it from Gloria's point of view.'

'Uh-huh.' His dimples winked as his mouth twitched. 'Well, to answer your question – yes, she did suggest that she required... extra services. I turned her down flat. She didn't like it.'

'I bet.' I pictured a thwarted Gloria forced to watch Ryan working in the garden without getting what she wanted, and I beamed – not only at the mental torture it must have caused her, but the fact that I'd had a taste of something she couldn't have. And it had been as delicious as her tormented imagination must have told her it would be.

'Weren't you even tempted?' I asked him.

He shook his head. 'I've told you before, I'm only interested in women I feel comfortable with, and I felt about as comfortable with Gloria as I would with a boa constrictor. Besides, I respect Rupert too much. It was never going to happen.'

I smiled. It was good to know that old-fashioned values were still alive and well in the younger generation.

Ryan deftly changed the subject. 'I hear you're entertaining tonight.'

I gave a noncommittal grunt. 'Rupert's entertaining tonight. I'm the mug he's roped into helping him.'

'I'm sure that's true, but don't forget it's all for your benefit.'

'In what respect?'

'Alain is coming, and I notice I haven't been invited.'

We went into the kitchen and I tackled the coffee. 'Maybe Rupert thought it would be too middle-aged for you.'

Ryan laughed. 'Don't worry, I'm not offended. I don't expect to be at every soirée Rupert arranges. You, on the other hand, need to be less naive if you're going to keep Rupert as a close friend and ally. He's trying to fix you up with a respectable accountant to make up for the last one, and he doesn't want your part-time lover mucking up the works.'

I gave an irritated sigh. 'I'm well aware of that, and believe me, I wish he wouldn't interfere, but there doesn't seem to be any stopping him. For God's sake, I've been single less than a fortnight. It's bad enough that I've slept with one man, without him trying to find me another.'

'Thanks a lot!'

'Sorry. I didn't mean it like that. It's just that... Well, I never really thought I was that kind of girl.'

His response was a loud laugh. '*That kind of girl?* Where did you get that expression from, your grandmother's parenting manual?' He reached across to touch my hand. 'Don't feel guilty about what we did, Emmy, or you'll make me feel bad, too.'

I nodded unconvincingly. 'Okay.' I gave him a sullen look. 'That still doesn't mean Rupert should be fixing me up with the first man that comes along. I go home this weekend. What's he going to achieve?'

'He doesn't want to lose you.'

I thought about Rupert's schemes last night – and my rejection of them. 'He won't. We'll stay in touch.'

Ryan put his empty cup in the sink. 'Emmy. Rupert wants you to have as many reasons as possible to keep coming back here as often as possible. He's worried that this place and his company won't be enough once you get back to your old life. He won't see any harm in throwing another temptation in your path.' He shot me a sympathetic smile. 'Thanks for the coffee.' Walking to the door, he turned back. 'By the way. Is he?'

'Is who what?' My mind was still on Rupert and his machinations.

'Alain. A temptation?'

'I barely know him,' I answered, as a perfect snapshot of Alain's toffee eyes popped unbidden into my head. I might barely know him, but it seemed that hadn't stopped me from memorising his face in perfect detail.

'But?'

I thought about my harsh words at the café yesterday, the anger I'd felt when I thought he was bullying Rupert and the way his face had turned ashen when he found out the truth about his friend's health. His anxiety to protect Rupert from the devastation that Gloria could wreak.

Ryan's eyes were twinkling. I could see he wasn't jealous, and we'd made our peace already.

'Well, I don't suppose I'd turn him down for a drink if I stuck around.' *If only to patch up yesterday's misunderstandings.* 'But since I'm leaving, it's not an issue.'

'Enjoy tonight, then. I'm sorry I can't be there. As a spectator, I mean.'

He waved, and as he headed off to his weeds, I tried hard not to be moved by the sight of his torso in a tight T-shirt.

Rupert and I would have to have words about him meddling with my love life, if not my life in general, but for now, since both the Kennedys and the Stewarts were leaving this morning, I had their rooms to clear and then Rupert to help with his blasted dinner party. The last thing I needed was for him to collapse with exhaustion before the meal and leave me with several strangers to amuse for an entire evening.

While I was busy upstairs, Madame Dupont did a cleaning stint downstairs. As was our habit now, we took a break together with a cup of *thé au citron*.

'Madame Dupont, has Rupert asked you about help for *La Cour des Roses*?' I asked her.

She shook her head, and I made a sound of pure frustration.

Somehow, between my earnest desire, her patience and an impromptu sketching session on the back of Rupert's shopping list, I managed to get across my dilemma.

'I leave on Saturday.' I drew a boat on choppy waters. 'Rupert needs help.' I drew a stick lady with a pan in her hand that looked disconcertingly like an axe. Art was never my strong suit. 'He needs lots of help.' I drew another lady making a bed.

At this, Madame Dupont gave a decidedly dirty laugh for a sweet old dear, but when I realised she must have got the wrong end of the stick and scribbled it out to start again, she winked to indicate she'd been kidding.

'Don't worry, Emie,' she said, and to my surprise, she pulled a tiny mobile phone from the depths of her skirt pocket and got to work. Several calls and a second lemon tea later, she'd written down a couple of names and phone numbers.

'You must make Rupert phone them with the details of what he wants and when he wants it.'

'*Merci beaucoup.*' I heaved a sigh of relief as I took the piece of paper, and a tear rolled down my face before I could stop it.

Madame Dupont reached across to wipe it away and patted my cheek, releasing a string of impossible French, but I got the gist – I was a good, kind girl. Coming from this formidable little woman, that meant a lot to me, and the sincerity with which it was said made my heart sing.

I stayed in the kitchen after lunch under the guise of helping Rupert to cook, but in reality to have a go at him about his penchant for meddling – but he was adamant about not letting me help.

'You've done enough unpaid slaving around here to last you a lifetime,' he said. 'It was me who decided to have people for dinner, so I shall be doing the work. I want you to relax for a change.'

I swallowed down the lecture I'd been about to deliver. Just because Rupert went about things in a bull-headed way didn't mean I wasn't touched by his motives, even if some of them were downright selfish.

'I don't want you overdoing it,' I warned.

'I won't.' When I still hovered, he relented a little. 'I might need help clearing up later on, when I've finished the prep.'

'Right. No problem.'

Feeling too restless to sit in the garden, instead I went for a stroll along the lanes. The temperature was just right, and it felt good to get some form of gentle exercise other than housework. There was a verge at the side of the road wide enough to protect me from speeding cars, and I enjoyed the bucolic views of fields and vines.

As I walked, I thought about the impending dinner party and sighed. If Rupert thought it would help Alain and I fall madly in love with each other, then he was sadly mistaken.

I felt awful about how I'd spoken to Alain yesterday. The way I'd rounded on him, even jabbed my finger at him. He hadn't known about Rupert's health. He'd only been looking out for his friend's welfare the best way he knew how, and the look on his face when I'd told him about the angina had been one of shock and concern, bordering on panic.

How we were going to brush by tonight, I didn't know. Even if I wanted to apologise – and I was beginning to think that I did – I might not get the opportunity in a room full of people.

I got back mildly sweaty from my exertions, and headed upstairs to shower and change. I needn't have bothered. When I came back down looking more presentable, the kitchen looked as though Rupert had taken part in a competition to see who could use the most pots and pans.

By the time people began to arrive, I was nervous at the prospect of facing Alain and not in a frame of mind conducive to socialising with Rupert's motley collection of guests.

First to arrive was Alain, who had been called upon to act as taxi driver to Jonathan, a favour Jonathan declared himself worthy of as his age meant he was unfit to drive on an evening out.

'Reactions are slow enough as it is,' he told me cheerfully. 'Add in a heavy meal, and I'd be falling asleep at the wheel.'

I looked awkwardly at Alain and he gave me a half-smile back. I glanced at the clock. Ten minutes before the others were due. *Just get on with it, Emmy.*

'Alain? Would you lend me a hand fetching napkins and... stuff?'

It was weak at best, pathetic at worst, but Rupert would just think it was a ploy for me to get Alain on his own – which it was – in order to seduce him, which I had no intention of.

Startled but politely compliant, Alain followed me into the guest lounge. 'Do you really need napkins?'

I took a small pile of linen squares from the sideboard. 'Yes – but I don't think I need your help to carry them.' I tried a smile. 'Alain, we got off on the wrong foot yesterday, and I'd like to apologise. Even though I was upset about what you were doing, I was unnecessarily rude, and I certainly had no idea that Rupert hadn't told you the full story about his hospital stay. I'm sorry.'

He nodded. 'I'm sorry too. I thought a lot about what you said yesterday, and with hindsight, you were right. I hadn't meant to be so negative or to panic Rupert, but I honestly had no idea how ill he's been. It's just... I know Gloria. I only wanted to make him more aware, before she hits him between the eyes.'

I smiled sadly. 'I take it you mean financially-speaking. Because emotionally-speaking, she already did.'

'I know.' He closed his eyes a moment. When he opened them again, his expression was sincere. 'Emmy, you and I want the same thing. We're both concerned for Rupert. We're just seeing it from different angles.'

I nodded, and there was an awkward pause. I waved the napkins at him and smiled. 'How long can it take to get napkins? You'd better bring – er – a couple of cushions?'

Back in the kitchen, Rupert and Jonathan exchanged knowing looks. I could have cheerfully throttled the pair of them.

Next to arrive, on time to the minute – and once I'd met her, I doubted time would ever dare try to get one over on her – was Ellie Fielding, the estate agent Rupert had recommended to the Stewarts. Somewhere in her late forties to early fifties, tall and straight as a beanpole, with closely-cropped bright red hair and violently clashing fuchsia lipstick, she had an immediate presence and confidence I could only imagine possessing in my wildest dreams.

People settled on various perches around the kitchen. While Jonathan requisitioned the comfy chair by the window and Ellie Fielding plumped for one of the bar stools at the counter – which made her taller and therefore twice as formidable – Alain settled for the windowsill. I threw him a cushion, which he caught gratefully.

'So, Rupert, what delights have you cooked up for us tonight?' Jonathan enquired as Rupert handed out drinks.

Rupert laughed. 'What difference does it make? You'll eat the whole lot like a starving man, no matter what it is.'

Jonathan took no offence. 'When you get to my age, the antici-pation is often more fun than the actual pleasure,' he muttered.

Rupert rolled his eyes. 'We'll assume you're still talking about tonight's menu, shall we?'

Further arrivals thankfully prevented any retorts. Philippe, Ellie's partner-in-crime at the estate agency, was her exact oppo-site – short, round, conservatively dressed in a shirt and tie and soft-spoken to the point where I had to strain to hear him, even though his English was impeccable. When he stood next to Ellie,

I tried not to laugh. I assumed they played "good cop, bad cop" with the customers. Philippe's elegant wife, Martine, was even shorter and quieter than her husband.

Sophie arrived next, and I was immediately grateful for her company. We kissed on each cheek and I introduced her to everyone. She was already on nodding terms with Philippe and Ellie because they worked in town, she knew Martine as she did her hair, and it turned out that Alain was her accountant.

Roaring up on his motorbike, the last to arrive was Bob. As he greeted everyone, I wondered how on earth he fitted into this group. I knew he and Jonathan hung out in the same bar, but it turned out he was a freelance photographer who took Ellie and Philippe's photos for them, Alain did his accounts, and Rupert... Who knows? Everyone knew everyone around here, it seemed. I didn't even know the names of my neighbours back in Birmingham. Nathan and I referred to them as "that old bloke two doors down" or "the noisy bugger above" so this casual camaraderie was like another planet to me.

With all the guests ensconced on their various perches like mismatching birds, Rupert allowed us to sample his amazing *canapés*: tiny, crumbling pastries with slivers of smoked salmon and dollops of creamy cheese, miniature wraps rolled around something spicy, marinated olives – seventh heaven.

We moved to the table for Rupert's homemade *pâté*. With half an ear on the conversation, I toyed with my starter. Rupert had made no secret of the fact that the dinner party was a cover for inviting Alain socially. But after his mad ideas about me living at *La Cour des Roses* last night, if I were to dig deeper... Did he want me to meet all his friends to show me that I wouldn't be isolated if I was daft enough to move here?

'So, will you do it, Emmy, do you think?' Jonathan asked, jolting me out of my thoughts.

'Huh?' I asked intelligently. 'Sorry. I was miles away. Do what?'

'Rupert tells us you're thinking of moving out here. Setting up your own business.'

How could I have missed that? I really needed to pay more attention where Rupert was concerned. Sophie was watching me intently from the corner of her eye. She looked as startled as me.

I shot Rupert a thunderous glare, but he was suddenly busy gathering up used plates to make room for the next course and wouldn't catch my eye.

'Rupert's exaggerating.' I tried to keep my voice light and even. 'He asked me last night whether I would consider coming to live out here to help, and maybe to try to build up my own business.'

'But?' This from Bob.

I looked pointedly at Rupert as he limped back to the table with dishes of steaming vegetables. '*But* I have a secure job to go back to. I can't see how Rupert's idea would be practical in real terms.'

'Depends on your perspective and how much you like what you're going back to.' Bob held his hands palm up like weighing scales. 'Money and security? Or a change and a challenge – and possibly poverty.' He nudged Jonathan. 'Jonathan here would be desperate to pay you a minimal proportion of his pension to do all his running around for him, wouldn't you, pal?'

Jonathan reached for a bread roll. 'You wait another twenty years, young Robert, and see how much you'll need an Emmy yourself by then.'

Everyone laughed, and I bit my lip as Rupert awkwardly ferried garlic potatoes and a fragrant roast chicken to the table, wafting scents of lemon and tarragon in his wake. He began to carve with a vicious-looking knife that I was glad I didn't have a hold of right now. He had a nerve. It was one thing foisting his ideas on me when it was just the two of us, but it was quite another to announce them to all and sundry.

As Rupert passed out slices of succulent, buttery chicken, Sophie gave me a sympathetic smile.

'So it is not something you would seriously consider?' she asked.

I shrugged. 'I don't think it's a good idea to give up a perfectly good job to live in a country I don't know very well with a language I can only just get by in. Besides, I'd have the same problems as back home, wouldn't I? I'd still have to get used to being single again. Earn a living. You French might have leisurely lunch hours and better haircuts, but at the end of the day, you still have to work and go on dodgy dates just the same as we Brits.'

She smiled. 'I suppose that is certainly true.'

To my surprise, Philippe decided to put in his two euros' worth. 'It would not be impossible, you know, Emmy.' His accent and quietness made him hard to follow, even though his English was fluent. 'Rupert has a good business here. I am sure that if he says he can afford to pay you, then that is so.'

I was about to say that of the many things I doubted about Rupert, his ability to pay me a minimum wage wasn't one of them. Whether I wanted to live off it was another matter. But before I could voice the thought, Philippe moved on.

'With regard to a part-time business for you, that is possible. I do not know what business you would like, but there are a lot of British people here.' He waved his arm around the room for emphasis, as though the group at the table represented the whole of the Loire. 'The economy is not so good,' he admitted. 'Nobody knows that better than an estate agent. But those who already live here do not want to rush back to Britain, and there will always be more who want to come.'

He looked to his business partner for support, and Ellie gave a predatory smile.

'What dear, unassuming Philippe isn't telling you, Emmy, is that it never does our business any harm to be able to recommend someone like you to our clients. It's a bit like those birds that feed off the hippos' parasites. Often, the only thing that stands between us and a sale is the confidence of the buyer. The more worries they have, the more they're put off from taking the plunge. Rupert says you're in marketing?'

I nodded meekly. The woman scared me to death.

'Well, I'm sure there would be a market for that – pardon the pun.'

Everyone chuckled politely. I think they were all scared of her as well.

'If we can allay those worries by recommending reliable people like Ryan, Alain, or indeed you – whatever you choose to offer – then we have that much more chance of a sale.' She turned to Rupert. 'Which reminds me. Thanks for giving my number to those guests of yours. The Stewarts. They came to see me before they went home. Lovely people. Very amenable. Very keen. I'm sure they'll be back.' She licked her fuchsia lips, presumably at the thought of an impending commission. 'See, Emmy? Back-scratching. Good for the soul. And for business.'

With that, she tucked into her chicken with more gusto than was quite feminine, a signal for everyone else to do the same.

CHAPTER SEVENTEEN

I glanced at Rupert, and he gave me an apologetic shrug. The sly bastard. Holding a dinner party for me to make friends whilst secretly hoping they might tempt me to move out here was mild enough a machination. But to put my future out to tender, knowing I'd hate people discussing it? I could only presume he'd taken a gamble that my fury would be outweighed by the persuasive abilities of the gathered company, but I didn't like being ganged up on, even if Rupert thought it was in a good cause – his.

Sophie caught my hand under the table. 'Are you okay?' she whispered.

I turned to her. 'How long do they give you for murder over here?'

She shook her head and smiled. 'You wouldn't joke if you weren't okay.'

I grunted. 'Who said I was joking?'

As I looked back at the group, I caught Alain's eye. Besides Martine, who I suspected was quiet because her English wasn't as good as her husband's, Alain was the only person who hadn't yet joined in the debate. Gazing briefly into those caramel-brown eyes of his, I saw sympathy for what Rupert had put me through – but I could glean no idea as to whether he agreed with the others, despite the fact that as an accountant, I would have thought he was one of the best-placed there to have an opinion. He cast me a half-smile, and for a brief moment I found myself wondering how his lips would feel on mine – until I reminded myself I'd sworn off accountants for good.

I was relieved we'd found the opportunity to apologise to each other. My conscience felt so much lighter. Alain was clearly a good bloke who cared very much about Rupert. He was also a bloke who wasn't above apologising – something very much in his favour. And of course, that smile was always going to be a bonus.

In a change of subject for which I was thankful – and which made me wonder if she was kindlier than my first impression of her, and was deliberately getting me off the hook from Rupert's bullying tactics – Ellie launched into a tirade against a seller who wanted them to market his house at a preposterous sum despite its many defects, which she listed with steel-sharp humour.

'Rising damp in the walls,' she told us. 'Electrics that must have been installed just after Edison discovered the lightbulb. A kitchen from the nineteen-fifties if we're being generous, and a bathroom in that hideous eighties avocado that makes you want to vomit.' She shuddered. 'All of which would be fine if he wanted to market the house accordingly – a house that needs substantial modernisation, if not demolition. But no. What had he done, Philippe?'

Philippe laughed. 'He had every wall in the house painted magnolia. Every single wall. And because of this, he claimed the house had been modernised and wanted a top price for it!'

Everyone laughed – although it took another glass of wine and dessert before I began to relax. It was hard not to be moved by Rupert's air-light mini lemon mousses and crumbling sweet pastries filled with chocolate ganache. By the time coffee was served – full strength, none of that British decaf-because-it's-practically-bedtime malarkey – I'd almost forgiven him his blundering methods. In fact, as I sat nursing my cup, what I predominantly felt for him was envy.

His kitchen was filled with fragrant smells and animated chatter and happy faces. It was well after eleven o'clock midweek, and yet there was no sign of anyone rushing off home. As I looked around, I knew without a shadow of a doubt that every single person sitting at the table was here because they wanted to be. I couldn't remember the last time Nathan and I had had anyone other than our parents to dinner.

Jonathan was eliciting sympathy from Sophie by lamenting the size of his pension, while Rupert told Philippe and Martine about the delightful English practices of gazumping and backing out of house sales days before exchanging contracts.

Alain turned to Ellie. 'I can't stand that kind of thing. There comes a point when business shouldn't be allowed to come before common decency and people's wellbeing.'

I raised an eyebrow. An accountant who didn't put business and figures first. An accountant who cared about his friends and enjoyed their company. One with soft brown eyes and a sexy smile, whose hint of an accent definitely lent him an edge of Gallic sex appeal. Hmmm...

'Emmy, did Rupert ever tell you about the time one of my suitors hit on him?' Jonathan pulled me out of my reverie, and as I turned wide eyes on him and everyone laughed good-naturedly at my reaction, I felt warm at the sound.

These people had taken me as they found me and had no preconceived notions, other than that I had been a good friend to Rupert. To them, I was just Emmy. Not Nathan's Emmy, Nathan's girlfriend, Emmy from work, Nick's sister, Flo and Dennis's daughter. Just Emmy. And I liked it just fine.

It was well after midnight before anyone began to make a move, and I couldn't stop yawning.

Sophie laughed as she kissed me goodnight. 'You British, always in your beds so early.'

I grinned, then suddenly remembered the present I'd bought for her yesterday. 'Wait there,' I told her as I shot off to fetch it from my room.

'What is this for?' she asked as I handed her the gift-wrapped package.

'To say thank you for being so kind to me last week.'

She unwrapped it, took the cork out of the bottle and sniffed. 'Perfect! There was no need, but thank you. I love it.' Another kiss. 'I'm very busy at the salon this week, not even time for lunch, but I would like to see you again before you go – just the two of us. Can you meet me for a quick coffee tomorrow?'

'I can't think why not. What time?'

'Twelve-thirty again?'

'Perfect. Thanks for coming tonight.'

'Thank you for inviting me.' She winked. 'Now I can picture all your stories perfectly.'

Alain and Jonathan were the last to go because Jonathan insisted on helping Rupert clear the table. Between Jonathan, who needed his stick all the time, and Rupert, who was not using his tonight so his limp was back in full force, they were like a comical duo from a convalescent home. In order to speed up the process, Alain and I chipped in, but we all kept bumping into one another. When the bulk of it was done, I stood out of the way at the door with Alain while Rupert packed up leftovers for Jonathan, messing about with plastic containers.

I shook my head. 'They're like two old women,' I said, stifling another yawn.

Alain smiled. 'You look tired.'

'Not been sleeping well.'

'That's hardly surprising.' He hesitated. 'Are you doing anything tomorrow night?'

Startled, I looked up at him. 'No, I don't think so. The next guest meal is Thursday. Why?'

'I... wondered if you'd like to go out for dinner.'

'Oh! I – er – well.'

I glanced across at Rupert, who was suddenly terribly busy putting all the plastic boxes in carrier bags for Jonathan. Meddling old sod. Still, accepting would be a way to make up for my rudeness yesterday, a chance to reassure myself that I was leaving Rupert in good hands... And yes, the hypnotic effect of Alain's gaze *might* have had something to do with it.

'I'd love to. Thank you.'

Alain smiled. 'I'll pick you up around seven, then. *Au revoir.*'

I felt a frisson of... something... at the sound of him speaking French.

He took Jonathan's carriers from Rupert, helped the old man out to the car and waved as they drove off.

'Do I detect a date in the offing, lovely Emmy?' Rupert asked as I closed the door.

'Date, no. Dinner, yes.'

'Same thing, isn't it?' His eyes were full of victory. I could have slapped him sometimes.

Sophie was just finishing with a customer when I arrived the following day. We went to the café across the square, and since there was a threat of drizzle in the air, we chose a table inside at the window and ordered coffee.

'So, did you enjoy the dinner party last night?' she asked, her dimple flashing.

I narrowed my eyes. 'Yes and no. Yes, because it was lovely food and nice people. And no, because Rupert has no qualms about crossing boundaries.'

Sophie thanked the waiter as he placed our coffees on the table. 'You didn't like him telling everyone about his plans for you?'

'No, I didn't. He'd only asked me the night before. And we'd both been drinking. I'd barely had time to absorb it all.'

'Perhaps he wanted to push...' Her pretty brow crinkled up as she thought. 'There is an expression...'

'Push home his advantage?'

'That's it!'

'Well, he can push all he likes. He went too far.'

'Hmm. I can sense that you are tempted, though.' There was a mischievous gleam in her eye.

I harrumphed. 'I don't know about tempted. More that now the idea's lodged in a corner of my brain, I can't make it go away.'

Sophie nodded. 'There is much to consider. A lot of it depends on Rupert – because he is who you would work for and live with. But you have to think about what you would leave behind in England, too, and how much you would miss it.'

'Yes, well, I won't know about that until I go back, will I? I would have said I'd miss it all very much – but that was before, when things were good with Nathan.'

'But now Nathan will not be keeping you in England.'

'No, but my family and friends are there. My job.'

'And how do you feel about leaving Rupert on Saturday? *La Cour des Roses*?'

'I...' My voice hitched.

'What? Tell me.'

'Sophie, I know this sounds stupid – but *La Cour des Roses* already feels like home to me.'

'No, not stupid. Some places... They become a part of us, *n'est-ce pas*? In here.' She placed a hand over her heart. 'Maybe for you it should be called *Le Coeur des Roses* – the heart of roses!' She smiled. 'Well, only you can decide. But if you do come back, remember you already have friends here. Me and Rupert, at least!'

'How is it that you have your own salon?' I asked, anxious to change the subject. 'You must be quite young, surely?'

'Twenty-nine,' Sophie told me. 'I started the salon just one year ago. I always wanted my own business. The rent is not expensive and I only employ the young girl you saw there. It does not make me rich, but I like being my own boss.'

'Don't you worry about financial security?'

Sophie shook her head. 'I make enough to buy what I need. I do not expect to make a fortune.' She finished her coffee. 'I'm sorry I didn't have time for lunch. Will you eat something back at *La Cour des Roses*?'

'Yes. Maybe just a salad.'

'You are not on a diet, I hope?' she asked with disdain.

'No. But I am out for dinner tonight.'

'Oh? With Rupert?'

I blushed. 'No, actually, I – er – it's...'

Sophie gave a little squeal of delight. 'You have a *date?*'

'Well...'

'Tell me!'

'It's all Rupert's fault, trying to set me up with someone so I'll be tempted to come back,' I said grumpily. 'I shouldn't have accepted the invitation yesterday after the dinner party. But I was tired and I didn't want to reject him in front of Jonathan and Rupert...'

'Someone at the dinner party?' Her eyes widened. *'Alain?'*

When I nodded, she grinned. 'Mmm. Very handsome. Rupert has made a good choice for you. A lot of women would like to go out with Alain, you know.'

That didn't surprise me. 'Really? Did you...?'

Sophie laughed and patted my hand. 'Don't worry. I like him, but he is not my type.'

'Oh? What is your type?' I asked her, desperate to deflect her from my dinner date.

'I like men who work with their hands – men with muscles,' she confessed with a comically dreamy look on her face.

A vision of Alain striding across the courtyard at *La Cour des Roses* leapt into my brain. He didn't look like the weightlifting kind, but he was tall and tanned and he looked pretty fit to me…

I mentally shook myself and laughed at my companion's expression. 'Oh? Are there many of those around here, Sophie?'

On the way back, I called at the supermarket. Since spotting the gift stall with the pretty glass bottles at the market on Monday, I'd had neither the time nor inclination to follow through on it, and I wanted to see if I could buy the goods I wanted here before I messed about ordering anything online.

My luck was doubly in. Not only did they sell economy-sized bottles of lovely, natural-looking products, but the household section also sold plain but pleasingly-shaped glass bottles with screw tops – although I was hoping to replace those with corks. Adding pretty-bordered sticky labels from the stationery section to the trolley, I headed for the checkout with another niggle checked off my to-do list.

By the time Rupert wandered into the kitchen after his rest, the table was covered in bottles filled with pastel-coloured bath crystals and oil, shampoo and conditioner, all neatly labelled and divided into groups, one for each room or *gîte*.

'You've been busy!' He frowned. 'How much has that little lot cost me?'

I handed him the receipt. 'Less than all those fiddly sachets, I suspect. *And* you're doing the environment a favour. *And* you can't put a price on class. The bottles to refill with are in the broom cupboard in the hall in a plastic box. This lot will have to go in there too, for now. Each time you have a room or a *gîte* changeover, make sure you start with the new regime.'

'Yes, Miss.' Rupert glanced at the receipt, then added it to the others he owed me from my various shopping trips. 'Don't you *dare* let me forget to write you a cheque before you go.'

I thought about my credit card bill and winced. 'Don't worry. I won't.'

He glanced at the clock. 'Shouldn't you be getting ready for your date with Alain?'

'Rupert, it's only five o'clock. How long do you think it takes me to get dressed?'

'I know you women. There are baths to be had, hair to be washed and dried and brushed. Accessories to be chosen.'

'Rupert, I'm going out for dinner, not taking part in a dog show!'

Even so, I scurried up to my room pretty sharpish.

Glancing at my phone on the bedside table, it occurred to me that Kate was due back from the Maldives today. I switched it on long enough to text her to let her know I'd stayed an extra week, but not to worry. She texted back to say she was pleased I'd extended my holiday and expected full details upon my return.

I took my time in the shower, smoothed on body butter, dried my hair, then opened the wardrobe and flicked through its contents. Hmmm. Good moral form prevented me from wearing the blue dress I'd worn for my dinner with Ryan. I'd been flirty with him, and I didn't want to be that way with Alain. He might be a handsome half-Frenchman, and I might be on the verge of forgiving him for being an accountant, but flirting might lead to complications and entanglements I would do well to avoid. I was going home on Saturday. All I wanted from the evening was to reiterate my apology for my behaviour and ensure he would look out for Rupert to my satisfaction.

I changed three times before I settled on navy linen trousers and a matching cotton shirt.

Alain called for me at seven as promised, and we drove into Pierre-la-Fontaine.

As he clambered out of his car, I asked the question I'd had in the back of my mind ever since I first saw him arrive at *La Cour des Roses*.

'Why do you have such a small car? I mean, you're a tall bloke. It's like trying to fit a mackerel into a sardine tin!'

He laughed – a natural, warm laugh that rolled over me and made me feel a little fuzzy. 'I think it must be the half-Englishman in me. I hate parking, but the French don't mind how close they get to your bumpers. Since I visit quite a few of my clients in local towns, I tend to feel more comfortable in a smaller, nippier car.'

I shook my head. 'You'll give yourself a hernia twisting in and out of it like that.'

Smiling, he led me down the street to the restaurant he'd chosen. The tables were separated by trellises wound with silk roses – a twee touch, but it lent an element of romance... And privacy.

The waiter handed us menus, and Alain surprised me by taking glasses from his pocket and slipping them on. As I surreptitiously studied him studying the menu over the top of *my* menu, I decided they only made him more attractive in that I'm-an-academic-so-I-need-someone-to-look-after-me sort of way that some men convey.

He helped me translate and once we'd ordered, we settled into comfortable chatter. With our mutual apology behind us, it was easy to relax in each other's company.

I mmm'd over my starter of warm goat's cheese salad. Remembering the sample I'd tried at the cheese stall, I'd turned my nose up at the idea as I'd studied the menu, but Alain had promised me it would be mild, creamy and delicious, and he was right.

'Is it good, after all?' he asked with a twinkle in his eye.

'Gorgeous!'

'So. How do you feel about going home this weekend?'

'I can't say I'm looking forward to all the explanations and gossip,' I admitted. 'But it'll be good to get back into a routine.'

'How did you get into marketing? Was it something you always wanted to do?'

'Ha! Not really.' He raised his eyebrows in surprise, and I laughed. 'When I was at school and everyone was choosing university courses, they all seemed to know exactly what they wanted to do, but all I could think was, "Shit, I haven't a clue what to pick." I liked most of my subjects, but I didn't have a favourite. The careers teacher suggested business studies because at least it might lead to a good job. So that's what I did.'

'Did you enjoy your course?'

I finished my starter and took a sip of my water, swilling it surreptitiously round my mouth in case I had bits of salad leaves stuck between my teeth.

'Yes and no. To be honest, I found the economics a bit of a mystery. Too much maths.' I made a face. 'And I guess I'm admitting that to the wrong person.'

Alain smiled. 'I loved maths. And economics.' He winked. 'But each to his own.'

'Hmm. Well, I muddled through those bits, but luckily I discovered I had a flair for other aspects of the course. I got a placement at a marketing agency in my third year, and they offered me a job when I finished my degree. I've been there ever since, and I'm assistant manager now. It's manic and I work long hours, but I enjoy it.'

'Do you have any plans for the next step? Manager or director?'

I rolled my eyes. 'Unfortunately, that would involve putting arsenic in my boss's tea. He's there for the duration. And as much as Carl is a self-serving idiot with a penchant for stealing the credit, I don't think he deserves that.'

'So if you wanted a promotion, you'd have to move?'

I nodded. 'Probably. It's been on my mind for the last year or two. But it might involve moving towns, let alone companies, so I never considered it seriously because of Nathan.' I dropped my head in my hands. 'Oh God, I don't even want to think about going back to work. Seeing Nathan there every day.'

'It will be awkward for him, too,' Alain pointed out. 'I certainly hope so, anyway – he deserves it. At least now you'll be able to think about what you really want to do, where you want to go, without taking him into consideration.'

The waiter arrived with our main courses. I took a taste of tender steak in a mouth-watering mushroom and red wine sauce, and managed not to moan out loud with pleasure.

'Of course, now you have an extra option to consider.' Alain looked across and held my gaze.

I rolled my eyes. 'I really don't think that's under serious consideration at the moment.'

He seemed about to say something, then stopped and just nodded.

'I am worried about Rupert, though. When I go back, I mean. We're sorting some help out, but I'm not sure he can cope on his own.'

Alain smiled warmly at me. It was a heart-melting smile, and my pulse pepped up the pace a little.

'Don't worry too much, Emmy. He has plenty of friends to watch out for him. People are inordinately fond of Rupert, for some reason. Gloria, on the other hand, was not overly popular. Many of Rupert's friends and acquaintances merely tolerated her for his sake.'

I nodded. I'd suspected as much. 'I wasn't sure how to take him myself at first, but he grows on you in an irritating sort of way. Nathan didn't take to him at all. Then again, I didn't take to Gloria, but Nathan obviously did.'

Alain closed his hand briefly over mine. When he took it back, I felt a little bereft. I'd enjoyed that brief touch of his palm covering my fingers. 'If it's any consolation, I think you're the better judge of character.'

'If I was any judge of character, I wouldn't have moved in with the boring, cheating bastard in the first place!' I quipped, then immediately kicked myself. 'Sorry.'

'Don't be. You're entitled. I felt much the same way when my wife left me.'

CHAPTER EIGHTEEN

I almost choked on my broccoli. I had no idea Alain had been married, let alone that his wife had left him.

'I had no idea you were married.' There they went again – my thoughts pouring straight down from my brain and out of my mouth.

He shrugged. 'It was a few years ago now.'

'How long were you married?'

'Just under a year.'

'A year!'

'I know. Pathetic, isn't it?'

'What happened?'

'She decided she'd married the wrong brother.'

My eyes widened. 'Oh, Alain, that's awful.'

'Not necessarily,' he said calmly. 'They have two young kids and are living happily ever after in Kent, where Sabine is popular because she's considered exotic, being a Parisian.'

'Do you still see them?'

'Now and again. I'd be lying if I said it wasn't hard at first, but we patched it up. I have a niece and nephew now. Grudges are of no use to any of us.'

'And haven't you...?'

'I'm not still holding a torch for my sister-in-law, if that's what you're thinking. Quite the opposite, in fact. I suspect I had a lucky escape.' He grinned. 'She bosses my brother around like an army general.'

'Serves him right! But what I meant was, haven't you ever...?'
I hesitated, looking for the right words.

'What? Found anyone else?'

I nodded.

'I'm thirty-six years old, Emmy, so yes, I've dated since, but...'
He paused. 'It's a cliché, I know, but I never really felt I'd found
the right girl yet.' He looked down at the table, and an awkward
moment passed between us before he looked up again. 'You're
going to be all right. Rupert told me he's in no doubt about it,
and I trust his judgement.'

'That only means *your* judgement's impaired!'

We laughed, banishing any awkwardness.

'So, how come you're half-French?'

'It's a very romantic tale,' he warned me, a glint of humour
in his eyes.

'I can handle it,' I assured him with mock severity. I wasn't so
sure I could handle him, though – the way his voice flowed over
me like velvet cognac.

'My mother is French. She was on a student exchange in
London at the tender age of nineteen and forgot to look the
opposite way while crossing the Kings Road. Dad grabbed her
hood and yanked her back, saving her from certain death under
the wheels of a bus.'

I placed a hand over my heart. 'That's sweet.'

'Sugary sweet, as it turns out – they've been inseparable ever
since. As soon as Dad finished his engineering degree, he got a job
with an international firm outside Paris. They had the obligatory
two children and are still living their happy-ever-after existence
in the suburbs.'

'Have you spent your whole life in France? You don't have
much of an accent.'

'Dad spoke to us in English, Mum in French, so we had double
the choice. I chose to stay here.'

'But your brother lives in England.'

'He went to university over there and decided to stay. He comes back for family visits, of course... Which is how he met Sabine.'

I waited a second for him to elaborate, but when he didn't, I didn't feel I could push. 'Weren't you tempted by the lights of Paris?' I asked him instead.

'I worked for a big firm there for a few years. It's an amazing city, and I met Sabine there.'

'So how did you end up in Pierre-la-Fontaine?'

'My dad had an accountant friend down here – we used to come and stay with them every summer when we were growing up. He asked if I'd like to be his partner. I already loved it here and I was getting tired of Paris by then. Sabine and I had just got married, and she seemed happy to make the move. I think she thought it would be a good place to bring up a family.' He pushed his food around his plate with his fork. 'But my brother came for a couple of visits that year and... She decided to have a family with him instead.'

'I'm sorry.' I wished I could think of something to say, but words failed me. I thought he might appreciate a change of subject. 'So, do you still work with your Dad's friend?'

Alain shook his head. 'He retired a couple of years ago, and I carried on by myself. I like it here. It's beautiful. I have good friends and a good business, and I can keep my own hours. What more can a man ask for?' He paused. 'Other than someone to share it with, perhaps.'

He gave me a smile and called for the dessert menu before we could take the conversation in a direction neither of us wanted to travel.

'Will you be busy packing on Friday?' Alain asked on the drive back.

'I suppose so. Why?'

'I wondered if you'd like to go out for the day.'

'Won't you be working?'

'I only have a couple of appointments. I can alter them.'

'Oh, well...'

'I know you might have a lot to do on Friday,' he said, sensing my hesitation. 'But I'm afraid I have to work tomorrow.'

I thought about spending my last day mooching around at *La Cour des Roses*, Rupert and I circling each other with the heavy cloud of my departure hanging over our heads, already missing each other before I'd even left.

'No, I can pack tomorrow instead,' I said, my mind made up. 'A day out on Friday would be great. Thank you.'

At *La Cour des Roses*, Alain left the engine running.

'Thank you for a lovely meal,' I managed.

'You're welcome. Thank you for your lovely company.'

In the shadows, I couldn't read his expression. My pulse was racing. It would have been so easy to lean in for a kiss. And yet... What would be the point? For either of us?

I gave him a small smile. 'Goodnight.'

'Night, Emmy.'

As I opened the car door, the light slanted across his face, his eyes intent on me, a self-deprecating half-smile on his lips, as though he too had wanted the kiss and was cursing himself for not being forward enough.

I slept in the next morning, but it was an unsettled, fitful doze. It had been a restless night, recalling snippets of my conversation with Alain and haunted by the possibility of a kiss I hadn't had the courage to taste.

I finally crawled downstairs in my pyjamas – no guests, so why should I care? – only to be stopped at the kitchen door by an even blearier-eyed Rupert.

'Upstairs. Get dressed. Guests!' he growled, pointing at the window as a car drove into the courtyard.

'Urgh. Right.' Off I scurried to shower and dress, thereby delaying any caffeine or nourishment.

Reappearing twenty minutes later, I plastered a smile on my face for the benefit of the early birds who were enjoying Rupert's coffee.

'Emmy – Caroline and Andy Bedford.'

We shook hands and I shot Rupert a silent plea for my morning fix.

'Emmy's been helping me out for the past couple of weeks,' he explained as he jumped to at the coffee machine. 'Unfortunately, she leaves on Saturday, so I hope you'll bear with me if things don't go quite so smoothly once she's gone.'

'I'm sure it will be fine,' Caroline Bedford said graciously. 'It certainly looks beautiful so far.' She glanced through the patio doors. 'Won't you miss all this, Emmy?'

I followed her gaze out to the garden. 'Yes, I will.' For a brief moment, my throat closed over. As soon as I could breathe again, I changed the subject. 'You made good time.'

'We set off far too early,' her husband said, a hint of blame aimed in his wife's direction. 'Drove through the night and got to Dover miles ahead of time. They let us take an earlier ferry.'

'More time here, then,' I said in as cheery a voice as I could muster. In only two days' time, I would be heading in the opposite direction, trying to judge how much time to allow and juggling with maps and the satnav and manic lorry drivers. On my own. I took a gulp of coffee and allowed it to potter its way towards my bloodstream.

When they were ready, I took the Bedfords up to their room. Caroline Bedford was bowled over, exclaiming over the fresh flowers and the little antique glass jewellery dish on the dressing table; the lace coverlet I'd found and used as a bedcover; the view over the garden. Her compliments made me feel more homesick by the minute... For here.

Back downstairs, Rupert was busy scribbling lists. 'Right, Emmy, we need to get a shift on or we won't get everything done. Good job we were here when they landed. Wasn't expecting them till lunchtime.'

He sounded as grumpy as I felt, but I let it be. Since I would be out tomorrow, this was his last chance to boss me about and be chauffeured around. Why *that* should make me sad, I couldn't imagine.

'How did your date go?' Rupert asked as we drove to the supermarket.

'Fine. Nice restaurant. Delicious meal. *Non*-stinky goat's cheese followed by steak.'

'Anything... afterwards?'

I glanced at him, ready with a tongue-lashing, but his interrogation was frankly a bit lacklustre for him. He looked tired.

I frowned. 'Coffee and a drive home. Nothing else.'

He only nodded, so I decided to throw him a titbit of hope. 'Alain's taking me out for the day tomorrow.'

'Oh?' That perked him up a bit. 'Where?'

'Dunno.'

'What time will you be back?'

'No idea. Does it matter?'

'Well, you – er – you'll need to pack.'

'I'll do that this afternoon.'

'Ah. Well, I'm sure he won't bring you back too late, knowing you have to get off early the next day and everything.'

He fell silent again. Crikey. This conversation was like pulling teeth.

'When are you going to try driving again?' I asked.

'Soon, I hope. Can't rely on other people forever.'

I gave him a doubtful look. 'Okay, but I don't think you should go alone the first time or two. Someone should go with you.'

'Already sorted. I asked Alain. He said he'd come over when I felt ready.'

'That's good of him.' There was a pause as I negotiated a junction I'd yet to find reliably friendly. 'You have rung those numbers, haven't you? The ones Madame Dupont gave me?'

'Yes, Emmy, I have.' His tone was impatient. 'Someone called Juliette will come in on guest meal days and help me cook. Madame Dupont has promised to be in the next day to clear up – except for Sunday, of course, because she goes to church. And some young girl will help her on Saturdays with the *gîtes*.'

'Good. And what about...'

'Oh, for God's sake, Emmy, give it a rest. It's all sorted!'

My mouth dropped open in shock. Rupert had never spoken to me like that before. For a second, I bit back a retort – and a tear or two while I was at it – but all the sleep-deficient nights and worry were wearing my restraint thin. Beyond thin.

'How *dare* you?' I asked him, my voice low and dangerous.

'What?'

'How dare you speak to me like that? After all I've done?'

'Emmy, I...'

'You ungrateful bastard!' My knuckles were white on the steering wheel as I fought to keep the tears from blinding me.

'Emmy...'

'I have run around after you. I have cleaned for you and cooked for you. I have fetched you your beers and your cups of tea. I have listened to your drunken ramblings with sympathy and understanding. I have tended your guests and your chickens. I have risked my good standing at my job for you, all for another week of the same.' I shook my head. 'I only wanted to know if everything was in place so I could go home with a little peace of mind. I didn't think it was too much to ask.'

'Emmy, I don't think you should get so upset when you're driving.'

'Oh, you don't?' I screeched the car to a halt, half on the road, half on the grass, narrowly avoiding a shallow ditch. The driver behind screamed his horn in outrage as he passed – or possibly admiration, if he was a native.

'What the hell are you doing?'

'Apparently, I'm not fit to drive. Perhaps you'd like to take over.' I unbuckled my seat belt.

Rupert's face was ashen-grey with shock. 'You know I can't.'

'Exactly. So I suggest you put up and shut up.' I refastened my seatbelt and screeched back onto the road.

'Emmy. For God's sake!'

'Save it, Rupert. I've had enough!'

He took me at my word. Either that or he was too petrified by my driving to speak. We drove on in silence, parked up in silence and trooped round the supermarket with monosyllables and stony faces. As we left the car park, Rupert asked me to turn towards the town centre.

'You bought chilled stuff. It'll go off,' I snapped.

'No, it won't. We won't be long.'

Stubborn old sod. I drove in and parked where I was told.

'Where do you need to go?'

'Couple of places. No need for you to come. Why don't you go get a coffee? I'll meet you there.'

'Fine.'

I sat and sulked as I nursed my coffee. I had no idea why he'd got out of bed on the wrong side this morning. Whatever it was, I didn't see why he should be taking it out on me. I was only trying to help. And inevitably, any satisfaction I might have had when I'd yelled at him was now overridden by guilt at behaving so badly.

Ten minutes later, Rupert reappeared, huffing and puffing –
and limping, to add to my guilt. He ordered a coffee and, when
he'd caught his breath, startled me by taking my hand.

'Emmy. I owe you an apology. I was horrid. I'm sorry.'

I didn't go so far as to pull my hand away, although I wanted
to. 'You're tired. We both are.'

'It's no excuse. I'm not coping with the idea of you going home,
that's all. I didn't want to say so because you already know how
I feel about it and, well, you've got enough to contend with.' He
took a sip of his coffee and I noticed his hand was shaking. 'I don't
want us to fall out, Emmy. Please. We've been through too much.'

I fought back yet another deluge of tears. They seemed to want
to come thick and fast lately.

I squeezed his hand. 'I'm sorry, too. I shouldn't have said what
I did. I'm bad-tempered about going home.'

Rupert nodded and drained his cup. 'Come on, then, love.
Chilled goods in the car.'

'I told you that forty minutes ago.'

By the time we got back, unpacked the shopping and pretended
to be interested in lunch, we were more or less on an even keel,
but I still felt dreadful about what had happened and I suspected
he did, too. Under the guise of his going for a rest – which it
looked like he desperately needed – and me going to pack, we
went our separate ways.

I dragged my suitcase down from the top of the wardrobe
and opened it out on the bed. Gazing into its yawning mouth
reminded me of the day Nathan had told me he was leaving, his
suitcase open on the floor by the window next door, the dust
motes dancing in the sunlight. It all seemed so long ago, another
lifetime – and in many ways it was. My life had irreconcilably
shifted without my permission or input, and all I could do was

go with the flow for now and hope I would come out somewhere nice – or at least somewhere acceptable – at the end of it all.

I started to pack the things I wouldn't need for the next thirty-six hours, defiantly throwing my stuff into the case higgledy-piggledy. None of Nathan's precise folding. How he could do that at the same time as telling someone he was leaving them was beyond me. The man was an emotional runt.

I thought about my day with Alain tomorrow and sighed. I had no idea where we were going. Choosing an outfit that might suit all eventualities from my already limited wardrobe wasn't easy.

Leaving out a smart pair of cream chinos that I hadn't worn this holiday due to all the manual work I'd been subjected to, a teal T-shirt, light sweater and pumps, I packed everything else so I couldn't second-guess my choices in the morning.

When I'd corralled my toiletries into one heap in the bathroom and my cosmetics into another heap on the dressing table, I checked the wardrobe and drawers and under the bed for anything I'd left behind. Only one odd sock of Nathan's languished at the back of his bedside drawer. I fished it out and dropped it in the bin, delighted at how much it must have upset his equilibrium to get to wherever he was going with Gloria, only to find he had an infuriatingly lone sock.

Staring around the bare room made me feel out of sorts, so I mooched downstairs. Madame Dupont was there, so she put the kettle on and we sat down for our usual garbled conversation over lemon tea.

'Did you enjoy the dinner party?' she asked with ill-disguised curiosity.

'Yes, thank you. The food was delicious and it was nice to meet Rupert's friends.' I did my best to tell her who was there and what we'd eaten. As she listened, I noticed she didn't correct me much. Either my French had improved, or she didn't have the heart so near to my leaving.

'I went out for dinner with Alain last night,' I admitted.

Her eyes lit up and there was a string of mischievous praise for the man, with nods and nudges in my direction. The old woman must be thinking along the same lines as Rupert. Heaven knows, she was just as meddlesome – and as well-meaning.

'Will you be here tomorrow?' I asked her. When she nodded, I told her, 'I won't be, I'm afraid. Alain has invited me out for the day.'

Her face transformed into a combination of smiles at possible future romance and sadness that this was to be our last cup of tea together.

'Reviens nous voir bientôt, Emie,' she crooned as she stood up and patted my cheek, then drew me into a tight hug against her wiry little body.

Come back and see us soon.

Heading out into the garden, I went around the corner of the house to the old orchard where I could indulge my misery away from prying eyes, but I was brought up short by the sight of Ryan pulling at weeds. I hadn't noticed his car or heard him arrive.

'Hi, Emmy. Are you okay?'

I gave him a wobbly smile. 'Just had a fond farewell with Madame Dupont. Thought I'd better come out here so we wouldn't have to do it all again when she finishes her work.'

'Ah.' He pulled me in for an affectionate and thankfully, non-sexual, hug. I couldn't have coped with that right now. Plus, I'd begun to experience the unnerving phenomenon that whenever I thought of Ryan and me rolling around together, along with the accompanying tingle and idiotic grin, a perfect image of Alain's face would disconcertingly superimpose itself across my memories.

'You must be an absolute superstar to have softened the old dragon – you know that, don't you?' he said as we drew apart.

I shook my head. 'I only did what anyone would do in the circumstances.'

'No, Emmy, you didn't. Most people would have gone straight back home, or at the very least, blamed Rupert for allowing his wife to run off with their man.' He took my face in his hands, planted a light kiss on my forehead, then bent to pick up his tools. 'I'm off,' he said. 'Have a good day with Alain tomorrow.'

My eyes widened. 'How did you know about that?'

'Rupert told me. Have a safe journey home, Emmy. And come back soon,' he echoed Madame Dupont's words as he disappeared around the corner of the house.

I dropped down under the nearest tree, my back resting against its trunk, eyes closed against the afternoon sun. As I heard his engine start up, I wondered if Ryan really had finished his stint in the garden or whether he was being tactful, knowing I was upset by Madame Dupont's farewell and not wanting to prolong ours. He was a nice guy. A little too happy-go-lucky for me, but some woman somewhere down the line would be well blessed with his genuine nature and easy-going personality.

My melancholy drifted towards a doze, until a light patter of feet and a wet something in my lap brought me rudely back to the present and my eyes shot open to find a dog's nose nuzzling at my hands. When the initial shock had abated and I'd satisfied myself that the stupid mutt wasn't going to amputate any appendages, I ruffled the curly hair on its head and scratched behind its floppy ears.

This must be my friend of old, the dog who'd come charging through the hedge to bark me awake after my outdoor session with Ryan. Glancing back to where the deed took place, I could see now that it was indeed only a few yards from an open window – presumably Rupert's bedroom. He must have been able to hear *everything*. I blushed at the thought, but my embarrassment was softened by the memory of Ryan's words when I'd questioned the wisdom of the location: "You're not trespassing. You belong here." I knew he'd meant as a *bona fide* guest, but it all seemed so prophetic after Rupert's invitation to live out here.

'They're all barking mad,' I said to the dog, lifting its muzzle to look into its appealingly dopey eyes. 'Just like you.'

'*Framboise! Framboise!*' The resigned call came from the roadside.

The dog turned its head towards the sound and, with an apologetic slobber in the general direction of my arm, shot off back through its secret hole in the hedge.

Framboise? Didn't that mean raspberry? What sort of a name was that to give to a poor defenceless animal? I stood up to brush hair and slaver from my person. Why Rupert was so keen on getting a dog, I couldn't imagine. Then again, as I thought of its appealing eyes and slave-like devotion to its owner's voice, I realised there was no contest. I'd choose a dog over Gloria any day. At least dogs were faithful.

When I went back inside, Madame Dupont had gone and Rupert was getting ready to cook. I slipped in to work beside him, neither of us saying much for fear of damaging the fragile peace between us. Once the prep was done, we sat for our customary tea break.

'I won't be seeing much of you tomorrow, then,' he said quietly.

'I don't know where we're going, but...'

'In that case, there's something I want to say.'

My heart sank at his serious tone. We were already treading on eggshells. 'Rupert, I don't think...'

'Please, Emmy, let me say it.'

Helpless, I nodded for him to go on.

'I know you think I've been bulldozing you a bit, getting people to side with me about you coming to live out here.'

'A bit!' I spluttered.

'All right. A lot. I wanted to show you that it wasn't as hare-brained a scheme as you think.' His brow furrowed as he sought the right words. 'You know how much I want you to come back, so there's no point in me going on about it. And I wouldn't have suggested it if I didn't think it was viable. But...'

'But?'

'At the end of the day, it's your life. You should do what *you* want. You should follow your heart, Emmy. That's all I want you to do.'

'And you think my heart belongs here?'

He drained his mug and got up. 'That's not for me to say, is it?'

CHAPTER NINETEEN

The following morning, I peered at myself in the bathroom mirror in dismay. Ugh. I looked like a sleep-deprived harridan.

I showered, fluffed my hair into a pale imitation of what Sophie had intended, and dressed in the outfit I'd left out. Making a beeline for my make-up bag on the dressing table, I pulled out the works – but when I looked in the mirror to decide where to begin, I stopped short. Despite the image that had greeted me when I'd first woken, a tanned, lightly-freckled, healthy-looking face was now there in its place.

I stared at it in genuine surprise. Back home, if I'd got up looking and feeling like I had this morning, it would have taken a good half-hour of creams, cosmetics and hair straighteners before I could even think about going out in public. Over here, it seemed all I needed was a quick shower, two minutes with the hairdryer, a slick of moisturiser, mascara and lip gloss, and I was done. Crikey! If I was daft enough to do what Rupert wanted, it wouldn't matter that I'd be earning a pittance – I wouldn't need to spend half as much on expensive props, for a start.

Alain called for me promptly at nine, Rupert wished us a good day out – startling me by the absence of his usual crass comments – and we headed off.

'Where are we going?' I asked, curious.

Alain shook his head. 'It's a surprise. Don't worry, it's not far. And it's one of my favourite places.'

We made small talk in the car, and I realised I was grateful for Rupert's matchmaking interference, after all. Not for the reasons he might imagine, but because yesterday had been so hard, packing and saying painful goodbyes and winding things up. A distraction today was more than welcome.

We hadn't been driving long when Alain turned into a large car park. I looked around, startled. 'We're here already?'

'Yes.'

'Where?'

He climbed out of the car and pointed across the road at the gigantic signs.

My eyes widened. 'We're going to the *zoo*?'

'Correct.'

Standing with hands on hips, I was unable to hide my surprise – and dismay. I'd imagined a civilised drive through the countryside, a bit of sightseeing, a spot of lunch. Not in my wildest dreams had I envisaged being brought to the zoo.

Alain wasn't fazed by my obvious lack of enthusiasm. Taking in my expression, he threw back his head and laughed – a deep, velvet sound that made my stomach lurch pleasantly.

'Don't look so worried, Emmy.' He opened the boot of the car and started piling sun cream, snacks and drinks into a small rucksack. 'You're going to love it.'

Realising I was being a little ungrateful, considering he'd rearranged his work schedule especially for me, I plastered a smile on my face.

'I'm sure I will,' I said politely, noting that every car arriving contained a family. Alain was an accountant, for goodness' sake. Zoos were for kids. What was he thinking? The last time I'd been to a zoo, I was nine years old and hated the cement paths and bored captives in dreary cages.

Slinging his rucksack over one shoulder, Alain started across the car park. As we joined the queue of parents and grandparents and excitable kids, I felt more than a little foolish. Confusion was added to it when we got to the front and Alain asked for one ticket.

'Only one?'

He smiled. It crinkled the lines at his eyes. My palms started sweating.

'I have an annual pass,' he explained, taking out his wallet and showing it to the woman at the counter.

'You have a pass for the *zoo*?'

'Why not?'

'Why not, indeed,' I agreed, but since my acting experience was limited to a waving willow tree in the school pantomime when I was seven, I suspected I wasn't convincing anyone.

'You're going to have a great day, I promise. Come on, we need to buy popcorn.'

'Popcorn?'

'To feed the animals.' He gave me an innocent look as I gaped at him. 'What? Accountants can't have fun, too?'

His laugh was infectious and I managed a weak but genuine one myself. 'Not the ones I know.' My smile broadened as I imagined what Nathan would say about spending a day at the zoo. He would be staid and boring and scathing. Defiantly, I decided to be more open-minded about the experience. It may seem a strange choice for a day out, but since my entire time in France had been bizarre, it would fit right in.

I needn't have worried. Alain's enthusiasm was big enough for the both of us, and it soon rubbed off on me. He knew the place inside out, and he was right – it wasn't anything like the zoo I remembered being dragged around as a child. Built on the site of an old quarry, this one was beautifully landscaped, shaded with bamboo and acacia, scattered with carved wooden animal statues – and the animals themselves were breathtaking. I oohed and aahed at the snow leopard's paws the size of dinner plates, sighed at the cuteness of the shy red pandas and delightedly took photos of dozens of scarlet ibis clustered in a tree, looking for all the world like giant pink fruit.

I loved the aviary. With the quarry rock acting as walls on all sides, it was fantastic watching the colourful birds fly overhead, especially the hyacinth macaws flitting from one side to the other like bright blue jewels. Fantastic, that was, until I felt something pelting my head and looked up to find a particularly stroppy green-and-red macaw chipping chunks of rock out of a nearby wall and lobbing them down at people on the path below.

My favourites were the comical antics of the monkeys and gibbons as they performed their aerial acrobatics along the trees and ropes like circus performers on a sugar high. I could have watched for hours, but thankfully Alain could recognise a woman who needed to eat.

'Let's go get you some lunch,' he said, dragging me reluctantly away. 'If we don't beat the crowds, we won't get a prime table.'

I couldn't imagine what could be prime about a table in a zoo restaurant, but sure enough, we got one overlooking the giraffes and zebras. I'd never been head-height with a giraffe before and I watched, spellbound, as it took a branch in its mouth and began to manoeuvre and manipulate it, using its long black tongue and rubbery lips to systematically strip the leaves, then unceremoniously dropped the bare branch to the ground. It was only when it loped away for further greenery that I could concentrate on my steak and *frites*.

'Have I converted you?' Alain asked me.

I grinned. 'Absolutely. I gather you come here quite a lot?'

He nodded. 'I think of the animals as old friends. When I'm at a loose end, it's fun. If I'm feeling low, it cheers me up. If I'm bored, there's always something new to see. It seems to suit any occasion. And I'm sure that sounds silly.'

'Not at all. It must be good to know where to go when you're feeling out of sorts.'

'You don't have anywhere?'

I thought about what I did back home when I felt down or needed to get away from Nathan for a while. Ignoring the obvious retail therapy – invariably an expensive mistake – nothing sprang to mind... Which was a shame, because I had a suspicion I would be feeling out of sorts quite a lot in the near future.

'Nowhere special.' My throat felt tight. How could I tell him I'd been so content at *La Cour des Roses*, I hadn't felt the need for a haven? That *La Cour des Roses* was my haven?

Talking of which...

'Alain, can I ask you something?'

'Of course.' He started to look worried. 'I think.'

'The other night at dinner, when Rupert was busy telling everyone about his idea of me moving to France and working for him, setting up a business...'

'Yes?'

'Well, I couldn't help but notice that everyone gave their opinion except you. And yet you're an accountant. I would have thought you'd have something to say about it from a professional standpoint.'

He put down his knife and fork, staring at his plate for a moment before looking up. 'From a professional standpoint, maybe. My problem is from a personal standpoint.'

I frowned. 'What do you mean?'

'Emmy.' He gave me a direct look. Those cinnamon eyes took some beating. 'I like you. You know I do. So any opinion I might express would be biased, wouldn't it? I could tell you Rupert's idea was viable, but I might be telling you that just so you'd come back here. That wouldn't be right.'

I gave him a direct look right back. 'Pretend I'm your sixty-year-old aunt. What would you tell me then?'

He cocked his head to one side as if he was trying, then abjectly shook his head. 'I can't.'

I reached across to slap him on the arm. 'Try harder.'

'I would tell you what you already know – that it's a gamble to leave a well-paid, steady job, especially since Rupert's business is so seasonal.'

'He said he would allow for the off-season.'

'Okay, so let's say he pays you a base wage evened out across the year. Living rent-free would make that go a lot further, but you wouldn't have any real security. I also think you could get bored after a while. That could be resolved by the challenge of setting up your own business, and I'm sure you'd be able to find a niche that uses your skills.' He hesitated. 'It all depends on how much you love your job back home. Whether you're ready for a change. And if so, whether you see a more precarious existence in a new country as a challenge and an adventure – or a potential nightmare. If you go ahead, I suspect you'd be more than capable.' He smiled. 'Be warned, though. The French do love their red tape – but I'd be more than willing to help you with that.'

I smirked. 'Hmm. Rupert said you would.'

Alain blushed just a little. 'Rupert needs to learn to stop interfering.'

'I won't argue with you there.' It was time to change the subject. 'Come on, hurry up. I don't want to miss the vultures being fed.'

I'd never seen anything like it – gigantic birds with evil beaks ripping pieces of meat to shreds in minutes and scrapping over the leftovers. Alain mocked me mercilessly for my girlish squealing as their gigantic wings flapped against my knees. As we left the horrid things to fight over the last strips of gristle, dark clouds began to form oppressively overhead and the air felt humid and close. I fanned at my face as Alain studied the sky.

'Looks like rain,' he pronounced solemnly, at which I burst out laughing.

'What's so funny?'

'Even I can tell it might rain, Alain. You wouldn't need to be a meteorologist!'

'Sorry.'

'No, I'm sorry.' I touched his arm. 'I shouldn't make fun of you. I don't know you well enough yet.'

'I wish you did. And I don't mind being made fun of. By you, anyway. My mother used to tell me that people only tease people they like, so I'll take it as a good sign.'

His words echoed Ryan's the first time we'd kissed. I felt I should be bothered by that somehow, but I wasn't. Ryan and I had enjoyed what we'd shared for what it was and moved on to an easy friendship. There was never any question of it being anything more.

Things were different with Alain. It all seemed so much more tentative... More important. I was glad he hadn't taken offence.

I was jolted out of my thoughts by a loud, deep rumble that started low and built to a deep crescendo, reverberating through the air and into my bones to make me jump.

'Thunder!' I exclaimed.

Now it was Alain's turn to laugh. He shook his head and pointed to a nearby enclosure. 'Not thunder. Lions.'

Turning, I saw a group of lions lounging on a rock formation. The male, his mane scraggy and almost black, was the source of the racket. The sound must have been heard across the whole zoo.

It was then that the heavens opened, building from a smattering of heavy, warning splashes to torrential rain in less than ten seconds. With a shriek, we headed for the nearest shelter, a covered viewing platform a few yards away. Storming up the wooden stairs, we shook our sodden clothes like dogs coming out of the ocean. The rain on the tin roof was deafening and as it pounded down, more and more people scuttled up the steps to join us until we were all jammed together like sardines. I tried hard not to think anything of the fact that Alain and I were now chest to chest, practically nose to nose, but I could feel the inevitable flush spread across my cheeks.

'Don't worry. It'll be short and sharp, I think,' Alain said.

'That's okay.' I peered over his shoulder at the lions sitting calmly on their rock, unfazed by the heavy drops of water literally bouncing off the ground. 'It's quite atmospheric.'

Alain chuckled. 'That's one word for it.'

We looked into each other's eyes. There was little choice – we were packed so tight that any turn I made, even if I could turn, would be an obvious avoidance tactic. Besides, I didn't want to avoid Alain's face. It was a nice face. Kind and oh-so-subtly sexy. No glasses, giving me an unobscured chance to look into the velvet brown depths of his eyes.

'Do you only wear glasses for reading?' I blurted my thoughts out yet again. I would have kicked myself, but there wasn't enough room.

'Yes. For reading and seeing things up close.'

'Hope I'm blurry enough, then. I'm not sure I bear up to close scrutiny nowadays.'

Alain frowned. 'Oddly enough, you're not at all blurry. And I think you're bearing up very well. On all fronts.' He paused. 'Emmy, I need to ask you something.'

'What?' My palms were damp again. I surreptitiously rubbed them against my legs.

He hesitated. 'If things were different, if you hadn't just had the worst time of your life – would you have considered the possibility of us... seeing each other?'

I stared at him, wide-eyed. 'Maybe. Probably.' Hypnotised by the rain and the golden flecks in his eyes, I murmured, 'Yes.'

As yet more people squashed into the shelter, we were forced deeper in until my back was hard against the glass and Alain was hard against me. Literally.

He blushed. 'God, Emmy, I'm sorry.'

I blushed to keep him company. 'It's okay. It's not your fault.'

'I think, under the circumstances, I ought to explain.' His mortification couldn't have been clearer, and I tried hard to concentrate on his face instead of the way his body felt against mine.

'No, honestly, Alain, you don't.'

'Emmy, I wish you weren't going home tomorrow. I know you've overstayed and you have to go, and I'm not worried I'll never see you again, because you'll be back to see Rupert. But I wish we'd had more time to get to know each other.' He frowned. 'Your life is upside-down at the moment, and any decent bloke wouldn't dream of putting you under pressure at a time like this. I only want you to know that under different circumstances, I think we could have been more than friends – and I would have liked that very much.'

I felt a sharp pang of regret, almost a physical pain, deep in my gut. He was talking about us in the past tense already, even though our friendship was so new. The possibility of it being anything more was too unlikely. I lived and worked in England. Alain lived and worked in France. We barely knew each other. I had no intention of uprooting myself for some ridiculous rebound romance, and I was sure Alain wouldn't want me to, only to end up taking the blame when it all went wrong.

And yet the thought that this gentle yet powerful something we'd only just found would die at the end of the day filled me with sadness. A tear threatened at the corner of my eye and I blinked furiously to stop it from falling, but it escaped anyway to roll blatantly down my cheek. Alain freed an arm and reached up to brush it away with his thumb.

'I'm sorry,' I murmured. 'I'm being stupid.'

'No, you're not. You've had a hard time.'

I sighed. It was now or never. I had to know if this burgeoning attraction was more than a cry for attention on my part, a need for comfort, a desire to know that I was attractive to someone after being so cruelly dumped. My unexpected fling with Ryan had reinstated my confidence a little, given me back some faith in myself – but that had been an experiment, a tentative step in forging a way forward. This thing with Alain... There was something else here, running way under the surface, but I'd been through so much over the past couple of weeks, I couldn't trust my own instincts any more.

Suddenly, I needed to be sure. In real terms, it would make no difference to what was already an impossible situation. But if I left France not knowing, I would always wonder.

'Now it's my turn to ask *you* something,' I ventured.

'Okay.' Alain was hesitant, a worried frown-line creasing his forehead. I would have found it comical if I hadn't felt so nervous.

'I don't want to appear too forward or anything.'

'I think we're already past that,' he muttered, embarrassed. He'd managed to retreat the inch or two that the huddle of damp humanity at his back would allow, but our bodies were still touching, the intimacy still potent enough to make us both ill at ease so early in our budding friendship.

'Here goes.' I cleared my throat. 'Would you mind kissing me?'

If his eyebrows could have shot up any higher, they would have hovered over his head in thin air, the way they do in cartoons.

I took a deep breath. 'I need to know.'

He gazed deep into my eyes, then nodded his understanding. In slow motion, the anticipation warm and sweet, he lowered his head until his lips met mine, feather light and velvet soft. We stayed like that for a long moment, oblivious to the multitude around us, until a jolt at his back forced that smidgeon of extra pressure and the kiss grew firmer, laden with possibility and impossibility, desire and regret mingling in soft desperation.

Alain pulled back, his eyes never leaving my face. 'Did that answer your question?'

I struggled to speak. 'Yes. Thank you.'

'You're welcome.'

The crowds were beginning to disperse as the rain slowed to a drizzle, then stopped as suddenly as it had started. A pair of middle-aged ladies gave us disapproving looks as Alain took my hand and we followed them out of the shelter. The sun shone again, burning brightly to dry the gravel pathways. I shivered a little.

Alain squeezed my hand. 'Are you okay?'

'I'm fine.'

'You're quiet.'

'That's because I don't know what to say.'

'Je comprends.'

The sound of him speaking French made my heart miss a beat. That and the knowledge that he *did* understand. I had to go home tomorrow. The likelihood that this could ever lead to anything was slim at best and would rely on me taking massive action and a huge leap of faith. I knew I was in no position to do that right now, either emotionally or in practical terms. Alain knew it, too.

We didn't leave until the zoo was ready to kick us out. While I excused myself to visit the loo, Alain disappeared into the gift shop where I tracked him down at the tills, pocketing his wallet and clutching a paper bag.

He held it out to me. 'To remind you of your grown-up visit to the zoo.'

And to remind you of me. As the unspoken words floated between us, I took the bag from him and peered inside at something grey and fluffy. Intrigued, I reached in and pulled out a soft toy – a gibbon with long dangling legs and arms and a cute baby on its back.

'It goes around your neck. Look.' Alain pointed to a little girl leaving the zoo proudly sporting hers. While I was distracted, he stretched the gibbon's arms around my neck and fastened the hands together. 'There.'

Embarrassed and inordinately pleased at the same time, I stroked the velvety fur. 'Thank you. I can't remember the last time someone bought me a soft toy.'

'That's what will make it a unique and treasured gift.'

I smiled. A ridiculous gift it might be, but I already knew he was right. I sported it all the way to the car, where it was removed so it – and I – wouldn't be throttled by the seat belt.

Alain glanced at the clock on the dashboard. 'Damn. We need to get back.'

'Oh? Do you need to be somewhere?'

His cheeks reddened a little. 'No. Ah. Well, yes. And you must have things to do.' He went quiet and fiddled with the radio. I was happy not to chat. All I could think about was our kiss and whether anything could ever come of it – but moving to a foreign country for all the wrong reasons simply wasn't on the cards.

When we arrived back at *La Cour des Roses*, the courtyard was crowded with cars.

I frowned. 'Who the hell are all these people?'

Alain cleared his throat. 'Come on, let's go in.'

'Alain, thank you, but you don't need to escort me in. I'm a big girl now.'

'Need a quick word with Rupert,' he muttered.

Shaking my head, I got out of the car and headed up the steps into the kitchen.

'Emmy. Have a nice day?' Rupert came through from the guest lounge.

'Yes, thanks. What are all those cars doing out there? We could barely park!'

He shrugged. 'I decided to have a party. Come on through and join in.'

'But Rupert, I'm tired,' I whined. 'Can't I just go for a bath?'

Rupert snorted, pushing me down the hall. 'Hardly, love. Not when you're the guest of honour.'

'I'm... What?'

But it was too late. I'd been propelled into a room of revellers.

CHAPTER TWENTY

There were greetings and cheers at my appearance. I spotted the crew from the dinner party – Ellie, Philippe (although no Martine this time), Bob and Jonathan. The Bedfords were there, along with some of this week's *gîte* guests. Ryan with Brenda and Richard. Sophie grinned at me from across the room and raised her glass in my direction.

I turned to Alain. 'You knew about this, didn't you?' I hissed.

He gave me a sheepish look. 'Knew about it. Didn't have much say in it. I've learned to do what I'm told where Rupert's concerned.'

His hangdog look made me laugh, and as a glass of wine was pushed into my hand, I figured I might as well give in and enjoy the evening. As Alain said, it was best to do as you were told where Rupert was concerned.

The sideboard groaned with nibbles that my host must have spent all day preparing while I was out of the way. I worried he might have overdone it, especially with *gîte* changeover day tomorrow, but he seemed in high spirits and I told myself that as of tomorrow morning, he was no longer my responsibility. My heart sank a little at the thought.

Jonathan ambled over and gave me a tight bear hug. 'Rupert's going to miss you, Emmy. God knows what he's going to do without you.'

'Stop making the poor girl feel guilty, you old fool,' Ellie said, coming swiftly to my rescue. 'Ignore him, Emmy. Jonathan and

Rupert are the absolute champions at emotional blackmail – as I'm sure you know by now.' She winked. 'Come and have a girly chat with me and Sophie while Jonathan gives Alain a list of all the little favours he needs doing in the next week or so.'

Alain gave me a smile as he turned fondly back to Jonathan, and I allowed myself to be dragged across the room.

Sophie kissed me on both cheeks. 'Did you have a lovely day?' When I couldn't help but grin, she squealed. 'I knew it!'

Ellie shook her head. 'The poor girl has only just got rid of one useless man,' she grumbled. 'Why everyone seems to think she needs another is beyond me.'

'But Alain is very handsome, don't you think?' Sophie asked her earnestly.

Ellie studied my date from across the room. As though he could feel her gaze lasering in on him, Alain turned and gave us a puzzled look.

'If you like that sort of thing,' Ellie agreed.

'You are not the romantic type, Miss Fielding,' Sophie chided.

'Please. It's Ellie. And no, I haven't got a romantic bone in my body, thank goodness. Needs, yes. Romance, no.' She shuddered, making us both laugh. 'Now, tell me, Sophie. Why have I never been to your hair salon when you've done such a wonderful job on Emmy's hair?'

Well, fancy that. I was beginning to warm to Ellie Fielding.

An hour or so in, the party was going great guns. Not too big to be impossible and not so small that it was just a gathering of friends. Rupert – as ever – had got it just right.

In the unlikely event of Nathan and me hosting something similar at home, people would come because they were Nathan's friends or because there was a work connection, an angle of some sort that might benefit them. My friends had nothing in common with Nathan's, so we tended not to mix them. There would be no camaraderie like there was here, with people happy to greet old friends and make new ones, embracing each other's differences.

I crossed the room to speak to the Bedfords. 'Did you have a good day today?'

'Lovely,' Caroline Bedford confirmed. 'Nothing too strenuous – just drove into Pierre-la-Fontaine for coffee and a look around, then lunch.' She smiled sheepishly. 'And then we spent the afternoon in the garden.'

'Do you have any sightseeing recommendations for us?' her husband asked.

I laughed. 'Not as many as I'd like, I'm afraid, what with helping Rupert. But I did take a lovely drive last week...' I described the day with my parents around the *château* towns. 'I'm sure Rupert would be happy to give you the itinerary in more detail. And...' I hesitated, then thought, what the heck. 'And then there's the zoo.'

'The zoo?'

'I went there today, actually. It's a wonderful place, very conservation-minded and beautifully landscaped. I think you'd like it.'

There was a loud clank of a spoon on glass.

'Ladies and gentlemen,' Rupert announced as the chatter died down. 'I would like to say a few words before I get too drunk to say what I want to say properly.'

A good-humoured chuckle rippled around the room. Some of those present obviously knew Rupert's drinking habits of old.

'First of all, welcome to my humble abode.'

At this, there was a loud snort from Jonathan who, as a pensioner, clearly lived in more straitened circumstances than his friend.

'I think you all know I'm not one for making speeches.'

He glared at Ellie's murmured 'Thank the Lord for that!' and continued undaunted.

'But since I *am* making one on this occasion... Firstly, I would like to apologise to those of you who don't know me well for having to put up with this outpouring' – he nodded at the Bedfords and the *gîte* guests – 'and secondly, at the risk of embarrassing you all, I would like to say how grateful I am to have good friends around me at such a difficult time.'

I glanced around at the array of bewildered faces staring back at their host, a man who was not renowned for sentimentality or any show of emotion.

'However, the main reason for breaking my embargo on speeches,' he carried on, 'is that I would like to propose a toast to my very own angel, Emmeline Jamieson.'

He winked at me, and I spluttered at the combination of being the subject of his toast and his use of my much-hated name in front of all these people.

'Emmy has just gone through the hardest time of her life,' he said, all trace of joking gone. 'And yet she has rallied round a man she barely knew to help him through the hardest time of *his* life. She is one of the friendliest, most unselfish people I have ever met, and I can only say how privileged I feel to have been at the receiving end of her warmth and generosity.'

He paused for a moment as though deciding whether to go on. 'At the risk of making you all nervous by becoming sentimental... I never had children. I'm well aware that every single one of my friends knows I would have made a terrible parent, and they'd be right. But if I'd ever had a daughter, I couldn't be more proud of her than I am of Emmy. And in the absence of being able to adopt her, I hope she will continue to be my friend for many years to come, however she chooses to map out her future.' He raised his glass. 'To Emmy.'

The echo came back. 'To Emmy.'

I would have curled up and died of embarrassment if it wasn't for the genuine way in which everyone responded, whether they knew me or not. Rupert may have been many things, but the one thing that was indisputable was that he was much-loved by his friends. Despite my discomfort at being the centre of unwanted attention, I knew that if there really were vibes in the atmosphere, all those coming my way were positive and heartfelt.

With the moment over and no way to segue from awkward silence to casual conversation, Rupert was saved by Bob, who declared it a moment for a professional photographer. He shot outside to his motorbike for his camera and returned to take several group photos, by which time everyone had relaxed into easy-going chatter again.

My face flushed from all the attention, I escaped into the kitchen. Away from my fifteen minutes – or fifteen seconds – of fame, I gave into the many mixed emotions storming around my system and burst into tears.

I didn't doubt for a minute that Rupert's speech had been genuine and heartfelt. If I hadn't been sure of that, I might have been suspicious that it was yet another ploy to add to his grandiose plans for my moving to France and his clumsy attempts at matchmaking. I wished he could see past his selfish motives and try to understand that he wasn't helping me cope with going back home to a presumably empty flat and stressful job and to face all my family and friends, by being as busy as a bee in the background, putting ridiculous notions of sunny hotel management and rather moreish accountants into my head.

Hearing a soft footfall behind me, I assumed it was Rupert. The last thing I wanted was to hurt his feelings by letting him think he'd upset me after such a lovely speech. In a panic, I swiped at my eyes with a tissue and turned to flash a beaming smile his way. But it wasn't Rupert. It was Alain.

'That smile isn't going to fool anybody,' he said gently.

'I thought you were Rupert.'

'He's busy ordering Bob and his camera around. Are you okay?'

'I'm fine.' I promptly burst into tears again.

He hesitated. 'Do you need a hug? Or do you want me to back off?'

'Hug,' I sniffled, lurching towards him as he folded his arms about my shoulders, towering over me so my head landed somewhere in the middle of his chest, where I sobbed until I realised I'd drenched his shirt with tears and possibly less desirable substances. Recovering myself enough to wipe my nose on the tissue before pulling away, I took a step back and hiccupped away any remaining tears.

'I'm so sorry,' I said, mortified. 'I don't know what's the matter with me. PMS on top of everything else, I think.' I winced and bit my lip. 'Sorry. Too much information.'

Alain inclined his head in a bemused gesture. 'That's okay. If Rupert's going to go getting all sentimental, he should at least make an effort to fit in with your hormones.'

I stared in horror at his chest. 'I'm sorry,' I said again. 'Look at your shirt. What will people think?'

Alain glanced at the spreading damp patch on the dark blue fabric. 'I could have spilled my drink. Don't worry about it. And stop apologising.'

'Sorry.'

He rolled his eyes and stepped nearer again, lifting his thumb to wipe under my eyes. 'Mascara,' he explained.

'Do I look like a panda?' I asked him anxiously.

'The truth?'

'Yes.'

'No. You look vulnerable and beautiful.'

I gaped at him, wide-eyed, as a wave of raucous laughter drifted in from the lounge.

'Come along, Emmeline Jamieson.' He tugged at my hand. 'You're missing your own party.'

As we walked back in, Alain retrieved his sparkling water from the sideboard and knocked against Ellie, successfully coating himself – but not Ellie or there would have been bloodshed – in the exact same spot where I'd shed my copious tears, bless him.

Only Rupert seemed suspicious of Alain's clumsiness – I saw him suppress a smile. Meddler. I wouldn't put it past him to have deliberately made me cry in the hope Alain would come after me and fold me in his arms and... Oh. Hmm.

Sophie found me not long afterwards. 'Are you okay? I would have come after you, but Alain got there first.' She was smirking.

'Don't you start,' I chided.

She plastered an innocent look across her face. 'So. What happened today?'

'We went to the zoo.'

She slapped my arm. 'You know what I mean. Anything exciting? A kiss, maybe?'

My blush told her everything she needed to know. 'Ah. Romance!' Her face fell. 'But you are going home tomorrow.'

'Yes.'

'And if you weren't...?'

I gave her the titbit she wanted. 'Then maybe.'

She nodded sadly, then looked at her watch. 'I have to go. An early appointment tomorrow.' Throwing her arms around me, she squeezed tight. 'I will miss you, Emmy. When you walked into my salon last week, I had no idea there would be so much excitement! *So* much more interesting than Madame Fournier's dog having puppies or Madame Laurent's husband's attempt to build a garage. You will come back soon?'

I nodded, unable to speak. My throat was clogged with tears.

By eleven o'clock, the party was still in full swing and I began to worry. I had to get up early for the ferry and Rupert had a busy day ahead, but there was no sign of anyone leaving yet.

I found Alain talking to Jonathan. 'You two. I need your help.'

Jonathan frowned. 'Of course, love. What is it?'

'We need to start breaking up the party, or Rupert's going to be exhausted tomorrow. Either of you ready to go home yet?'

Jonathan smiled. 'Your concern for Rupert is touching, Emmy.'

I rolled my eyes. 'Yes, well, it's not as selfless as you think. I have to get up at six in the morning.'

Alain nodded. 'What do you say, Jonathan? Ready for beddy-byes if I give you a lift home?'

Jonathan gave an exaggerated yawn. 'Guess I am pretty tired. Better go tell our host.'

'That's the idea.' I beamed at them. 'Be really loud about it, so people take the hint.'

Off they went to say goodbye to Rupert, Jonathan hamming it up all the way there and back. He should have been in amateur dramatics. Maybe he had been, once upon a time.

As I saw them to the door, I was gratified to hear a couple of murmurs along the same lines from other guests.

I popped a kiss on Jonathan's cheek. 'Well done. You're a star.'

He blushed and kissed me back. 'Take care of yourself, Emmy. Keep in touch. Give me your car key, Alain.'

'What for?'

'Takes me ages to get in that tiny thing. You two can stay here for a minute while I battle with it.'

Shaking his head, Alain handed him the key and watched him shuffle down the steps and across the gravel. 'He's as bad as Rupert. I'm not sure which of them should get the prize for interfering.'

I grinned. 'They mean well, though.'

'Yes, they do.'

He turned to me, all trace of joking gone. His eyes were hypnotising in the light from the doorway, golden flecks shimmering amongst the brown. We looked at each other for a long moment, and then he leaned towards me and cupped my neck in his hand as he drew me to him. His kiss was soft and gentle, and his lips felt so perfect on mine that I could have wept for joy at finding him and sorrow at losing him already. I allowed myself that small moment of bliss before pulling away.

'Bye, Alain.'

'*Au revoir*, Emmy.'

My alarm jolted me out of a fitful sleep at six for the drive to Calais. Despite not getting to bed until well after midnight by the time I'd cleared up after the party, I wanted to allow plenty of time for getting lost, tail-to-tail traffic jams, the car breaking down, a tyre blowout or any other manner of possible travel catastrophes.

Rupert had scoffed at my planned departure time, but when I wouldn't budge, he only said, 'Maybe that's best. Whatever you're comfortable with, love. *Bon voyage*.' Then he'd kissed my cheek and headed off to his room without another word. He knew there was more than practicality behind my early start. An emotional goodbye in the morning would be hell for both of us.

All I had to do was shower and dump the last few things lying around into my bag. When I scanned the room that had been my home for the past three weeks, the empty furniture stared back at me, lifeless and uncluttered, ready for the next guests.

I crept downstairs and out to the car. As I opened the boot to toss my bags in, I looked around me one last time. It was getting light, and I knew there would soon be dappled sunlight pushing through green leaves to twinkle on the gravel. Brightly-coloured flowers, climbing vines, fragrant roses, birds chattering, bees zinging, chickens clucking.

My throat closed over. Panicked, I heaved my chest in an attempt to drag air into my lungs, but it felt like they were shut tight. I clutched at the car door, lowered myself into the seat and pulled on my seat belt. Still, I could barely breathe. The engine spluttered to life, shattering the early morning peace, and I set off across the courtyard, down the drive, onto the lane. Half a mile down the road, I pulled into a lay-by, clambered out and dropped to all fours, gulping in the air that *La Cour des Roses* had denied me.

A car pulled up behind me and a middle-aged man in a business suit rushed out. *'Est-ce qu'il y a un problème, Madame?'*

'Non, merci. Merci beaucoup,' I managed between gasping breaths, standing shakily. Since my French didn't stretch to explanations of lack of oxygen or the symptoms of panic attacks, I resorted to thumping my chest in a dramatic manner and then forced a smile to show my kind Samaritan that all was well now. He touched my arm, judging whether it was safe to leave me, then smiled back and climbed into his car.

I did the same. As I navigated the junction onto the main road and picked up speed, my chest felt as though someone had opened it up and sewn a stone inside in place of my heart.

Remarkably, considering my frame of mind, I managed to get myself to Calais in plenty of time without running out of petrol or detouring to Germany. I drove onto the ferry without plunging into the sea, and parked bumper-to-bumper in that terrifying way they insist on without rear-ending the car in front. I even had the presence of mind to memorise which level and staircase I was at.

This was one good thing about Nathan's absence, I supposed. Since he'd buggered off, I'd been forced into doing things for myself again, and in the spirit of finding a silver lining, I told myself it was good for me. Sink or swim. Although come to think of it, that wasn't such a good expression, considering my current mode of transport.

I stood out on deck for the ferry's departure, my stomach leaden and my heart hollow. Logic told me I should be relieved to be returning to the familiar, but my heart told a different story. The feeling that I was being wrenched from newfound friendship and solidarity, from a place that had felt more like home in the past three weeks than my own flat had for the past three years, was suffocating. As the French coast slipped further into the distance and I was drawn inexorably towards my homeland, I clutched the rail with white knuckles, gulping in sea air until I could taste salt on my tongue, praying this sort of thing was only a temporary blip.

When my breathing reached a more acceptable level, I became conscious that I was taking in more second-hand smoke than fresh air. Weaving my way through the windswept figures clutching their cigarettes, I went back inside in search of caffeine. My purchase did little to lighten my mood. As I sat nursing the plastic cup, all I could do was compare it with Rupert's magic brew and sulk.

Scrabbling in my copious bag for a tissue, my hand closed around an unfamiliar object and I pulled out a small package. Puzzled, I turned it over in my hand, until curiosity got the better of me and I pulled off the ribbon and tissue to reveal a neat black box.

I lifted the lid and gasped. A pendant glinted back at me – the head of a rose, crafted in white gold, with a tiny diamond at its centre.

A note was tucked into the lid. Unfolding it, I immediately recognised Rupert's familiar letterhead and scruffy handwriting.

Dear Emmy,

Don't be mad with me – I know it's an unspoken sin to go into a woman's handbag uninvited. I wanted to give this to you in person, but in the end, I took the coward's way out. Please accept it as a token of my appreciation for all you've done. I hope it will remind you of La Cour des Roses... And I also hope it might make you think about coming back someday soon.
Much love and gratitude,
Rupert.

Blinking hard to stop the tears pricking at the back of my eyes, I fingered the pendant. It was exquisite – a simple, elegant design. Spotting the jeweller's address printed inside the lid, I realised Rupert must have bought it on our final foray into town. How he'd found something so appropriate, I had no idea. And I'd been sitting in the café nursing my grudges while he chose something so beautiful for me.

I knew he wasn't happy that I'd refused payment for the work I'd done, but he shouldn't have spent money on such an expensive gift instead. Still, as I lifted it from its box, fastened the chain around my neck and felt the weight of the rose against the hollow of my throat, all desire to be cross with him vanished. Instead, I chose to enjoy the thought that had gone into the gift and what it represented to me.

Friendship. A place that was dear to my heart. Somewhere I knew I would always be welcome. Newfound confidence in myself, and the welcome rediscovery of aspects of my old self that had somehow gone missing for a while.

Arriving home was a surreal experience. I'd set off on holiday with a boyfriend, and here I was battering my way back into the apartment without one. It felt like a chapter of my life had started and not been finished properly.

Kicking the post out of the way, I staggered to the bedroom, threw the suitcase and bags onto the bed and looked around. Everything was exactly the way we'd left it the morning we set off, from the tick list of things to remember still wedged in the mirror frame to the unwashed water glasses on the bedside table.

Taking a deep breath, I flung open the wardrobe doors. Half of Nathan's things were gone. His business suits and shoes. That ludicrous electric rotating tie rack his mother had bought him for Christmas. His laptop from the safe place under his jumpers on the shelf.

Nathan was back from France, then. Where was he living? Was he still with Gloria, or had they already tired of each other? Did he wonder where I was when he came to get his stuff and found the flat untouched and empty? I hated that he'd left me with so many questions.

Dazed, I wandered into the kitchen to put the kettle on. A note was propped against it. I picked it up with shaking fingers.

Emmy,

Not sure where you are right now - I can only presume still in France, as all your stuff is still here.

I thought it only fair to let you know that I've resigned and moved to a job in London. I'll be in touch about the flat and the rest of my stuff when the dust has settled.

Hope you are well.

Regards,

Nathan.

I wasn't sure whether to laugh or cry. He thought it only fair to let me know? He hoped I was well? *Regards?* After five years together, how much more impersonal could he get?

The content of his note filtered through to my overtired brain cells. He'd quit work and moved to London. How had he got another job so quickly? Why wasn't he working out his notice at our place?

Taking a deep breath, I let it out with a whoosh. The thing I'd dreaded most – tiptoeing around him at work under the scrutiny of all our colleagues – was no longer a threat. Whatever he was playing at, he'd done me a favour.

And then an awful thought struck me. What if he'd done a more thorough job of leaving me than I thought, and had emptied our joint bank account?

Feeling sick, I rushed to the bedroom, dug out my laptop and charger and fired it up, holding my breath as I logged in.

No negatives or overdraft charges, thank goodness – only the usual direct debits, my own cash withdrawal the third week in France and a couple more which must have been made by Nathan. I looked at the dates. One the day after he left me, the other the following Friday. So, he'd stayed in France for the whole of that second week. I frowned. I might be none the poorer, but I was also none the wiser.

Rejecting the instant coffee granules in the cupboard with a shudder worthy of a true Frenchwoman, I made black tea – no milk in the fridge – and moved through to the lounge to sit on the sofa, listening to the silence fill the space.

I glanced around the room. It was like seeing it for the first time, and I was surprised to find that I didn't like what I saw. How was it possible to walk out of this place three weeks ago, loving its sleek, modern minimalism, only to walk back in now and find it soulless and so damned unwelcoming? I got up and paced around, trying to get the feeling back – the feeling that I was home – but it was like viewing a show home, as though it had nothing to do with me any more.

I told myself it was late. I was exhausted. I would feel differently tomorrow.

But that feeling stayed with me for the rest of the weekend. I couldn't shake it off. On Sunday morning, I made a start on the chores and unpacked. As I stuffed dirty laundry into the washing machine, a bundle of grey fur caught my eye and I rescued the gibbons from a watery death just in time. Clutching them to me, I closed my eyes to concentrate on the memory of Alain's face so close to mine in the shelter at the zoo. The noise of the rain pounding on the roof. The colour of his eyes. The feel of his lips on mine. If only...

Stroking my inanimate friends apologetically, I carried them through to the bedroom to sit them on the pillow next to mine. Nathan's pillow. The gibbons would probably be better company than he'd been the last few months – at least they wouldn't sulk or ignore me when I tried to talk to them.

CHAPTER TWENTY-ONE

By Sunday night, there was still no word from Nathan. That was fine by me. I had more pressing concerns, namely the hurdle of returning to work. What had he told them in his resignation letter? Would our colleagues realise we'd split up? Well, I'd find out soon enough.

I did, however, get a call from Kate, back from sunning herself in the Maldives with her man.

'Was it spectacularly wonderful?' I asked her.

'Oh, Emmy, it was fabulous. Five star hotel, wonderful beach, great food... Lots of sex. How about you?'

I snorted out a laugh. 'You're asking me how much sex I had on holiday?' *Little does she know.*

'No, silly. I got your text saying you were staying another week. What's all that about? Shall I come round?'

I needed smiles and sanity and wine. 'God, yes.'

Two hours later, we were curled on the sofa with a bottle of white, and Kate was up to speed on everything – and I mean everything. Even Ryan and Alain. It was such a relief to be able to talk to someone who knew me inside out, without worrying about the consequences. Laughter and tears ensued.

'God, Emmy. Can't I leave you for two minutes without your life turning upside-down?' she concluded.

I laughed. 'Doesn't look like it.'

She fingered the pendant at my throat. 'That is so beautiful! Rupert must think an awful lot of you.' She hesitated. 'This proposal of his, for want of a better word. You say it's mad, but are you secretly considering it, somewhere in that twisted subconscious of yours?'

Like I said – she knew me too well.

'I'm trying hard not to,' I told her. 'I mean, it's in there, but I'm trying to keep it buried. My common sense is telling me it's idiotic. But Rupert says I should "follow my heart".' I made quote marks in the air.

'And what does your heart say?'

I shook my head. 'I'm refusing to listen to it right now. I need to get back to work, Kate. At least I won't have to face Nathan there, but it's still going to be pretty weird. I have a presentation coming up. I can't afford to let my mind wander off into the clouds.'

'And what about Alain?'

I glared at her. 'What about him?'

'Come on, Emmy. It's obvious your fling with Ryan was just that... And I enjoyed the titillation very much, by the way. I never had you down as the type to roll around in the shrubbery!'

I swiped at her, but she carried on undaunted. 'Alain, though... Now that sounds like something with real possibilities.' She sipped her wine, then burst out laughing. 'I can't believe you've fallen for another accountant, after everything that's happened with Nathan!'

'I haven't *fallen* for him, Kate. He's just... Well, I suppose he's the sort of bloke I could see myself going out with way down the line, *if* I ever feel up to dipping a toe in the water of relationships again.' Definitely time to change the subject. 'Now, are you going to show me these sickening photos of paradise from your hols or not?'

On the commute to work on Monday morning, crushed between a man determined to read his fully-spread newspaper and an old dear who thought it was a good idea to bring her dog for a ride in rush hour, trepidation coiled in my stomach. I felt disorientated, as though I'd forgotten how to do my job. I'd never taken such a long time off before. France and Rupert and *La Cour des Roses* were still bright and colourful in my mind, while work felt blurry and faded and out-of-focus.

There were too many early birds to walk past to get to my desk, and I told myself I was only imagining the curious stares as I draped my jacket across the back of my chair. With something bordering on despair, I took in the mountain of crap dumped on my desk. I couldn't breathe. My chest felt tight. I clutched at the back of the chair. Another panic attack.

Heaven forbid I should be allowed to enjoy it in peace. Carl shot out of his office the second I'd lowered myself onto my seat.

'Emmy. Welcome back. I need a word.'

I followed him into his office, gulping at the recycled air pumped out by his permanently malfunctioning air-conditioning unit.

'Take a seat.' He sat behind his desk, his fingers drumming agitatedly on the fake wood. 'You look like crap, Emmy.'

'Thanks, Carl.' He hadn't been on any training courses for tact while I was away, then. 'Long journey, that's all.'

'Everything alright now? Your friend okay?'

So far, so good.

'Not bad, thanks. The extra week really helped. I appreciate it, Carl. I know it was inconvenient, but...'

He waved away my thanks with a flap of his hand. 'Don't worry about it, Emmy. If it couldn't be helped, it couldn't be helped. I know you'll do whatever it takes to catch up.'

I held back a sigh. Carl would make sure the full three weeks got taken off my holiday allowance, but I would still be expected to work all the hours God sent to make the time up. I didn't know why they bothered giving you a holiday entitlement at all.

'You know I will. As always.'

'Right, well, we'll need to go through everything. I'll fill you in on Dave's presentation to the Kellys, maybe later this morning. I'll let you settle in first.'

How gracious. 'Thanks.'

'There's something else.' Carl looked distinctly uncomfortable, and my heart started thumping so hard in my chest, I wouldn't have been surprised if it had broken loose and skittered across his desk. This had to be about Nathan.

'It's about Nathan.'

'Oh?' I tried for a noncommittal tone. No point in giving anything away yet. Indeed, since I had very little idea what was going on myself, there wasn't much I *could* give away.

'Emmy, you must appreciate that the extra week you took made things difficult for me, especially after the way Nathan's behaved. But I'm on your side. I've made it clear to the powers-that-be that you're a valued member of this department and must be treated as an individual. You shouldn't be tarred with the same brush as Nathan just because you live together.'

My frown became a wide-eyed stare. I was puzzled by the idea that he thought Nathan and I were still together despite Nathan's sudden move to London. Carl had always had about as much understanding of personal issues as a grain of sand, but surely even *he* must have worked it out.

'Once the dust has settled, I'm sure people will understand that his poor decisions shouldn't reflect on you,' he went on, oblivious to my consternation. 'I only hope you can cope with the extra pressure at home.'

'Extra pressure?'

'Well, I can't imagine it'll be easy with Nathan commuting to London every day. I wouldn't like to think it might put any strain on you and affect your work. We care here, but we do run a business, after all. We can only give so much leeway...' He finally faltered.

I reached for the water jug on his desk, poured myself a glass and drank shakily. 'Carl, I need you to do me a favour and answer some questions for me.'

'What for?'

I rubbed at my temples where a headache was forming. 'Just humour me for now, okay?'

'Okay.' His confusion was as transparent as mine must be. 'What do you need to know?'

'When did Nathan resign?'

'You don't *know*?'

'No. When?'

'The day after you rang me. He sent an e-mail to Derek giving his notice.'

'He's not been back in?'

'No.'

'Why isn't he working out his notice?'

Carl shifted uncomfortably in his chair. 'He's defected to a rival company, Emmy. We couldn't be seen to be chasing after him, nor could we allow him back in the office. Too dangerous.'

'I see.' Carl had practically made me beg for the extra week – and yet here they were, blithely accepting Nathan's unorthodox resignation because it suited them not to have their industry secrets exposed to a rival company. Ah, the mysteries of private enterprise.

'It's not our preferred way of going about things and he won't get a reference, of course,' Carl added, keen to stop me thinking they'd allowed Nathan to get away with murder.

Something jolted in my brain, setting off a rollercoaster of confused thoughts. Nathan had e-mailed while he was in France. How could he have got a job in London while he was still over there? With no reference?

'So how did he get the job?' Might as well ask straight out. I'd already proved I was in the dark. One more question couldn't hurt.

But Carl was beginning to tire of my questions. 'I have no idea, Emmy. I presume he must have contacts we didn't know about. Now, I think I've been patient enough. How can you not know any of this? What's going on?'

I took a deep breath and reviewed my options. There didn't appear to be many. 'Nathan and I split up while we were away.'

Carl sat up straight in his chair, shock and the desire for gossip warring openly on his face. 'You did? When?'

'The end of the first week.'

'But you said... So all you told me on the phone...'

'I didn't lie to you, Carl. I *was* staying with a friend and he *was* in genuine need. At the same time, Nathan and I separated. He went to stay elsewhere and I stayed to help the friend.'

Carl's eyes narrowed as he presumably weighed up how much he believed me. 'What on earth brought that on? You and Nathan have been together for ages!'

I hesitated. Nathan leaving the company in such a dramatic fashion must have led to a fair bit of speculation (other than by Carl, who was a complete numbskull) and I didn't mind people knowing Nathan and I were no longer together. But the ignominious nature of Nathan's betrayal was nobody's business but mine and his, and I wanted to keep it that way.

'We'd grown apart, nothing more to it than that. The holiday showed us we didn't want the same things any more.'

'That's it?'

'That's it. Happens all the time. Now, if it's okay with you, I think I should start making an effort to scale Mount Everest back there on my desk.'

'Fine. I'll be out in a bit to go through it with you.'

I rose from my chair, headed for the door, then decided a little spine was in order and turned back.

'Oh, and Carl? About Nathan and me being tarred with the same brush? I wouldn't have appreciated it even if we were still together. We weren't joined at the hip. But since we're *not* together, I won't take any crap about the way he's chosen to behave. Any discrimination against me, and I'll take it as far as I can go. Do I make myself clear?'

The shock on Carl's face was plain to see. I'd never spoken to him that way before. Usually, I allowed him to be the big boss while I chipped away making things the way I wanted them, letting him think it was his idea all along. This sort of plain speaking was not within our usual limited range, but my time away had given me three weeks' perspective. It was time to stand up for myself. Besides, since I did half his workload on top of my own, Carl couldn't afford to alienate me.

I'd barely got back to my chair when Cathy, one of the marketing assistants and unofficially my deputy, came over to perch on the edge of my desk.

'Emmy, it's great to have you back!'

'Thanks.' I grinned. 'How's it been?'

She lowered her voice. 'Bloody nightmare. Carl's been like a bear with a sore head the whole time you were away. So, how was your holiday?'

'It was okay, thanks. Hard work, you know, with this friend to look after.'

'What about Nathan's new job? Is he enjoying it?'

I took a deep breath. No doubt I was doomed to have this conversation numerous times over the next few days. Or maybe not. If Cathy relayed it back to everyone, it would save me the bother.

Might as well get it over with. 'I have no idea. We broke up.'

Her eyes went wide with shock. 'Oh my God, Emmy! We assumed he'd be commuting to London. Carl told us you'd taken the extra week to look after a sick friend!'

'I did. But Nathan and I also split up. I'm not unhappy about it, but I *am* happy for you to spread the word so I don't have to.'

I gave her a pleading look. 'Do you mind being the office gossip for a while?'

She patted my shoulder. 'You can count on me.'

I gave her a wry smile. 'Thanks. Now bugger off. I have things to do.'

At ten o'clock, Carl came out of his office to go through things – a euphemism for dumping all his deadlines and unwanted projects on me – and to discuss our follow-up plans for the Kelly account. As predicted, they had opted for the vintage route, and we needed to firm up ideas before the next presentation.

By eleven o'clock, it was as though I'd never been away. That was fine by me. I loved deadlines. I loved sinking my teeth into new projects – even Carl's unwanted ones. I was grateful to be back in a routine, corralling the mayhem on my desk into some order of priority.

At lunchtime, I stuffed a sandwich into my mouth without even noticing the filling. No more leisurely lunches followed by a quiet doze. By two o'clock, my automatic pilot was fully operational and by five o'clock, the images in my mind had switched places. Work was now stark and monochrome and highly defined, and *La Cour des Roses* was faded and discoloured, like an old instant snap from my mother's photograph albums.

But as that first week wore on, the routine lost its lustre a little. Up at six-thirty each morning, a rushed breakfast of cardboard cereal and cardboard toast, sweaty bodies jammed onto the train, raincoats smelling of soggy dogs. Daily phone calls with my mother to reassure her I wasn't suicidal. Desultory attempts at evening nourishment – beans on toast, egg on toast, a takeaway so stodgy it made me feel sick. Sick to the stomach and sick at heart, because it was so far from the vine-ripened tomatoes and fresh vegetables and creamy cheeses I'd left behind.

I told myself it was natural to feel a little down after being on holiday.

At work, I'd expected a ton of stuff to catch up on and I'd expected awkwardness once people found out about Nathan and me. I got both. But I'd also expected to settle back into the hectic days I'd always enjoyed, and that wasn't happening.

The job itself was fine – planning the presentation to the Kellys and getting the team on board, liaising with clients, troubleshooting. I liked the busyness and the challenge, same as ever.

What I didn't like was fending off curious glances from colleagues – or worse, their frankly impertinent questions about Nathan's sudden departure.

'Hi, Emmy. Nice to see you back. So sorry to hear about you and Nathan.' This from Hazel in the accounts department, on an innocent foray to the ladies'.

'Thanks.'

'Have you heard from him in London?'

Is it any of your business? 'Well, I only got back at the weekend...'

'Oh, yes. We heard you had to stay to look after a poorly friend. We *thought* it sounded odd.'

Who the hell was this collective "we"? I bristled. 'Actually, I *was* looking after a poorly friend.'

'Ah,' she said, a knowing look sliding out from under her eyelashes. 'A female friend?'

I held my temper. 'No. A male friend.' Her eyes lit up, and I hastened to put her straight. 'An *elderly* male friend.' I sent a silent apology through the ether to Rupert for referring to him as elderly, but I knew he would understand that this line of enquiry had to be stopped.

'So, who's this woman that got Nathan his new job, then?'

Talk about cutting to the chase. 'Why, what have you heard on that impressive grapevine of yours?'

'I know someone who moved to that company a couple of years ago. She rang to tell me another of ours defected to them. Got the job out of the blue, without it even being advertised. Rumour is, the woman who got him the job is a cousin of one of the directors and pulled a few strings. A friend of Nathan's, is she?'

The mystery woman she'd referred to could only be Gloria. Swallowing down nausea, I spoke mildly. 'I would hope so, if she went to all that trouble for him.'

I held onto the knowledge that the gossips would soon lose interest in me and that I had a slob session with Kate planned for Friday night.

She texted me on Thursday.

Stinking cold. Sodding air conditioning on flight, probably. Sorry can't come tomorrow. Don't want to share! Kate xx

I immediately phoned Nick, declaring my intention to grab a train down to London after work on Friday and crash out at his place for the weekend.

God love my little brother, he didn't bat an eye. 'Er – right, fine. I – uh – need to cancel a couple of things.'

'Oh, don't cancel anything for me,' I said knowingly. 'I can tag along.'

I imagined I could hear him blush. 'You know damn well you can't.'

'Nick, I don't want to spoil your weekend,' I whined.

'Don't worry, big sis, it's nothing that won't improve for the waiting. Absence makes the groin grow fonder and all that.'

I laughed. 'You're sure you don't mind?'

'You know I don't. What do you want to do?'

'Popcorn, mindless action movies, large vats of wine – oh, and some decent food for a change. No ready-meal crap. I've had my fill of that here.'

I left work dead on time, a sin punishable by death on every day except Fridays, when there was a mass exodus for the door at five o'clock.

By the time I landed at Nick's flat, which could kindly be described as bijou, I was tired and grumpy. He gave me a sympathetic hug, steered me to the sofa, propped me up with cushions, placed a large glass of Pinot Grigio in my hand, a tray of deli delicacies between us, and switched on a mayhem-ridden movie. Perfect.

While Nick tossed and turned on the sofa, I wallowed in his king-size bed and had the first proper night's sleep I'd had since arriving back in England.

On Saturday, we took the tube to the National Gallery, not because it was my favourite art museum – although I was happy to pay it at least, oh, twenty minutes' respect before I got bored – but because I liked the café there. Nick, grateful that he wasn't being dragged on a self-pity-fuelled shopping spree, happily tagged along and even paid for the coffee and fancy cakes.

'Do you like your work, Nick?' I asked him as we sat basking in the weak sunshine leaking through the windows.

'Most of the time. Depends where I'm working and what I'm working on.'

Nick did something with computers that was frankly beyond my comprehension, but I gathered he was a genius at it, because he'd already built up a fearsome reputation and operated on a consultancy basis. This netted him twice the money he would have earned working at one firm and allowed him to take as much time off as he required or could afford – with the added bonus of meeting a large number of women as he flitted from place to place like a bachelor butterfly, tasting the flowers on offer but never committing himself to one in particular.

'Why, don't you like yours?' he asked.

'Of course I do. Only...' I searched for a way to describe what I felt. 'You know how you watch an old film because you remember seeing it years ago and you loved it? But when you watch it again, it's like watching a different film altogether because you're seeing it with different eyes and it's lost something, lost that magic somehow?'

Nick nodded and put the last of his cake on my plate. He was such a sweetie. 'You could pick another movie. A brand new one.'

I polished off the cake. 'I'm a bit worried about jumping from the frying pan into the fire right now.'

'That's understandable. You've been through a lot. Maybe you just need more time to get back into things.'

'Maybe, but...' I tried to put my finger on what was wrong. 'I always thought I fitted in pretty well there. But since I got back from France, I feel like an outsider all of a sudden. I don't know whether it's to do with Nathan leaving the way he did, or people resenting the extra week's holiday I took. Marketing's okay, but people from accounts barely nod at me in passing, as though it's all my fault that Nathan did what he did.'

Nick gave me a sympathetic look. 'You're gossip of the month. They'll move onto someone else soon.'

'I'm sure you're right. But...'

Images floated into my mind. Jonathan embracing me and praising me to high heaven at the café the first time we met. Brenda and Richard, so friendly with me and my parents at the restaurant. Madame Dupont's kindly acceptance of my plight and acknowledgement of my hard work. Sophie's bubbly friendship. Rupert's kitchen full of laughter and joshing banter and goodwill.

'But?' Nick prompted.

'You know, I met a few people while I was at the guesthouse. Rupert's friends and acquaintances.'

'So?'

'Well, I can't understand how people I only met once or twice in France could be so warm and friendly and well-meaning, and yet people I've worked with for years can give me the cold shoulder and talk about me behind my back like this.' My voice hitched a little.

Nick cocked his head to one side as he thought about it. 'Maybe that has less to do with them and more to do with you.'

'What do you mean? Are you saying this is all my fault now?'

'Not at all. I'm saying they've probably always been that way, but you haven't really noticed because you were so caught up in your work or with Nathan or it wasn't directed at you.' He paused. 'You can ride it out, Emmy, but there's nothing to stop you seeing what's out there. You're good at your job. I'm sure you could find another – preferably somewhere where they appreciate you more and treat you to the occasional pay rise. And it's not as though you're tied down by Nathan now.'

'I'll think about it. But I've been at that place ever since I left university, and I've worked damned hard to get to where I am. That's a lot of time and energy devoted to one job. I'm not sure I'm ready to throw it all away yet.'

Nick shook his head. 'You're looking at it from the wrong angle, Emmy. You devoted your time and energy to developing your *career*, not necessarily that particular job. If they can't offer you promotion, then maybe it's time to find somewhere that can.'

I rolled my eyes. 'It's not an easy job market out there.'

'How about doing what I do?' He held up a hand when I snorted. 'I don't mean *exactly* what I do – obviously – but you could try going freelance. There must be loads of places that need skills like yours on a temporary basis. You'd only need to market your talents properly – which, since you're in marketing in the first place, shouldn't be that hard to do, when you think about it.'

'Hmm. It's not exactly secure, is it? Living from one contract to the next. However Nathan and I wrap things up, I'll still have rent or a mortgage to pay. Bills. Running a car. Living expenses.'

'I manage alright.'

I swiped at him. 'Yes, but you're a genius and people fall over themselves to employ you.'

Nick reached across to ruffle my hair. 'Poor, predictable Emmy. Isn't it time you took a chance for a change?'

I thought about Rupert's half-baked offer of a half-baked job, and his half-baked ideas for my half-baked business – but I suspected that wasn't quite the high-flying freelancing lifestyle Nick had in mind.

Sunday morning saw heavy rain driving against the windows, so Nick and I curled up on the sofa with a large cafetière of coffee and a brick-sized pile of Sunday papers. Solicitous of my precarious state, he'd volunteered to get drenched going to the newsagent, a gesture which made me feel much loved.

As we lounged amidst the paper pigsty, I felt an unexpected wave of regret. This was how Nathan and I had spent our Sundays. Staring unseeingly at the article I'd been reading, I willed away tears before Nick looked up from the sports section.

Too late. 'What's up?'

My chin wobbled. 'I was thinking about Nathan.'

'And?'

'This is how we spent our Sundays together.' I imagined Nathan sitting in the armchair – imagined feeling cosy and comfortable with him, a companionable silence. I closed my eyes, wallowing in self-pity.

Nick came over to put his arm around my shoulders. 'Do I detect rose-tinted specs this morning?'

Scrubbing away the tears with the back of my hand, I looked across at Nick's empty chair. Now, in my mind's eye, Nathan was oblivious to my presence, lost in the financial pages, murmuring at the odd thing I read out without looking up, not remotely interested in what I had to say. That Sunday ritual, so perfect for the first couple of years, had slowly deteriorated into an excuse to lose ourselves in our own worlds on the one day of the week when we had enough time to pay attention to each other.

I sighed. 'Maybe.'

CHAPTER TWENTY-TWO

Arriving back home late Sunday afternoon, I fired up the laptop and checked my e-mails.

Good – one from Rupert. I'd e-mailed him that first weekend to let him know I was home and to thank him for the beautiful necklace. He'd replied to say he was glad I'd got myself back in one piece, but then nothing further.

My intuition told me he was being kind, keeping his distance to give me a chance to settle back into my old life, but after a week, I'd begun to worry whether he was coping. I needn't have.

Hi Emmy,

Hope your first week back at work wasn't too monstrous.

Things are going well here. The people Madame Dupont enlisted are doing a good job. Juliette comes in on the days I have to cook, does some shopping for fresh stuff – I finally took your advice and I'm doing one Internet shop a week – and helps me prep. A girl called Émilie comes in on Saturdays to help with changeover day. Madame Dupont has taken to doing any midweek room changes herself, which is good of her, but to be honest I'm not sure how long she'll be able to keep it up. Juliette is capable but has no sense of humour, and Émilie is young and nervous. I don't think she likes me accidentally shortening her name to Emmy, but she's too shy to tell me off.

To fill my time in the evenings, I've been looking at the website as
per your instructions, and I've made a note of what needs changing.
Took some photos, too. I know you're probably up to your eyes,
so no rush.
Missing you.
Love, Rupert

I imagined him joshing around the kitchen with stone-faced
Juliette. He wouldn't give up until he dredged a smile out of
her, which would make her all the more stoical. And poor
young Émilie was probably scared stiff of him. I wasn't happy
about Madame Dupont overdoing things, but for now Rupert
had the help he needed, and that was all that mattered. He
hadn't mentioned his leg or general health, so either he was
improving and hadn't felt the need to, or he wasn't but didn't
want to worry me.

God, I missed him. I missed his jokes. His obvious fondness
for me. The banter we shared while we were cooking together.
Let's face it, with the crap I'd been eating lately, I missed his
cooking, full stop. I even missed his selfish demands – but I
comforted myself with the thought that I could go back for a
visit soon.

I opened the row of attachments. Wording to change. A copy
of the bookings spreadsheet we'd set up, so I could think about
an availability page. Several new photos.

At these, tears welled in my eyes. Furious that just looking at
La Cour des Roses could make me so homesick, I shoved my chair
back and stormed off to the kitchen for a healing herbal brew. As
I waited for the kettle to boil, I thought about Rupert's website
and sighed. It had been my idea to update it, after all, and I'd
promised to do it, even if that promise had been dragged out of
me somehow. Ah, well. Better make a start.

⬡ ⬡ ⬡

The following week at work was no better than the first, and I started to worry in earnest. I should be getting back into my stride by now.

Inexplicably blaming everything on the inadequacies of instant coffee, I splashed out on a shiny little espresso machine, praying that all my ills would be solved by a decent cup of coffee each morning. The irony wasn't lost on me that the one effort I'd made to feel more at home in good old Blighty was to replicate one of my pleasures in France – except I didn't have a huge, high-beamed kitchen in which to make it or a beautiful, lush garden in which to drink it.

I spent my evenings on Rupert's website, tackling the text and photos first. When I started on the availability page, I realised it would be a pig to do because of all the different rooms and *gîtes*. I e-mailed him with the complications and possible solutions. He e-mailed back to say he'd think about it and that Juliette was a pain in the arse.

The only bright point of the week was another text from Kate.

Germs under control. Thursday eve any good?

I texted back. *Absolutely. I don't give a sod about the germs. I need you!*

When Carl called me into his office on Tuesday, my mood was so low, I thought a bollocking couldn't make it any worse. Despite trying to concentrate on the Kelly account, I knew I'd been on the listless side and hadn't been grafting at my usual manic rate. Assuming he was panicking about tomorrow's presentation, I perched uncomfortably on the edge of a chair.

'Emmy.' He cleared his throat. 'I wondered if you were busy this evening.'

'After work?'

'Well... Yes.'

Great. More unpaid overtime. Typical Carl tactic – drag me in to haul me over the coals for not working hard enough and then ask me to stay behind, knowing I couldn't refuse if I wanted to avoid the reprimand. I arranged my features into an expression resembling something like willing.

'Nothing specific. Why? Are you worried about tomorrow?'

Carl frowned in puzzlement. 'What? Oh, no. Not at all. I wondered if you'd like to go for a drink. Maybe grab a bite to eat.'

Oh, bloody hell. I hadn't seen that one coming. The willing expression I'd plastered on my face just seconds before was suddenly horribly unfitting to the occasion, but I had no way of removing it without letting my face fall. I toned it down by tiny degrees as the pause stretched between us.

'Oh? Who's going?' I asked innocently, hoping against hope that he meant a whole crowd of us and playing for time as my mind raced. What on earth had brought this on? There had never been any indication in all the years we'd worked together! Then again, I'd been with Nathan before. Now I'd been abandoned, perhaps I was fair game in Carl's eyes.

'Er – I was hoping just the two of us, actually. What do you think?'

Crap. He was my boss. Refusing would be bad, but the idea of playing along for an easy life was too unpalatable. I had no interest in Carl whatsoever. Drinks and dinner would lead to other things I really couldn't stomach.

'I...' Damn. I'd already told him I wasn't busy. If I suddenly dreamt up a forgotten appointment with the hairdresser or the vet or the local taxidermist, he would only ask again sometime. This had to be nipped in the bud. 'I'm sorry, Carl. I don't think that's a good idea.'

His face fell and he started fiddling with the knot of his tie. I almost felt sorry for him. It must have taken quite a bit of nerve to expose himself to rejection like this. That or his hopeless inability to read others' emotions had allowed him to think he was in with a chance.

'May I ask why?'

Yes, Carl, you may. You're ten years older than me but look more like it's twenty, you've been divorced twice, your beard is scruffy and unappealing and you have no insight whatsoever into the female psyche. Not only that, but you allow me to mop up all the excess work and take all the flak, and you take all the credit.

'I don't think it's wise to mix work with pleasure,' I ad-libbed.

He frowned. 'You met Nathan at work.'

Ah, but I fancied him. He showed promise. For a while, anyway.

'Yes, but he was in another department. Besides, look how that turned out. These things are all very well until they go wrong and make everyone feel awkward.' Carl's expression was still hopeful. I couldn't bear the idea that he hadn't got the message. 'To be honest, Carl, I think I've got a long way to go before I'd feel comfortable with anything like that. It's only a few weeks since Nathan and I split up. I'm not ready to move on yet.'

'Ah. Of course. Yes. Right, well, in that case, I need to speak to you about the presentation tomorrow. The way I see it...'

I let him drone on, wondering whether he'd leave it at that or whether he'd have another go when he deemed that enough time had passed for my heart to heal. Maybe moving to France wasn't such a bad idea after all.

Still reeling over Carl asking me out, by lunchtime I was desperate to get out of the office for a while. Walking along the street with no particular destination in mind, I jumped when a hand grabbed my arm.

'Emmy! God, I haven't seen you for a while. How are you?'

Lucy used to work in the accounts department with Nathan, and although I didn't know her well, she'd always been pleasant in passing. She'd since moved on to bigger and better things as some sort of high-flying bank executive, making my career path look like a half-beaten track through the undergrowth.

'Hi, Lucy. How are you?'

'Fine. On a quick lunch break. Are you? We could grab a coffee. What do you say?'

'Sounds good.'

Lucy dragged me into the nearest café, bullied a couple who were thinking about leaving into being snappier about it, and flung her coat across a chair before anyone else could get near.

As we waited for our drinks to arrive, we batted "How are you?" and similar platitudes around for a while until I galvanised myself into enquiring about her career. She filled me in on the last eighteen months' worth of her achievements, making me feel more like a failure by the minute.

'So, how about you?' she finally asked. 'Still at the same firm? Still with Nathan?'

'Nathan and I split up, actually. He's moved to London.'

'*Really?* But you two seemed so right for each other!'

I frowned. 'Did we?'

'Of course. Working at the same place since forever. That lovely flat of yours.' *Being so bloody boring together*, she might as well have said, since it was clearly what she was thinking. 'It was all so perfect, wasn't it?'

'Until now,' I pointed out.

'I suppose so.' Lucy took a surreptitious glance at her watch. 'So how about work? Any promotions in the offing?'

My heart sank. It was embarrassing to admit I was still in exactly the same position she'd left me in a year and a half ago.

'No, 'fraid not.' I knew that wouldn't cut it with Lucy, so tagged on, 'I'm currently looking for a position elsewhere.' *When I get round to it.*

Lucy curled her lip. 'Well, good luck with that. God knows, it's about time you had a change, but it's not going to be easy moving companies in this economic climate. It could take you quite a while to find something.'

The bloody cheek!

'Actually, I've been asked to move to France.' It popped out of my mouth before I could stop it.

Lucy frowned. 'To *France*? To do *what*?'

Her tone of voice suggested she doubted I had any skills that might be exportable, and my hackles rose further. Shit. I'd done it now. I could hardly tell her I'd be skivvying for an ageing ex-pat, could I?

'I... It's a marketing contract,' I told her with as much conviction as I could muster. 'For a tourist business. They need hands-on help on a consultancy basis, and they're willing to help me establish my own business out there as well.' God, I was going to burn in hell for that one.

Lucy didn't bother to hide her surprise – whether about my considering a move to France or the fact that someone might want to employ me, I wasn't sure.

'Well, I can see why you might want to move companies,' she said. 'But moving to France on a whim – isn't that a bit reckless? One consultancy contract and then setting up on your own? What about financial security?'

My brain was desperately trying to tell my mouth that this was absolutely none of her business – but she was being so patronising.

'That's not guaranteed even if I stay here, is it?' I pointed out. 'People get made redundant in our business all the time.'

'But do you even speak French?'

'Actually, I speak it really well,' I exaggerated, smiling as I imagined Madame Dupont cackling at the suggestion.

I drained my coffee, stood and grabbed my jacket. 'Well, it's been nice seeing you again, Lucy. Take care.'

Wednesday's presentation to the Kellys was the first I'd been so nervous about in a long time. I felt that I had a great deal to prove. It was me they asked for every time, me they trusted. In the past, they had never been entirely happy with our proposals, going along with them half-heartedly because they paid us good money to come up with ideas, knew our reputation and trusted my judgement. But the fact that they were never quite on board meant the results were never what they might be. I was thrilled they had decided to go along with our vintage theme – but it felt like a last ditch attempt, somehow, and as I'd already told Carl, it was quite a gamble.

Gamble or not, it went down a storm. The Kelly brothers were happy that we were playing on an aspect of their company they were comfortable with and proud of, and the younger generation were happy that their elders were finally enthusiastic about *something*. There was a lot of work ahead, but at least we all agreed that we were finally targeting the right markets with the right advertising and exposure.

'I hear it went well,' Cathy said as we took five minutes for lunch at our desks. 'I'm not sure Carl was convinced about your tactics, but you pulled it off as usual. Here. Have a cream cake to celebrate.' She pushed a plate in front of me. 'Been keeping it in the fridge all morning for you.'

'Thanks.' I sounded flat and tried to smile. I couldn't understand it – I usually got such a buzz from a success like that, but this time the buzz wasn't forthcoming.

'Is everything alright?' she asked, frowning. 'I would have thought you'd be floating on the ceiling after this morning!'

Shit. Is it really so obvious? I shrugged. 'So would I. Maybe I'm just tired.'

'Emmy, I hope you don't mind me asking, but did something happen in France? Other than splitting up with Nathan, I mean.'

Oh, something happened all right. I fell in love. With a place, and everything that goes with it.

◉ ◉ ◉

The day was not made any better when I was foolish enough to answer my mobile without checking caller display. Before I could get my bearings, my mother had elicited a promise from me that I would allow myself to be fed and watered at their house after work. Apparently, my daily phone calls weren't enough to reassure her with regard to my wellbeing, and she wanted to see for herself that I was still vaguely in the land of the living.

I wasn't likely to convince her. I still felt queasy after Carl's proposition and Lucy's snide attitude, so I couldn't say I was looking forward to an evening of fielding my mother's interrogations.

When I arrived late – as usual – Mum tutted at my lack of punctuality as she brought food to the table. Under the accurate illusion that I lived off convenience food and takeaways and might expire if I didn't have a decent home-cooked meal every so often, she always went to a great deal of trouble when she had the chance to cook for me.

'Well? Any news?' she demanded, as she loaded my plate with the carefully-planned vitamins and minerals that must last me until the next time she fed me.

Knowing she wouldn't be fobbed off with minutiae, I gave her the Carl-asking-me-out story as a titbit to get her teeth into. She enjoyed it and batted it around for a while, but it clearly wasn't going to suffice.

'I went to see Nick at the weekend,' I proffered.

'Oh? Any reason?'

I shrugged. 'I fancied the company, and I didn't want to stay in the flat on my own.'

'Why not?'

'I don't like it any more,' I admitted.

'What are you going to do about the flat, Emmy?' Dad asked.

'I can't afford to stay there on my own. Rupert thinks I should persuade Nathan to rent it out.'

Dad considered for a moment. 'Rupert's got a good head on his shoulders. I think he's probably right – if you and Nathan can sort it out amicably.'

'I think we can, if only because it's in both our best interests.'

'Well, then, perhaps you need to get in touch with Nathan sooner rather than later.' When I pouted, he pointed his fork at me. 'You'll feel better once it's done.'

I sighed. Dad was right. Nathan was hardly likely to carry on paying his half of the mortgage when he was no longer living there.

My shoulders sagged in defeat. 'Maybe at the weekend.'

Back home, when I checked my e-mails, there was one from Jonathan, of all people.

Hello, Emmy,

Hope you don't mind – I got your e-mail address from Rupert. Using Bob's laptop to send this. Bumped into him in the bar yesterday and we were wondering how you're getting on. Rupert says you're fine and to leave you alone, but we don't trust him. Besides, Bob wanted to send you the pictures he took at the party. He's attached them, he says – no idea what the hell he's talking about, but I hope you get them.

Hope you're settling in okay. Don't leave it too long before you come back to see us.

Love, Jonathan x

P.S. Called into Alain's office this morning to give him your e-mail address in case he didn't already have it. He looked pretty glum. How much damage can two people do to each other on a visit to the zoo?

I smiled. Jonathan, the old fool. I pictured him propping up the bar at his favourite café, swapping tall tales with the owner, and shook my head at the way he had everyone running around after him, giving him lifts and doing his errands – errands he would have *me* do for a paltry wage if he and Rupert had their way, the scheming duo.

Sipping at my tea, I thought about Rupert's offer and how swiftly I'd rejected it as unrealistic. Two weeks ago, that had seemed the right thing to do. Two weeks ago, I was still under the illusion that I loved my job and everything would fall back into place. But after the Kelly presentation today, I was beginning to wonder. I should have been over the moon – it couldn't have gone any better – but all I felt was mild satisfaction.

And after Carl asking me out yesterday, I might have to look for a new job sooner rather than later. The thought of us awkwardly dancing around each other was more than I could stand.

Would it be such a terrible thing to move to France? It didn't have to be forever. I had savings. I could go over for the peak season, help Rupert out, see how things went and if it didn't look viable, I could always come back. Hmm.

I re-read Jonathan's e-mail. It sounded like Alain was moping, after all. I hadn't suggested we keep in touch – although it wouldn't have surprised me if he'd wheedled my details from Rupert – but it seemed he was playing the martyr for my sake, bless him.

Allowing myself a few moments of self-indulgence, I remembered his smile and cinnamon eyes; imagined what could happen between us if I was in a position to allow it to. My gut instinct told me that Alain was settled in his own skin, with nothing to prove – that he would treat me well if I gave him the chance, maybe even cherish me. Yet another temptation calling to me from across the Channel.

Straightening my spine, I opened Bob's attachments. They had what I presumed was the desired effect of brightening my mood. Happy, smiling faces. Ellie with Philippe. Jonathan with his arm around Rupert. Alain. One of me with Sophie. I looked happy and relaxed and was wearing barely any make-up. I hardly recognised myself.

When Carl called me into his office on Thursday afternoon, my heart sank. Surely the Kellys hadn't changed their minds already?

'Emmy. I... realise I made a mistake asking you out earlier this week, and I'd like to apologise. I wouldn't want it to make things awkward between us.'

Should've thought of that before you did it, then. I drummed up a reassuring smile. 'That's okay. Let's just draw a line under it, shall we?'

He looked relieved. 'Thank you. I appreciate it, especially since I was in a meeting with the directors this morning...'

Oh God. Sounds serious.

'...and we were discussing you.'

Gulp.

'I told them all about the Kelly presentation. They're thrilled that we're finally making headway with the account.' He shuffled uncomfortably in the chair. 'I also spoke to... someone... in accounts yesterday. She – I mean, the person I spoke to – had a call from Lucy. I gather you might be considering leaving us.'

The traitorous... 'That was an informal conversation, Carl. I...'

He held up a hand. 'I'm sure. But it only confirmed what I was already worried about. I spoke to the directors about it this morning...'

Oh God, no.

'...and I told them we can't afford to lose you.' You work hard, your judgement is sound, our clients think you're the best thing since sliced bread – and you support me to the hilt.'

Ah. Now we were getting down to it. Carl was scared of losing his workhorse.

'To that end, in recognition of your valued input to the company, they would like you to consider the new position of Team Manager.'

When I simply stared at him open-mouthed, he hastily added, 'Which carries with it, of course, a very respectable pay rise. You and I both know you perform that role pretty much, anyway – but this would cement your seniority over the team and give you more scope. And as the agency expands, then hopefully the team will grow. What do you think?'

Great? Crap? I wasn't sure. The words "Five weeks too late" sprang to mind.

'Gosh, Carl, that's quite a bombshell. Unexpected. And kind of you, to push for it for me. I don't know what to say.' *Literally.*

Assuming in his usual hopeless way that I was overwhelmed with gratitude, Carl shook his head. 'No need, Emmy. Now, I know you won't really need to think about it, but as a matter of form, the directors have asked for your confirmation by the beginning of next week. Is that okay?'

I plastered on a beaming smile. 'Of course. Thanks.'

Kate's slightly germ-ridden appearance on Thursday was like someone throwing a lifebelt to my sanity.

She kicked off her shoes and curled up in the corner of the sofa, patting the cushion beside her. 'Sit! Tell Aunty Kate all about it.'

At which, I promptly burst into tears.

She mopped and soothed and quietly absorbed my garbled tale of my boss asking me out and the promotion and pay rise and how, even though my presentation was a raging success, I still felt like shit and I missed Rupert and I didn't know what was happening to me...

When I ran out of steam, she coaxed wine through my quivering lips. 'God, Emmy. What the hell are you going to do?'

I shook my head, spent. 'I don't know. I feel like I've been on some sort of hamster wheel, but it was a hamster wheel designed by me and Nathan as a couple. Now we're not together, I don't need to stay on it any more. But I don't know where to take it from there.'

'What about the promotion? Isn't it what you've been working towards?'

'Of course! I'd officially be in charge of the team, I'd have more say, and if the agency does well, that role could grow.'

'And don't forget the money,' Kate added.

'God, yes. That would make such a difference, now I'm not half of a joint income with Nathan.'

'Maybe you could even keep the flat?'

'Hmmph. Wouldn't want to. But it might mean I could afford something passably decent on my own.'

'And yet I'm not sensing the joy here, Emmy. Are you still thinking about going back to France?'

I shrugged. 'Part of me thinks I'd be bonkers to even consider it. Especially with a pay rise and a promotion in the offing.'

'Would you enjoy managing Rupert's business for him, do you think?'

'I enjoyed it while I was there, but maybe that's only because it was a novelty. Alain thinks I might get a little bored after a while – but that setting up my own business would give me more of a challenge.'

'Hmm. And about Alain. Would you consider starting a relationship with him?'

I closed my eyes for a moment. Saw his eyes, the way he looked at me when we said goodbye. 'I know he would like to give it a go.'

Kate shook her head. 'I asked if *you* wanted to.'

'Yes, I would. But my common sense is telling me not to go down that road again in a hurry.'

'Why?'

I sighed. 'My whole life, I've gone with the flow. University, dating, getting a job, meeting Nathan, moving in with him... I'm beginning to think I didn't make any choices at all – I just let it all happen. I think that's why I can't get excited about the promotion. It's more of the same, isn't it? Being swept along in the stream.' I sighed. 'I want my next relationship to come out of a conscious decision, not just let it happen by accident.'

She gave me a sympathetic smile. 'Trouble is, we can't always control when we meet someone, can we? Besides, isn't that what you're trying to do now? Make a conscious decision?'

'Yes, but that's not so easy with everything all jumbled up in my head.'

'Then unravel it. You tackle things like this at work all the time. Make a list of pros and cons. Give everything a mark out of ten for how important it is to you.' She gave my arm a nudge. 'I expect to be a ten, by the way.'

'Twenty, more like.' Tears pricked at my eyes. 'Would you visit me? If I moved?'

'What, with sunshine, fantastic food and sexy young gardeners on offer? You couldn't keep me away!'

CHAPTER TWENTY-THREE

An hour later, we'd worked our way through a large bag of tortilla chips, another glass of wine – and we had our list in Kate's neat, rounded handwriting.

She laid out the sheets on the coffee table in front of us. 'Interesting exercise, putting it in black and white, don't you think?'

She waited as I stared. The pros column was substantially longer than the cons. I genuinely hadn't expected that – especially since I'd played devil's advocate the whole time.

'So how's that jumble in your head doing now?' she asked.

'It's still there, only now it's bigger and on paper.' I sighed. 'What if I go out there and it's all a total disaster?'

Kate put a hand on my arm. 'Crikey, it's not a life sentence, Emmy. Nobody's buying you a one-way ferry ticket and forbidding you re-entry! You could try it, and if it didn't work out, you could come back.'

'Except then I'd be a lot worse off.'

'Not necessarily.'

'What, after giving up a good job and turning down a promotion?'

Kate shook her head. 'You'd just have to play on your time abroad as a valuable step in your career.'

'Yeah, right. So when I'm at an interview and they ask what I've been doing for the past... year, say, what am I supposed to answer? That I've been making beds and stabbing around in the dark trying and failing to set up a business?'

'You tell them the truth – that you took up the opportunity to manage a different kind of enterprise and to widen your experience of marketing on the continent, allowing you to add to your skills whilst reassessing your priorities and career.'

'God, Kate, you talk shit sometimes.'

'Ha! *You're* the one in marketing, not me!'

Nathan finally got in touch. In person. He didn't even ring the doorbell, the cheeky sod – just used his key, as though he had every right in the world to invade my space.

I'd sloughed off my work day in the shower, allowing extra time and posher products because it was Friday, and I'd just pulled on old trackies and a sweatshirt when I heard the noise. I assumed it must be burglars, and my heart started thumping in my chest so hard I thought I might have a heart attack.

In a panic, I raked my eyes over the junk corner of the bedroom for a weapon. Nathan's bowling ball looked too heavy and unwieldy, and I didn't think the semi-deflated exercise ball would cut it. Grabbing my old hockey stick, I crept down the hall and sprang into the lounge wielding my weapon of choice.

Nathan threw his hands defensively over his head. 'Emmy, it's only me! There's no need for violence!'

He looked so pathetic that fear gave way to amusement, and I started to laugh.

'I don't see what's so damned funny. You could have hit me!'

For a brief moment, I struggled to put on a straight face more suited to the occasion, but then it dawned on me that after weeks of no contact other than one curt note, he'd let himself in without phoning or even ringing the bell. Suddenly, that straight face wasn't so hard to find.

'You should have phoned first. How was I supposed to know you weren't some intruder?' That was exactly how I felt about him. An intruder.

'I shouldn't have to phone first.' His chin set in that stubborn pose he had. I used to think it was cute. Now, I couldn't for the life of me remember why.

'Of course you should, you arrogant bastard! I can't believe you let yourself in here like that!'

Nathan looked taken aback. 'What the hell's got into you?' He held up a hand in a conciliatory gesture. 'Okay, I could have phoned first. But it's my flat, too. I have every right to be here.'

'You have a *right* to be here? What right? Are you referring to legal or moral right? Because you relinquished all moral right to waltz in and out of here the day you drove off with Gloria. You left me high and dry. I had to look after an invalid *and* run his business for him, I had Mum and Dad flying over to find out what the hell was going on thanks to your interfering mother, *and* I had to make Carl furious by staying out there an extra week. That was how I spent *my holiday,* Nathan.'

'You didn't have to look after Rupert, Em. I don't see how you can blame me for that – it was your choice.'

Absolutely incredible.

'Did you honestly think I could walk away from a mess like that when it was my own boyfriend who caused it? You took away Rupert's wife when he needed her most, so yes, you were to blame, and no, I didn't have a choice, not being a selfish, heartless bastard like you!'

This was exhausting. I wanted to stop shouting now. My throat was sore.

'Anyway, it's all water under the bridge,' I said flatly, all anger spent. 'You went. I stayed. And it wasn't so bad, after all.'

'Oh? You and old Rupert became a bit of an item, did you?' His face had the edge of an ugly sneer about it.

It made me sick to the stomach. 'No, Nathan, we didn't. We became friends. There's a world of difference.'

'Friends, my arse. You can't tell me you spent all that time out there washing his socks and helping him to his bedroom without...'

'Shut up, Nathan.'

I couldn't stand this conversation any longer. I wanted it to end. I slapped his face.

The sound reverberated in the room. Nathan's eyes were wide with shock. So were mine.

He rubbed at the ugly red marks on his cheek. 'What the hell was that for?'

I felt sick. Sick at the marks, sick at my behaviour, sick at what we'd been reduced to.

'If you have to ask, then we have nothing more to say to each other.'

It was a prime exit line. All he had to do was take the lead and walk out.

'How about a cup of tea?' he asked instead.

I stared at him in disbelief. 'A cup of *tea*?'

He walked into the kitchen, put the kettle on, reached into the cupboard for the teabags and pulled the milk from the fridge, for all the world as though he'd never been away.

I watched him from the doorway. 'I don't want tea, Nathan. I want you to leave.'

He looked at me, his brow furrowing, then his expression cleared. 'You've had your hair cut. It's nice.'

It would have been funny if it hadn't been so damned annoying. All the time we'd been a couple, I could count the number of times he'd commented on a new outfit or hairstyle on the fingers of one hand. I desperately wanted to point out the irony, but I couldn't see what purpose it would serve other than provoking another shouting match, so I settled for a weak, 'Thanks.'

Nathan handed me a mug, walked back into the lounge and settled himself on the sofa. Left with no option, I followed him, perching on the edge of the designer reading chair neither of us read in because it was so uncomfortable. I noticed his hands were shaking a little.

'I deserved the slap,' he said quietly. 'For what happened in France and for running away instead of facing up to what was going on between us.'

Fazed by this sudden change of direction and his seemingly sincere contrition, I waited with a kind of detached curiosity for what would come next.

'I didn't come here to have a row, Emmy.'

'Then what did you come here for?'

'To apologise. I know I haven't gone about things the right way.'

Talk about an understatement! I sipped my tea. It was too hot and burned my tongue. He hadn't put enough milk in. Three cups of tea a day for five years, and he still didn't know how much milk I liked.

'I know I behaved badly, but it takes two for things to go wrong,' he said. 'If we're going to work through this, we need to try and meet in the middle somewhere.'

'*What?*' I stared at him, open-mouthed, not sure I could have heard right.

'I said we need to find a way to work through this together. I've told you I'm sorry. Can't we move on?'

'You're saying you want to come *back*?'

'Yes.' There was a sureness, a cockiness in the one syllable. Not "if you'll have me" or "if that's what you want". Just a resounding "yes".

I hardly trusted myself to speak. 'So what you're saying is: you've been unhappy with our relationship for quite some time but didn't think to speak to me about it, you've slept with another woman, you've left me, you've not been in touch, you've changed jobs and moved cities, and now you want to come back. Just like that.'

A sulky look passed over his eyes and I watched with interest as he fought to control it. Nathan never liked having his shortcomings pointed out.

'No, not just like that. Of course I understand things are less than perfect, but we could still make a go of it.'

'And what about London?' I choked out. 'Your new job?'

He winced. 'I'll get something nearer as soon as I can. To be honest, I'm not enjoying it down there anyway.'

Ah, now we were getting down to it. It seemed the grass wasn't greener after all. Talking of which...

'What about Gloria?' I asked him.

He jolted and put his tea on the table, out of harm's way. 'What do you mean?'

'I mean, Nathan, what about Gloria? The woman you left me for?'

He shifted uncomfortably in his chair. 'I didn't leave you *for* her, Emmy. I left *with* her. There's a difference.'

'There is?'

'Of course there is. You and I were unhappy, Gloria and Rupert were unhappy, and after we'd... Well, it seemed sensible to go together. I didn't promise her anything.'

'But she got you your new job. That would suggest to me that you're more than a momentary convenience for each other. Or is the convenience all on your side and not hers?'

'How do you know she got me the job?'

'Come on, Nathan, ours is a pretty small world. Word gets around.' I shook my head. 'You've burned a lot of bridges. They'll never take you back at our place, and your new company won't give you a reference after just a few weeks. How do you expect to get another job up here?'

His shoulders sagged for a moment, then he straightened. 'I'll have to commute until I've been there long enough to get a reference. Or I'll lean on Derek. He owes me a favour or two. It'll work out, Emmy. I'll do whatever it takes.'

For a moment, I was impressed by his determination. He must want to come back, to give up a prime job in the capital. The burning question was: did he want to come back because he loved me? Or because his new job and his new life and his new woman weren't all he'd expected, and I was the comfortable option, the safer bet?

'You didn't answer my question,' I said quietly.

'Question? What question?'

'About Gloria. I presume you're living with her.'

'Sort of. They have that flat in Kensington, so I moved in while I got settled. It wasn't meant to be permanent.'

I couldn't believe their cheek, using Rupert's flat as their love nest. 'So you're still there?'

'For now.'

'I see. And does Gloria know it isn't meant to be permanent?'

'How do you mean?'

'I mean, Nathan, does Gloria know you've come up here to see me? That you want to come back? To work. To be with me.'

He fiddled with a stray thread on a cushion, winding it around his fingers and letting it spring back.

'No. I didn't want to upset her. She's been very supportive, sharing the flat and helping me with the job. I thought it would be better to tell her once you and I sorted ourselves out.'

I shook my head with something bordering on despair. 'My God, talk about hedging your bets! You went off with Gloria, gave her the impression you two were together, allowed her to pull strings to find you a job – and now you've come up here to ask me to take you back without even *telling* her? You didn't split up with her first?'

'No, because...'

'*Because*, Nathan, you want to come back here where it's nice and easy and safe, but if I say no, you can still go back to Gloria, pretend nothing has happened and make a go of it with the runner-up.' I laughed, but the sound came out harsh and cold. 'I can't believe I actually feel sorry for her! And I can't believe how little you're committed to making our relationship work.'

'I do want it to work,' he whined. 'I want to make a go of it. I love you.'

A cold, hollow feeling flooded my veins. All those months before the holiday when I wished he would tell me that more often, to reassure me that things weren't going sour. The nights in France after his betrayal, when I would have given anything to hear the words.

But no. He had to say them when I least expected or wanted it. I thought back to our early days when he'd told me he loved me all the time, and I felt so sad. Did he mean it now? Or did he just think he did?

The mug I'd forgotten I was holding slipped through my fingers and clattered to the floor. I watched as the steaming liquid spread across the laminate, the broken handle lying forlornly on its own in the puddle, the mug still rolling.

Nathan jumped up, fetched a towel from the kitchen and started to mop up the mess.

My lips felt numb, glued together, so I spoke through my teeth, forcing the words out. 'Why don't you leave it, Nathan?'

He looked up from where he knelt. 'What?'

'This mess. Just leave it alone.'

'I can manage. It's nearly done. What's the matter with you, Emmy? Haven't you got anything to say? I'm talking about our future.'

I looked at the man I'd once loved. 'So am I, Nathan. So am I.'

The next morning, I'd hoped for a lie-in, but when I realised that wasn't going to happen, I headed blearily to the kitchen to make an espresso. While the water hissed its way through the life-saving grains, I fired up my laptop at the kitchen table.

Dad was right – it was time Nathan and I got the flat sorted out, and since last night's conversation had gone so spectacularly pear-shaped, I figured an e-mail was the safest way to broach the subject.

Clutching my coffee, I logged on to find an e-mail from Rupert. The subject line read: *Emmy's Future*.

I almost dropped my coffee in surprise, cursing as the strong black liquid sloshed onto my white robe. Dabbing ineffectually at the stain, I opened the e-mail.

Morning, Emmy. I imagine you're huddled over a strong espresso about now.

How well he knew me. *Yes, I was, Rupert, but I've just chucked it all over myself.*

Life has been rather faded and dull since you left.

Interesting. Those were pretty much the same words I would have used to describe my own life at the moment.

We've been ticking along, though, and I've been moving about more, getting in everyone's way.

I bet you have.

The extra help is okay, but it's not the same as the way you did things. What we need is a bit of oomph around here. All the suggestions you made, all the ideas you had. I tried putting a few into place – I'm not such a lazy old sod as you think – but it would all go so much better with you at the helm. Now, before you start getting cross and tapping your foot in that aggravated way you have...

I stopped battering my foot against the laminate.

> *...I want you to read this carefully. I mean it, Emmy. Don't just glance at it and assume it's a load of old bollocks from an interfering old fart. It's not – and I like to think I'm not. I know my stuff. I wouldn't be lounging around in relative comfort the way I do with the assets I have if I didn't. We were both a little drunk when we first discussed it, and if I'm being honest, I was guessing at what I was saying. Well, I'm not guessing any more. It's all laid out right here, and most of the ideas which the alcohol and I came up with were good ones, though I say so myself. So, read this. Think about it. Take it seriously and look into it. Please don't dismiss it before you've given it a chance. In my humble opinion...*

I snorted, and the coffee I was sipping went up my nose, making me choke. Rupert was many things. Humble wasn't one of them.

> *...you need a real change, Emmy, not a holiday. It seemed to me when you were here that your life is in a bit of a rut. I know you said you love your job, your flat, and I'm sure you think you do.*

I thought I did, Rupert. Now I'm not so sure.

> *But you don't have that drip Nathan holding you back any more, and at the risk of sounding mushy, you looked a darned sight happier at the end of your holiday after three weeks of crisis and crap here than you did at the beginning when you'd just arrived from that perfect life of yours. You don't have to burn any bridges. You could try it for a few months, then go back to your old life. Or not. No one's life should follow the same long road without a diversion here and there, Emmy. Think about it.*
> *Love, Rupert.*

Frowning, I opened the attachment. Reams of figures blurred in front of my eyes. Ugh. This was going to take some time. I made toast and another coffee, then settled down to work out what the old fool was playing at.

It soon became clear that this was Rupert's ultimate gambit to get what he wanted.

He started with my incomings, outgoings and assets as he understood them. I logged on to banks and building societies to verify, entering my more accurate figures next to his.

Next, he dealt with the likely rent from the flat, confirming it would cover our mortgage and maintenance costs.

The following section concerned what would happen if I moved to France. I looked at the figure he was offering to pay me and almost laughed at how low it seemed compared with my current salary, but only for a moment. With no mortgage, rent or bills, and only my own living expenses and a small car to run, it wasn't too far from my current disposable income – a fact which surprised me.

The final part concerned setting up my own business. He didn't presume to tell me what sort of business, but he had asked all his friends what rates they paid for various services they already used relating to their property, and what other services they might be willing to pay for. Did they have a website and who maintained it? If not, would they like one? Did they use an agency to advertise, and were they happy with it? (Not always, it seemed.) He hadn't stinted on the possibilities and permutations, even though it was all speculative at best.

I realised he must have spent hours on this.

With my shoulders stiff from hunching over the laptop, I dragged my aching bones to the bathroom, ran a deep, hot bath and sank into it, my head filled with figures and projections and possibilities. It was hard not to be influenced by them. Rupert could be convincing with his verbal skills alone – add in hard evidence, and it was damned near impossible not to be drawn into his way of thinking.

It was clear I would be busy helping Rupert from spring through to autumn. The problem was the winter months.

And yet a quiet voice in my head told me to use my imagination. I could use those months to build up my own business. I remembered what Nick said about freelancing. If I was kicking my heels in the off-season, I could look at taking on proper contracts from the UK. Everything was done online nowadays.

The hot bath and the thoughts spinning in my head made me feel slightly sick, so I gave it up as a bad job, made a huge mug of tea, sat back at my laptop and e-mailed Nathan, laying out the arguments for renting rather than selling and even cribbing some of Rupert's wording and figures.

Wondering if the temperature I seemed to have developed was induced by the bath, I walked back into the lounge and decided there was no harm in getting a few things done. If I was going to contact letting agents, the place needed to look its best.

Slowly and methodically, I cleaned the flat to within an inch of its dreary life, cleared out cupboards (my stuff and joint stuff only – Nathan could sort his own crap out), and decluttered what little clutter there was.

Sorting through the magazine rack – God, did Nathan *ever* read those nerdy tech magazines he insisted on subscribing to? – I came across last year's batch of holiday brochures and gave a snort. A fat lot of use they'd been! I could only presume the brochure for the Seychelles had been wishful thinking on my part, and the one for golfing holidays in Portugal hidden at the bottom was something Nathan might have been planning without me.

A glossy cottage brochure caught my eye, and I flicked through it. My marketing eyebrow raised in approval. These people certainly knew how to take a photo and write a blurb. Every single cottage came across as a paradise. With professional curiosity, I turned to the front, where they declared themselves specialists in their region of England, offering both homeowners and holidaymakers a service above and beyond. I thought about what Rupert had said in his e-mail about agencies. What I'd said to him at the café about advertising with someone more specialised. Hmmm... Interesting.

The rest of the brochures went in the recycling bin. That one didn't. It accompanied me to my laptop, where I ate a sandwich whilst composing a thoroughly cheeky e-mail asking if they would be willing to chat to me sometime about how and why they set up their agency and whether they would share some of the nitty-gritty, hastily adding that I had no intention of treading on their toes, or even in the same country.

When I'd finally finished with the flat, I realised I hadn't been listening to what my body was telling me – or more accurately, screeching at me: that I was really ill. When I stood still long enough to realise I might fall down, I just had time to stagger to the bedroom before nausea and dizziness kicked in with a vengeance, and a headache joined in the fun.

Alternately piling covers on for the shivers and throwing them off for the sweats, I made my way through a restless evening and miserable night, to the accompaniment of cymbals clashing in my head.

CHAPTER TWENTY-FOUR

By morning, the headache had eased a little and the queasiness was gone, but I still felt hot. And cold. I reached for the mirror on the bedside table and stuck my tongue out to peer at it, but all it told me was that I had no idea why people did that.

I lay inert, staring at the ceiling. The lining paper had a fault and there was a ridge right down the middle of the room. I was surprised I'd never noticed it before.

When my internal caffeine alarm jangled at my nerves, I toddled blearily through to the kitchen, rejecting coffee in case my stomach rebelled and settling for tea instead. Back in bed, I sat with my knees pulled up to my chest and checked my phone for texts and e-mails.

There was no reply from Nathan... But there *was* an e-mail from Alain. I almost spilled my tea.

Hello, Emmy

Sorry I haven't been in touch. I wanted to contact you, but I knew you had a lot to contend with back home and I didn't want to complicate things for you or put you under any pressure.

I gather Rupert has had no such qualms, however – he told me all about the numbers he sent you, so I figured I couldn't make things any worse.

I thought I should let you know that I demanded a copy from him and went over it. That day at the zoo, you said that as an accountant, I

should have an opinion. Well, I do. It all looks pretty sound to me.
Setting up your own business is the unknown quantity, of course,
but I'm sure you'd be able to come up with something viable – and
Rupert is busy garnering plenty of support for you at this end in his
own inimitable bull-in-a-china-shop way.

Emmy, you already know how I feel, and I appreciate that there
are wider issues for you to consider – but I want you to know that I
haven't changed my mind since you left. I think we have something
going between us. It's small at the moment, but it's there... And
it could grow.

Take care. Alain x

I closed my eyes. It was hard not to be influenced by the knowledge
that Alain was so keen on a relationship – but if I went to France,
it had to be because I wanted to experience life in a new country,
take up new challenges, make new friends... *Not* because there
was a delicious half-Frenchman keen to help me settle in.

Idly flicking back to the photos Rupert sent me for the website,
I stared at one taken from the bottom of the garden looking
back towards the house. Knowledge of what lay behind each
blue-shuttered window in its handsome façade was imprinted
on my brain, the plants and shrubs in the foreground still so
familiar. It was probably only the lack of proper food over the past
twenty-four hours, but suddenly I felt light-headed, as though I
was being drawn down a tunnel into a 3D memory of sights and
sounds and smells and sensations. They felt so good. So right.

When the doorbell interrupted this psychedelic experience,
I ignored it, but it kept on sounding at twenty-second intervals
until I crawled out of bed, pulled on my robe and dragged myself
to the door.

Mum and Dad. Great.

Mum pushed her way inside. 'Why didn't you answer? Were
you still asleep? You look awful. Are you poorly?'

I nodded.

She put a hand on my brow and frowned. 'Hmm. Hot. What else?'

Meekly, I listed my symptoms.

'Right. Dennis. Sofa,' she commanded before storming off to the kitchen.

Dad dutifully plunked me on the sofa, propped my head with cushions, fetched the duvet from the bedroom and covered me up like a five-year-old, while Mum bustled back in with mugs of tea and a pot of out-of-date vitamins she'd found at the back of a cupboard.

'You're run down, Emmy,' she declared with a mother's conviction. 'You're tired and you haven't been eating properly. It's not surprising you're coming down with something.'

I marvelled at the way she could sound so sympathetic and so cross with me at the same time.

'I'll be fine,' I said, warming my hands on the mug she handed me. 'Why are you here? You can't tell me you *knew* I was ill.'

'We're on the way to Aunt Jeanie's for Sunday lunch,' Dad put in. 'Your mother wanted to see if you were alright.'

I plastered on a smile. 'I'm fine.' To distract Mum from fussing over me, I told them about Nathan's visit.

'To think he had the nerve to waltz in like that!' Mum declared when I'd finished.

Dad set his empty mug down on the coffee table. 'But unfortunately, he has every right.'

Mum gasped at her husband's perfidy. 'Dennis, how can you say that? He left our daughter for another woman. He moved to London, for God's sake!'

Dad laid a hand on her arm to shush her. 'We're not talking about morals here, Flo, or Nathan's lack of them. We're talking about legality. The fact is, the flat and mortgage are in joint names.' He turned to me. 'Did you speak to him about that?'

I shook my head. 'We were too busy yelling at each other. I e-mailed him yesterday about renting the flat out. He hasn't replied yet.'

'But Emmy,' Mum cut in, 'Where will you live?'

I chewed my lip. Wasn't it time I told my own parents that I'd been asked to move to France?

I started to tell them, hesitantly at first, but it soon came gushing out – Rupert's drunken offer of a life in France, my cynicism, his e-mail yesterday. In the interest of full disclosure, I threw in Carl's offer of promotion while I was at it. I was too delirious to pick and choose – I just dumped the lot for them to sift through themselves.

When I'd finished, for once Mum was at a loss for words. I'd expected a flood of questions and a very vocal opinion of Rupert's sanity or mine or both... But no. She simply sat staring at me for a while and then looked to Dad for his reaction.

He smiled. 'It's down to me, is it, ladies? In that case, do I get to see Rupert's figures, or do I have to rely on my crystal ball?'

I scurried off to fetch my laptop. He scrolled through the document without looking up once, whilst Mum and I waited with disguised impatience for our oracle to speak.

Well, my impatience was disguised. Mum didn't have time for that crap.

'Oh for heaven's sake, Dennis. Would it work or not?' she demanded.

He carefully placed the laptop to one side and steepled his fingers together in business mode. 'Have you checked any of this, Emmy?'

I nodded. 'It's about right.'

'Well, then. I'm afraid I wouldn't feel qualified to comment about building a business in France, but as for the rest... If I were to trust Rupert's judgement – which I'm inclined to – I would say it was feasible, if it's what you want to do.' He glanced at my mother, who was still surprisingly quiet. 'No comment, Flo, love?'

'Only that I'm proud of you, Emmy, for even thinking about such a brave move. If you do go, we'll miss you so much. But I'm worried you're only considering this to get away from everything that's going wrong here. It's an awfully big thing to do for the wrong reasons.'

'I know.' I gave her a small smile. 'But I think it's time for me to do *something*, don't you?'

She nodded. 'Whatever you choose, we'll back you all the way, you know we will.' She batted my father on the arm. 'Come on, Dennis. Jeanie's roast will be drying out.'

With a peck on the cheek, they were gone, and I honestly felt much better – whether from the moral support or the expired vitamins, I had no idea.

The vitamins obviously weren't potent enough, because when I woke on Monday morning, I knew there was no way I was going to work. I phoned Carl, who was predictably unimpressed, but my voice was croaky enough for him to admit I sounded awful. That done, I made myself a large mug of tea. By the time I'd finished it, my voice was back to normal. Oops.

At nine o'clock on the dot, I phoned two letting agents and arranged for them to come early that afternoon, keeping fingers crossed that I could remain upright long enough to show them around. I slept the rest of the morning away, crawling out of bed just in time to get dressed before they landed.

Both told me the flat was a desirable rental property due to its position on a commuter route into the city and its decor. No clutter or personal touches. People didn't like to feel they were intruding in someone else's home.

Nathan and I had spent over three years in this flat, yet apparently we'd left no mark on it at all. Our first home, our pride and joy, reflected so little of our personalities that it was ready for strangers to move in at a moment's notice.

I thought of *La Cour des Roses* and its clutter. The mish-mash of modern gadgetry, expensive antiques and tasteful old tat. Rupert making pastry at the scrubbed pine table. The glorious, shiny coffee machine. Wandering down to the chicken run, clutching a strong espresso and breathing in the scent of the flowers, the dewy grass between my toes. The den with its antique desk and squishy cushions and eclectic selection of books. *La Cour des Roses* was a home. It could be *my* home.

Still, it was all very well getting the thumbs-up from the letting agents. What I needed was a thumbs-up from Nathan. I checked my e-mails – and found one from Ryan.

Emmy,

Hope you're settling in and that everything's going the way you want it to.

Wasn't sure how much news you were getting from our end, but since I know you're probably worrying about Rupert, I thought I'd tell you he's fine. His limp's improved and it looks like he's lost a bit of weight, which I presume is good for him – he told me about the angina. Otherwise, the man's as grouchy as a bear. One minute he's monosyllabic and moping, and the next, he's in manic planning mode.

He's got it into his head that he needs to make improvements. You'd think he'd have enough on keeping the place going as it stands. Anyway, he's got this granny room in the extension that they built for Gloria's mother, and he wants it completely refitting. Redecorated, new carpet, light fixtures, furniture – even its own entrance. I asked him why he wanted another guest room, especially next to his own quarters, but he was very cagey. All he would say is

*that it has to be tasteful and he only trusts me to do it, so I didn't feel
I could let him down. It could be me developing angina at this rate!*

*Anyway, I bet we can both guess who he has in mind to occupy
the room...*

Take care of yourself.
Ryan.

I smiled. Ryan was a good friend, giving me the news as it was,
not how he thought I would want it to be.

As for Rupert, the cheeky bastard was already sorting out a
room for me! I didn't know whether to be touched by his faith
or pissed off with him for being so sodding presumptuous and
stubborn.

Nathan phoned that evening, waking me from a fitful doze.

'I got your e-mail about the flat,' he said, by way of a greeting.
'I took the weekend to consider.'

I tried to think of something pleasant to say that might heal
the hurtful rift of Friday night, but my mind was a blank. 'Thanks
for phoning back,' was the best I could do.

'If we did let it out, when were you thinking of?' he asked.

'As soon as possible.'

'You don't waste time, do you? Got another boyfriend already?'

I imagined his sneer at the other end of the line, and it made
me sad.

'No, Nathan, but I do have a life to lead and I want to get on
with it. What do you think, then?'

'It makes sense. I can't afford to buy you out. Especially now
I'm in London. You wouldn't believe the cost of living down here.'

Perhaps Gloria was already leading him a merry dance on the
expenses front. I sincerely hoped so.

'What about the furniture?' I asked awkwardly.

'I don't have any use for it at the moment. How about you?'

I couldn't stand the stuff. 'No.'

Nathan's tone was brisk. 'We could let it out furnished, then. Are you happy to sort out the agents if I deal with the legal side?'

This took me by surprise. How could he be so calm and business-like just a few scant days after asking me to take him back?

'Er – okay. Thanks.' I failed to hide the puzzlement in my voice.

Nathan sighed. 'I'm not stupid, Emmy. You made yourself clear on Friday. I thought it was worth a shot and I lost. You said you want to get on with your life. That's fine. I have a life to get on with, too.'

With Gloria. The words floated unspoken between us.

'What about the car?'

'You keep it for now,' he said. 'I've got a company car.'

'Okay, thanks.' I wasn't going to argue.

There was an awkward pause. 'Where will you move to?' he asked. 'Somewhere smaller, nearer work?'

'I don't know,' I said honestly. Then, for devilment mainly, 'I might move to France.'

'To *France*? Are you mad?'

'No, Nathan, I am not mad.' My tone was icy steel. '*You've* seen fit to leave me, give up a good job without a reference, move to London to shack up with an older woman...'

'Oh, and I suppose moving to France to shack up with Rupert is no different?' His voice was ugly and bitter.

'Actually, it's *very* different. If I do go, I'll give proper notice at work, retain the right to a reference and put my life in order. And I would not be shacking up with Rupert. I would be working for him whilst setting up my own business – but I would *not* be sleeping with him. It's called friendship. You might like to try it sometime.' I clicked off the phone and let my aching head fall back onto the cool pillow.

Drugged up to the eyeballs with painkillers and still sporting an exciting fever, I drifted in and out of sleep.

What if I went to France and it turned out that Rupert had written the whole thing while drunk and it was a load of twaddle and I ended up penniless and homeless?

At one in the morning, I was sweating so much that the wet sheets were making me cold. I got up to change the bedding.

Running off to France wasn't my only option. I would soon be rid of the flat, and then I could find somewhere that suited me here. If I accepted the promotion, I might get my passion back. I could even use my contacts to start freelancing in my spare time.

At three o'clock, I only just made it to the bathroom in time to throw up.

Mum and Dad could come out for holidays. Nick could bring his latest conquest over. I would miss Kate terribly, but she could come to stay, too. It wasn't as if I didn't know anybody in France. Rupert and Sophie. Ryan. Jonathan and Madame Dupont. And then there was Alain. Mmmm... Alain.

At four o'clock, I threw up again. Twice.

When the alarm shrilled at seven, I jolted out of a deep, dreamless sleep. My headache was gone. My temperature was down. I felt hungry. And everything was clear.

I lay staring at the ridge in the ceiling, knowing I should get up for work but making no move to do so.

The text alert on my phone jolted me out of limbo. I plucked it up from the bedside table, expecting it to be my mother making sure my virus hadn't turned into pneumonia.

It was from Rupert, and I opened it in a panic. Perhaps his leg was worse or his angina had been playing up or one of the girls helping had mucked something up or he was cross with me for not acknowledging his e-mail.

Three little words. *Come home, Emmy.*

I thought of my once-loved job with its trendy offices. Working alongside people like Carl. The exhausting commute to work. This flat with its cold sleek lines and no heart.

I didn't want a minimalist life any more. I wanted warmth and noise and clutter and colour and friendly chatter and pleasant aggravation.

I wanted to live again.

EPILOGUE

I could smell lavender through the open window as I slowed the car to a stop, the crunch of gravel causing a group of chattering birds to explode from the vines above the *gîte* doors.

As I clambered out of the car, nervous knots in my stomach mingled with a welcome glow of homecoming. I pushed open the gate, and a blur of black bolted straight for me. My heart jumped into my mouth, and instinct had me holding out my hand for the hound to sample. Relief washed over me when it sniffed, licked, then threw itself wantonly onto its back for me to tickle its tummy. This was no hound. This was a gormless, harmless mutt.

'Gloria!'

Rupert's voice from inside the house made my stomach clench and my veins freeze. All the blood drained from my face. She was back, then.

Rupert peered out of the doorway. 'Emmy. Thought it must be you. It's wonderful to have you back.'

He launched himself down the steps to suffocate me in a tight bear hug, which was brought to a halt by the jealous headbutting of the dog.

I wanted to say something along the lines of, "Why the hell didn't you warn me your bitch of a wife's back so we could put a stop to this arrangement before I paid my ferry fare?"

'You got a dog,' I said numbly instead.

'Yes.' Rupert pushed the dog's head away. 'For God's sake, Gloria, let Emmy breathe!'

My eyes widened. '*This* is Gloria?'

'Of course. Why, what did you think... ?' Rupert took in my pale complexion, started to laugh, then stopped before I could hit him. 'Oh, Emmy, I'm sorry. You look like you've seen a ghost.'

'You called your dog *Gloria*?' I asked incredulously, already flooded with relief. 'Is that fair on the dog?'

Rupert grinned as he tickled the dog behind the ears and she snuggled adoringly against his leg. 'Why not? She's a bit past her prime, she needed rescuing, I couldn't resist her – and she's a bitch.'

I smiled back, fondled the dog's waiting head and leaned up to kiss Rupert on the cheek.

My heart soared. I was home.

LETTER FROM HELEN

Thank you for choosing to read *The Little French Guesthouse*. I hope you enjoyed Emmy's journey to France and self-discovery as much as I did! If you were as sorry as I was to reach The End and you are wondering what will happen between Emmy and Alain, you will be pleased to know that a sequel is on the way!

As for my inspiration for *The Little French Guesthouse*, I'd had the opening scene in my mind for a long time, but I didn't get around to doing anything about it until, on one of our family holidays to France, I stumbled upon the region and location that felt just right for it. Creating *La Cour des Roses* was only a few steps away in my imagination, and everything flowed from there. I sometimes forget it isn't a real place!

I absolutely loved being in Emmy's world – and head. She feels like a close friend to me. Writers often say their characters take on a life of their own, and that was certainly true with this book. Rupert, in particular, did not turn out how I'd initially intended - but I like him so much better the way he led me to write him, and I'm very fond of him. It seems others are, too, from the comments I've received.

If you enjoyed the read, I would love it if you could take the time to leave a review. It makes so much difference to know that readers have enjoyed my book and what they liked about it . . . and of course, it might encourage others to buy it and share that enjoyment!

You can sign up for news about my new releases here:

www.bookouture.com/helen-pollard

You can also find me on Facebook, Twitter and Goodreads, and at my website and blog.

Thank you!

Helen x

🐦 HelenPollardWrites

📘 @helenpollard147

www.helenpollardwrites.wordpress.com